This story is dedicated to all of us.

Praise for James Grady

'Grady is a master of intrigue'
John Grisham

'Here, in this delicate but haunting noir, the young characters are beautifully crafted, the story is dramatic and utterly believable, and the time period is vividly evoked'
Booklist* on *The Smoke in Our Eyes

'Though the threat of violence looms throughout the narrative, Grady delivers a spare tale of domestic tragedy, rich with nostalgia and memorable characters'
Publishers Weekly* on *The Smoke in Our Eyes

'*The Smoke in Our Eyes* is a love letter to simpler, bygone days when people's sense of awe and wonder could be brought out more easily'
Washington Independent Review of Books

Also by James Grady

Six Days of the Condor
Shadow of the Condor
The Great Pebble Affair
Catch the Wind
Razor Game
Just a Shot Away
Steeltown
Runner in the Street
Hard Bargains
River of Darkness
(reissued as *The Nature of the Game*)
Thunder
White Flame
City of Shadows
Mad Dogs
Last Days of the Condor
This Train

JAMES **GRADY**

THE SMOKE IN OUR EYES

NO EXIT PRESS

First published in the USA in 2024 by Pegasus Crime,
an imprint of Simon & Schuster LLC,
New York, USA

First published in the UK in 2024 by No Exit Press,
an imprint of Bedford Square Publishers Ltd,
London, UK

noexit.co.uk
@noexitpress

A CIP catalogue record for this book is available from the British Library.

ISBN
978-1-83501-115-7 (Paperback)
978-1-83501-116-4 (eBook)

2 4 6 8 10 9 7 5 3 1

Typeset by in 11 on 13.25pt Bembo Std
by Avocet Typeset, Bideford, Devon, EX39 2BP
Printed and bound in Great Britain by
CPI Group (UK) Ltd, Croydon CR0 4YY

FSC www.fsc.org
MIX
Paper | Supporting responsible forestry
FSC® C171272

This is fact: There is no Montana town named Vernon. No characters in this story are real. Regretfully, painfully, there was a time when real people all over the USA talked, thought, and acted like in this novel, a time that made *who* and *where* we are now.
We have to face that – to know that – to change that.

As Ziggy Marley said:

'… *you don't know your past,*
you don't know your future.'

This is fiction: This is a novel. A coincidence of yesterday's ghosts and angels of imagination. Phantoms in the author's imagination striving to create fiction that tells the truth.

'... take a good look around. This is your hometown.'
—Bruce Springsteen

SUNRISE SERVICE

Lucas Ross was ten years old that Easter Sunday morning when he found diamonds on the highway.

'Wake up,' whispered his mother as he snuggled in his bed. 'It's near dawn. Be quiet. Let your father sleep.'

Mom padded out of his dark bedroom.

His bare feet swung around to press the gray carpet. He rubbed the sleep out of his eyes. Shuffled into the hall. His parents' bedroom door was closed.

He eased into the dark bathroom. Shut the door. Snapped on the light because, *well*, you have to see where you're aiming. Barefooted his Batman-pajamaed way through the living room to the yellow-walled kitchen.

The coffee percolator vibrated on the gas stove burner's ring of blue fire. Two breakfast places faced each other on the oval kitchen table. Glasses of fresh-squeezed orange juice. White bowls for cereal. Silver metal spoons.

He sat with his back to the picture window framing their dark backyard.

Puffy-robed teenager Laura shuffled upstairs from her basement bedroom with its pink walls and *Don't touch!* rules. Settled in her chair across from Lucas.

Dad mumbled 'Morning' as he appeared in the kitchen.

'*Don!*' said his wife. 'I thought…'

'Couldn't sleep.' He stared at the percolator's steam of bubbling coffee.

'Do you want the radio on?' said Mom.

'For what?' grumbled Dad. 'I got the real news yesterday.'

But he spun a knob on that black box on the counter.

A man's voice without a body filled the family's kitchen.

'—has matched Russia rocketing into outer space with those science machines called "satellites," so the Soviet Communists are not ahead of us.'

Yes! thought Lucas.

'Meanwhile, there are reports of violence stemming from a federal judge ordering Virginia to stop segregation in its public schools.'

What's 'segregation'? thought Lucas. *Does my school have it? Or schools in other towns in Montana that aren't as special as Vernon?*

'The Civil Aeronautics Board says "pilot error" caused the Iowa plane crash on a snowy night last month that killed a teen music star and three other people.'

Lucas remembered hearing Laura and her best friend Claudia play that guy's record over and over after the plane crash:

'That'll be the day, woo-hoo, that'll be the day, woo-hoo…'

Will the radio talk about me when I die? wondered Lucas.

'The Post Office confiscated a magazine that published excerpts from a novel called *Naked Lunch*. Sorry for dropping that on you folks here on Easter, but here on KRIP's Sunday News Corral, we don't make the news, we just wrangle it.'

Wrangling, thought Lucas. *Like Grampa being a cowboy.*

'Wrangling it,' said the DJ for this local AM station. 'Some days… Sometimes it's too damn hard.'

Laura froze, her hand holding the spoon of milk and cornflakes.

Their parents, standing by the stove, frowned.

'Martin County residents today are waking up to news of a tragic one-car accident on the highway south of town last night that killed one local teenage boy and left another one in the hospital. Authorities identified the two boys as Hal Hemmer and Earl Klise, both juniors in Vernon High School.'

'Oh God!' Laura's spoon clattered into her bowl.

'You know those boys, don't you, Laura?' Mom wiped a dishrag over spilled milk. 'You're a sophomore, but everybody knows everybody in high school.'

Laura whispered: 'I don't know anything about that accident!'

Mom washed the dishrag in the kitchen sink.

Dad got the just-delivered big city newspaper from the front porch.

Laura gripped her orange juice glass like it was a carnival carousel pole.

And Lucas knew she'd lied about not knowing anything about the accident.

But he also knew Laura was not, *nope*, never had been a liar.

'Better get ready,' Mom told her. 'You've got that God-damn church thing.'

Laura hurried downstairs.

'You better get a move on, too,' Mom told Lucas.

She'd laid out his clothes the night before. Lucas wanted white socks to match his white shirt, but black ones waited in his dress shoes.

Lucas frowned at the bathroom mirror's reflection of his wild brown hair.

The mirror reflected the white bathtub. *What a cool idea!*

Lucas folded the bathmat onto the tub's floor. Knelt both knees on the mat. Gripped the 'C' handle. Stuck his head under the faucet. Turned the handle.

Cold waterfall tumbling over his skull: *ten, nine, seven-five-onezero!*

Lucas pulled out of the torrent.

The mirror showed victory: his hair lay flat on his head.

He marched into the gray-walled living room.

His mother's anxious voice in the kitchen stopped Lucas mid-step:

'Don't worry, Don. It was just a wedding. Just talk.'

'At the reception,' said Dad. 'Watching him work it. Alec watching him, too, right beside me but almost like I wasn't there. Or it didn't matter if I was there.'

'It was his daughter's wedding, Don. That's all. Alec had a lot on his mind. Probably a little drunk, too. I would have been. That wasn't like he ever wanted.'

Dad said: 'Out of nowhere, Alec says: "*I think he'll fit in just fine.*" And he's looking at that college boy who just married his daughter. Fran Marshall is now Mrs Ben Owens. "*Fit in just fine.*" All I could do was stand there. Say nothing.'

'You don't know that it means anything.'

Cold cupped Lucas's groin. He looked down.

A dark half-moon of tub splash covered the crotch of his tan khakis.

Oh God, it looks like I peed my pants!

'Lucas,' called his mother in the kitchen. 'Come here.'

Stand sideways in the kitchen doorway and—

'You look fine, dear,' said Mom. 'Laura! Irwin will be here any minute!'

Dad shuffled out of the kitchen. 'Last thing I need now is Irwin.'

'I better put something else on.' Mom fingered her pink terrycloth smock as she hurried behind her husband toward their bedroom.

The hands on the clock above the kitchen sink read 6:41: "You have to get up at six because Irwin will pick you up at a quarter to seven."

Four minutes.

Mom and Dad in their bedroom. Laura downstairs. His crotch smeared dark, wet by *HONEST IT'S NOT PEE!*

Lucas jammed a kitchen chair against the sink. *Three minutes!* He pulled the toaster next to the sink. Climbed on the wobbly chair. Put one shoe in the sink. Spun the toaster knob to DARK. Pushed the lever down. Lowered his soaked crotch close to the two slots of glowing toaster coils.

BAM! BAM! BAM!

Knocking on the front door!

'Lucas!' called his mother. 'Let Irwin in!'

Aaah! Lucas fought to keep his balance. *Still dark all over my crotch and OW! The hot toaster! Get out of the sink! Off the chair! Run to the—*

NO! Get the chair back where it belongs!

BAM! BAM! BAM!

Hunch over. Keep one hand in front of your… Open the front door.

Red-haired, pudgy teenager Irwin stood on the front porch. His smile turned to a sneer when he saw it was just Laura's little brother.

'Didn't you hear me?' said Irwin as he pushed past Lucas into the house. 'Aren't you guys ready? Hi, Mrs Ross.'

'Did you hear what happened?' said Mom as she entered the living room.

'The car wreck and Earl and Hal? Do you know which one is alive?'

'No,' said Mom. 'It's awful. Sure glad it wasn't you or Laura.'

'That wouldn't happen to kids like us,' said Irwin. 'Bet they were drinking. They have those beer parties at the river.'

'Don't tell me what I don't wanna know,' said Mom.

'Bet it was that car they rebuilt. Mrs Sweeny's '57 Chevy. The one that somebody sugared the gas tank. Remember they bought it off the junk heap?'

POP! *The toaster.*

Mom frowned toward her kitchen.

Laura hurried up the back stairs, through the kitchen, into the living room.

'Go,' she said. 'Let's just go.'

'You coming, Mrs Ross?' asked Irwin. 'See your kids do Sunrise Service?'

'I went to that wedding,' said Mom. 'Only so much church a body can take.'

Lucas kept his back toward them as he edged toward the front door.

Irwin stood where he was. Swayed like a cobra. 'What's the guy Fran married like? Kind of… sudden, and on the Saturday before Easter.'

'You get married when you get married,' said Mom. 'I didn't really talk to him. We got invited because Don manages the trucking firm.'

'We're going now,' said Laura as she hurried Lucas and Irwin outside.

Snow had been gone for a week that March day. Hills of gray dirt and last year's yellowed weeds rose from the rumpled prairie three blocks away. Dawn pinked Montana's big sky above the flatland valley cradling Lucas's hometown.

'Laura!' called Mom. 'Aren't you supposed to bring music books?'

The teenage girl marched back into the house.

Irwin and Lucas waited on the lawn.

Irwin said: 'Look across the street to the hospital. That's the Hemmers' car. And Dr Horn's Dodge. Don't know the other three.'

The American flag swayed atop its steel pole in front of the hospital. The hospital staff had forgotten to lower the flag at sunset. Forgotten *again*, Lucas noted. Like I forgot to check last night so I could make things like they should be. Lower the flag without letting it touch the ground. Take it into the hospital.

'You seen your new neighbor Falk's car?' said Irwin. 'He's a lawyer. Has a new car. Well, not "this year" new. Not a 1959. His is a '58. Only other Cadillac that new in town belongs to your dad's boss, Mr Marshall.

'The Falks got a daughter younger than you,' Irwin leered. 'Now she's your Girl Next Door. The girl you're going to marry.'

'*I am not!*'

Laura ran down the front steps. 'Get in the car!'

Lucas dove into the backseat of Irwin's parents' car. Irwin ground the engine to life. Gravel crunched under tires as the car pulled away from the curb.

Lucas looked down at his khaki pants' crotch. *Still a shadow left!*

'I'm in bad trouble,' whispered Laura.

She whirled to her little brother. 'Don't you dare tell Mom and Dad! Hope-to-die promise me you won't tell them or anybody anything!'

'I promise!'

Laura slumped in someone else's car carrying her somewhere.

'I was there. Last night. That party by the river. With Earl and Hal.'

'*What?*' yelled Irwin. 'You couldn't have been! That's not what we do!'

'I know, I know, I know! But I did. And now one of them is dead and I, I—'

'You didn't do anything... *really wrong*, did you?' whispered Irwin.

'A few sips from one beer. I was careful. Held the bottle the whole time.'

Lucas shouted from the backseat: 'They can get your fingerprints off the beer bottle! My FBI book says so!'

The teenagers ignored him.

'Claudia took me,' said Laura. 'But I felt... weird. Then it was after ten.'

'You broke curfew!' said Irwin.

The car he drove idled at the intersection where a steel girders tower rose from the fire station. The tower's whistle blew every night for that ten o'clock curfew for everybody under eighteen, plus every noon and every time it needed to summon the volunteer firemen to risk their lives fighting someone else's blaze.

'We drove home on the gravel roads and through alleys so the cops didn't catch us. I snuck in the back door.'

Irwin spun the steering wheel left and drove a block to the tan stucco church where amplifiers in the belfry filled the morning with a spinning black disc on a record player turntable freeing chimes of faith.

'I saw them leave,' she said as Irwin pulled to the curb. 'Earl and Hal. They went to get more beer. I saw them drive away from the bonfire and the parked cars and the shadows of trees along the river and now they're dead.'

'Only one,' said Irwin.

'And I'm part of that,' said Laura as they all entered the church.

Shocked teenagers from the Youth Fellowship Program who'd been volunteered by tradition to take over the Easter Morning Sunrise Service clustered by the altar with its golden cross. Their hushed voices flitted through the church sanctuary: "*When will they say who? What's gonna happen?*"

The three arriving souls said nothing.

Laura had volunteered Lucas after their mother asked her to "*get him out of his books.*" YFP teenagers practiced their march-in from the side door and along the rail separating rows of pews from the pulpit with its choir benches, organ, the altar with that empty gold cross. Irwin would sit Up There. Kids who'd pass collection plates or read Bible verses would sit in a front pew with Lucas.

Laura sat at the organ. Said nothing. Stared at the black and white keys.

Tear-streaked high schoolers put Lucas in the hall by the side door leading to the sanctuary. He heard mutters and thumps on the other side of the door.

Grim-faced Chris Harvie – the junior in high school who was Claudia's boyfriend and who'd gotten into Big Trouble two years earlier for what he did to Elvis Presley – snapped a match and put blue flame to Lucas's candle lighter. Laura struck organ keys. Lucas followed the blue flame as he led the others into the sanctuary. Fifty-some well-dressed adults and children stood in rows of pews. Laura played the organ while they sang 'Christ the Lord Is Risen Today.'

Lucas lit the altar candles. Made it back down the pulpit steps to the front pew without tripping. The organ crescendoed. The congregation sang: '*Ah-ah-men*.' Minister for a Day Irwin asked everyone to sit.

Church for Lucas meant dust dancing in shafts of sunlight through color-stained glass windows. The organ vibrating heavy air. Uncomfortable clothes.

Here Lucas felt weird. While he knew that these walls were special and that Jesus was a Jew turned Catholic rightfully rebelled into a Methodist, Lucas couldn't buy that just being a church person got you into his Father's heaven.

Wish I knew what got you there, thought Lucas as the pew pressed against his spine. *That must be one of the things I'll find out when I'm grown up.*

But right now, he needed to stay awake.

Which would have been hard if he'd paid attention to Irwin's big sentences about '*youth today who will become our leaders well into the twenty-first century*.'

Lucas let his mind run like wild horses.

His sister's hands crashed down for the organ's final *Amen!* that freed Lucas to the sunlit Fellowship Hall. The Ladies Auxiliary chattered in the kitchen with its steaming cocoa and gurgling coffee. Lucas spotted trays of donuts on the refreshments table. Parishioners shuffled into the big hall. Lucas grabbed a chocolate donut. Slid through the crowd.

There was Mom's sister Aunt Dory with her curls of hay-colored hair and quick smile, in from the farm with Uncle Paul, who looked like a cowboy movie hero, a toothpick in his smile and all dressed up in his Sunday sport coat.

There was another farm family, Mr and Mrs Herbst with their two kids who went to a one-room country school. Mr Herbst was bald.

Lucas saw Irwin buttering up a suit and tie boss for the power company.

Saw—

'Got you!' A claw grabbed Lucas's arm. Pulled him closer to her.

Humpbacked and twisted. A black veiled bonnet. A snow of rose-scented powder covering her hatchet face. She opened the maw inside her ring of ruby lipstick and yellow teeth to expel vapors of dead cigarettes.

'Praise be, we got you now, little man!'

'I didn't do anything, Mrs Sweeny! Honest!'

'You got a guilty conscience?' The claw trembled his arm.

'No, ma'am, I—'

'You belong to a Conner girl.'

'My grandma is Meg Conner. I'm—'

'Cora's boy. Married that Ross man who came to town.'

The claw shook him.

'Maybe you're one of the good Conners. Like your Aunt Dory and her Paul. I let them farm my land. They come to church. Not like others in Meg Conner's family. Heard she's in the hospital. Good thing we got you churchin'. You need it, what with your uncle the *Eye-talian* papist and that evil red house on the hill. Plus, your Aunt Iona's husband worked for that thieving slanter McDewel.'

'But I don't know about papes or slanting!'

'Don't know much, do you? Got a mind to write a letter about that. The schools have gotten shameful. A town like this is a curse for the virtuous.'

Bald farmer Herbst ambled toward the boy in the clutch of an old crone.

Mrs Sweeny's rancid breath bathed Lucas. 'You *sure* you're a good boy?'

'I promise I try!'

'Not like those two I just heard about,' she hissed. 'You hear they wrecked my car I sold them? You know what I think?'

'Honest, I don't!'

'I think they were who sugared my gas tank in the first place. Broke the car. Then tricked me into selling to them dirt cheap. But God showed them, didn't he? You remember that. God gets them that does wrong. Everybody pays.'

Then bald farmer Herbst was there. 'Happy Easter to you, Mrs Sweeny!'

The crone had to free Lucas to shake his rescuer's hand.

Herbst winked at the liberated boy.

Lucas dodged through the crowd. *Where's Laura?*

Aunt Dory gave him one of her thousand-watt smiles. 'Did you have a good chat with Mrs Sweeny? Paul can listen to her for hours. Don't know how he does it.'

'I'm a helluva guy,' said Uncle Paul with the cowboy hero looks. 'Mrs Sweeny won't write no letters complaining about me. Remember when she was on her high horse about the city road crew?'

'Have you seen Laura?' asked Lucas.

'Just talked to her,' said Uncle Paul. 'Damn shame about those boys. We stopped for coffee out the truck stop. Ran into Sheriff Wood. He said their car rolled a half dozen times. Threw 'em both out.'

'Which… Which one…'

'Was the Klise boy who died: Earl. That Hal Hemmer – nice kid – he's banged up, concussion. Woke up lying on the highway, red lights whirling. Like I told Laura, damn shame that ain't the all of it. Both kids was beered up. Whichever one was driving'd be up for a hard charge.'

'Who was it?'

'Nobody knows. Hal can't remember diddly from all yesterday. Doc Horn thinks he never will. Could have been either one of them behind the wheel. The hell of it is, the law's gotta balance it out.'

'Mrs Sweeny says they did that sugar thing to her car so they could—'

'Weren't those kids. Wish it was poor dead Earl Klise who was driving for sure. Wouldn't make it any better, but then it won't get no worse.'

Lucas scanned the crowd. 'Where's Laura?'

She was outside. Alone in the passenger seat of the parked blue car.

Rolled the window down. 'Find Irwin. We've got to get out of here.'

Irwin drove them away.

'Not home!' said Laura. 'I can't go there.'

Irwin headed up the long slope of Knob Hill.

'What were you thinking?' said Irwin. 'Why did you do it?'

'Because I could! Because I had a chance to!' Laura shook her head. 'Claudia picked me up after the wedding. Rode around with her. Cruising Main Street. Going nowhere. Like always. Claudia said she knew about a party. She was mad at Chris. I sat there in the front seat. Sat there like I am now, only…

'Only I'd just sat through that wedding. Fran graduated from high school when we were in junior high. Now there she was, standing up in front of everybody, wearing a white dress that I know is a lie.'

Lucas frowned. 'How can a dress lie?'

'Shut up, Lucas!' said the teenagers.

'She got married,' said Laura. '*Bingo!* She wasn't Fran Marshall anymore. I didn't know who she was. *She* didn't know who she was. But it was over. She walked down that aisle and all of a sudden, she was just like her mother. And mine. And I just… I said: "*Yeah, I'll go to the party.*"'

'You know what this means?'

'The National Honor Society.'

Lucas said: 'Were they there?'

'Be quiet, Lucas!' said Irwin.

'But that's the point,' said Laura. 'They weren't there. It's not enough to keep a B+ average. Oh no, you've got to keep the pledge.'

'That was going to be so easy for us! That's the kind of kids we are!'

'Sure, everybody knows who we are. This town has you pegged the day you're born. You, me. Get in the Honor Society. Pledge no drinking. No lawbreaking. Or they kick you out.'

'That's the smart thing to do,' said Irwin. 'Especially for you!'

'*Lau-ra's smar-ter than you are!*' teased Lucas.

'Not anymore,' she whispered.

'We got in this year,' said Irwin. 'As sophomores – first time we were eligible! In a month, they'll announce the scholarships old man Fruen set up with his oil money. A thousand dollars each for a senior boy and girl in the Honor Society. Was nice of Fruen to include girls even though they're… You're the smartest girl in our class. Smarter than most of the boys—'

Smarter than you, thought Lucas in the backseat.

'—but you've got to be *in* the Society! A whole thousand dollars is waiting for you in two years and you… you…!'

They crested Knob Hill. Vernon spread out below them. The car turned around. The road swept down the hill past weathered houses. Past the tan brick high school and Lucas's Blackhawk Elementary School. The street dead-ended at the east-west highway, and beyond that, the railroad tracks.

Three indigo crags chiseled from the vast blue sky ruled the northern horizon: the Buffalo Hills, geologies too slight to be called mountains in this vast geography where sixty miles away, the sawtooth peaks of the Rocky Mountains cut the western skyline. The Buffalo Hills sat almost thirty miles beyond the town. Another ten miles of prairie behind them waited Canada.

West Buffalo looked like the number 9 on its back and was Lucas's favorite. Middle Buffalo rose like a pair of praying hands. East Buffalo stretched across the horizon like a pile of crumpled socks.

Irwin rode the brake down Knob Hill's road.

'You'll need that money,' Irwin told Laura. 'I'm lucky, we own the bank. You keep saying that scholarship is your only ticket out of this town. How it will let you go out of state to college, not just to Montana U. Fran went to the U and look where she is today! And last night... You blew it!'

His sister choked a sob in the same instant that Lucas yelled: 'Look!'

A maroon Mercury coupe sat face-out on the sidewalk of a brown house. A two-wheel haul box rode the coupe's rear bumper. Slid out of the haul box doors and onto the lawn was an upright, saloon-style black piano.

'Who's moving here?' asked Lucas.

'Your new teacher, dummy,' snapped Irwin. 'Forget about that.'

Irwin's words to Laura were soft: 'What are you going to do?'

She shook her head. Shrugged. Refused to let tears win.

They rolled past the brown-brick high school.

Lucas looked out of the car as they rolled past his school. His old teacher Mrs Bemiller broke her hip. His new teacher had a black piano.

'What's that?' said Lucas when they reached the two-lane highway.

Way down toward the corner to Main Street: a... a *jumble* across the road at the Texaco gas station.

'How come your brother squints all the time?'

Laura waved that away as Irwin turned their vehicle toward the jumble.

'Oh God!' said Laura. 'It's the car.'

Three men stood near the wreck. One wore a hat.

The charred Chevy's roof dangled from the frame on the passenger side. None of the windows had glass. One wheel was gone; the other tires were blown. The driver's door hung open. A hydraulic lift jacked-up the car's rear end.

Irwin drove into the Safeway supermarket parking lot, the west end turnaround for teenagers who'd loop back down to Main Street to the east end of town's railroad crossing, then circle back: '*dragging Main*.'

A rusted station wagon skidded to a stop at the Texaco. Out of it staggered Jim Klise dressed in a polka-dotted pajama top and baggy pants, a work boot on his right foot while his left foot wore a black slipper. That one-kid dad stumbled to the wrecked car his dead son loved. The three men standing there started toward Klise. His waving arms shooed them away.

His eyes locked on the mangled Chevy. His jaw hung open like the battered driver's door. He circled around the front bumper arrowed-up between the heap's hollow eyes. Around the crunched passenger side door to the jacked-up back end.

A meadowlark chirped.

A freight train clattered into town.

Klise jerked the long pipe handle out of the hydraulic jack. BAM! He crashed the pipe down on the Chevy's sprung trunk. BAM! The freight train blew its whistle as it rumbled past. BAM! Round and round the mangled car charged Klise. BAM! BAM! On the roof. The hood. The glass-gone windshield. BAM! BAM! BAM! Over and over until Klise's face melted. The pipe fell from his hands. Clattered on the pavement. He dropped to his knees.

Irwin nudged their car to the highway out of town. Stared at the windshield. Laura didn't look back. Lucas's backseat eyes bounced to the rearview mirror and a shrinking glimpse of a man crumpled by a wreckage.

'You know where we have to go,' said Laura.

Irwin steered the car onto the two-lane blacktop out of town to the river. Their lone car followed the two-lane highway south through a gold and brown chessboard of farmland. They drove past a gravel road leading from the highway through wheat fields to a barbwire-topped chain-link fence that caged huge bulldozers, backhoes, and cranes beside a hill of excavated earth.

One of the new missile sites, thought Lucas. *The Russians will shoot their missiles and send their bombers across Canada. Our radar will spot them. In secret places where wise men rule America, our guys will push buttons and whoosh! Mushroom A-bomb clouds will spike up all over our blue globe. Even where cities aren't blasted into holes, firestorms or radiation will kill everybody. But the Russians won't win. And the Wow! thing is that in Vernon, we'll see the missiles roar up from our golden wheat fields, streak white contrails across our big blue sky. We'll be the first regular people to know It's All Over.*

Irwin told Laura: 'Nobody knows you were there.'

'Claudia and the other kids who were there, they know. And Hal—'

'Your uncle said Hal can't remember. Claudia and the others: you think they'll tell the cops that they were there? As long as you don't say anything—'

'Somebody will.'

'Somebody *might*. But—'

'But it's an *honor* code. I'm supposed to tell. Not lie about it.'

'You made one lousy stupid mistake. It wasn't really that bad! Don't ruin your only sure thing to get what you want and deserve for your whole damn life!'

'Earl's dead.'

'And you confessing does *what* to help him?'

'One moment,' said Laura. 'That's all it takes. You do some little thing. Suddenly the whole world changes.'

Lucas squinted. Saw only the farm fields. Mountains. Sky. Blurry road.

'What about Hal?' said Laura. 'My uncle told me the police need to know if he was driving. Then it's more than just drinking. Then it's a kind of murder.'

Irwin shook his head. 'Hal got punished enough for a lifetime last night. Waking up on the road like—'

He shot his finger at the windshield. 'There!'

A black tire propped up by its sheared axle lay on the road's shoulder.

Irwin parked the car on the edge of the highway beside the broken axle. They stepped into the cool air. Blacktop crunched under church-shined shoes.

'There's no cars!' Lucas stood tall on the two-lane highway. Wild! Free!

'It's early,' said Irwin. 'Everybody will come see before dark.

'Look.' He pointed down the road toward the river's canyon. 'Skid marks. Then that big paint scrape. Middle of the night, black as hell. The driver's drunk. Swerves. Loses control. The car flips. Rolls over and over.'

Lucas frowned. *What is that sparkling?*

'I can't do this,' said Laura.

'That's what I've been saying,' Irwin told her. 'You can't.'

A ten-year-old boy walked heel-to-toe along the dashes of white-line center stripes on the highway like Batman on a steel girder atop Gotham City.

'I can't be trapped out here,' said his sister.

Lucas *heel-toed, heel-toed* ever closer to the gray highway's sparkles.

'I've got to go home,' said Laura. 'Tell my folks. Tell… *whoever*, too.'

'*What?*' yelled Irwin. 'Are you crazy? Get kicked out of – That won't do any good! That's like… like Mr Klise beating a wrecked car! Didn't change a thing!'

'But it was real. And so is something I can do.'

'It'll sure as hell hurt you. Will it help anybody? Will it help Hal?'

'I don't know.'

'Oh, great! You're going to do something just because you can!'

'I've got no choice. Whatever I do, I do something.'

'This isn't about you!'

'It is now. I didn't want any of it. But I was there, so now it's about me, too. I can't forget that. Wait. Hope. Pretend. If I do, then I'm stuck on this road forever.'

'Guys!' yelled Lucas. 'Hey, guys! Come here, quick! Look! On the road! Sparkles like diamonds!'

Irwin shoved Lucas. 'That's beads of glass! Busted glass from a wrecked car. There's a dead guy just like us on a slab in the undertaker's parlor. Your sister's going to screw herself. And you see damn diamonds on the highway!'

Irwin sneered: 'You don't see what's there. She wants to throw it away.'

They got in his car.

Stone-faced Irwin drove fast and hard.

Laura sat straight and silent in the front seat.

Lucas rode behind them.

Stared out the windshield at the highway rumbling beneath the wheels.

BORDERS

She walked into Lucas's class the next day and he forgot everything else.

Forgot about his whole family at the Monday morning breakfast table when it was usually only him, Laura, and Mom with her newspaper crossword puzzle set aside until after her kids went to school and Dad woke up, left for work.

The kitchen's picture window framed the world outside where purple blooms swayed on the lilac hedge that made the border of their backyard. KRIP AM radio filled the kitchen with the Swap & Bulletin Board, hog 'n' cattle reports, crop futures, and polka music Lucas hated – '*oom-pah-pah, oom-pah-pah.*'

'Lucas,' said Dad, 'if anybody asks you what's going on, tell them nothing.'

'Tell them nothing about what?'

'Nothing about everything. Especially about Laura. And that car wreck.'

'Who's going to ask me anything? I'm a kid.'

'Doesn't matter who asks you. The point is, you don't know anything.'

Laura stared past the five-years-younger brother who sat across from her.

'Is everything OK?' asked Lucas.

'You can say that,' Dad told him. 'Sure, you can say everything is OK.'

But Lucas forgot about all that when she walked into his classroom.

Forgot about that and about arguing with Wayne and Kurt before school, three fifth graders huddled in the chaos of kids on a packed-sand playground.

'You're so wrong, Lucas!' said Kurt. '*The Blob* is worse than *The Thing*! *The Thing* is like a man, so you can just hide from it until the Army gets there, but *The Blob* is huge and red and takes over everything!'

'Nu-unh!' argued Lucas about great movies. 'Monsters who are like you are the worst. They know how to get you.'

He waved his arms *Dah!* The pink eraser flew out of his grip to crash in front of a pair of black-and-white sneakers worn by a boy named Marin.

First Bell rang.

Children stampeded toward the school doors.

Wayne didn't move.

Kurt didn't move.

Lucas didn't move.

Marin stared at them. He was the same size as them. In 5A like them.

But Marin had just moved to Vernon.

They'd lived there forever. Been Cub Scouts. Didn't join Boy Scouts—

—which was a relief for Lucas. There was something about the scoutmaster that made him feel… creeped.

The week they'd started fifth grade, Lucas, Kurt, and Wayne trudged to the National Rifle Association's nighttime gun safety class at Knob Hill's indoor shooting range. Lucas blinked as the safety instructor walked past dozens of sitting-on-the-floor elementary school kids with a rifle jauntily riding his hip. The death bore pointed to the dark night beyond that ceiling.

Loaded gun, thought Lucas. One look at Kurt and Wayne watching the instructor told Lucas they didn't get it.

So when the preacher of gun safety 'accidentally' pulled the trigger—

BANG!

—besides the startle and now safety-taught fear that whacked Lucas, he felt the joy of "*I was right!*"

I got it, he told himself. I saw what was there *for real*.

Now he saw a fellow fifth grader named Marin standing there staring back at him as he decided the fate of a lonely pink eraser on a packed-sand playground. Marin had jet-black hair. Skin the color of coffee with cream.

Four hard-beating-hearts, blue-jeaned boys stood on that sand playground.

Marin underhanded the eraser toward Lucas. Glided into the school.

Lucas bobbled the catch.

Bobbled it *of course* just as Anna, *oh Anna,* and Bobbi Jean flowed past.

'Phew!' said Wayne. 'That was lucky. I didn't know if he'd give it back.'

'Come on,' said Kurt. 'We'll be late.'

Wayne whispered as they ran inside: 'You know Marin is a half-breed.'

Lucas only knew that he'd bungled a catch in front of Anna.

But he forgot about that.

Like he forgot about how as they hurried into their 5A classroom, Kurt said: 'Why isn't Ralph poking people this morning?'

Like he forgot about the Secret Magic Plan as he sat at his desk and bathed in the vision of Anna with her golden angel hair. She sat to his left, giggling with Bobbi Jean, who was whip skinny and had hair the color of mud.

The Secret Magic Plan.

All Lucas had to do was align the universe.

He fingered his math sheet. The turn-in box sat on the teacher's desk. After the call for homework, kids would straggle to the box. When Anna rose, he'd race for one of two chances at eternity. He'd either slide his paper under or drop it on top of hers and thus create destiny. They'd be together. He couldn't decide which move was better, but that became just another mystery he forgot *when*.

Final Bell clanged through the school.

Everyone in 5A shut up and sat still.

Except, of course, for Nick, whose right hand always twitched.

And Ralph, who'd poked nobody yet and now shifted around in his desk.

Lucas let no one see him watch Anna out of the corners of his eyes.

Principal Olsen exploded into the classroom.

Lucas tensed. *Please please please don't see me!*

Then he saw who followed Principal Olsen and forgot everything else.

'Sit up straight!' bellowed Mr Olsen. 'Pay attention! You! Nick Harris! If you can't keep your hand still, we'll nail it to the desk!

'No more easy street!' Principal Olsen slashed his forefinger across the fifth grade faces. 'Mrs Bemiller's hip broke and you thought you were going to get the rest of the year with *substitutes.* But I got you a real teacher. You jump when she says jump or you'll come down the office and jump for me.'

A sucking wind pulled the breath out of every kid.

Principal Olsen said: 'This is your new teacher, Miss Jordan Smith.'

The song of her name: 'Miss Jordan Smith.' *Miss*: she wasn't married. Soft sunlight waves lit her midnight hair. Her violet eyes were wide and bright. Those lips curled in a slow smile. She evoked The Secret Of The Truck Shop but Lucas banished such thoughts. A noble warmth filled him.

Jordan Smith, thought Lucas. *You have a black piano.*

Her voice was husky, magnetic.

'Thank you, Principal Olsen. We appreciate you taking time

out of your busy day.' She stepped past him toward the class. 'Now it's up to me to—'

'Nope!' said Principal Olsen. 'I'm not the kind of skipper who'd leave you high and dry on your first day with this bunch. I set up a lesson to start you off.'

'Is that necessary? You are the principal, but this is my class now.'

'No bother. You can just sit over there.' He pointed to the windowsill.

'I can just…' She made a smile for Principal Olsen. 'Sit… over… there.'

The second hand swept the clock above the classroom door.

'Well,' she said, 'guess we better get you going so you can be gone.'

Lucas saw the principal blink.

'Just give me a moment to take my place,' said Miss Jordan Smith.

But instead of sitting *over there* on the windowsill, she marched to the back of the room and wedged herself into an empty desk just like all the kids.

'We're ready, Mr Olsen,' she said from behind the students. 'Please begin.'

He marched to the blackboard. 'Listen up, people! This is how life is.'

The principal jerked down a roll-up map.

That flattened vision of the world faced 1959's fifth grade students.

Lucas knew the shapes of America and Canada. Of desert Mexico south of the Alamo. The squiggle of green was always England. The big hook was the lions/gorillas/elephants of Africa. 'Unexplored Territory' labeled a patch of Africa's map the size of Kansas, while across the blue ocean were more jungles in South America where escaped Nazis hid and blowgun darts tipped with curare *puff-thwack-'Aah!'* made you dead. Yellow deserts with oil and Arabs on camels. Then there were the they'll-be-frozen-forever snow-white Arctics.

Red shaded a third of the world map.

'There's us and there's them,' said Principal Olsen.

Asia, thought Lucas. *Russia. China. The east end of Europe.*

'Communism!' snapped Mr Olsen. 'They're dying to take over the world. Put us men in prison camps. Take your moms and you girls and – We won't get into that. They'll make you work for no money. Tell you who to marry. Not let you worship Jesus like Americans are supposed to. Not let you say what you think. Try anything and they'll put you up against a brick wall and *rat-a-tat-tat*.'

He punched the map.

'This world is like a prison. Places like Hungary where they threw rocks at Russian tanks. West Berlin where Miss Smith taught the kids of our soldiers. Everything *Red* is run by the big boss in the principal's office called Moscow.

'That's how it is,' he said as he assumed the Navy's command pose. 'So be glad you're an American and not trapped in a place that's run like the Reds.'

The red second hand made a full circle around the black-numbered clock.

From the back of the classroom came her voice: 'Truly amazing.'

'Thank you, Miss Smith.'

'Oh yes.' She walked to the front of the classroom. 'I think we all learned something. In fact, you've given us a lot to work on.'

'Teaching is what you're here for.'

'Yes,' she said, 'it is. And you're welcome to stay and learn.'

Before he could respond, she added: 'Perhaps, though, first could you please do us a favor? I don't know how to open the window and it's stuffy in here.'

Like a man should, he opened the stiff metal window. Turned from that…

… and realized he was *over there.*

Miss Jordan Smith stood in front of her class. Cool air flowed over them.

'Hey, kids,' she said. 'When you look at this map, what do you see?'

Lucas squinted as hard as he could.

'It looks like one big thing, but you see all these lines called "borders." When you cross over those lines, those borders, you're someplace else. When you cross a border, it feels the same as where you were *and* completely different, both at the same time. Sometimes you don't know when you've stepped over the line until suddenly *whoops* – there you are. Some borders are OK to cross. Some mean there are different rules. And crossing some can be dangerous.

'We all come from inside the borders of one place out into a big world. And Mr Olsen over there will tell you this is true: you can't know where you are if you don't know what else is out there.'

Mr Olsen *over there* wanted to say something but he'd lost his tongue.

'So let's figure this out,' said Miss Smith. 'We'll make teams. Everybody on a team will help on a big report about a foreign place. What's it like to live there? Was it a colony like us before our revolution? Did Hitler occupy it? Did they have no borders like Montana did when it belonged to the Indians?'

'Miss Smith! Miss Smith!' Of course, it was Eileen waving her hand, then bursting out with: 'That doesn't count because we got rid of all the Indians.'

'*Not quite,*' said Marin.

The room stopped breathing. Frank Stiff Arm became a rock in his seat. Faye Inman made herself so still no wind could shake her black hair. Bobby Dupree and Penny Miller burned in their forever tans. Lucas saw twenty-one milk-skinned kids struggling to find a safe place to point their eyes.

Me, too, he thought. *Me, too.*

A dragon cloud from Mr Olsen snaked across the room to Marin.

Miss Smith sent Marin a smile. 'Great point. And we're glad about that.'

She's right, thought Lucas.

And Marin was right to say *un-un* to Eileen.

'We'll have four kids to a team,' she said. 'Start choosing up during recess, then tomorrow, I'll assign people who still can't make up their minds. We'll—'

The Recess Bell rang.

Scrambling fifth graders swept Lucas into their evacuation.

He glimpsed Miss Smith smiling beside her new desk.

Saw Mr Olsen sitting *over there*, glaring like something was off.

Lucas caught up with Kurt and Wayne on the packed-sand playground.

'We gotta choose a fourth for that project,' said Kurt as they passed first graders spinning on the merry-go-round. 'Or she'll stick us with somebody.'

Lucas said: 'How about Marin?'

His friends stared at him.

'He's smart,' said Lucas. 'I saw him at the library.'

Wayne said: 'Marin is… He probably wouldn't do any of the work.'

'Will so,' said Lucas. ''Sides, the only one else who'd be good is Bobbi Jean.'

'Forget it!' snapped Wayne. 'We can't have a girl!'

Kurt shrugged. 'Bobbi Jean's probably already with Anna.'

'Who cares about them?' fibbed Lucas. 'We have to pick him while we can.'

'Then you do it,' said Wayne. 'And I don't want to end up doing his share.'

'You won't,' said Kurt. 'But he's right, Lucas. You gotta be the one to ask.'

Lucas found Marin flying high through the cool air on a swing.

You see me, thought Lucas. *Please stop.*

The other boy whipped past him as far as the swing's chains allowed. Higher and higher, until the only thing left to do was let go. Let the rush suck him out of the swing's seat. Power back, *whoosh* forward... *Let go.* Fly free into blue sky.

Marin—

—quit pumping. Flowed out of the swing to face Lucas.

'I was thinking,' said Lucas. 'Me, Kurt, Wayne. Would you be on our team?'

'You want me? For that project she gave us?'

Lucas nodded.

'*YOU!*'

Principal Olsen's yell blasted the two boys. They whirled. Saw him so close his spit spray hit them. '*Marin!* You might have other people fooled, but I know a troublemaker when I see one! And, mister, I got my eye on you!'

Rocks crunched under Mr Olsen's black shoes as he charged away.

'You still want me on your team?' whispered Marin.

Lucas nodded.

Marin walked away.

Kurt and Wayne met Lucas in the middle of the playground.

'What happened?' asked Kurt.

'Beats me,' answered Lucas.

Bobbi Jean ran up to them. She pointed toward the brown brick fortress a long block away. 'Hey, Lucas! Is that your dad's car over at the high school?'

Squinting, Lucas couldn't be sure, but Bobbi Jean would know Dad's company car, a black station wagon with white letters: MARSHALL TRUCKING.

'What's he doing there?' she asked.

'I don't know anything! I mean... It's... It's OK. He's doing nothing.'

'High school's a funny place to do nothing,' said Bobbi Jean.

The ringing bell killed recess and they all ran inside.

'So,' said Miss Smith as they sat in their desks, 'do we have any teams?'

Of course Eileen's hand shot up: three *not-as-bossy* girls on her team.

'Miss Smith?'

'Yes, Marin?'

'I'm with Lucas Ross. And those guys there: Kurt, Wayne.'

Lucas flew home for lunch past the high school doors that teenagers slammed out of as the noon whistle blew. He ran the whole six blocks home. On the way to the back door, Lucas turned between his house and the Dentons'—

—spotted Mr Denton, a squat man scrunched beside a tree in his own yard, peering toward the north end of town with binoculars.

'Hey, Mr Denton!'

He whirled to the neighbor boy. Binoculars tucked behind his back.

'What are you doing?' asked Lucas as he ran to join the gruff old man.

'Ah… Nothing, I—'

'What are you looking at with those binoculars? Can I see?'

'*No!*'

Lucas peered where the binoculars had pointed: north over Main Street, past the railroad tracks, past the houses there to the hills at the city limits.

Denton said: 'I was looking at birds. Go eat lunch. Nothing's going on here.'

Nothing's going on everywhere, thought Lucas. As his fingers touched the back door to his house, Lucas remembered Mrs Sweeny's sour-breath hiss:

'*Your uncle the Eye-talian Papist and that evil red house on the north hill.*'

He squinted toward the north side. A new box-like house was there, he knew that, but all he could see was its reddish blur. No uncle. And no evil.

Lucas ran into the kitchen. Saw his whole family already home for lunch, sitting around the table with tuna fish sandwiches and milk.

Shouted: 'I got the greatest new teacher!'

'That's nice,' said Mom as Lucas sat in his place.

'Hey, Dad: How come you were at the high school?'

Dad used *that voice*: 'Do you remember what we talked about?'

'Yeah, I know nothing, but you were there. I saw the car at recess.'

'Lucas,' said Dad, 'some things have to stay in the family.'

'I'm in the family,' said Lucas.

'But you're not—'

'*Old enough*. When will I be "*old enough*"?'

'This is all we can tell you,' said Dad. 'There was a car wreck. Earl Klise died. Hal Hemmer didn't. Laura's on the line because of something she did. Now she's doing the right thing. She's helping the sheriff and county attorney. We're still figuring out what that means.'

'I think—'

'*We* doesn't mean *you*, Lucas,' said Dad. 'And there's one rule everybody agrees on *besides* you saying nothing: Laura can't talk about it at all. She has to be able to swear to that in a court of law.'

'Hand on the Bible,' said Lucas.

'I hope it doesn't come to that,' said Dad.

'What about the Honor Society?'

Laura said: 'He knows about that. Yesterday, riding around… He knows.'

'The Honor Society,' said Dad. 'This morning I pointed out to the high school that the county attorney says Laura can't tell anything to anybody. Otherwise the law might get screwed up.

Lots of rumors, but since nobody can tell the Honor Society anything, there's nothing the Honor Society can do.'

'Not yet,' sighed Laura. 'But—'

'I'm too tired for more buts,' said Dad. 'What with this and that wedding.'

'We should leave that alone,' said Mom. 'Let sleeping dogs lie.'

'They wake up,' said Dad.

'Mr Denton watches birds,' said Lucas.

'What?' said Mom.

'Next door. Mr Denton. He watches birds. With binoculars.'

Dad said: 'The only thing Denton ever used for birds is his shotgun.'

'Well, he's watching the north side for them now.'

Lucas couldn't translate the glance his parents gave each other.

Mom said: 'If you've finished your sandwich, go back to school.'

Lucas stood. 'Her name is Miss Jordan Smith.'

And that afternoon she turned 5A inside out and upside down with a multiplication game where each student whirled to face the desk behind him, shouted out the name of the kid they saw and threw him or her a *what* times *what* equals *what*. They answered, whirled to do the same to the kid behind him, all around the room, faster and faster, louder and laughing and cheering—

The door flew open.

Mr Olsen loomed in that passageway to the rest of the world.

'Isn't it great!' said Miss Smith. 'Your kids will be math champions!'

She gave her boss an innocent smile.

Mr Olsen blinked.

Then called out to the hall: 'Get in here!'

A dusty-haired girl shuffled in. Kept her eyes pointed down.

'You got a new classmate.' Mr Olsen stepped into 5A. Gestured for the new girl to step beside him and she did.

Raised her eyes.

'Her name is Donna Schultz,' said Mr Olsen as he scanned the room.

He spotted Lucas. 'Ross! Are you the last of the Rs?'

'*Yes*—' said Lucas, being absolutely sure to add: '—*sir*.'

'Are there any Ss?'

No was the answer born in silence to the front of the classroom.

'All you kids behind Ross, change your seats one further back. New girl—'

Miss Smith interrupted: 'Donna Schultz.'

'—take the desk behind the Ross kid there. What are you all waiting for?'

Lucas was torn between watching his classmates last-named T through Z rearrange their daily lives and staring at the new girl in school.

She sat in the desk behind Lucas. Only had a notebook and one pencil.

'Oh,' said Principal Olsen. 'I forgot. Come up here, Donna.'

His eyes pulled the new girl to the front of the classroom.

'Good,' he said. 'Now turn around and walk back.'

Her right shoulder moved up and down with each clumpy step.

Donna was beside Lucas when Principal Olsen proclaimed:

'See, class? That's how somebody who's had polio walks. That's why all of you who whined about those vaccination shots we lined up for in the gym should be thanking your lucky stars for American science.'

The desk behind him thudded into Lucas's back as Donna collapsed into her assigned place. He heard her sob once. Sob twice. Strangle all other sobs.

Mr Olsen turned to face a stunned Miss Smith. 'They're all yours.'

He slammed 5A's door shut behind him.

Miss Smith took in a deep breath and let it out.

Picked up the class's three schoolbooks.

Faced her students with a soft smile.

'It's almost time to go,' she said. 'You've all been checking the clock. But here, now, we got some time just to ourselves.

'Before you go home,' she said as she walked up and down the aisles, 'I want you all to start thinking on something I'd like you to do for me.'

She paused at Nick's desk to slip a pencil into his skittering hand and slide a sheet of paper under that so he could see what he'd scribble. And if he could see more of what he was doing, maybe he could do something better.

'What I need you to do,' she said, walking on, 'is give me a project next Monday that tells me about you. I already know your names. Heck, if we shout them out anymore, we'll all get in big trouble!'

Somebody snickered.

And like that, relief eased the room.

Eileen waved her hand. 'What do you mean: *something about us*?'

'That's what you'll show me,' said the teacher. 'Could be a letter introducing yourself. Could be a poem. A story about where you went with your family. A drawing you do. Could be a pretend story you make up. I don't know – and you'll find out. The only way you can get it wrong is not to do it at all.

'Isn't this what school's for? Finding out about you and the world? We've got all these ideas we wrote on the blackboard this morning about the world and questions to think about for your group report. You all have your notes on that.'

Lucas glanced at Kurt. Got the nod.

'But what I need to know is not what's written on the blackboard or in books. I need to know about you. You're the only one who can give that to me.'

The clock said *Not Yet*, so she let them copy more from the blackboard while she walked the aisles between the rows of their desks. She stopped next to Ralph, who hadn't poked or shoved or twisted an arm of anyone all day.

'Hey, Ralph,' she said. 'You've been all tense in your desk since I got here.'

'Nothing's wrong, Miss Smith!' said Ralph. 'Honest!'

She stood waiting beside the desk of the class bully.

'I just, *um*, hurt my back,' said Ralph.

'Let's send you to the school nurse.'

'No! Don't do that! I'm OK, honest! Please – Am I in trouble? Not for this!'

'*Naw.*' She gently pulled Ralph's collar away from his spine and looked.

That quick hiss of sucked-in air wasn't Ralph, thought Lucas. *Was her.*

And then she was standing right behind Lucas.

'I'm glad you showed up,' Miss Smith told the new girl. 'Now I'm not the only *S* in the room.

'These are for you,' said Miss Smith as she put the three textbooks on the desk beside the staring-straight-ahead Donna. 'Same as everybody else.'

Now she's standing right beside me! Lucas sat straight and tall.

The sway of her black hair electrified past his face as she stared bent down to look at the empty page in his notebook. She said nothing. Walked away.

Dismissal Bell clanged.

Lucas turned to smile *Hi!* to the new Donna. He'd figured out *exactly* what to say to her so she'd feel at home: 'My grandmother had polio, too!'

Donna's face looked like a bull about to charge. 'I'm not your *anything.*'

Miss Smith's voice rang out above the din of fifth graders headed home:

'Lucas Ross: sit back down. Please stay after class.'

Mistake! All the kids knew that was a mistake as they scrambled to get out of there. His friends stared at him: Kurt and Wayne, Anna and Bobbi Jean. Marin. Lucas was one of the good kids! Him staying after school had to be a mistake!

He faced Miss Smith from his desk at the back of the empty classroom.

She stood leaning back against her desk at the front of the room.

'I don't know about you,' she said, 'but I've had a heck of a day.'

'Yes, ma'am.'

'I think I'm going to like it here. What do you think?'

'I… I hope so.'

'Me, too. I noticed something, and I wonder if you'd do me a favor.'

Hard as he could, Lucas nodded.

'Sitting right where you are, would you read me what's on the blackboard?'

'Wha-what?'

'Just up there behind me. All the instructions I wrote up there for your team project. I noticed you weren't taking any notes and kept squinting.'

'Kurt's on my team. He takes notes for the project so I don't have to.'

'What about when you're not on a team?'

'Mostly I get it when I read the books, but I can always call him. Or Wayne. Once I called Bobbi Jean, but *please* don't tell anybody I did: she's a girl.'

'I keep secrets, Lucas. Apparently, so do you. Please read what's on the blackboard.'

Heart pounding. Eyes squinting. Promising anything to God *if…*

The blackboard stayed a blur.

'Come sit in the front row,' she said. 'Bring your notebook.'

Took him a decade to walk to the front and sit in a strange desk.

'Now can you read it for me?'

'*Imagine how people live. What they do for work. Are they like us? What's it like to be a kid there? Do they have dogs? What—*'

'That's fine, Lucas.' Miss Smith moved behind her desk. 'While you copy all that, I'll write a note to your parents to get your eyes checked for glasses.'

'Oh please *no*, Miss Smith! Glasses will ruin my whole life!'

'*What?*'

KNOCK-KNOCK – on her open door.

'Am I intruding?' said the man silhouetted by afternoon sunlight.

He's just a sixth grade teacher, thought Lucas. *He's tall. No glasses.*

'I'm Neal Dylan,' he said to Lucas's teacher. 'Just down the hall from you.'

So stay there! thought Lucas. *Go away. I'm here.*

'I'm the new kid in school. Jordan Smith.'

Mr Dylan said: 'Sorry I didn't get a chance to meet you earlier. There's something I had to work on, a car accident.'

'This weekend. Two high school kids. What do you have to do with that?'

'Somebody has to help.'

Don't lose this chance to change her mind! thought Lucas. But he'd copied everything from the blackboard. *You can stay as long as they see you keeping busy. Start the special homework! Write her...*

Write her a cool story! Like the ones that keep waking up in your head.

'What are you going to do?' she asked the man in the room.

The breeze from the window Principal Olsen opened stirred her black hair.

The hero of the story will be a soldier, thought Lucas. *And he'll be stationed in West Berlin. And he'll rescue an American woman teacher from the Reds.*

'About the accident,' she said. 'What's going to happen?'

'We're trying to work it so nobody gets hurt even more.'

Neal Dylan glanced at the Ross boy in a desk scribbling in his notebook. 'Did Mr Olsen... share his theories on education with you?'

'You could say that,' she said.

Realization hit Lucas: *If she reads about a soldier and West Berlin and a teacher, she'll think – That's what she'll think and don't let her know that!*

'I don't want to say the wrong thing to the wrong person at the wrong time in the wrong place,' said Miss Jordan Smith.

They swung their eyes to Lucas.

'You don't need to worry about me,' said Mr Neal Dylan.

I don't need to worry about him, thought Lucas. *He's married.*

'Something came up in class today,' she said. 'Actually, a couple things happened that just… I don't know how the system here in Vernon works, but…'

'We could grab some coffee,' said the man who spent his days down the hall from her. 'Maybe I could help you figure out what to do. When you're done here.'

Lucas felt their glare. But he could trick them into letting him—

Wait! The story could be about a spy!

'That would be great,' Miss Smith told Mr Dylan.

Then she said: 'I've finished your note, Lucas.'

And the spy meets a woman who might be a killer but is really cool and has hair the color of a raven!

Miss Smith told her colleague: 'If I can help you, I will. With the accident.'

Mr Dylan nodded to her as Lucas closed his notebook.

'How is this town?' she asked her colleague as Lucas packed up.

'I grew up here,' he said. 'Didn't mean to come back, but… things happen.

'*How is this town?*' he said. 'Terrible. Wonderful.'

'So it's like everywhere else.'

Lucas watched her lasso the moment with her smile.

THE SHAPE OF THINGS

Tuesday surprised Lucas as Tuesdays shouldn't.

Sunday is Rest & Get Ready Day: *Here comes another week.*

Monday whams you with: *What you've got to do.*

Tuesday should be: *OK, you're in it now.*

Tuesday was Day 3 of the week, thought Lucas. A *no surprises* day. Has you already doing what showed up on Monday until Friday night when – if you're lucky – you get to go to the movies at the Roxy.

Plus, three is one of the *means something special* numbers. A triangle has three sides. Dad told Lucas that in his one year at engineering school before he came to Vernon, he learned that the triangle is the strongest shape.

Wouldn't it be cool to discover a new shape! thought Lucas.

He'd planned to keep that Tuesday's shape strong and free of surprises.

Failed before he'd even finished his OJ and buttered toast while reading the comics in the newspaper as he sat alone at the breakfast table.

KNOCK-KNOCK! The front door.

In from the farm walked smiling Aunt Dory.

'Hey, guys!' she said. 'Morning. You ready, Cora?'

Mom bustled out of the bedroom. Frowned. 'Where's everybody else?'

'Hell, you know Iona's got her hands full getting her kids off to school, and Beryl… Beryl says she's gotta run the taxi this morning.'

'The hell you say,' said Mom.

'Nope,' said Aunt Dory. 'The hell *she* says. Says Johnny's busy with—

'—doesn't make any difference,' continued Dory, the youngest of the Conner sisters. 'I'm here, you're ready, and Doc Horn don't need all four of us.'

Then Mom and Aunt Dory were gone out the slamming-closed front door.

Lucas rushed to school. Was about to scramble into 5A's classroom when *she* walked out with another teacher: *Playground Duty.*

Lucas *casually* strolled through the growing pack of grade school kids on this fine spring Tuesday morning. He circled around wherever Miss Smith walked. Reached the monkey bars where kids scrambled. Slipped/kept on climbing. Hung from their arms and slid down its fireman's pole.

Lucas watched Miss Smith create a triangle.

Her gravity eyes pulled him to her.

She threw a smile and a *come here* nod toward the new girl, Donna, who stood by herself near the teeter-totters.

Turned to her left and summoned Bobbi Jean.

Three ten-year-old American children of the generation that survived the Spanish Flu of 1918 and the Dust Bowl Depression and won World War II shuffled into an ordered triangle in front of Jordan Smith on the packed-sand playground.

'I'm glad I caught you guys before class,' she said. 'Donna, you know Lucas, right? I mean, you sit right behind him.'

'I know who he is,' came Donna's flat reply.

'I've gotta ask you a favor,' Miss Smith told Donna. 'Lucas has trouble seeing the blackboard. And I don't want to disrupt the class by making people change seats *again* to put him in the front row. So when you all have to copy down what's on the blackboard, would you help out and pass your notes to him?'

Donna's brow wrinkled. 'He needs *my* help?'

'We all need help.'

Donna's voice softened. 'OK.'

'Great,' said Smith. 'Bobbi Jean, I need you to tell all your friends that these two are not breaking the rules and passing notes during class. Things work best when we all know what's going on.'

'I'll tell everybody!' said Bobbi Jean.

'Be sure to tell them it's all *cool*.' Miss Smith used that word like she was one of those big-city jazz musicians Lucas heard Laura tell Irwin about or in that old James Dean movie about teenagers and a gun with no bullets.

'One more thing, Bobbi Jean: Do you and Anna have your report team?'

'Anna's still trying to make up her mind.'

'Today I'm assigning teams that aren't ready. You two are now with Donna. Unless you're already on a team, Donna?'

The new girl in school shook her head *no*.

Miss Smith told Bobbi Jean: 'You better find Anna, tell her.'

Bobbi Jean smiled to the new girl. 'Later, Donna!' Ran off.

Lucas said: 'What… what about me?'

'You've got to do what you've got to do,' said Miss Smith.

Walked away with whatever that meant.

Lucas looked at Donna. 'I guess I should say thanks.'

'You *guess*?' She shrugged. 'I *guess* that's better than nothing.'

Limped away like nothing mattered.

Recess meant Wayne and Kurt hurried to Lucas. Lucas waved over Marin.

Now we're four, he thought. *Like the Musketeers their second time around.*

Kurt said: 'You seen the digging they're doing for the new high school?'

'Laura'll be in the first senior class to graduate from there,' said Lucas.

Shut up! You know nothing about Laura-high-school-accident!

Wayne said: 'It's on the northside.'

The northside.

They were all southside kids. They went to Blackhawk Elementary, not the northside's Mountain View Elementary or the mysterious Catholic school.

The northside.

The tough side of this town of nearly four thousand people. Across the railroad tracks. Where the *second*-toughest bar was the Bucket of Blood. The *toughest* bar was the Oasis, a block away. The tall wooden fence, no-roof 'bullpen' out back of the Oasis was where they threw drunks to sleep it off or fight it out.

The northside.

Where bulldozers had scraped flat the yellow prairie inside wooden stakes for a new high school to help Republican President Eisenhower's genius plan to educate *every* American kid in *everything* to help us Stay on Top and Beat the Russians. Plus, the new high school would serve the stampede of children as Vernon grew bigger with the good times that were never ever going to stop.

The northside.

Where blocks of new houses created a neighborhood with fathers who worked in offices and mothers who always wore lipstick and raised children who'd someday bus across the tracks to the gray-castle junior high beside the old high school's fortress of brown bricks one long block up from the playground where Lucas and his three friends stood that Tuesday morning.

The northside.

Dad's trucking company with The Secret and garages for rows of parked silver tanker trucks filled a block on the northside. Aunt Beryl and Uncle Johnny lived on the northside. Kept the blue taxi parked at their white house. And on the far side of the northside, past the edge of town but easy to see from Lucas's backyard with good eyes or binoculars, stood a new two-story box house painted red.

'OK,' said Lucas to his three buddies on the playground during that morning's recess. 'We picked France for our country to report on, so—'

'So we gotta divide up the questions and stuff from the blackboard,' said Wayne. 'Then put it together in one report.'

Kurt said: 'Plus whatever else we each can find on our own for—'

'YOU FOUR!' Principal Olsen pounced out of nowhere. 'What're you doing?'

Lucas blurted: 'We're working on the group project we gotta do!'

Kurt said: 'From off when you showed us the map!'

'*Hmmph.*' Principal Olsen looked at all of them. Stared at Marin.

Stabbed his finger at these fifth graders. 'No gangs!'

He stormed away as his wake swirled them into what he'd forbidden.

The Recess Bell called everyone back inside the school for math class.

Lucas watched his buddies take their seats as he sat in his desk in front of Donna. Realized that if he, Donna, and Bobbi Jean had been a triangle, he and his three new gang buddies were four corners of a square. Like a box. And if four corners made a box, he and his family were a box too, but…

He blinked. *But we didn't get to decide the shape of our family.*

Or what's in that box.

Maybe he'd learn about all that in the new high school on the northside.

He frowned. Northside and southside made a line. A border, like Miss Smith talked about yesterday. A border that kids crossed into being new junior high school kids when they got older and so maybe the border… went away.

So maybe two things create one new thing: 1 + 1 = 3, not just 2.

Morning Dismissal Bell sent Lucas and all his classmates scurrying home except for Bobbi Jean and other country bus kids who brought their own lunch. Wayne, Kurt, and Marin walked with him until their paths changed. They each said 'See ya!' as they headed toward where they slept.

Lucas walked into the kitchen, where his family sat around that day's lunch of bologna and catsup sandwiches on white bread with glasses of milk just as Laura told her parents: 'Nobody says anything, but everybody stares at me.'

'That's just your imagination,' said Mom. 'Eat your lunch.'

Laura stared straight ahead. 'I know what I know.'

Lucas ate a homemade chocolate chip cookie while walking back to school, where everything stayed Tuesday OK until twenty-seven minutes before afternoon recess when a sixth grade girl knocked on the open door and told Miss Smith:

'Principal Olsen says Marin's supposed to go to the office.'

Miss Smith shot up her hand to stop Marin as he stood out of his desk.

Asked the messenger: 'Why does Mr Olsen want to see Marin?'

The girl shrugged. 'I'm just doing what I'm supposed to do.'

All the kids in 5A knew what Marin's long walk down the tiled floor toward the office meant. Lucas saw that realization grow on Miss Smith's face.

Lucas watched his friend leave the safety of 5A, out the door, gone.

Miss Smith rushed through explaining that the 'built by' WPA sign on the county courthouse that Bobbi Jean had raised her hand and asked about was a federal government program to save the country from the Depression by bubbling money up through working people like in Vernon to a place called Wall Street back east in New York that helped cause the mess in the first place.

'Lucas,' she called out as she scribbled on a pink hall pass. 'Go to the office. Give this note to Principal Olsen. Tell him you'll wait for his answer. Hurry!'

Lucas didn't break the no-running rule, but he hustled through the flat-walled hallway shaft like he was being tracked by The Thing.

A chill grabbed Lucas when he saw no one sat in Mrs B's secretary desk in the outer room of the office. When Principal Olsen did something with the bad kids, Mrs B always left her desk for somewhere else.

SLAP!

Muffled sound came through the wooden door to the inner office.

SLAP!

A man's shout: *'Are you getting it yet?'*

Some other sound like... *whimpering.*

SLAP!

Make it stop! Make it stop! Lucas pounded on the door with his fist.

Jumped back. Stood trembling at attention.

Principal Olsen exploded out of his Inner Sanctum—

—saw the Ross kid standing there, pink hall pass in his shaky hand.

Olsen flashed on that this kid's sister was a star when she'd gone to this school. Remembered that folks on Main Street and the school board liked Lucas's dad. Who was a boss. Remembered the tough-town Conner women.

'What do you want?' snapped Principal Olsen.

'Miss Smith said I had to give you this note and get an answer right away!'

Principal Olsen grabbed the pink slip.

Marin stood shaking by the principal's desk.

'Why is she bothering me about this now?' muttered Principal Olsen.

He scrawled something on the pink slip of paper, shoved it back to Lucas.

Principal Olsen jerked his head in that direction. 'This guy a friend of yours?'

Lucas bobbed his head. 'And we're on the same project team!'

'Remind him how lucky he is to be here. Maybe he should've been shipped off to one of them Injun boarding schools. Let the nuns shape him up 'n' save him from his red blood. Or he should've stuck to his reservation.' Principal Olsen waved for Marin to go with Lucas. 'Now you two get back to class. Don't let me catch you in here again like this.'

Principal Olsen stalked back into his inner office. Shut the door.

Lucas saw red marks on Marin's pale-coffee face.

Saw tears Marin hadn't been able to stop.

'We've got a hall pass,' said Lucas. 'Let's go to the bathroom.'

He led the way into that sanctuary with two gray stalls, low-mounted urinals across from a wall of mirrors and sinks. Chemical smells whiffed into a scent like pine with the stench of urine.

Marin hurried into a gray stall.

Lucas's reflection stared back at him from the mirror above the sinks.

He unfolded the pink slip.

Miss Smith had written: 'Can I lower the temperature in my room?'

Principal Olsen's angry scrawl read: 'Don'T caRE!'

Lucas folded the message so important it interrupted *whatever.*

Marin flushed the toilet in the gray stall like he'd used it. Walked out to the sinks. Turned the cold water on. Splashed his face over and over.

Lucas handed him paper towels.

Wondered what shape this Tuesday made.

SPIES

Lucas lay on his bed Saturday morning before the first explosion.

Dressed. Ready. Thinking about the movie his parents let him go to the night before: *The Bat*, a crazy killer loose in a mansion full of trapped people in some place where they had such things as mansions. None of his friends had gone, nor had Laura, but because Lucas delivered handbills door-to-door for the Roxy, he got a free ticket to any movie his parents let him see.

Now as he lay there after breakfast waiting for his other job to start, his parents' words crept through his open bedroom window from the backyard.

'All I'm asking is for you to steer what could happen anyway,' said Dad.

'If you look for trouble, you find it,' said Mom.

'I'm not looking for trouble, but we have to know if it's there.'

'Isn't Laura and that car wreck enough?'

'Things don't come like you want. If anybody in this town knows what's going on, it's you guys, the Conner girls.'

'We have to figure out about my mother tonight,' said Cora.

'That's perfect! That means nobody will notice what you're asking.'

Wait! thought Lucas. *This is like being a spy for my story! Who are the bad guys? Do there always have to be bad guys? There's a woman with raven hair. The spy lies under the Berlin – no – under the East Berlin open window.*

'You've got to do this, Cora. It's our best shot.'

The back door opened, slammed shut. Dad called: 'Come on, Lucas.'

'I cut these for Gramma,' Mom told Lucas in the living room as she showed him a handful of purple lilac blooms. 'Hospital rooms smell.'

'We all do what we can to help,' said Dad. As his wife glared at him, he told Lucas: 'Put your bike in the back of the station wagon.'

Driving to the shop, Lucas said: 'Dad, how come you always wear a sports jacket? You wear it outside *and* at your office. If it's a jacket, why wear it inside?'

The white-logo-painted black station wagon obeyed a red stop sign.

'You'll understand when you grow up. When you're a lawyer.'

'It's silly.'

'*NO!*' Dad's fists strangled the steering wheel. His face burned with a rage Lucas'd never seen before. 'When you're the boss, a manager, you wear a boss's jacket! How you get treated! That's the job you got! The respect! *Who you are!*'

The polite *Toot!* of a car horn came from behind them.

Their rearview mirror showed gray-haired Mrs Wiggan waving at them.

Dad pried his hand off the station wagon's steering wheel. Waved *OK!*

The station wagon emblazoned MARSHALL TRUCKING rolled forward.

'Didn't mean to yell like that.' Dad tossed a hollow smile to Lucas.

We're almost there, thought Lucas. *Don't say anything! Think about the spy story. Think about The Secret Of The Truck Shop and how you won't get caught. Don't dare get caught, not today – not after this blowup!*

Marshall Trucking sprawled near the highway to Canada and the north country oil fields. Gleaming silver steel tanker trucks lined the packed-earth lot. The gray clapboard house next door had a sign in the window that read: Office.

Act normal, thought Lucas as he walked with his father to an open garage bay and the truck backed in there. *Be a spy.*

A man in greasy overalls turned to them from the truck's open hood. 'Damn, Don, some Saturday I'm gonna look up and you won't be walking in here.'

Dad's smile came hard. 'Lucas had to go to work.'

'*Sure*, you're just here 'cause of the kid. Least here, we know what we do. At home talking to the wife? That's tricky. This is just the job. How're you, Lucas?'

'OK, Harry.'

'Then why you standing over here when the broom is shaggin' it over there by the tool bench?' Harry McNamer swung his steel-braced right leg he brought back from D-Day around the pivot of his good limb. 'Had a damn good excuse for missing work last Saturday to go to the big *whoop-tee-do*, but I bet you two was in on Sunday even though it was Easter.'

'You'd lose that one,' said Dad.

Lucas grabbed the push broom from beside the red emergency shutoff button for the hydraulic lifts. Listened to hear if they suspected. *You're a spy.*

The East Berlin factory where the killer might be hiding smelled like gas, silver wrenches, and rubber tires. And oily floor dust herded by a push broom.

'So,' he heard Dad say to the head mechanic, 'did you like the wedding?'

'I got damn good 'n' drunk. But so did the old lady, so what the hell.'

Lucas swept back and forth across the garage's cement floor.

'Can't believe Fran got hitched,' said McNamer. ''Member when we was in the old place? After Alec had the big heart attack, brought you on. Alec didn't have no twenty-three trucks then. Like maybe five. Fran'd line up sockets on the bench.'

Lucas turned the broom to push its dirt pile back toward them.

And to The Secret.

'So at the wedding,' said Dad, 'any talk about the guy she married?'

'Ben, ain't it? Ben Owens.'

'Yes,' said Dad. 'Ben. I wonder what he's going to do now.'

'Get a job. A boss job. Push paper. Ain't that what all college boys do?'

Lucas swept around the arms of a hydraulic hoist on the cement floor.

'But I was just wondering,' said Dad. 'Fran, him: What'll they do?'

'Don't figure they'll come back here,' said McNamer. 'Ain't no place for him. ''Less he's hankering to drive a truck. Me, I just don't see that.'

'No,' said Dad. 'Me either. How's the rebuild going?'

Spy Lucas pushed the broom.

He saw Dad walking to his office, McNamer bent under the truck hood.

Back in the shadows waited the mechanics' desk. Garage smells. Metal slots on the walls: Time cards. Run slips. Work orders. ICC reports.

An overhead bulb no one ever turned off lit that corner with pale light.

Lit The Secret Of The Truck Shop.

That hung-up calendar logged 1949. The year Lucas was born.

But the time hung up on that wall is forever.

She lives in a rectangular world of red satin. Red satin cushion on the bed. Red satin draping the wall behind her.

She's naked.

Flesh like a smooth swirl of vanilla and strawberry.

Awe gripped Lucas from his first sight of her. His first sight of *any* woman in a picture or in person who looked like her. A soul who wasn't a wife or mom, a teacher or a high school/college/works at the bank girl-gone-woman.

She curls her bare legs up as she sits on the red bed. Her right arm makes the triangle she uses to rise up. Her fingers press the red satin. '*I choose to be here.*' She arches her back. Turns to face the world. Her left arm bends back over and behind her head and shields her heart-side eye.

Her breasts yearn free. Their swollen red-dot tips search like a second pair of eyes. Her face is a pink-rouged slide of high cheekbone and sleek jaw. An arched tan eyebrow and black lashes make a *see-you* slit for her dark gaze that says she knows. Says you don't. Her red lips smile. Their burning kiss.

Golden curls splay out behind her. Hair like September wheat shimmering in the camera's flash. Lucas knew the different shades of those flowing curls and her dark eyebrows meant that she'd taken the color God gave her—

—and rebelled.

Maybe you gotta rebel against who you're supposed to be to be who you are.

Yes! realized Lucas. Rebel! *The spy knew that her dyed raven hair hid its true color of… like a wheat field. She painted her lips—*

'Lucas!' yelled McNamer. 'You fall in a hole back there?'

'No! I mean – Almost done!'

He shoveled his dust piles into the trash bin. Swept the office while Dad clattered typewriter keys at his desk surrounded by file cabinets full of paper.

Lucas cleaned two toilets. Volunteered to get a form for McNamer from the forever-lit mechanic's desk. Went back there *again* to be sure he'd closed the drawer. Biked home for lunch with Mom before she went across the street to visit Gramma Meg in the hospital. Wrote words of the spy story and played until dinner, after which Dad *of course* went back to work.

Lucas had just finished drying the dishes Mom insisted on washing the exact correct way when Aunt Iona and Aunt Dory marched into the house.

'Hey, Lucas!' said Aunt Dory. 'What'd you do today?'

'Nothing! Honest!'

Dory laughed. 'Does "*nothing honest*" mean *dishonest*?'

'Lucas ain't that kind of kid,' said Aunt Iona.

Iona was darkest of the Conner girls. Iona came after Beryl, but before Lucas's mom and 'baby' Dory. Three Conner brothers were scattered across the west by wind, women, and whiskey, so the sisters who'd stayed in Vernon were the ones who counted, the ones the whole town knew and who knew the whole town.

'I'm ready,' said Mom as she walked into the living room.

'Sure, *now* you are,' said Iona. 'Half an hour ago, Dory and I damn near died when Meg wanted to wheel down to the nursery to look for new babies.'

Dory said: 'We'd just snuck Beryl down thataway to work the new place.'

'Did Meg catch her?' asked Lucas's mother about her own.

'Hell no!' said Iona. 'Beryl gets away with everything.'

'Oh.' Dory smiled. 'Like you never do. Why don't you reach in your purse and give Lucas one of the breath-cleanin' Lifesavers you're always sneaking? We've already seen our mother tonight, and your Orville's back over in Butte, so you won't be needing to use them now.'

Cora Conner aka Mom announced: 'Lucas is going riding with us.'

Her sisters stared at her.

Mom argued: 'Laura's over to Shelby with the choir. Don's working.'

'Well, yeah,' said Dory, 'but… Lucas's been staying by himself for a year.'

And I want to watch the new TV! thought Lucas. *Or read a Hardy Boys.*

Dory said: 'If he comes, the talking's going to have to be all around him.'

'He's gotta go and that's that.' Mom shrank in her shoes. 'Or… Or maybe, since I gotta watch him, maybe we shouldn't go. Leave all that for another time.'

'I don't get it,' said Iona. 'You're the one for us talking and now...'

'Forget it, Cora,' said Dory. 'You're coming. Lucas: Grab your jacket.'

They left the house and climbed into the blue taxi idling at the curb.

Aunt Beryl waited behind the steering wheel. She was the oldest of the Conner girls, but Lucas knew her hair'd gone gray *way* early.

'Hell, kid,' said gray-haired Beryl as her nephew opened the taxi's back door. 'Didn't expect to see you. Be careful not to kick those two big green tanks on the back floor, or we'll have bubble water all over the place.'

'What?' said Lucas as he rested his sneakers on a heavy cylinder.

Iona slid into the backseat beside him.

Driver Beryl said: 'Carbonated water. Pressurized. For the – your uncle Johnny's business. It's not set up for 'em yet.'

'What isn't?' said Mom as she climbed in the other back door and wedged Lucas between two Conner sisters.

'It's just a cathouse thing,' said Iona. 'We don't need to never mind.'

'What's a cathouse?' asked Lucas.

Dory looked at Beryl. Beryl pointed her eyes to where Lucas's mother sat trapped in the rearview mirror. Iona stared out the window and started to hum.

Dory said: 'It's some kind of thing somebody will have to have a talk with you about pretty quick.'

'Don't look at me,' said Mom.

'Hell,' said Beryl. 'We know better than that!'

All the Conner girls laughed. Even Mom.

Four sisters and a boy rode away through the geography of their lives.

But not through my town, thought Lucas.

There's the town the kids know. Which ant hills are red and

which are black. Which crab apple trees ripen first. Which car dealer puts out donuts when the new models come in and doesn't yell at grabby kids. Which houses are haunted. Which give good stuff at Halloween. Where you can run to. Where you can hide.

Teenagers know another town. Where someone special lives. Which road takes you out where no one else can see. How many times you can cruise Main Street before curfew blows.

Adults know a town of lists. Where's the job. Where's the school. Where's the hospital. The bank. The firehouse. The post office. The mechanic. The grocery store. And probably where's the cathouse.

'How's your new neighbor Falk?' Aunt Dory asked Mom as they drove past his house. 'I saw him parked in front of Mrs Sweeny's.'

Lucas asked: 'What's a slanter?'

'Huh?' said Mom.

'Mrs Sweeny said Uncle Orville used to work for some slanter guy named Mickey something, but I don't know what a slanter is.'

'Oh God, don't ask your uncle!' said that man's dark-haired wife Iona.

'A slanter's a thief,' Iona told Lucas. 'A guy who fixes his oil rig so he drills at a slant off his land underground to your land to suck up your oil. Mrs Sweeny is mad at Orville because he worked for a guy named McDewel. She thinks McDewel slanted her land. She's so damn certain she's sitting on a fortune, she's never agreed to any drilling deal. But McDewel died broke, so go figure.

'Hell,' said Iona, 'these days I wish Orville was a slanter. He says work in Butte is slowing down and if he doesn't find some jobs, he's going to have to lay off his crew. But that's his worry, the son-of-a-bitch, I got six kids to keep clean.'

'Hey,' said gray-haired Beryl as she commanded the steering wheel. 'Did you hear that new guy Falk's starting a Civic League?'

'What the hell is that?' asked Iona.

'Some new thing he's brought to town with him. Like now there'll be Civic League kind of folks and then the rest of us.'

'Not in Vernon,' said Dory.

'Not when we all grew up knowing who didn't have a Sears catalog for wiping in the outhouse,' said Mom.

'Maybe it's a good thing,' said Dory. 'Got to try something new.'

'Why?' said Mom.

Dory said: 'So what are we going to do about—'

Mom blurted: 'The Falks invited us to dinner but the last time we went out anywhere was the Marshall wedding!'

'Ah… Well, good, Cora.' Her baby sister frowned.

Words sprayed out of Cora Ross: 'So we went to the Easter wedding and I was wondering if anybody said anything, anybody heard anything!'

Beryl frowned at Mom's rigid image in the rearview mirror. 'Hell, Cora, everybody in town knows why they had to have the wedding when they did.'

Iona said: 'Wonder how much Gramma Meg knows about her *what's what*.'

'Look!' Beryl pointed through the windshield. 'There's Garth!'

A tall, thin man marched through the spring evening, eyes lost a thousand miles beyond the horizon, his never-takes-it-off gray winter hat jammed on his head, earflaps pulled down and buckled under his chin.

'Let's honk the horn so he'll go berserk like a chicken with its head cut off,' said Beryl.

'Don't do that!' said Iona. 'What if he smacks into our car?'

'You guys are no fun anymore,' said Beryl.

'Look at them bandages on his face,' said Iona as they drove past him.

'Shaves himself every day,' said Dory.

'We should take up a collection,' said Iona. 'Buy him an electric razor.'

'What if he hung himself with the cord?' said Mom.

'Or somebody else,' said Dory.

They turned past Lucas's school as he said: 'How come Garth's like that?'

'Shell shock in the war,' said Dory. 'Cannons shooting at him all day and night. Now along w' everything else, loud noises make him go *boom boom*.'

'He was fun in high school,' said Iona. 'What were we talking about?'

Mom blurted: 'The Marshall girl's wedding and what's going on there!'

'No,' said Dory, 'we were talking about our mother, Meg.'

Metal cylinders clanked together as Beryl swung the taxi into a parking space alongside the Tastee-Freez drive-in.

'Shit, Beryl!' cried Iona. 'Careful! What if these things back here blow up?'

'Then somebody'll have a hell of a story to tell.' The too-soon-gray sister turned off the taxi's engine. Her eyes locked out the windshield. 'Least it's only one stop to deliver those. For the vending machines, I drive all over the county.'

'You guys want Cokes or what?' asked Dory.

'Nickels and dimes,' continued Beryl. 'That's what I collect. Johnny brings in the folding money. All goes into the same pot. Paperwork shipped off. Plus now we got a damn taxi business.'

'Hey, Beryl,' said Iona from the backseat. 'Are they the same people Johnny's working for on the… the you know?'

Beryl lit a cigarette. 'Everybody does business with somebody.'

Iona leaned forward from the backseat. 'These carbonated water thingies here: Are they going to have a pop machine or bar out t' the house?'

'Beats me what they're going to have,' said Beryl. 'I just drive the taxi.'

Iona laughed. 'Hey, let's drive out and look at the house.'

'Hey,' countered Beryl, 'let's drive down to Butte. We'd get there past midnight, but that place never closes. See the big city. The copper mine. The mile-wide, mile-deep damn Berkeley Pit. See what holes your Orville is drilling.'

'What the hell do you mean by that?' snapped Iona.

Dory jumped in. 'Say, Cora—'

How come Dory's yelling? wondered Lucas.

'—what's Laura gonna do this summer?'

Dory's face pleaded for an answer.

'Not gonna talk about her and that car wreck!' said Mom. 'She's stopping Saturday waitressing. Got an operator job at the phone company. *Oh!* Laura said a woman got off the train today. Came to the café. Asked about the doctor.'

'Another one,' Dory said. 'I heard there was a girl and her mom into the Totem Pole Motel the other day all the way from Chicago. Doc Nirmberg's a hell of a thing for us to be famous for. You wonder how they hear about him.'

'You get in trouble, you'd be surprised what you hear,' said Beryl.

'Know what I heard?' said Iona. 'Somebody asked Doc Nirmberg if he was worried about the law. He said something like: "*Worry about my patients. If Sheriff Wood don't like that, leanin' against my office wall's my shotgun.*"'

Car driver Beryl shook her gone-gray-too-soon. 'But it's us women who always get shot.'

'That's why the cathouse is such a good thing,' said Dory. 'For all the gandy dancers slinging sledgehammers for the railroad and such. Guys with no wives. The… the house saves a lot of… a lot of problems. Keep our girls safe.

'But hell now,' she said. 'We're just jabbering away here and Lucas is dying for a Coke. Come on, Beryl, let's you and me get 'em. My treat. Come on.'

His two front seat aunts got out, walked away from the slam of their doors.

In the backseat, Mom glared at her sister Iona.

'What?' said Iona. 'What did I do? I was just talking. And then so was she.'

Familiar cars crawled through the drive-in loop in the evening light. Parents and their toddler joined his aunts at the walk-up window. Lucas watched Dory "*How you doing?*" them. Beryl's gaze seemed locked on somewhere else.

The taxi doors opened. Dory passed ice-jiggling paper cups to the backseat.

'They're all the same,' she said. 'Figured we're all family.'

Beryl climbed in behind the steering wheel. Pulled her door shut.

'I was saying to Beryl,' continued Dory, 'we're lucky we got Dr Horn and don't have to have Doc Nirmberg. I mean, his specialty ain't Gramma Meg's deal!'

Mom and Dory laughed.

But not Beryl. Not Iona.

Beryl cranked the taxi to life. Steered the cab through the neighborhood west of Lucas's school. Past the closed round outdoor swimming pool.

Dory rushed out a river of talk as the car drove through town – on and on, until Lucas heard Iona sigh.

Then Beryl whispered: '*Aw, hell.* Forget about it.'

Dory took a deep breath and let it out.

'So,' she said, 'what are we going to do about – *Lucas*: Look straight ahead there! Isn't that the sixth grade teacher's car? Neal Dylan?'

Lucas squinted through the windshield. He noticed a car prowling the street toward them. Saw the brown house that held a black piano.

'Poor Neal,' said Iona as the two cars neared each other. 'If the cathouse woulda been there a couple years back, maybe he wouldn't've been trapped.'

'But it all worked out,' said Dory. 'That baby Rachel's cute as hell. He takes her with him every chance he gets.'

'Don't look like he's got the baby now,' said Beryl as Neal Dylan's car receded in her mirrors. 'He's all alone, driving around.'

'He should have taken Rita to Doc Nirmberg,' said Iona.

'Don't say that!' said Dory.

'Besides,' said Beryl, 'Rita's too sharp to let a good man like him get away.'

The spy prayed that the guard at the factory gate wouldn't check his identity papers. The window glowed in the factory office. Maybe she's in there, he thought. Maybe if she looks out, she'll see me, thought the spy. Maybe I can see her. Does she know I know about her raven hair?

'Gramma Meg,' said Beryl.

'I ain't gonna be the one to tell her!' Iona unrolled another Lifesaver.

'Let's drag Main.' Beryl turned the taxi in that direction. 'Pretend we're kids.'

'I am a kid!' said Lucas.

'You're in a taxi now,' said Dory. 'Same as us.'

'Someday it'll be you and Laura riding around like this,' said Mom.

Heartbeats of silence filled the taxi.

The blue taxi carried the adults who'd carried Lucas forward through time down the Main Street of their lives. He rode with them. Knew he always would.

Their taxi purred past the Conoco gas station with two garage bays. Past flat-faced stores. Neon-sign bars. A bus depot. The dime store. One of five clothes stores. The drugstore. The Chat & Chew Café. The Capital Café. The dreams-haunted Roxy movie theater and the Whitehouse ice-cream parlor.

'Look who's holding up the wall of Teagardens,' said Beryl as they drove past that bar. 'Harley Anderson, back against the bricks. Got a boy your age, doesn't he, Lucas?'

Lucas squinted at the big man with the battered fedora and the belly over the belt of his tan workpants. The man's beady gaze followed the cruising taxi.

'Ralph's in my class,' said Lucas.

Said nothing about the noogies, the arm twists, the shoves.

'Well, Harley was in your Uncle Vaughn's,' said Dory.

'Was a mean son-of-a-bitch back then, too.' Beryl shook her gray head. 'Seems like there's always a mean son-of-a-bitch just waiting to run into you.'

'Ain't that the truth,' said Iona.

'But,' said Beryl, 'a mean son-of-a-bitch is better than no son-of-a-bitch.'

'You just gotta laugh and keep on going,' said Iona.

'Sure as hell don't want to get drunk.'

'Is drunk what it was?' said Iona. 'I thought somebody got all itchy.'

'A girl can't help it if she's got to scratch!' said Beryl.

The sisters laughed.

Mom said: 'Maybe somebody should have worn a glove.'

Lucas frowned. *Adults are so weird! Hard to scratch with gloves on.*

'Come on now,' said Dory. 'This is getting us nowhere.'

'Right,' said Beryl. 'Let's go see the house you're all so fired up about.'

The blue taxi growled under a sunset sky. They turned off Main Street to cross the tracks, motored north toward the dump where lost seagulls glided above gullies filled with garbage. They passed the baseball park. A sign that said VERNON CITY LIMITS. The town's rough pavement became a gravel road. Beryl steered the blue taxi up a long driveway toward that red-walled stucco house.

'Ain't nobody in it now,' she said as Lucas stared at curtained windows on both floors of the box-like red house. 'Course it'll be open in time for the fair. I'll see a lot of this road then. Taxi is the only way you can come out here.'

'I could walk out here,' said Lucas. 'Or ride my bike. And Dad could drive out here easy as—'

'Your dad's not coming out here!' snapped Mom.

'Well, *he* ain't,' said Beryl. 'But if Lucas saves up, when he's older…'

Mom said: 'When he's older, I'll give him the cash.'

'Cora!' cried her sister Dory. 'Why I never—'

'You think I'd rather pay Doc Nirmberg? Or go to an Easter wedding?'

'Why do I need cash to come out here, Mom? To pay for the taxi?'

'Hell, Lucas,' said Aunt Beryl, 'I'll ride you out here for free!'

The Conner sisters laughed.

Beryl said: 'You show up some way other than our taxi, the house woman who runs things 's got a straight razor.'

'How will the people who live out here come to town?' asked Lucas.

'That won't happen much. But comes time for the runs to the regular clinic checkups – Doc Horn came up with that idea – that's a taxi job.'

'What's it like inside?' asked Iona.

'I don't go inside,' said Beryl.

'Oh, hell,' said Iona. 'I could never do that neither.'

'Think it'll make money?' asked Dory.

'Johnny says we'll have the most profitable taxi in Montana. If we ran a meter, I'd be cranking it all day and all night to total up what'll be on the books.'

They headed back to town. Beryl pulled on the headlights.

'I suppose it's just good business,' said Mom. 'Makes sense.'

'Sure,' said Dory. 'That's what we all think. The mayor and cops say it's a good deal. They know what's what and how to work the law, so it must be OK.'

'You betcha,' chimed in Iona.

'I just drive a taxi,' said Beryl. 'I just drive a cab.'

'Somebody's got to do it,' said Lucas because that's what you say.

The taxi *bumpity-bumped* over the half dozen railroad tracks.

Dory said: 'We still got Gramma Meg to figure.'

'Then hell,' said Beryl as she sent the taxi down the alley behind Main Street, 'let's drive down here. Our Meg likes the back roads.'

Evening blended toward night.

''Member how when she was midwifing she'd round up us kids and march us off to see when babies were going to be born strange?' asked Iona. 'Don't you wonder why?'

'I gave up wondering why when I figured out it didn't do any good,' said Mom. 'I'm just glad we don't got to do that no more.'

'Ah, hell,' said Beryl as they cruised the alley past the dimly lit backs of Main Street's businesses. 'It was always good for a story and – *What's that?*'

The metal cylinders clanked as Beryl hit the brakes.

Lucas and his aunts jerked forward in their seats.

'Beryl!' said Dory. 'You almost put me through the windshield!'

'Wouldn't that have pissed Johnny off,' said his wife. 'Look over there.'

Her sisters looked at the back of the Coast-To-Coast hardware store and its window in a gray cinderblock wall not far from the back door to the Mint Bar.

But Lucas watched the blur at the edge of the taxi's headlights.

Garth. Jumping away from the yellow eyes of the alley crawler. Lurking in the shadows. You think if you pretend you don't see us, we won't see you.

'Look,' said Beryl. 'That orange shimmer in the Coast-To-Coast window.'

The spy saw the shape of the killer standing deep in the shadows.

'Let's go look,' said Beryl.

'You go look,' said Mom. 'I'm staying here.'

'Iona, slide out and go see,' said Dory.

'Why is it always me?' said Iona. 'Remember that time at the river?'

Lucas yelled: 'I'll go look!'

Before Mom could forbid him, Beryl said: 'See, Iona? Somebody's got guts.'

'Ah, shit.' Iona opened her door as her sisters shared a sly smile.

The cylinders on the backseat floor clinked as Lucas and Iona stepped out onto the graveled alley. Lucas saw worry tighten Mom's face.

Streetlamps and the taxi's headlights showed Aunt Iona leading him to the hardware store's gray cinderblock wall.

Iona pressed her palms against the cinderblocks, stood on her tiptoes, but only her curly dark hair reached the bottom of the store's window.

She looked at Lucas. 'Maybe I can lift you up to see.'

From beyond the buildings in the alley came the sound of a cruising teenager honking his family's car horn on Main Street. Inside the nearby Mint Bar, a dime dropped into the jukebox for Hank Williams's 'Jambalaya.' Laughter and music echoed out to the alley through that bar's propped-open back door.

Aunt Iona stood behind Lucas, put her hands in his armpits…

'Don't laugh!' she whispered. 'Jesus Christ, you'll get us caught.'

He strangled nervous, tickled mirth. She chuckled, too.

Iona pushed up under his armpits, harder, harder…

His sneakers never left the ground.

From the taxi, Mom yelled: 'Come on! Let's go!'

'Wait a minute,' said Iona. 'Lucas, get down on your hands and knees beside the wall, then I'll stand on you and be able to see.'

'Won't that hurt?'

'Oh hell, kid, only for a minute or so.'

He dropped to all fours. Rocks gouged his palms and knees.

Iona's feet drilled into his back and her weight crushed his hands and knees into the alley. Lucas knew that in the shadows, a man wearing a buckled-earflaps cap on an April night watched a housewife stand on the back of a schoolboy bent beside a cinderblock wall. Watched her stretch her neck to peer into a window where orange light danced to an invisible jukebox's song. Watched three other conspirators keep the motor running in the getaway car.

'Can't really see much,' whispered Iona.

Iona wiped off the glass. Her pressure parted the windows a crack.

Whump!

Fire inside the hardware store sucked oxygen in through the cracked-open window. Erupted with a roar. Shattered the window. Blasted orange flames out into the night. Knocked Iona backward off Lucas's back.

She landed on her butt, bounced up like a basketball. Ran screaming as her sisters tumbled out of the idling taxi: 'SON-OF-A-BITCH I'M ON FIRE!'

Iona danced madly in the alley as the jukebox played Hank Williams. Her hands beat at her smoking hair. Flames shot out of the shattered window.

Mom hugged her dancing sister but couldn't make her stop.

Beryl grabbed a fifty-pound canister of carbon-dioxide-charged water like it weighed no more than the cupful of ice-slush Coke that Dory threw on her dancing sisters. Beryl muscled the canister spigot. Trickled useless liquid at Iona.

'Ahhh!' A screaming apparition in a buckled-earflaps cap charged out of the shadows. Wrestled the CO_2 canister from Beryl's hands. Wrestled the spigot all the way open. Drenched the dancing sisters. Ran off screaming into the night, the canister clutched in his hands. *'Ahhh!'*

Aunt Dory grabbed Lucas. 'Run, go quick, tell them in the bar!'

Lucas ran through the Mint's open back door. Raced down the back stairs past stacked cases of beer. Past doors branded GENTS and GALS. Bounced like a pinball through dancing couples. Yelled at the bartender:

'FIRE NEXT DOOR AND MY AUNT IS SMOKING!'

Adults rocketed around him. A woman who smelled of

whiskey hustled him out the front door and across Main Street. The fire tower's wail cut the night air. A fireball erupted through the tar roof of Coast-To-Coast Hardware.

Fire engines came screaming. Firemen with long hoses sprayed water. People rushed to Main Street from all over town. Patrons at the Roxy abandoned *The Bat* movie to race outside for the real show. Cops directed traffic. Red lights spun. Lucas coughed smoke of burning rubber as he stood bathed in dry heat.

Then he heard it.

In the distance, from the east end of Main Street. Coming closer. Louder.

'… Fire! Fire! Fire! Fire! Fire!'

Garth raced through the crowd, the CO_2 canister clutched in his hands. Threw the canister into the swirling yellow heart of the blaze.

Whump! The exploding canister mushroomed hot air out to the sidewalk and rocked Garth back on the heels of his brown boots.

He fled toward the darkness at the west end of Main Street.

'Bomb! Bomb! Bomb! Bomb! Bomb!…'

The true killer died when the spy got him with a great shot from the spy's .45, but the killer fell on the switch for the bomb, and the East Berlin factory exploded in a ball of fire that lit the whole night. The spy picked himself up. Looked back at the burning building where the doomed raven-haired woman had saved him with her scream. He knew now that she was innocent and really had wheat-field hair. But he never knew if she'd really loved him.

Beryl huddled beside Iona on the dropped tailgate of a pickup truck.

Iona's dark hair lay matted on her head. A waitress from the Sports Club spread pats of butter where Iona's eyebrows used to be. Flies buzzed around her face. One of her hands shooed them away. The other hand brought a cigarette to her lips. She spotted her nephew. Took a deep puff. Exhaled her tobacco breath.

'I got no Lifesavers and don't give a good God-damn about what Orville or Meg or any other son-of-a-bitch smells on my breath tonight!'

Lucas ran to the edge of the crowd where his parents stood.

Got close enough to hear Mom say: '... then on top of all that, *no*, I didn't find out anything more about you-know-what because Lucas came with us.'

A man grabbed Lucas's shoulder. 'Hey, boy! I hear you're a regular hero!'

Dad's boss Alec Marshall let go of Lucas's shoulder. Stood with his hands thrust in his pants pockets, hat tilted back. His grin beamed down at the boy.

'All I did was run somewhere screaming.'

'Sometimes being a hero means knowing when to run like hell. Hey there, Don! Cora: you OK? I seen your sisters. Should have known if there was some excitement, there'd be a Conner girl around somewhere close!'

He laughed. Jiggled his hands in his pockets. Smiled at Dad.

The two men gravitated together.

'This is what I keep telling that new son-in-law of mine,' Alec told Dad. 'You want excitement, why, Vernon's got as much as anyplace.'

'Really,' said Dad. 'So what does he say?'

'Oh hell, Don, he's just a kid, you know. But a smart one. A damn lucky one, too, to get my Fran. Not that she didn't do good, no sir. Ben's a fine boy.'

'Seemed nice at the wedding.'

'Glad you think so. A man's glad to know his only child got a nice man. And that they'll be OK. A man doesn't need the weight of worrying about his grown kids, no sir. It can kill a fellow, worrying about his kids.'

'I know what you mean.'

Shelves inside the hardware store collapsed with a shower of sparks.

'Yup,' said Alec, jiggling his hands inside his pockets, 'they'll do just fine. Ben'll finish up down there at the U. Have a degree in business. That's more than I got. Hell, even more than you got, Don, and you're the smartest guy I know.

'And that's a damn good thing, too,' said Alec. 'Between us, why, we can make sure he works in just fine when he comes on board.'

Dad's voice froze the flames. 'When he comes on board?'

'Ben, yeah, after graduation, they're moving up here. Fran'll start coming up next week. Setting up a house I got 'em over on the westside. He's a-coming in June. Working with us in the trucking company – OK, hell, who am I kidding: working with you. This damn heart of mine, thank God I have you to run things.'

Exploding ammunition boxes in the fire went *rat-a-tat-tat*.

'Woo-hoo!' Alec jumped back from the flames. Scurried back down Main Street to his parked car. 'Sounds like a damn war out here! See you guys later!'

Then he was gone in the smoke and the dark.

Dad slumped in his shoes on their exploded Main Street.

Mom put her hand on his arm. Nodded for Lucas to walk away.

Laura will be sorry she missed this! thought Lucas. Volunteer firemen sprayed water at the fire raging in the hollow center of what had once been a grand building. The air smelled of wet soot, burned wood, black rubber smoke.

Aunt Dory smiled. 'Damn, Lucas! Ain't this a hell of a Saturday night!'

MIRACLE DAYS

Sunday afternoon filled the hospital window near where Megan Conner sat on the bed. Long sleeves on her black dress hid her lumberjack arms. Pinned above her heart was the silver brooch her husband won in a poker game at the Palace Hotel saloon. She told her grandchildren that their dead Grampa Harry knew the cards he dealt for the gambling houses during winter as well as he knew the ranchers' cattle he cowboyed from spring roundups to autumn auctions.

Gramma Meg loved to wear the brooch. '*Make the things you got work for you,*' Lucas heard her tell Laura. The silver ornament grabbed your attention when you saw Megan Conner. Made her beautiful white hair seem like heaven's cloud. That gave her green eyes time to trap your gaze and make it hard to stare at the clumpy black shoes in the steel stirrups of her leg braces.

'Don't just hang in the doorway,' she told all-alone Lucas. 'Come on in.'

'Mom told me to come over and keep you company before they got here.'

'You should have come sooner,' said Gramma. 'Shooed away Elly Sweeny. She asked about you guys. Pretending to be Christian social, but really snooping about your new neighbor Falk. Like I just off the train from Dumb Town.'

'We're having dinner at the Falks tomorrow night,' said Lucas.

'Don't tell them about Elly coming to see me. You hear? You don't know nothing about that.'

'Gramma, I keep knowing more and more nothing!'

'You must be growing up.' She leaned closer. 'You gotten fixed yet?'

Blood rushed to Lucas's head. His heart thumped. *No! Not again! Please!*

A nurse carrying folded sheets and fresh towels bustled into the hospital room. 'Well, hey there! How are we this afternoon?'

'You sound pretty damn chipper,' said Gramma. 'As for "we"…'

Please don't, Gramma! Please don't!

The nurse said: 'This is your Cora's boy, isn't it? Aren't we getting big?'

'So damn big you wouldn't hardly believe what he's still got to have done.'

'Glasses! That's all, Gramma, honest, please! They want to see if I need—'

'Glasses are no problem,' said Gramma. 'You know what his problem is?'

But then she frowned as the nurse draped folded white bed sheets and hospital towels over the visitor's chair.

'The morning girl already changed my bed,' Gramma Meg told the nurse.

'We're all just fine here. Don't you worry now, missy.'

'Who?'

The nurse froze in her white shoes. 'I'm sorry, what did you—'

'No, it's you. *Please* don't say you've gone nuts or all senile-old-lady.'

The nurse laughed. 'Why, why no, what are you talking about?'

'Well, I don't know who you're talking to,' said Gramma. 'Talking to yourself, maybe. People who are touched in the head or too old for their own good do that. But don't worry. I won't tell the boss doctors. I'm here to help you.'

'Help me? I don't need—'

'Well, you must need some help. You made a mistake.'

'I didn't make any… What mistake did I—'

'You were talking to somebody who isn't here.'

'Who isn't here?'

'Why, a whole lot of people. Just look around.'

Lucas knew the nurse couldn't help herself. Looked around the room where an old lady in a black dress sat on the bed. Where new sheets draped the visitor's chair. Where a boy might need glasses.

'See?' said Gramma. 'Nobody here but us chickens. Nobody named Missy. I had a husband, been dead fourteen years. That means I can't be a "miss." Course, you might not know my name. Or forgot. They say that's another sign of being senile. Or nuts. Just like talking to yourself and people who aren't there.

'But,' continued Gramma, 'as I recollect, they wrote my name outside the door. *Lucas!* See if that sign is still up.'

The nurse snapped: 'It's still there!'

'Then there shouldn't be any mistakes. Aren't we happy about that?'

The nurse looked like a gorilla slapped her. 'I guess so.'

'You're the nurse. As long as you guess so, we must be right.'

Then Gramma's smile curved like a sword. 'So why is it that you fetched another bunch of clean sheets and towels in here?'

'I'm not supposed to – I just do what they tell me.'

'I bet you do,' said Gramma.

'I've got work.' The nurse turned toward the door.

'Don't you want to know Lucas's problem?'

Oh God no, Gramma, no!

'I mean,' the old lady told the rigid back of the frozen-still woman in the white uniform, 'you're supposed to care about the sick and crippled up.'

Self-defense made the nurse turn.

Look away! Please don't look at me!

'His thingy. They said he was too little when he was born early. I figure nothing's so little you can't cut off more. If God didn't want men cut, He wouldn't have given us knives.'

The nurse said: 'I don't know what you're—'

'Circumcised! Lucas ain't been fixed yet. It's broken and looks that way. Say, you're a nurse. You girls do the real work. We're here and we got the boy. A little snip-snip. We'll make things right, then everybody will be happy.'

Blinding wind roared Lucas from that hospital room. He couldn't feel. Couldn't think. Couldn't see. Like in other places and other… *dones* by Gramma.

'Lucas!' *Her voice.* 'Lucas! What are you doing?'

He blinked.

The nurse had left.

'You were just standing there,' said Gramma Meg.

'What else was I supposed to do?'

'Do what you got to and have a little fun.' Drool trickled down her cheek. She wiped it away with a handkerchief from her sleeve. Hit him with her green eyes. 'For a second there, thought maybe you was the one who had the stroke.'

'I wish Dad and Uncle Paul would get here.'

'If wishes were horses, beggars would ride. Now fetch my wheelchair.'

'We're supposed to wait. They're coming to—'

'You wait long enough, you end up with a long wait. I want to go. You're big enough to push the chair. So wheel it on over.'

He did what she said.

'Pull it alongside me. Fetch my crutches.' She smiled at her grandson. 'Look at that: they nearly fit you.'

No they don't!

'Don't worry,' she said as though she'd heard him. 'You'll grow into them.'

Gramma swung her weight off the bed. Stood in front of the wheelchair with her steel-braced legs locked tight as she took a crutch in each hand.

'Get behind the chair.'

Lucas's seventy-nine-year-old Gramma Meg pushed down on

the crutches and rose like an Olympic gymnast. Lowered herself into her chariot.

Lucas gripped the handles on her wheelchair.

'How come you do that?' he said. 'Say those things about my… about me?'

'Isn't it the truth? Let me see. Come around here. Give us a look.'

'No! I mean – they won't let me here.'

'They let you do what you do. We probably don't have time for a good look anyway. Maybe later. But isn't it true? The truth is the truth. Aren't I right?'

'Yeah, but… I don't want to talk about it to people. That makes me feel…'

'You beat the world to the punch, it won't hurt so bad.'

'I don't understand.'

'You will. You better. Let's go. Leave the crutches.' Meg folded her hands.

Lucas pushed with all his weight. The chair inched forward.

'See?' she said. 'I was right. You're strong enough.'

Lucas swung the chair to the left.

'It's like a ghost town in here since that Hemmer boy from the car wreck went home,' said Meg as they rolled down the hospital corridor. 'Come nighttime, I'd hear him in a dark room down the hall. In his bed. Crying. Poor kid.'

Two nurses working behind the desk spotted the wheelchair rolling toward them. Hurried away as if answering the wail of a phantom ambulance.

'*Don't look back!*' Gramma whispered as Lucas pushed the wheelchair to the elevator. 'If those nurses ain't gonna say good-bye, then the hell with them.'

Lucas pressed the elevator call button. 'They just didn't see us.'

'They're working hard at *not* seeing.' The doors slid open. 'Back us in.'

Sweat soaked Lucas's shirt. He threw his weight so that the

wheelchair circled to the right and rolled his grandmother into a silver box. The doors closed.

Meg said: 'Aren't you going to push the button?'

Lucas stretched – barely managed to press the black button that waited inches from her folded hands. The elevator lurched. The box they rode in sank.

'Wonder what those nurses weren't going to look at or say?' said Meg.

The elevator whined as Lucas said: 'Who knows? Who cares?'

'You better. What people don't say, likely that's what's going on.'

'I don't have to figure that out until I'm older, Gramma.'

'Really? Not until you're older? Not until *then*? You know when *then* is?'

The elevator lurched. Stopped. Its mirror doors slid open to a sunlit hall.

'Welcome to *then*,' she told him. 'We're here. You're there. Let's go.'

The boy pushed his grandmother into the hospital corridor. Muscled her toward the front entrance where the glass doors stood propped open.

'Why are you stopping?' she asked Lucas.

'Gram, I got you here, but there's two steps down to the sidewalk!'

'So? You just have to turn me around, wheel us down backwards.'

'I can't! I'm not big enough. I'll run get Dad and Uncle Paul.'

'They didn't show up when it was time. It's *then* now. Your turn. You can't always run across some street and get help. You gotta do what you gotta do.'

'But—'

'That's right. Turn around so we go down butt first.'

'If I lose control or the wheelchair tips or—'

'Don't.'

Lucas eased the wheelchair around so it stood on the front stoop facing the glass doors of the hospital that caught their reflection: Gramma with her hands folded in her lap. Him behind the wheelchair.

Meg said: 'Hold tight, honey, and give it hell!'

Lucas pulled. The wheelchair didn't move. He leaned back—

Oh God here it comes! Steel rods driving through my arms to my back! Lock legs – BOOM! *Down one step and Gramma's bouncing, hands coming up but* BOOM! *Down the second step – Tilting, side to side it's – settled. Stopped.*

Lucas clung to the wheelchair handles. His head draped between his sore arms. He didn't look up as he swung the wheelchair so Gramma faced across the street to his house where Mom and Dad would—

'Why is the police car stopping at your house?' said Gramma Meg.

A black cruiser with red lights on its roof and gold stars on its front doors parked in front of Lucas's house. Sheriff Bill Wood got out of the car. Didn't notice the boy and the old woman in the wheelchair watch him put on his Stetson.

Meg cried: 'They're after my girls for burning up Main Street last night!'

Her arms. Those black-dress-sheathed arms that had carried her on crutches since she was nineteen. Lumberjack arms that swung her nine-times-pregnant weight through years of washing clothes, kneading bread, and midwifing. Those massive muscled arms of Megan Conner snapped up from her wheelchair lap.

Her hands clamped onto the chair's wheels and spun them like tires on a teenager's car rocketing forward to burn rubber and signature the street.

Lucas clung to the chair speeding down the sidewalk.

Tripped. Staggered. Fell.

Held on as the chair hurtled toward the curb, dragging him

behind it. Rushing concrete banged his knees. His arms screamed in their shoulder sockets.

Gramma spun her wheels like a roulette wheel. 'Push harder!'

The curb.

Meg threw her weight backward. Her ride's front wheels flipped up…

The wheelchair shot off the hospital sidewalk, crashed down to the gutter.

Charged across the street.

Dragged clinging-on Lucas behind it.

Shot up the neighbor's driveway.

Whirled in a ninety-degree turn.

Snapped Lucas behind it like a whip.

Braked at the sidewalk's stairs leading up to the Ross home.

Gramma Meg yelled: 'Good thing you got here to help, Sheriff!'

On the front porch, Sheriff Bill Wood turned from pressing the doorbell. Frowned at the old lady in the wheelchair on the sidewalk.

'Hey, Mrs Conner, good to see—'

A hand popped up over the old lady's right shoulder.

Then came the tousled hair of a dazed, staggering-to-his-feet boy.

The sheriff blinked. 'Who's that?'

'Just my grandson. Laying down on the job, but don't blame him. I'm a lot of lifting for only me and a little boy, so that must be why they called you.'

'Nobody called me,' said Sheriff Wood.

'Well then,' said Meg to the badge on the porch, 'I guess it's just good policing you showing up here when you did. The kind of smart work that made me sure to vote for you and tell everybody else to, too.'

'Hey, Sheriff,' said Don Ross, stepping out to his front porch with his brother-in-law Paul. Their wives crowded the doorway behind them.

'Well, *Bill*,' said Meg, 'long as you're here, it's a shame my sons-in-law have to pack me up the stairs all by themselves.'

'Be glad to help,' said Sheriff Bill Wood.

Mom and Aunt Dory stepped onto the front porch as the three men walked down the stairs to the old lady in the wheelchair.

'Gramma,' said Mom, 'where are your crutches?'

'I knew there'd be good strong men here. If you got a dog, why bark?'

Sheriff Wood took one side of the wheelchair. Uncle Paul grabbed the other. Dad gripped the handlebars. They carried Megan Conner up the concrete steps.

Lucas shuffled behind the men and their burden.

Mom met him on the porch. 'How'd you get so dirty? Go wash up.'

They were crowded into the living room when he finished.

Dad and Mom in the gold chairs. Aunt Dory in the green chair. Uncle Paul stood beside her. The sheriff on the couch. Laura leaned against the wall. Gramma Meg in the middle of the gray rug, her wheelchair turned so her smile shone straight at the man with the badge on his chest. The room felt close. Tight.

Aunt Dory was telling the sheriff: '… is just a family Sunday dinner.'

'We have 'em two, three times a year,' said Gramma Meg. 'At least, that's how often I get invited.'

'Still, I'm sorry,' said the sheriff. 'But some things can't wait.'

'That fire was just an accident waiting to happen,' said Meg.

'Excuse me, Mrs Conner?'

'That's what the nurses told me,' she said. 'They know about things. I don't see how anybody can blame anybody for what was going to happen anyway.'

'Fire?' Sheriff Wood frowned. 'Oh, that was an electrical. Nobody's fault.'

'Thanks for dropping by and telling us,' said Megan. 'Are you sure you can't stay for dinner?'

'No, ma'am, thank you. But—'

'Well, it's good to see you. Be sure to drop down to my house come election.'

'I'll do that, Mrs Conner. But today I came to see Don and Cora and your granddaughter for a private talk.'

What's that noise?

Lucas swept his gaze over the faces of his family in the room. They seemed not to hear the faint clinking of metal on metal that came from—

From the old lady in the wheelchair. From the steel stirrup brace around her right foot as that leg trembled the stirrup against the chair's metal footrest.

'Sheriff,' said Dad, 'whatever you got to say, we'll all know it soon.'

The lawman nodded. 'Things ain't going like we hoped.'

'They never do,' said Gramma.

'Mother, please!' snapped Lucas's mom.

'We were all set to write it up as an accident of unknown origin,' continued the sheriff. 'That would have put a cap on it, but Mrs Klise—'

Gramma stabbed her forefinger toward the sheriff: 'The car wreck!'

'Yes, ma'am. As I was—'

'That poor Hemmer boy was laying up the hospital with me. That was an accident, too. Just like the fire. And if it wasn't, why, seems like I'm the one in our family closest to the law on it.'

'Not quite, Gram,' whispered Laura.

'Oh, honey, when anything happened, you were probably off in the weeds somewhere all puking drunk, so there's nothing here for you and the law.'

'Anyway,' said the sheriff, 'the smooth deal we hoped for won't do now. Mrs Klise, Ruth... She's making a hell of a fuss. Won't listen to nobody. Her husband Jim, it's like he ain't here. Ruth, she's hell-fired demanding law action.'

'Her only child died,' said Dad. 'She's dying for something to hold on to.'

'That's how I figure it,' said Sheriff Wood. 'You get hit with that kind of pain, something has to happen. Ruth is threatening to go to the state attorney general. If we let that happen, then we can't help nobody, including her.

'Judge Guthrie says the law provides for a special public inquest – locally. Could do a grand jury, but that would be secret.'

'Got to be out in the open so everybody can see,' said Dad.

'Yup. And to give Ruth Klise her due so she can't go crazy for more.'

'Laura has to testify,' said her dad.

The sheriff nodded.

Lucas saw his sister sag against the wall.

'Testimony is all she's facing,' said the sheriff. 'She's on no other line. Nobody wants anything like that. Hell, nobody wants anything like this.'

'Except Ruth Klise,' said Lucas's mom.

Dad stood.

Everyone except Gramma followed his momentum. The adults jabbered as Gramma sat trapped in her wheelchair. Held Laura's arm as the lawman left.

Outside, the sheriff's car drove away.

Inside, metal tinkling hammered the silence.

Gramma said: 'Aren't we going to eat? I don't want to miss my program.'

Suddenly the house smelled of roasted chicken and brown gravy, of canned corn and mashed potatoes and the beets Gramma had jarred that Mom would silently compel Lucas to plop purple on his white plate and eat even though he hated them and they'd fill stomach space he wanted to save for the two freshly baked apple pies that perfumed the kitchen air.

The Conner family crowded around the table. Gramma in her wheelchair sat jammed next to Lucas. Silverware clattered.

'Laura,' said Gramma Meg. 'Don't be so sad. The law ain't gonna hurt you.'

'I know, Gram. Thanks, but it's more than that.'

'You worried about that scholarship thing. It'll work out fine, 'cause if you don't get it, then there won't be no need for you to leave Montana.'

Mashed potatoes fell off Laura's fork.

'Say,' announced Uncle Paul. 'I seen in the paper we shot another rocket off into space. Now it's up there just like that Russian satellite thing. They were saying on the radio how the next thing they're going to do is shoot some damn monkey up there. Can you imagine that? A monkey in a rocket ship?'

Gramma said: 'How dumb can the Russians get? I seen monkeys at the circus in Great Falls. You lock one of them up in a rocket, shoot it up in the sky, I bet the monkey goes crazy, screaming and running around, carrying on. Those stupid Russians are gonna be all day cleaning up monkey shit out of that rocket.'

Her leg spasm thumped the table. Silverware clinked a chorus with the steel of her brace hitting the wheelchair. Milk trembled in Lucas's glass.

Dad said: 'I think it's America going to put the monkey up in our rockets.'

'Us?' said Gramma.

'*Oh!*' said Lucas. 'In school, Miss Smith told us the Russians say they're going to use dogs. Shoot dogs off in their rockets.'

'Dogs? Monkeys?' Gramma shook her head. 'Gotta be an easier way to get rid of them. When animals got old or lamed up, your Grampa Harry'd just take them t' the hill and shoot them. Had the boys dig a hole. Who needs a rocket?'

'Any way you look at it,' said Dad, 'we live in some pretty amazing times.'

'Pretty damn scary and stupid if you ask me,' said Gramma.

'One minute you're walking along minding your own business. Next minute you get clobbered by monkey shit falling out of the sky.'

'That won't happen!' said Lucas. 'Miss Smith says all the stuff we shoot up there will burn up when it falls back down.'

'Oh great,' said Gramma. 'Imagine the smell of burning monkey shit.'

'Mother!' said her daughter Dory. 'We're trying to eat Sunday dinner!'

'I didn't bring it up. What do I know about monkey shit?'

'That wasn't where we were going in the conversation,' said Dad. 'We were talking about amazing times. And we got to have a serious conversation here.'

Mom said: 'Laura, why don't you and Lucas go to your rooms.'

Gramma said: 'Aren't we going to have pie?'

'What?' said Mom and Aunt Dory together.

'Apple pie. You got two of them sitting over there on the counter.'

'Well, yes, Ma,' said Lucas's mother. 'We figured we'd save it for later.'

'Why? We ate dinner, so it's dessert time. No reason why we can't eat pie and talk at the same time. That way we'll be done in time for my program.'

'Well...'

'Plus, you don't want to cheat the kids out of their dessert, do you, Cora?'

'That's OK, Gramma.' Laura edged away from the table. 'I'm full.'

'I want pie!' said Lucas.

Dad's eyes thrust a sword through Lucas's chest that pinned him to his chair. He couldn't take back his words no matter how much he wanted to.

'See?' said Gramma. 'The boy's gotta eat, and so do I.'

Mom and her sister Dory cleared away the dinner plates, cut

the pie, and served it as savvy Laura fled downstairs. Lucas sat sword-pinned in his chair.

'So like we were saying,' said Dad, 'we live in amazing times.'

Eat your pie! Lucas told himself as he picked up his fork. *If you don't, you're guilty of wasting food on top of not knowing when to shut up.*

'It is like it always is.' Gramma's hand shook as she aimed her fork. 'Yesterday, today, tomorrow: time is time and we're stuck with it.'

Lucas attacked the cursed slice of pie the Best Way. First used his fork to scoop out the guts of cinnamon-baked apples from inside two layers of crust.

'But things are always changing,' said Uncle Paul.

'Tell me about that,' said Gramma. 'I hate that.'

'Now, Mom,' said Dory. 'Gotta admit indoor toilets are a good deal.'

'I thought we weren't supposed to talk about things like monkey shit at Sunday dinner.'

'But things like the polio shots Lucas and Laura got,' said their mother to the woman who polio robbed. 'Those things.'

'Medicine, doctors,' said Dad. 'They've come a long way. Made things good.'

'They still ain't fixed Lucas.'

'We're not here to talk about Lucas,' said Dory. 'We gotta talk about you.'

'Oh.' Gramma cut a bite of pie.

Lucas forked off the crust point of his wedge of apple pie.

'So we gotta talk about me,' said Gramma. 'That's why we're here. I thought this was – What did you tell the sheriff, Dory? "*Just a regular family Sunday dinner.*" Did you forget what I told you kids? Lying to the law is trouble.'

'Nobody lied,' said Mom. 'That's what it is... and kind of isn't, too.'

'It is or it isn't,' said Meg. 'Everything is one thing. No matter how many doodads you hang on it, a Christmas tree is just a dead pine nailed to a board.'

'It is what you make it,' said Dad. 'That's for sure. And what we gotta talk about is how to make the best of what we got here.'

'Make the best of me.'

Gramma watched her daughters and their husbands nod.

Lucas forced his jaws to chew apple syrup crust.

'You had a stroke,' said Lucas's mother.

Gramma said: 'Don't forget the polio.'

'That's right!' said Dory. 'And together, they put you in a real rough place.'

'The hospital's not so bad. I've been getting better and getting the nurses—'

'The hospital nurses aren't there to take care of you like you need taking care of,' said Mom. 'The stroke changed you.'

'I didn't vote for that any more than I did for that damn sheriff.'

Dad smiled. 'Life's a rigged game, Meg. You know that better than most. But you're still at the table. You can still do fine.'

Gramma stared at him. 'If?'

'If you do it smart. Don't fight what you can't beat. Get the best you can.'

'Smart words, but I'm the one who has to live them.'

'We all do,' said Mom.

'You can't stay in the hospital,' said Dory. 'There's nothing more they can do for you there. The trembling from the stroke. The muscles it screwed up that make you drool. They aren't changing. With your leg going off like it does, you can't use crutches easy no more. Can't do for yourself alone like you used to.'

'All my life I been trying to get my leg to move. Now it goes crazy and does it on its own.'

'You need someone to help you full-time,' said Dory. 'Be there if you need it. Help you get to the bathroom. Hell, aren't we glad we got them indoors now!'

Lucas's mom Cora said: 'Even if we found a live-in hired woman for you at the house, that wouldn't be enough. And we'd like to, but none of us can—'

'Iona's got so damn many kids,' interrupted Dory. 'Us five in our family are out on the farm where if something went wrong, you'd be stuck. Don and Cora had to build into the basement to get Laura her room. Lucas is in the only other. Besides, there's too many stairs here. If there was a fire, getting you out… And can you imagine Beryl asking Johnny? Or living with him?'

'Spit it out.'

Lucas choked on the last mouthful of pie crust.

'You can't live in your house no more,' said Mom. 'You can't stay in the hospital. Can't come in with any of us.'

'There's special rooms right in that other wing of the hospital,' said Dory.

'The nursing home! You're putting me in the nursing home!'

Mom said: 'It's not like *we're* doing it. It's just… That's all we got left.'

'Wheeling me off to die locked up with the loonies and the gone-softs!'

'No,' said Dad. 'But we have to be practical and find you a way to live.'

'You call the nursing home *living*?'

'We love you, Mom,' said Dory. 'This isn't the best thing, it's the only thing.'

'But you won't lose your house,' said Mom. 'Cousin Becky, she's struggling. She could live there and keep the house in the family. Still yours.'

Megan's leg rebelled in a spasm of thumping that shook Lucas's chair.

'It's the stroke,' said Cora. 'You could have another. Or

heart trouble. And we wouldn't be able to help. There, you got professionals who know what to do.'

Dad said: 'Sad truth is, the choice you got left is whether you fight against what's going to happen or whether you fight for more with it.'

'Besides,' said Uncle Paul, 'this isn't like you're one of the ones who got crazy wind in their noggins. You had a stroke. A medical condition. Like we was talking about before, we live in amazing times. Science, doctors: Who knows what they're going to come up with? Stuff that maybe could fix strokes right up again.'

'Amazing times,' whispered Gramma. 'Watch out for monkey shit.'

Lucas stared at his empty pie plate to make himself invisible.

'You've got this all set up, don't you?' said Gramma.

'Hell, Megan,' said Uncle Paul. 'You don't have to worry about a thing.'

'*Gee*, that's a load off my mind. But when?'

Mom looked at Aunt Dory, who looked back.

Gramma sighed. 'So this starts tonight?'

'Well, that's a good idea!' said Dory. 'That's a plan.'

'Oh, I figured the plan.'

Everyone sat silent and still on a Sunday evening in a warm kitchen.

Until Gramma said: 'What time is it?'

Dad read the clock on the wall. 'A couple minutes past the top of the hour.'

'My program's on. Lucas, wheel me into the living room.'

Dory said: 'Let us get that, Mom.'

'Lucas can do it. He's young. All of you best remember what that's like while you can.'

But the adults helped Lucas muscle the wheelchair into the living room and face Gramma to the Ross family's first-ever TV set they got that year. Dad turned the knob. Hurried away while the set was warming up. Uncle Paul followed him when the screen glowed snowy white. Mom whispered in Lucas's ear: 'Keep her company!' She hurried back into the kitchen as the TV screen shimmered alive with black and white ghosts.

'Turn it up loud,' Gramma told Lucas. He walked to the TV box. Spun the volume dial so they couldn't hear the adults whispering in the kitchen.

A pudgy man in a black suit clutched a microphone as he stood in front of a choir and shouted through the TV screen:

'—here at Jimmy Pearl's Days of Miracle Ministry! That's why we need all the pennies you good folks out there in TV land send to help me, Jimmy Pearl – *God's humble servant* – help you. We know, *oh yes we do!* Know there are miracles just waiting to happen. If we pray. If we believe. If we sacrifice.'

'Look at those poor fools,' Gramma told Lucas, her eyes on the TV screen. 'Hobbling up to the stage with crutches and canes and bent backs.'

She shook her head.

Whispered: 'Amazing times. Miracle days.'

She fished the handkerchief out of her sleeve, but instead of wiping away drool, she pressed it higher up on her cheeks, by her eyes.

'Didn't have TV *back when*,' whispered Gramma. 'Monkeys in rockets. Push me closer,' she commanded Lucas. 'Real close to the TV.'

He got her so close her knees almost kissed the glass screen.

'Stand here beside me,' she commanded. 'You need healing, too.'

Her muscled hand pressed against his butt.

Pressed his uncut crotch close to the bathing black and white light.

Gramma yearned toward Jimmy Pearl's fervent benediction. Toward his outstretched palm. Toward a black and white savior coming to her in the screen.

'Hey, you two!' said Dory. 'Doesn't that music mean the program is done?'

'We'll all take you over, Meg,' said Uncle Paul as Mom turned off the TV set.

Their sundown parade crossed the street toward the hospital. Lucas pushed Gramma up the sidewalk toward the hospital's front doors. The four adults drifted apart from the rolling old woman and the pushing boy.

Only Lucas heard Gramma say: 'You know how far you can push me?'

He said, '*No.*'

'Not far enough,' she whispered. 'Not far enough.'

Uncle Paul and Dad carried her up the hospital steps. Wheeled her inside. Down the main corridor toward the elevator they'd ridden earlier.

But Aunt Dory hurried beyond that. Swung open a huge door. Light streamed toward them through that portal. The walls beyond were pink, not hospital green. Benches waited along the walls. Dory called out: 'Come this way!'

They rolled toward a desk where a hefty nurse smiled. 'Hi, Mrs Conner.'

'At least she got that right,' said Gramma.

'Sure she did,' said Lucas's mother. 'We made sure everything is right.'

They rode an elevator to the second floor. Shoulder to shoulder, crowded in its whirring metal box. Gramma stared at her reflection in the shiny doors…

… that slid open and deposited them into an invisible cloud of warm powder.

Old people, thought Lucas. *This smell means old people.*

Lucas pushed the wheelchair past a nurses' station. Past a big room with couches and chairs along the walls. Past a kitchen nook. Down the cream-colored corridor to a room with a door twice the width of any in the Ross family house.

'Well, hey there!' called gray-haired Aunt Beryl waiting inside as they rolled into that strange room. 'How we doing?'

Aunt Iona paced by a bed bolted to one wall. Band-Aids clung to where yesterday she'd had eyebrows. A Lifesaver clicked inside her nervous smile.

Dory chippered out: 'We're fine! We're all fine, aren't we, Gramma Meg?'

Days of Used to Be hung on a pale wall.

Snapshots of *when*, mostly black and white.

Seven of Meg's kids who'd lived clustered around the horse Zeke. Dory, Cora, Iona, and Beryl straddled the horse's bare back. None of them looked older than Lucas's ten. Three boys who were his uncles wore suspenders and baggy pants.

Lucas saw the kindergarten-era picture of him playing in the dirt yard of Iona's house. *I'm wearing a cowboy hat.* Laura's eighth grade graduation picture and a snapshot of her as a baby in Gramma's arms. Aunt Dory and Uncle Paul's three younger-than-Lucas kids posed on a bench. Grampa Harry sat tall in the saddle of his horse at the front of the state's last free-range cattle drive.

'See, Gram?' Iona's words clicked the spearmint Lifesaver against her teeth. 'Looks good in here, doesn't it?'

'I see,' said Megan Conner. 'Oh, I see.'

CLICKS

Neal Dylan stood like a hawk in the doorway of his classroom as Monday morning's First Bell rang through the school.

Look away! Lucas wanted to tell him. *Down here is trouble.*

Lucas shuffled toward Miss Smith's 5A in the school's sunlit hallway of dust and pine-scented mopped tiles. A kindergarten girl with blonde curls skipped around the corner. She stuck her tongue out at Lucas.

Watch out! Lucas wanted to yell, but she made it to her classroom without Principal Olsen charging out into the hall to scream at her about No Skipping.

'Am I glad to see you guys this morning!' Miss Smith's voice soared into the hall from 5A's open doorway only four, only three steps away from Lucas.

Lucas hesitated in the classroom doorway.

Crossed the border into 5A only as Final Bell rang.

'Hey, Lucas. I was afraid I'd have to send out a search party for you.'

Even though he was almost late, those lips smiled for him.

That made today even more grim.

Lucas forced himself to be the perfect student all morning. Shuffled home for a tuna fish sandwich lunch so his family would suspect nothing.

Mom said: 'When you're done, hurry home. We don't want to be late.'

During afternoon recess, he leaned on the tennis court's chain-link fence.

Bobbi Jean ran past and waved. His hands stayed in his pockets.

A teacher blew the whistle on kids by the teeter-totters. He didn't look.

Kurt and Wayne walked up to him. Then came Marin.

'We've got to work on that project!' said Wayne.

'Are you OK?' Kurt asked Lucas.

'Don't worry.' Lucas saw the blurred thousand hills surrounding the town.

'You guys!' said Wayne. 'Who's doing what? We gotta make sure it's fair.'

Marin said: 'Sure, that's what we gotta do.'

Recess Bell clanged and saved Lucas. He wordlessly led them inside.

Said nothing when Donna passed him her blackboard notes.

Said nothing when he passed them back.

When school ended, Lucas was the last kid to leave 5A.

Miss Smith sat at her desk checking homework.

Have you read my spy story yet? Lucas paused by her desk. His pounding heart hammered his tongue to the roof of his mouth.

She looked up. 'Hey! Thought you were already gone like the wind.'

'No, I, not yet, I...'

'Is something wrong?'

'I wanted to say good-bye.'

'So long,' she said. 'See you tomorrow.'

Don't look back! He shuffled toward the door. Do Not Look Back.

But he did. Black hair hid her face as she bent over the desk. Her leg bent back from her knee. He saw her slim white ankle, the smooth curve of her calf.

Mr Dylan spotted him in the hall. 'Hey, Lucas. Is Miss Smith still there? You going home?'

Lucas walked past him without saying a word. Without a lie. Men don't lie.

Home was to the south.

Lucas walked north, the direction Stuart Little took in the best book *ever.* Stuart refused to let the world make him only a brilliant mouse: he drove away.

Lucas reached the two-lane highway defined by the arc of the sun.

About a billion light-years to Lucas's right was Chicago, where Scarface Al Capone with machine guns in violin cases got beat by the cool Untouchables.

A long drive to Lucas's left – if he had a car, if he could reach the pedals, if he really knew how to drive from sitting on Dad's lap to steer – out that way rose the Rocky Mountains that almost killed explorers Lewis and Clark.

Dead ahead thirty-some miles away waited the border to another country.

Standing by the highway put Lucas in the wind gusts. A truck roared by. Beyond the highway waited the train tracks.

Lucas raced across the road.

His sneakers crunched scrub grass. Beyond the drainage ditch lay the train bed, steel rails, and tar-soaked wooden ties. Boxcars painted with exotic names like SANTA FE and GREAT NORTHERN. Doors on three cars gaped open.

A train whistle cut the air off to Lucas's right, east of town and barreling through. Came the clatter and roar. Came the *clickety-clack, clickety-clack* of steel wheels on steel rails. The black engine. Green and brown boxcars. Five black cylinder tankers. Couple flatbeds. A dozen slatted cattle cars. Red caboose and *whoosh*, gone out of town, the whistle crying *good-bye, good-bye.*

The afternoon sun glistened on empty steel rails just twenty steps away from where Lucas slumped in the dirt like a doomed Buddha.

Jordan Smith's voice: 'I bet there'll be another train along any minute.'

She stood silhouetted against the afternoon's blue sky. Her

dress flapped in the breeze. A man's windbreaker jacketed her. Midnight hair floated like a wispy black cloud around her face. She folded herself to sit shoulder to shoulder with Lucas on the embankment. Stared with him at the railroad tracks.

Said: 'When he was selling me on what a great place Vernon is, Mr Olsen bragged that thirty-nine trains a day come through town. Think that's right?'

Lucas couldn't stop his shrug.

'Listen,' she said. 'Off to the east. Here comes another one.'

A long train cry followed her words. A different whistle than the freight. A different rumble that stopped back in town at the depot.

'Passenger train,' she said. 'You can see the orange cars.'

Couldn't help himself, looked.

Couldn't see anything down there but a blur.

'When you're old enough,' she said, 'you can buy a train ticket and go where you want. Course, some people hop freights. Be like a hobo. Live in the cold with no family or friends or clean food. Nothing to protect you from bears or bad guys. Don't know why people think that's a great adventure. You'd have to be the luckiest guy in the world to not get hurt. Are you lucky?'

'I don't know.'

'Maybe you are, maybe you aren't. The thing about luck is, you never know where it is or what it is, you just get it, one way or the other. Can't control it. Can't wish it. And it changes.'

'Then it doesn't matter.'

'Well… we don't have cancer. They didn't drop the A-bomb – I know: *not yet*. My mom's still alive in Ohio. She took in sewing to give me piano lessons. Once I got to hear Billie Holiday singing in a bar I had to fetch my dad out of. The motorcycle wreck when I was seventeen left me with just a tiny forehead scar. I got a job that let me go to Europe. My car tire wasn't flat when I woke up this morning, and when I came out here to see what you were doing, Mr Dylan loaned me his jacket.

'Got bad luck, too. My kid sister… She died when I was ten – just your age.'

The cool breeze blew over them.

Train brakes hissed. The whistle blew. The engine chugged strong.

'Here it comes!' she cried.

An orange railsnake rolled past them, faster, ever faster, until the oval passenger windows on its side blurred into a silver stream gone in a blink.

'Wonder what those people think,' said Jordan Smith. 'Wonder if they even saw us.'

'They don't think nothing.'

'Lucas, *please*, I gotta at least pretend to be a teacher: they don't think *anything*.'

Lucas strangled a chuckle.

'You thinking about taking a passenger train? Or are you after a scary, lonely adventure? Going to hop a freight? Where do you think a train can take you?'

His arms were sore from pushing the wheelchair. 'Not far enough.'

'*Oh*, I get it. You really *are* just here watching the trains go by.'

She said: 'Where are you *supposed* to be?'

Lucas whispered: 'The eye doctor.'

'So you figure maybe if you're *here* when you're supposed to be *there*, then eventually maybe you won't *have to* go there.'

Lucas couldn't say anything. Couldn't look at her.

'That's an idea,' she said. 'Lot of people get it. Problem is, "there" is still *there*. Plus, you got parents who'll get you another appointment, get you there.'

'I… I…'

'It feels like life's falling into a shape you can't do anything about. So you just do something random even though it doesn't make things like you want.'

Lucas couldn't move.

She said: 'So it's a big deal, getting glasses?'

'I didn't do anything wrong! At least my sister, her whole life changed because she did one thing wrong. But I didn't do anything wrong. I just *am* wrong. Just ask my Gra – I just am.'

'Is your whole life going to change?'

'Before I even get a chance! You can't be an FBI agent if you wear glasses. You can't be a pilot or one of the guys they're going to send into outer space with monkeys. You're just stuck. With *glasses*.'

She sat beside him. Waiting.

'None of the heroes in movies wear glasses,' he said. 'Not one.'

The wind blew dirt on him. She threw a pebble at the tracks.

Lucas muttered: 'Girls don't like boys who wear glasses.'

'Maybe,' said Miss Jordan Smith. 'Maybe not. But let's pretend you're right. Girls don't like guys who wear glasses. But lots of women do. Or don't care.'

Wind brushed the prairie. His heart slammed against his ribs. He was in trouble, but suddenly he didn't know what kind.

She said: 'Glasses make you look intelligent. *Women* go for intelligent men.'

'Not around here.'

'I don't know about that. I just moved to town.'

'You gotta be cool or have the right stuff or be on the right team or look like a movie star or be tough and not have glasses. Smart doesn't matter.'

'Is that so?'

He wouldn't look at her. 'I'm not making this up.'

'We both wish you were.' She stared at the tracks. 'It's a big world, Lucas. Not every place is like here. Plus, things change. People, too. Even you.'

'Yeah, they're going to make me wear glasses.'

A car horn tooted on the highway behind them.

They didn't turn around to look.

'So you want to be like a movie hero?'

Lucas felt his face burn. Mumbled: 'Why be anything else?'

'What does the hero do?'

'He… wins. He gets the…'

'Are you sure? Or is that just how it turns out *sometimes*?'

'I don't know. Every movie is different.'

'He does what's right. Not what everybody thinks or tells him to do or what he likes. He does it for real. What he should do. What he has to do.'

Lucas's shrug said *maybe, yeah*.

'What makes a hero is that he does it when it's hard. When things aren't fair. Anybody can do the right thing when it's easy. But when it's hard, when you lose something and don't get anything back, that's when you're a hero. Even if nobody knows it. Even if they laugh at you. Maybe hate you. Leave you with nothing but what you did and lost and who you are.'

Lucas trembled.

'You know what you've got to do,' she said. 'Might not be as hard as you think. Might be worse. But you've got to do it. Can't hide from it. Can't run from it. Even if your mom and dad and me let you get away with it, even if you trick the world into thinking you don't need glasses, that would be just a trick. Not real. Not you. Not the best you could be.'

He crumbled into a slouch. 'This was so stupid!'

'Well, not an Einstein move. But you're still one of us humans.' She stood. 'Besides, figure it this way: if you get glasses, who knows what you'll see?'

She stood and gave him her hand. He was terrified she'd realize their touching flesh burned. Lucas didn't let his weight pull her down as he stood. She smiled. Freed their grip. Beneath the blue afternoon sky, they turned…

Saw Neal Dylan leaning on his old car parked on their side of the highway.

'What's he doing here?' said Lucas.

'Maybe he wants his jacket.' She walked toward Neal. Her

momentum pulled Lucas with her. 'He spotted you off on an unusual adventure and came to tell me. Loaned me his jacket. Wasn't that nice of him?'

'Yeah.' Lucas stared at his sneakers and *not* the grin on Mr Dylan's face.

'Hey!' Neal Dylan called out as the boy and the woman walked toward him.

'Hey, yourself!' She laughed.

'I figured you two might need a ride. So here I am.'

'A ride is always appreciated. Especially since Lucas is probably late.'

'Where are we going?' asked Neal Dylan.

She said: 'Lucas?'

'Dr Bond's,' sighed Lucas. 'On Main Street.'

'We can do that,' said the man. 'Hop in the back, Lucas.'

She got in the front seat.

'What did you guys find out there?' asked Neal as he turned the car's key.

'A bunch of trains we aren't taking.'

Lucas heard some kind of smile in her words.

That smile's for *me*! he telepathed to Mr Dylan. Not *you*!

'Good,' said Neal as the car engine caught life. 'I'd have missed you two.'

The car pulled out onto the road.

'We were talking about how getting glasses can change your life,' said the single female teacher.

Her married male colleague said: 'Wish I'd gotten the right kind of glasses when I was your age, Lucas.'

Couldn't help himself, Lucas had to ask: 'Why?'

'If I could have better seen *then* what was in front of me… maybe, who knows? *If* and *maybe,* Lucas. Two of the strongest words we can teach you.'

'And scariest,' she said. 'If—'

Both teachers burst out laughing.

'*If*,' she finished, 'if you try and dodge words like them.'

'Or not see them clearly and completely,' Neal added.

'Yes,' she said. 'Yes.'

Lucas said: 'I know.'

He actually didn't know what they were talking about, but he wouldn't let them leave him out or make him be just the kid in the backseat of their car.

The woman riding beside the driver said: 'Lucas and I were talking about good men who wear glasses. Cool guys, too.'

'Lots of good *glasses* men around town,' said hometown guy Neal. 'Chris Harvie, he's on the basketball team. He just started wearing – *That guy!* The singer who the high school kids love, what was – *Buddy Holly!* He wore glasses!'

Jordan said: 'I should have thought of that.'

Cold, flat-out, Lucas said: 'He died in a plane crash.'

'Yeah,' said Neal Dylan, 'but glasses helped make his dreams come true.'

The old car halted for a stop sign. Neal turned the radio's knob.

Nothing.

'You've got to hit a bump just right to get it to work,' he said.

Wham! Jordan Smith's fist slammed the dashboard above the radio.

Instant crackle and a man's slow soulful singing filled the car:

'*… must realize, smoke gets in your eyes…*'

'Hey, Lucas,' said Neal Dylan as violins soared on the radio. 'We're lucky. She's got the magic touch.'

Lucas said nothing.

'Of all the versions of this song,' said Mr Dylan, 'I like this one best.'

'Me, too,' she said.

The radio played. They drove Main Street. Past the Dodge dealership. Past the viaduct bridging over the railroad tracks. Past the drugstore and bus station, until the song ended and Mr Dylan stopped the car across from the Roxy.

Stopped the car in front of Dr Bond's office.

'Thanks for the ride,' said Jordan Smith, her fingers on the door handle.

'Don't go! I mean… I can take you… *wherever*.'

'I think I better – I mean, I want to walk.'

'Yes,' Neal Dylan told her. 'Sometimes it's good to just walk.'

She opened the front passenger's side door—

'Wait!' she cried. 'Your jacket!'

He smiled. 'If you're going to walk, you can at least use my jacket.'

She got out of the car. Her eyes pulled Lucas out of the backseat.

Lucas and Jordan Smith stood on the sidewalk. Saw none of the rest of the afternoon bustle on Main Street as they watched Neal Dylan slowly drive away.

'Miss Smith? Are you – Are you going to tell anybody about this?'

'What is there to tell?' Her smile seemed far away. 'We looked at trains we didn't take. We went for a ride. Listened to a song. We didn't go anywhere but where we were supposed to. Did what we had to do. And walked home alone.' Her smile hit him for real. 'Go on in now, Lucas. I'll see you later.'

She walked away, hair floating in the wind, that jacket holding her close.

Dr Bond's office smelled like electric dust. Lucas stared at the deserted receptionist's desk. Sat in a chair beside a stack of *Reader's Digest*s and a *LIFE* magazine with a cover picture of a bearded guy named Castro shouting into the microphone like he was Elvis Presley singing 'Heartbreak Hotel.'

Lucas shook his head. *What did Chris Harvie do to Elvis back two years ago that got Chris in trouble? Chris was only a freshman in high school then.*

A kindly old toad wearing thick glasses and a white smock

bustled into the waiting room. 'Sorry I'm running late, Lucas. Mrs McGiffert is just finishing up.'

That farm woman smiled at Lucas as she left.

Then it was his turn in the hard chair. Dr Bond pushed against his face with a black steel plate where clicking lenses fitted over his eyes.

'Which looks better? This one or that one?' CLICK! 'Now which?' CLICK!

'Did I get them right?' he asked when Dr Bond pushed the machine away.

'Question is, will we get you right. Answer is *yes*. Gonna get you glasses.'

Lucas sighed. 'How long do I have?'

'Eh, a week or so. Pick a frame from those four on the wall.'

Lucas chose black frames. Least they looked like the glasses Superman wore for his disguise as Clark Kent. 'How come my eyes went bad?'

'Sooner or later, everybody needs a little help to see.'

The gentle toad shooed him home.

'What took you so long?' said Mom when he got there. 'Go get ready.'

He washed his face and hands. Changed into the shirt she'd laid out on the bed. When he came out, Mom sat on the couch. She wore a fancy dress.

Dressed-up Laura came up from downstairs. Sat in the green chair.

Lucas glanced at the clock on the wall – couldn't be sure what it read.

'I gotta get glasses,' said Lucas.

'If you gotta, you gotta,' said Mom. Her legs were crossed. Her foot tapped the air. 'We'll leave as soon as your father gets here.'

'How come we always have to get ready and wait like this?' said Lucas.

'The sooner we get there, the sooner we can come home.'

The pointing black hands on Lucas's wristwatch said Dad parked the company station wagon out front at 5:16. He found them all sitting there when he walked through the door. Said: 'Cora, what's the rush?'

'They said to come after work. It's after work, so let's go. We're on their time now. The sooner we get it over with, the sooner we're back on our time.'

Dad fussed extra long to wash up. He called the night dispatcher 'just to make sure' the trucking company's phone was covered. At 5:33, he led his family out their front door.

Here we are, thought Lucas, *walking toward sunset. Dad wearing his dress-up sports coat. Mom in a special dress. Laura and me combed and fussed.*

The hospital sits across the street to our left. If Gramma still had her room there, what would she see as we walked past her window? If Miss Smith and Mr Dylan drove past in his green car, they'd turn their heads and see… *what?*

CLICK!

Through the evening's plate pressed against his face, Lucas saw Dad ring the doorbell on the Falks' house two doors up from the Ross family home. Saw Mom standing beside him. Saw Laura and himself waiting at the bottom of the porch steps. Saw a tall man with a loose tie on his white shirt open the door.

'Hey, ah… Don! Cora! Well, you're… Come in. Hi, kids. Call me Carl.' The man called Carl yelled back into his house: 'Nancy! The Rosses are already here!'

CLICK!

Mom and Dad sat on the couch in a stranger's living room. They held drinks with the cowboy days' name: *ditches.* Whiskey or other booze and water – like water scooped out of a ditch. Laura and Lucas held cold green bottles of Coke. Huddled on the piano bench. Carl Falk sat in a big chair with a smile on his face, his tie cinched tight around his neck. The house's mother/wife

Nancy wore an hourglass green dress. Rouge pinked her cheeks. She sat on a footstool.

'… over for dinner,' said Carl. 'Especially since we won't be neighbors for long.'

'You're leaving town?' said Lucas's Mom. 'You just moved here.'

'And glad we did,' said Carl. 'But we're just renting. Don't get me wrong. This row of five houses were great when they built them back before the war.'

'Yes,' said Dad. 'We like our place.'

'Good place.' Carl smiled. 'But a block of modern houses is being built on the northside – not the old northside, not the run-down or rough part.'

'I was born and raised on the northside,' said Mom.

'Then you know what I mean,' said Carl. 'We like being on this side of town, but over there we'll get a new house and be with our kind of people.'

Dad stared at his host.

'You know,' said Carl. 'The new pharmacist. The guy who owns the radio station. Vice president of the bank. People like that. Like all of us.'

'Everybody's pretty much the same here in Vernon,' said Mom.

Wife Nancy chirped. 'Very friendly!'

'That's why we moved here from the big firm in Missoula,' said Carl. 'Small-town America. Can't beat it. Good values. And in Vernon, a lot of opportunities. But you know that, Don. Everybody says you're one of our leading businessmen.'

'I do the work,' said Dad.

'That's what I mean. You're our kind of guy. Knew it moment I met you.'

'Carl's a great judge of character,' chirped Nancy.

'And Don here, he's the kind of guy who'll keep our new Civic League up to the right caliber of people.'

'I've been a little too busy to think about joining,' said Dad.

'Oh, don't worry, you will.' Carl took a pull on his drink. 'Say, that reminds me. Aren't you two related to Orville Dixon?'

Mom said: 'He's married to my sister Iona.'

'Somebody pointed him out. He's got the big Quonset hut west of town, right? The best drilling company in Martin county. Never met him, but when I saw him, I thought: *There's another kind of guy who'd be good for the League.*'

Mom laughed.

Dad said: 'You thought that when you saw him?'

'You can tell a lot about a man by the way he carries himself.' Carl leaned back in his seat to gesture with his hand that held his drink.

'Yes,' said Dad. 'I suppose you can.'

'Carl's real good that way!' Nancy fluttered her hands.

'You've never met Orville,' said Dad. 'But he knows how to carry himself, so you think he might be good to meet. To talk about joining your League, right?'

'Well, sure, that's why.'

'Sure, that's why. Would you like me to call him? Introduce you two?'

'Oh, don't go to that trouble,' said Carl. 'I'll hook up with him. But if he knows we're friends, why, that might make him more comfortable. It's all about people like us getting to know one another.'

CLICK!

Lucas frowned as he watched his father. *What's that look? That smile?*

'You know,' said Dad, 'I've got another brother-in-law you might want for your League. There's Paul, but he's a farmer and they got their own groups. But I'm also related to Johnny Russo.'

Lucas swore he saw *call-me-Carl's* face go pale. '*Ah*, well, I… We… He…'

'I can call him up,' said Dad. 'He'd love to join the League.'

'Well, I… I don't know him, but I…' Carl stared at the two sitting-there Ross children. At their mother, who watched him with no expression on her face. 'I know *of* him, if you know what I mean, and well, I don't know that he's quite right for the Civic League. If you know what I mean.'

'Yes,' said Dad. 'I think I know exactly what you mean.'

CLICK!

The Coke bottle warmed in Lucas's hand.

Carl swung his face toward his wife. 'Where's Erika? We've got company.'

Smiles twitched Nancy's face. 'They came so – She's just getting dressed. You know how little girls are.'

'Big girls, too,' said Carl. 'Am I right or am I right, Don?'

Dad's polite smile didn't waver.

The phantom little girl's mother stared at the teenage neighbor girl.

'You get it, Laura. She's putting on dress after dress. Getting perfect. She's only in kindergarten, but soon she'll be ready for makeup. Sorry she's – My fault, Carl. Should I go get her?'

'She knows what Daddy expects. You can get everybody another drink.'

CLICK!

Lucas opened the bathroom door as the toilet *whooshed* behind him. Out into the hall stepped a curly-haired girl in a frilly dress. She carried a hairbrush.

Lucas blinked.

She's the stuck-her-tongue-out kindergarten girl from this morning! The Falks' kid. New in town. That's why she didn't know to be afraid of Mr Olsen.

Erika, thought Lucas. *Her name is Erika.*

She's the girl next door who Irwin teased me about. The one I'm supposed to marry. She's just a little girl! But she might grow up to be like… like…

Lucas smiled at her, polite fifth grader to sweet kindergartener.

'That's my bathroom!' hissed Erika. Hit him with the hairbrush each time she said: '*Mine, mine, mine!*'

Skipped through the door to the living room.

I don't give a damn what I'm supposed to do! No way will I marry her!

CLICK!

From the Falks' living room came Daddy Carl applauding the prancing Erika. '*Here she is!*'

Lucas walked the other way, an unlit hall stacked with moving boxes. The dark air was thick with the scents of cardboard and baking roast beef.

Stopped in the arch leading to the kitchen, where he saw Mrs Falk.

She peered toward the door to the living room's mumble of conversation.

Reached inside a cupboard. Lifted down a recipe box rubber-banded shut. Grabbed a pair of glasses out of the box. Slid them on. Tiptoed back to the cookbook. Lucas watched her lips track what she read.

Something *thumped* in the living room.

Mrs Falk whipped the glasses off. Turned like a deer into some headlights.

Came the sound of Mr Falk: 'Whoa, precious! Too many spins!'

Lucas watched that little girl's mother slump with relief. She hid the glasses in their rubber-banded box in her cupboard. Turned toward Lucas—

Jump back deeper into the dark hall! You're a spy!

She didn't see him. Nancy Falk opened a glass-front cupboard door so its flat plane was between the shadowed hall that hid Lucas and where she stood. She moved the door's square glass pane in and out on its hinge, looking for—

There! She held the cupboard door in exactly the right place.

The window is a mirror on her side, realized Lucas as she used a silver compact pad to brush more pink on her cheeks.

Lucas blinked from where she did not see him as he watched her work.

You won't wear glasses you don't want your husband to see. So you sneak them. At least Aunt Iona sneaking cigarettes from Uncle Orville and Gramma Meg is doing something big. Hiding a bad habit. But hiding who you are—

Is just like I wanted to do.

CLICK!

Two families ate dinner around a big table. There was a platter of roast beef. Modern mashed potatoes straight out of a box. Canned pear and iceberg lettuce salad from a recipe in *Redbook* magazine. Precious Erika sat across from Lucas. Beneath the table, her feet swung back and forth, stabbing her black patent leather shoes into his shins.

As forks filled scraped plates all around the table, host Carl finished a story that Lucas didn't understand about How to Keep Mr Taxman Out Of Our Wallets.

'What's an honest guy to do?' said Carl.

Took a drink from his whiskey ditch.

'You know,' he said, 'I have to apologize.'

'Really?' said Dad. 'For which thing?'

'Well, normally Nancy leads the family in grace before dinner.'

Lucas saw surprise tremor hostess Nancy's face.

Her husband continued: 'But, being new in town, we didn't know quite how you folks do all that.'

'It's your house,' said Mom.

'But we're still figuring out things like that. Which church to go to.'

'Can't help you there,' said Dad. 'The kids go to Methodist Sunday School because their Gramma Meg got a heart throb for a circuit rider preacher.'

'I met someone who goes there,' said Carl Falk. 'A wonderful old woman: Elly Sweeny.'

Lucas blurted: 'Something's on your watch!'

Their host sighed. Put his elbows on the table. Made his arms like a tepee.

'Oh, Carl,' said his wife. 'I'm sorry, but you shouldn't be so modest.'

'Might as well come get a look at it, son,' said Mr Falk.

Lucas inched his chair back from the table.

Falk nodded at his wife. 'Nancy rigged this up and insists I wear it.'

'Well, I think it's important!' she said.

'You know how wives are,' Falk told Dad. 'Got to keep them happy.'

'Thank you, dear.' Nancy Falk flashed him a smile.

Flashed a different smile to Mom.

'They present it as a medallion,' said Falk as Lucas walked behind his wife's stiff hair, 'but Nancy insisted on getting a jeweler to rig a chain so it hangs on my watch band right out there for everybody to see.

'Here.' He stuck his wrist in front of Lucas's face. 'What do you see?'

'Like a little gold book. With weird letters.'

'They're Greek. Gamma Delta Zeta.'

His wife sounded like she was reading from a blackboard. 'The lawyers' national honorarium society. Only a law school's top graduates can join.'

Her husband held out his wrist for Dad and Mom and Laura to see.

'Good thing Lucas has sharp eyes,' drawled Mom. No one in her family twitched a smile. 'Otherwise we might never have known who you are.'

'You're a lawyer?' said Lucas, who kept hearing that he would be one, too.

'Hey, I know what you're thinking,' Carl Falk told the boy. 'I don't mess with that Perry Mason getting innocent people off murder stuff like in paperback books you buy off the rack in the drugstore or see on TV. That stuff is for guys who don't want to use the law to its full potential. Like I told Sheriff Wood when he asked me to advise that Hemmer kid from the car wreck, it's not just a question of billable hours that his poor mother couldn't swing, it's that I'd be lost in a courtroom. Why, I barely know where the courthouse is!'

'Then what is it you do?' asked Lucas.

Carl Falk winked at the kid. 'That's what you go to law school to find out.'

CLICK!

Lucas saw his family standing in front of the Falks' house.

Laura was already down the porch steps with him. Mom was muttering, 'It was good,' while Dad explained how he 'has to drive to the office,' how 'the kids have homework.' Streetlights winked on. Lucas saw a glint on the wrist of the lawyer who stood in his front door beside blind Nancy of the powdered smile.

As soon as they all hit the public sidewalk, Dad whispered: 'Keep walking.'

Mom sighed as they passed the Dentons'. 'And I put a girdle on for that.'

'I know where I'd like to put a girdle,' said Dad.

They all four laughed.

Suddenly the CLICKING was gone. Lucas was back where he belonged. Cool evening air filled his lungs between laughs where everything was real.

'Come on!' said Dad. 'Everybody in the station wagon!'

'Where are we going?' Laura and Lucas slammed their backseat doors.

'How about ice cream?' said Dad.

'Two desserts in one night?' said Laura.

'Whatever that orange thing was,' said Lucas, 'I wouldn't call it dessert.'

'Let's get our own,' said Dad. 'That's how our kind of people are.'

A station wagon rocking with laughter pulled out into the Vernon night.

'Hey, Cora,' said Dad. 'Remind me to find my Good Conduct medal from the Army, get Fred Farnsworth to make it into a—'

But whatever that jeweler was to do drowned in Ross family laughter.

This is what people should see when they look at us, thought Lucas as his dad turned onto Main Street. *Us going where we wanna in the car. Laughing.*

As Dad parked the car across from the Whitehouse café, Lucas said: 'Maybe it'll be good when I get my glasses.'

Dad opened the Whitehouse door for his family to go in—

—stepped back to hold it open for Neal Dylan coming out.

That sixth grade teacher held a baby girl against his shoulder and a cardboard carryout tray supporting three to-go cups. Dad and Mr Dylan exchanged *How-are-yous.* Mr Dylan nodded at Lucas. Hurried toward his parked green car. Dad led his family into the wonders of the Whitehouse.

They walked back out with ice creams – a cup of maple nut for Laura, a chocolate cone for Lucas. Drove to the northside so Dad could run into the trucking company 'to check on things' and thus not have lied to the Falks. Dad was in and out again before Lucas was halfway through with his chocolate ice cream cone or had a chance to see if everything was OK in the garage where one light burned.

'If we go home right away, they'll know,' said Mom.

So Dad meandered the station wagon across the viaduct that bridged the railroad tracks to connect the northside with the west end of Main Street. Drove past the Catholic church. Drove past the high school. Up Knob Hill.

'Hey,' said Mom, 'isn't that Neal Dylan's car?'

That green car with the radio that only worked with a good bump or the magic touch sat in front of Jordan Smith's brown house.

'Wonder what he's doing there?' said Mom as they rolled past.

'His jacket,' whispered Lucas as he watched the sliding away green car and brown house. 'He loaned her his jacket and he must be, needs his jacket.'

Darkness and distance vanished what he'd seen. Melting chocolate ice cream trickled down his fingers. A lonesome train whistle left town without him.

ELVIS

Lucas'd never felt any place as tense as the courtroom that trapped his sister Tuesday morning nine days after Gramma Meg went to the nursing home.

Laura and their parents sat with him on a bench by the railing separating those who came to *watch* and those who came to *do*.

Laura wore her best dress. Lucas wore his Easter outfit. His parents looked dressed for the church they never went to or the wedding they'd just seen.

Everyone obeyed when some man at the front of the court yelled, 'All rise!'

A judge in a black robe walked in. Banged a gavel. Everyone sat down.

'Laura Ross!' called the court clerk.

Laura stood. Dad patted her arm. Mom brushed off wrinkles in her dress.

The teenage girl took a deep breath.

Walked toward the clerk waiting beside the witness box.

Didn't look at where Ruth Klise vibrated beside her hollow husband.

Didn't look at where Pauline Hemmer slumped, her eyes darting from the mother of her son's dead best friend to her own son at the defendant's table.

Laura didn't focus on Hal Hemmer's white shirt and black tie as he sat beside his brown-suited lawyer who wasn't Mr Falk. Nor did she look at the table where prosecutor County Attorney Kohrman sat beside his scuffed briefcase.

The clerk held a black Bible under the teenage girl's hand. 'Do you swear to tell the truth, the whole truth and nothing but the truth, so help you God?'

Laura said: 'I do.'

Lucas scanned the prosecutor, Hal and his lawyer. He turned and looked over his right shoulder and saw the Government classes of high school seniors.

'*The more people who know what happened, the fewer people will bend the truth into trouble,*' he'd heard Dad tell Sheriff Wood. Now all eighty-some of those Government classes' field trip seniors meekly filled four spectator benches, while up front by the railing sat Neal Dylan.

What is he doing here? thought Lucas.

The judge looked down from his bench to Laura in the witness box.

'We want to be sure you understand what's going on. The prosecution has stipulated that you are not liable for any charges. This is an evidentiary hearing. You've already talked with Mr Kohrman and Sheriff Wood. We're going to ask you about what you told them so we can get it on the record. Is that clear?'

'Yes, Your Honor.'

'You're a minor, so let the record note that your parents are present.'

Me, too! thought Lucas.

The judge said: 'Mr Kohrman.'

'Laura,' said the prosecutor as he stood and walked toward her, 'everyone appreciates you doing the right thing. It takes courage to be in that chair.'

A nervous smile twitched on Laura's face.

'You were at the party near the river the Saturday night before Easter?'

'Yes.'

'Did you see Hal Hemmer and Earl Klise there?'

'Yes.'

'Had either of them been drinking?'

'Everybody stood around the bonfire. Some car headlights were turned on and... they were both holding bottles of beer.'

'And you saw them leave?'

Laura nodded. 'To go find more beer.'

'Who was driving?'

'They both were.'

'Excuse me?'

'They were laughing. Horsing around. Hal started the car. Earl shoved Hal over from behind the wheel. Hal fell out, ran around like a Chinese fire drill. That's where you stop at a red light, somebody calls it, everybody jumps out and runs around to beat the green light and—'

'We know what it is, Laura,' said the judge.

Kohrman said: 'Just tell us what happened with the driving that night.'

'Hal ran to the car, wrestled Earl over and got behind the steering wheel again. They drove off. Toward the highway.'

'Did you watch them go?'

'Five steps away from the bonfire was dark. You could hear the tires crunching on the gravel road. A few seconds after they started off, I saw brake lights flash and the headlights stop. Car doors slammed. Then the lights went toward the highway. Couple seconds later, I saw brake lights flash again. Headlights stop. Then the lights disappeared.'

'This changing drivers...'

'Hal and Earl did it all the time. Like a game they played.'

'What happened after you saw them leave?'

'Kids began to go home. We – I left.'

'Laura, you didn't see the boys after that. Do you know anyone who did?'

She shook her head *no*.

'Is it possible that they drove back to the party but everyone had left?'

Laura nodded her head *yes.*

'And who would have been driving their car then?'

'I don't know!'

Don't cry, Laura! urged Lucas. *It's OK!*

Her face pleaded for help as she said: 'Both of them!'

Kohrman looked at the judge. 'No further questions.'

The judge said: 'Mr Hopper?'

That brown-suited man sitting beside Hal said: 'No questions.'

'You can step down, Laura,' said the judge.

She'd only gone two paces away from the witness box when Mr Kohrman said: 'Your Honor, the People have nothing further to present.'

Laura was near the brown-suited lawyer as he rose, told the judge: 'Your Honor, the defense has nothing to present.'

Laura put her hand on the smooth wood of the railing gate as the judge said: 'The Court finds sufficient evidence to sustain criminal charges. Evidentiary and probable cause hearing is now closed. Proceeding to open court.'

'Your Honor,' said the lawyer in the brown suit, 'my client, Hal Hemmer, a minor, with the consent and consultation of his mother and the county attorney, would like to enter a plea and accept judgment.'

Laura slid into her seat between Mom and Dad on the spectator's bench as the judge said: 'Hal Hemmer, please rise.'

Mom patted Laura's arm. Dad whispered: 'You did fine.' Laura sighed. Lucas saw her wet eyes look straight ahead. Lucas stared at the white-shirted teenage boy standing beside the man in a brown suit.

'Young man,' said the judge, 'do you understand this is your chance to say what you want, to explain or defend yourself about what happened on that road?'

Hal's head bobbed up and down.

'Speak up, son,' said the judge. 'The law needs to hear your words.'

A whisper flitted through the courtroom: 'Yes, sir.'

'The Court is aware that your father died in the Battle of the Bulge—'

Lucas didn't know that. *Was that the Japs – No! Nazis, the 'Nuts!' time.*

'—but your mother agrees with your decision. Is that correct?'

Mrs Hemmer nodded. Tears plopped on her dress.

Hal said: 'Yes, sir.'

'Mr Kohrman?'

'Your Honor, the evidentiary hearing established that both boys were violating curfew, illegally procuring, possessing, drinking and driving under the influence of alcohol. Hal – the defendant – has no memory of the accident. Dr Horn testified that such amnesia came from the car wreck, is probably permanent and definitely *not* some story faked to cover up what happened. Definitely *not*. Testimony from Laura Ross—'

Cool! thought Lucas. *He said Laura's name!*

'—and evidence gathered by Sheriff Wood indicates that there is no way to establish who was driving the car and thus criminally liable for the fatal accident. In the interests of justice, the People accept Hal Hemmer's plea of guilty to one count of reckless endangerment.'

'Defense concurs,' said the man in the brown suit. 'With stipulations.'

The judge leaned toward the trembling boy.

'Hal, a terrible thing happened. Even though you didn't want it to happen, you helped set up the circumstances. You broke laws. You got hurt. Your friend Earl died. In life, you have to pay for what you do.'

'Yes, sir.'

The whole courtroom saw Hal tremble as he said: 'I... I want to. I should.'

'All the charges on your sheet could add up to a lot of time behind bars. You're a juvenile, so you'd get shipped off to the

Miles City Boys' Reformatory until you turn eighteen, then sent over to the penitentiary in Deer Lodge to serve out the rest of your term.'

'*Ohhn!*' Hal knew that groan came from his mom.

He kept his eyes on the judge.

'But what good would that do?' said His Honor. 'You weren't alone out there on that highway. Your friend Earl was there. So were your families. In a way, so was this whole town. You've already paid a terrible price that you'll feel for the rest of your life.

'Justice is about what should happen. The law is about what we can do. Maybe this is one time we can close the gap. If we follow straight law, send you down the prison line, then *two* of our town's boys are destroyed by that wreck on the highway. That's not justice. But it's also wrong to let you walk away with just your scars. Leave you to have to punish yourself *by* yourself. Plus, letting you walk tells all the other kids in town that the law doesn't matter.

'So, like people who care about you have worked out, you're going to jail.'

The sentenced boy's mother sobbed.

'But this is our town's tragedy, so we'll work it out our way. For your guilty plea to reckless endangerment, I accept the prosecution's waiver of all other charges and sentence you to three years' imprisonment. However, all but ninety days are suspended, with probation to run for the full three years. I'm remanding you to Sheriff Wood to serve your time in our county jail. While you're there, you will continue your education – and you *will* finish high school next year.

Neal Dylan stood, his hands on the rail.

'Your Honor,' said that sixth grade teacher, 'I've volunteered with another teacher to tutor Hal at the jail so he'll be ready for his senior year in the fall.'

'The Court thanks you, Mr Dylan, and your fellow teacher, too.'

Neal Dylan sat down.

'Hal,' said the judge, 'the law's given you punishment and a chance. Probation is more work than jail. You get in trouble, you break any laws – curfew, booze, speeding – then nobody can help you. A violation rockets you straight out of town to the state system. Prison can be worse than us judges intend. I don't want to see you locked up behind prison bars. Not you. Not one of us.'

'Yes, sir. I mean, Your Honor. I mean… Yes, sir. Thank you.'

Bang!

The judge's gavel shattered the glass fist gripping everyone in the courtroom. Lucas felt his father exhale. Hal's face turned toward heaven while Laura's hand shielded her eyes. A whirlwind swept people to their feet. The senior class students were shooed from their benches like a herd of sheep.

'*NO!*' screamed a woman. 'This isn't right!'

Lucas strained to his tiptoes.

There! Up front by the railing. Neal Dylan with a look on his face like he'd seen *The Thing* as Ruth Klise lunged away from where her husband slumped.

'My boy is killed and he gets – gets a vacation with the sheriff!'

Dad herded Lucas and Laura toward the exit. 'Hurry up! Move!'

Ruth Klise waved her arms. 'My Earl's dead and he gets away with it!'

Sheriff Wood charged the woman who bore, birthed and buried one boy.

Pauline Hemmer tore her gaze from her white-shirted lone son beyond the rail to the frantic woman she'd known all her life.

Ruth Klise screamed: '*Laura!*'

Fought grabbing hands. Pushed toward the teenage girl.

'*Laura! You tell them! Tell them the truth! Tell them what's right!*'

Dad shoved past Lucas to loom with Mom between their children and the frantic woman as he threw an order behind him: 'You two get out of here!'

Lucas grabbed Laura's arm. Hurried toward the double doors under the red exit sign. Pauline Hemmer cried: 'Sorry! Oh, Ruth, I'm, we're sorry, we're sorry!'

Laura flung open the doors, Lucas beside her as they heard: 'Sorry isn't anything! Isn't enough! Isn't—'

Sister and brother stumbled into the gray marble corridor outside the courtroom as the double doors *whooshed* closed behind them.

A teacher herded eighty chattering seniors down the main staircase.

'I can't go that way!' whispered Laura. A clouded glass door filled one end of the corridor. She plucked Lucas's sleeve. 'Come on!'

Lucas barely had time to read the black ink on the door's clouded glass:

COUNTY CLERK OF RECORDS & DEEDS

He and Laura blew through that clouded door and into a fluorescent-lit room. He smelled ink. Dusty paper. At a desk on the other side of a scarred wood counter sat a beefy woman mouthing a cigarette. Inside a radio on a gray file cabinet, Patti Page sang 'Cross Over the Bridge.'

The ember on the desk woman's cigarette glowed red. Her beady eyes probed the intruders while Lucas's heart slammed against his ribs.

Laura blurted: 'We're waiting for our parents! We'll just… wait.'

'Lots of "wait" in this place.' The woman flicked gray flakes into the ashtray. 'Your folks got papers?'

'I don't know,' said Laura.

'Papers is what this place is all about. You need forms to fill out?'

Lucas said: 'We already did that at school.'

Laura stepped on Lucas's foot to make him shut up.

'School stuff's another office,' said the clerk. 'Down the spiral stairway.'

Laura pulled him away from the counter. The clouded glass entrance door waited to their left. A brown door leading deeper into this office waited to their right. That closed inner office door had a brass lever handle.

Laura whispered: 'Be quiet! Stand here and don't make trouble!'

Of course I won't make trouble! thought Lucas. *I'm no dumb little kid!*

He leaned on the brass lever doorknob of the door behind him.

Spun backward as the door flew open.

Tumbled facedown onto the tile floor of the storage room.

Sprawled near the table where a man sat, metal shelves of boxes behind him. Lucas first saw the man's shined shoes and suit pants. Looked up.

'What are you doing here?' lawyer Carl Falk yelled to the boy on the floor.

'I don't know!' cried Lucas.

He saw a huge map unrolled on the table.

Falk tossed his suit jacket over the map. Slammed a ledger shut.

Yelled at the boy on the floor: 'Why are you here?'

'It was an accident!'

Falk blinked. His face turned red as he helped Lucas up.

'Of course it was,' the adult told the trembling boy and his teenage sister, who materialized behind him. 'Of course it was an accident.'

'Honest, I didn't do anything. I didn't see—'

'There's nothing to see.' The lawyer's firm hand urged Lucas and Laura out of that room. 'Nothing to tell. Wouldn't want you two to get in trouble.'

Laura grabbed Lucas, flung open the fogged glass door to the outside hallway. 'We're just waiting! But this is the wrong room. We're going.'

The fogged glass door closed behind them with a *click*.

They stood alone in the corridor of doors outside the courtroom.

'I told you not to make trouble!' snapped Laura.

'I didn't!' said Lucas. 'I just fell into it.'

'Watch where you lean.' She stared at the closed offices, the sealed doors to the courtroom, the wide staircase leading down. 'Where are Mom and Dad?'

'Why are you asking me? You're older. You're supposed to be in charge.'

'Then why can't I do what I want?' Laura's eyes went to the wide staircase. 'What if people are still down there?'

You don't mean "people," thought Lucas. *You mean those seniors. Big kids. Cool ones. Who might see you. Who saw you testify. Who might say… something.*

'That office woman said there was another staircase.' Lucas ran to a door with a brass plate instead of a knob or a handle.

'Lucas, don't—'

He pushed the brass plate on that door before Laura could finish her veto.

That opened door led them to a dim shaft of concrete walls centered by a black steel spiral staircase.

'Doors out of here gotta be down there,' said Laura.

They tiptoed down the black steel spiral stairs.

A shaft of light blew into the landing where the staircase curved beneath their feet. Laura jerked to a halt – almost fell when Lucas bumped into her.

An invisible man below bellowed: 'Just get in here, Harley!'

Shoes scraped on the metal landing below. The shaft disappeared as that door closed. Angry words from two men clanged up the black steel spiral staircase where the Ross children trembled.

The second man below yelled: 'Why the hell—'

'Because it's better for everybody in here.'

That voice. Lucas saw that Laura recognized it too:

Mr Makhem, the county superintendent of schools. Boss of all the teachers *and* even of Principal Olsen.

'You were upsetting my secretary,' Mr Makhem told the phantom Harley. 'Besides, you're complaining about people being in your business, but when you yell, you get more people in your business than made you mad in the first place.'

'You ain't running out on me, Makhem! You ain't dodging this one!'

The school superintendent said: 'Do you see me going anywhere?'

Lucas and Laura huddled on the spiraling stairs above the two phantoms.

'You've got to understand, Harley. Miss Smith is new in town.'

'That won't—'

'Doesn't excuse anything. Nor does it put her on the hook for doing her job.'

'Her damn job is to teach my kid and that's that!'

'According to Principal Olsen – and he's no fan of hers – she's doing that better than most. The kids are doing swell since she came on board.'

'She's got no right to tell me how to raise my boy! The law says—'

'Don't tell me about the law, Harley. Every day I juggle more law *dos* and *don'ts* and *What Fors* than you could haul in your pickup truck.'

'Somebody ought to school your Miss Smith on the *dos* and *don'ts* in this town. Saying I have to bring my damn boy to that county nurse. That's messing in my business!'

'She just wants the nurse to look your son over and see that he's alright.'

'If he ain't alright, I'll make him that way. I keep my boy on the straight and narrow. "*Spare the rod and spoil the child.*" The Bible says so.'

'Actually, that isn't in the Bible. But folks spout a lot of stuff as "Bible" that isn't. Easy to see how you'd be confused.'

'I ain't confused!'

'Good. So coming in here worked out just fine.'

'Don't go tricky on me, Makhem! If you don't straighten out that nosy no-man bitch, then somebody else will.'

'If somebody does more than talk like a gentleman to Miss Smith or any other teacher, then that somebody's got a hard guy like Principal Olsen to deal with. Plus me. And you know me, Harley. I don't have Olsen's easygoing ways.'

'Working man always takes it in the neck, don't he? Well, I'm a voter, so—'

'So hooray for America. My reelection comes next year. And don't give me that "working man" crap. I sweat as much as you do. Got anything else to say?'

'Figured you were a guy who knew better. Knew that folks who mess with the likes of me end up *in* a mess.'

'Do they. Well, life's an education, Harley. I hope you learned something today. I know I did.'

Departing shoes scraped the floor of the stairwell below. That door closed.

Below them, Harley bellowed: 'Son-of-a-bitch!'

The door they couldn't see crashed open and blew a shaft of light into the dim stairwell. Boots stomped away as that door swung shut.

'Now!' hissed Laura.

They ran back the way they'd come. Laura slammed the stairwell's door open to the main corridor outside the courtroom.

Mom, her face drenched with worry: 'Where the hell have you been?'

'Looking for you,' said Laura.

Mom scanned the deserted corridor.

'Your father went to work. Let's get out of here.'

She led them down the main marble staircase and out the side door.

Laura told her mother: 'I can't go to school. Not today.'

'Your Dad says that's OK for both of you. Take Lucas to pick up his glasses.'

'*Mom, no!*' cried Laura. 'I can't go downtown either! Not now! Not after…'

'It's always going to be "after."'

They'd reached the Lutheran church corner where Dad's boss's daughter got married. Home was to the right. Past the vacant shale lot across the street from the hospital. Past the house where a lawyer named Falk lived.

And lied about him and the courthouse, thought Lucas.

Mom nodded down the hill and past the alley to the passageway between two shops on Main Street. 'Go on now, Laura. Get it done before lunch.'

Then she hurried away to their white-walled, blue-roofed house.

In his green office, Dr Bond settled black-framed glasses on Lucas's face.

'There you go,' said the kindly toad. 'Step outside and check it out. Then come back and I'll tighten 'em up.'

Lucas held his hand over his glasses so he couldn't see. Stepped through the optometrist's door. Heard it close behind him. Took his blocking hand away.

Saw a new world. The same place but… *different.* Every shape cut by clean lines. A strange car rolled by. Lucas realized he could read the license plate.

'So how does it look?' The kindly toad slid the bows of Lucas's glasses back and forth through hot white sand to soften the plastic for shaping.

'All I could see was Main Street.'

'If you can see that and see it clear, you've seen it all.'

Lucas frowned as the eye doctor waved the glasses in the air to cool them.

'But it's just Vernon,' said the ten-year-old boy. 'There's a lot more out there. Dad said you were a tank guy with Patton in the war and saw everything.'

As Dr Bond settled the glasses back on Lucas, the kindly old toad shimmered into a grizzled young man wearing filthy Army khaki and a green helmet above bottomless eyes.

'You know what I saw? I saw the same sons-of-bitches, sad sacks, and fightin'-to-stay alives were everywhere. I still see 'em every day right here.'

Then a kindly old toad shuffled away to his back office.

Laura stood by the door to Main Street. Lucas's new vision scanned the doctor's deserted waiting room. Spotted the magazine cover of that bearded Cuban guy named Castro yelling into the microphone like he was Elvis Presley.

Lucas whispered to his sister: 'Tell me what Chris Harvie did to Elvis!'

Laura reached for the door. 'I don't need to relive any more trouble today.'

But her brother plucked her sleeve. 'That was two years ago!'

Laura looked through the glass door to Main Street.

'Wasn't just skipping school,' she whispered. 'Maybe fifty high school kids did that. None of us in junior high did, not even Claudia and she was already kind of with Chris, just waiting until she got to high school and old enough.

'I don't remember how but everybody knew Elvis was on the train coming through town from back east. Kids skipped school and went down to the train station. Stood on the depot platform. Waited. Excited. Chris made a banner: VERNON DIGS ELVIS!

'Train roars in. Orange passenger cars. Faces pressed against the windows. A mob of kids bouncing up and down on the platform. Yelling. Waving the banner.

'People got off the train. People got on. Ten minutes plus stop, just like now.

'Then the whistle blows and off it roars. Here then gone. And nothing. No Elvis. He didn't get off or stand on the train stoop or even open a window to wave. It was like we weren't even there. Like he didn't care. Like we didn't matter.'

He asked her: 'So what did Chris do?'

'That got him suspended from school for three days? The telegram. He wrote it. Collected money for it.'

Laura shook her head.

'Claudia has a copy the Western Union guy in the depot typed up for Chris after they sent it so it could be delivered to Elvis at the next station stop: ALL SAVVY STUDENTS HEAVE OFF LOVING ELVIS.'

'Huh?'

'Chris almost got away with it. Almost just got one detention like other kids who skipped school. Then the high school principal noticed the code.'

'What code?'

'You figure it out. I'll give you a hint: United Nations.'

Laura peered through the glass door. Saw no one nearby on the sidewalk. Opened the doctor's office door and led her kid brother out.

Lucas frowned as he followed Laura out into the brightness and the sidewalk. *United Nations? What does that—*

The vision grabbed him:

'Laura! *What if Elvis wasn't really on the train?*'

'Elvis was on the train. Elvis is always on the train that goes through town. And he doesn't get off and you can't get on.'

United Nations, thought Lucas as he walked beside Laura. He tried to use his new glasses to see the words of Chris Harvie's telegram. If the UN was the clue, did it mean something about war or peace or…

The UN. *'All Savvy Students—'*

What comes next? Oh, yeah: '*Heave Off Loving Elvis.*'

Hanging in the air, Lucas saw: A S S H O—

The door to the Tap Room bar swung open.

A woman pushed a baby carriage out to the sidewalk with a cloud of cigarette smoke, beer, and canned tomato juice. The bar door closing behind her chopped off some man's laugh as she spotted Lucas and Laura.

'Well, I'll be damned,' said the woman from the bar. 'It's the star witness.'

Lucas felt his sister burst into flame.

'You remember me, Laura.'

The woman's ash-colored hair brushed her shoulders. She had big brown eyes. Smooth pale skin. The blouse tucked into the waistband of her tan slacks billowed out with a fullness that made Lucas feel strange. He saw chips in her red nail polish as she leaned on the baby carriage. Put a brown paper sack into her purse. Fished out a pack of Lucky Strikes.

A cigarette went between her scarlet lips as she told Laura: 'I'd give you a fag, but a girl's gotta earn her own naughty things.'

The twenty-something mother lit the Lucky.

'Cat got your tongue?' said the smoking woman. 'Been so busy talking up there in the big time you can't say hi?'

'Hello…' Laura's voice trailed off into known uncertainty.

'You can still call me Rita. I remember babysitting you, even if you don't.'

'I sort of do.'

'*Sort of do?*' Rita laughed. 'What the hell. Who's the geek with glasses? He's awful short to be your boyfriend.'

The baby was strapped in so she couldn't escape. Sitting up, bright eyes and bouncing. She went '*Ooo! Ooo!*' as her soft hand summoned Lucas's finger.

'Should have guessed,' said the baby's mother. 'You go for the older guys, too, don't you, Rachel? He's a smart one, too. Figure that from the glasses.'

Rita turned to the now-teenage girl. 'You see my Neal up there at the show? He get to be a big shot?'

'He...' Laura settled herself. 'Mr Dylan did fine.'

'You call him *Mr* Dylan, you better call me *Mrs.*' The wife of that sixth grade teacher ground her cigarette into the concrete under her shoe. 'You know, he almost was a lawyer once upon a time. Funny how things work out.'

But she gave those words no laugh.

A breeze brushed over them.

Lucas's new glasses let him see Rita ride that breeze to a wistful vision of what used to be. Or maybe a vision of what was supposed to be.

Then she blinked back to this bright sun on a cracked sidewalk outside a Main Street bar in her hometown where she stood pushing a baby buggy.

'I babysat you,' she told Laura. 'Now look at you. A star up in the big time. Looking to dance on out of town, so I hear. Maybe you will, maybe you won't.'

Laura stood still as a wooden statue.

'You grow up some, your *wills* and *won'ts* can surprise you.'

Rita pulled a pair of sunglasses from her purse. Slid them over her eyes.

'Bright out here,' she said. Turned the stroller away from them. 'See you kids around town.'

The carriage hit a bump. Baby Rachel's head bobbled.

And Lucas heard those buggy wheels whirling like a train.

But where, oh where, is Elvis?

THE BLACK PIANO

Bobbi Jean ran through after-school sunlight to where Lucas stood alone in front of Miss Smith's house. 'What are you doing here?'

'Nothing!' Lucas alibied: 'My mom told me to come.'

A flicker jerked Lucas's new-glasses focus across the street.

On that house's white wall: the shadow of a man.

'Last night,' said Lucas, distracted by the shadow. 'She told me…'

All four Rosses sat at the dinner table. Pork chops and canned corn.

Mom said: 'I'm damn glad that courthouse thing is over.'

'It's not over.' Laura pushed yellow kernels around her white plate with a silver fork. 'Not for me. Not until the Honor Society meeting tomorrow.'

Mom shrugged. 'You did the right thing. If they don't like it, the hell with them. Think about what your Gramma Meg would do.'

'Nothing that would get her out of *that place*.'

Dad's voice rumbled: '*This place* puts a roof over your head, young lady.'

'Back in the Depression, we knew to be thankful for that,' said Mom.

Laura's shaking hands flew up by her face. '*No!* I don't want to hear about the Depression! How all the money disappeared. How people stood in line for charity bread. The sky so full of dust people choked. Clouds of buzzing grasshoppers so thick they were crawling all over you. They ate Grampa's shirt on the clothesline. Then the war. That's not what I want!'

'You never get what you want!' snapped Mom. 'That's that.'

The *clink* of Dad's fork on his plate killed that conversation.

'*Lucas!*'

'I didn't say anything, Mom!'

'This ain't about that. Mrs Clawson called. You can't take piano lessons from her anymore because they're moving to San Diego.'

His face exploded with a grin. *Yes! Done! Over! Free!*

'But I already fixed it,' continued Mom. 'And I don't want to hear any complaints. When Laura isn't using it, that piano just sits there, waste of good money. Besides, everybody says how swell it is for you to take lessons.'

'But, Mom!'

'You'll be under her thumb more 'n you want, but you have to.'

'Huh?'

'Your teacher, Miss Smith, she—'

'*Jordan Smith?*'

'Since when do you get to call your teacher by her first name?'

'Never! I never do!'

'Now you got to be extra careful about all that, because Mrs Clawson, she did the looking, now your schoolteacher's going to pick up teaching piano for you. Laura don't need teaching anymore. But you need it a lot.'

'I do! I mean, I guess so.'

'She isn't taking many students because she's tutoring Hal at the jail. I know you don't want piano lessons, but you'll thank me when you're older.'

He hid his smile when he said: 'When can – do I start?'

The next day, he met Bobbi Jean outside Miss Jordan Smith's house.

'Then she told me now,' he said. 'Half an hour after school got out.'

'Me, too!' said Bobbi Jean. 'Instead of taking the bus home after school, I waited at the oil company's office downtown until it was time to walk here.'

The shadow man moved on the white-walled house across the street.

'I ride the west bus fourteen miles,' said Bobbi Jean. 'Kids out east ride thirty miles to town, but their dads are farmers and mine's the geologist at the refinery. Do your parents ever try to make you believe something that flat-out can't be?'

Lucas blinked back from watching the shadow. 'What?'

'Do your parents ever tell you something that isn't true?'

'All parents do. Remember Santa Claus?'

'They keep telling me that I'll stop noticing the smells because our house is next to a refinery. Rotten eggs. Gas. Oil. When the smokestack blasts out bursts of flame – Dad says it's natural gas burn-off, methane – those *whoosh* flares of flames make the smoke sic your nose.

'The smells still get me. Always will. My parents say it doesn't soak into you. That where you grow up won't be how you always smell.'

Bobbi Jean softly asked: 'Lucas, do you think I… smell? I mean, like black smoke or rotten eggs or the refinery?'

'Never noticed.'

'Anna's my best friend even if she doesn't have enough time now to work much with me and Donna – Donna's smart but she doesn't talk a lot, you know what I mean? – and now Anna's hanging around with sixth grade girls just because I don't live in town, so she won't tell me if I smell because it would make me feel bad. Don't you wish Anna was taking piano lessons with us?'

Lucas's heart slammed in his chest. *Anna* and *Miss Smith?*

I'd explode!

Bobbi Jean whispered: 'Can you keep a secret?'

'I'm great at keeping secrets. Miss Smith said so.'

'Promise?'

'Cross my heart.'

'And hope to die?'

The shadow man across the street disappeared.

'OK,' said Lucas. 'Hope to die.'

'Can I ask you a favor?'

'I already promised *hope-to-die* and I don't even know what for, and now—'

'Now I'm asking you a favor! That's what you promised you'd keep secret!'

'That's so goofy. "A secret" and then it's "a favor" but that's *really* "a promise"? What are you talking about? I'm never going to understand girls!'

'Probably not.'

'What's your... *What do you want?*'

Her whisper came so soft he could barely hear it:

'Lucas... Would you smell me?'

Lucas knew that he and Bobbi Jean were suddenly in a *serious* new place.

'Smell me and tell the truth?' she said. 'The flat-out, whole nothing but the truth? About if I smell like rotten eggs or oil or the black smoke or... anything?'

Bobbi Jean closed her eyes.

Lucas leaned so close to her that he felt the warmth of her cheek. The tingle of her forearm. Strands of her brown hair floated across his glasses.

He nosed in the biggest breath under heaven. Let it out with a loud *whoosh*.

'Nope,' he said. 'No rotten eggs. No oil or smoke. You don't smell like that.'

Her grin stretched so wide its reflection almost broke his new glasses.

Bobbi Jean looked at his sneakers. Whispered: 'What do I smell like?'

'Guess you smell like a girl.'

They looked away from each other.

Lucas scanned his glasses over the street. *No shadow man.*

Bobbi Jean said: 'We better go inside.'

'You first.' He stepped between her and any bad shadows *because.*

'Scaredy cat!' Bobbi Jean led the way from the sidewalk to the brown house, her eyes on the porch with its swing. 'Was it cool going to court?'

'Yeah, but...'

'But what?' said Bobbi Jean as they climbed the front porch steps.

What he wanted to say was: '*But we lost.*'

Or so Laura'd claimed when she came home that noon.

'The Honor Society,' she'd told her family at the kitchen table. 'It's over.'

'That's too bad, honey,' said Mom. 'Sit down and eat.'

'How can I?'

'Because you're hungry even if you don't know it.'

'Mom, I – *Dad*: you know! You understand. Tell her. Everything's over!'

Dad shrugged. 'For now.'

Laura slumped into her chair. 'Everything's over and I'm trapped. Lost!'

'But are you done feeling sorry for yourself?' said Dad.

'What?'

'You heard me. Remember, you dealt this hand. But if you're done feeling sorry for yourself, then maybe you can hear what else you need to know.'

RING! went the black phone on the kitchen's yellow wall.

'There's nothing else to know,' said Laura.

'There's always something else to know,' said Dad.

Mom lifted the phone off its wall cradle. 'Hello?'

'For instance,' Dad told Laura, 'did you know that you can apply to Honor Society again next fall when you're a junior? They'll use the record you make from now until then to judge whether you're worthy. If you get in again, you'll be eligible for that senior scholarship.'

'Oh, hi, Alec… Nothing much. Finishing lunch.'

Dad's boss, thought Lucas. Probably in his own house, a short man holding the phone in one hand while his other stayed in his pants pocket jingling coins.

'Yes, Don's right here.' Mom cupped one muffling hand over the phone.

Laura glared at her father as he stood up from his kitchen chair.

'But that means I'll have to act like I'm in the Honor Society now! Follow all their rules just so *maybe* they'll let me back in to follow all their rules. That's like… like Hal! Like I'm on permanent probation!'

'Everybody's on permanent probation.' Dad took the phone. 'Hello?'

Mom's stare ordered her children to eat.

'Sorry I missed you… Yes, working at home. I can see how you'd lose track of time… I'll look at it with both eyes wide open… You do the same.'

Dad wrestled the phone back into its cradle with a motion that tensed his back. When he eased down in front of his sandwich again, his face was stone.

'So Alec's new son-in-law wrote a whole four-page business school report on modern trucking operations. Got a *solid* B on it. Alec told me he just left it on my desk for me to read and "think about." One quick visit gets "a solid B" four pages and I'm supposed to "think about it."'

He shook his head.

'See, Laura? Somebody's sure not worried about being "on probation," so why should you?'

Lucas said: 'How come Alec took that report to your office during lunch?'

'Because he knew I wouldn't be there.'

Lucas remembered his secret turn-in homework plan about Anna.

Dad shook his head. Looked at his wife. 'I'm the boss.'

She said: 'Yes, dear.'

Standing on Miss Smith's porch, Lucas told Bobbi Jean: 'Court was OK.'

Bobbi Jean knocked on the peeling white-painted screen door.

Lucas... *tingled.*

Whipped around to look behind him. His glasses almost flew off.

Saw no one there.

The wind blew. A meadowlark whistled. Out of sight blocks away, a city road crew *rat-a-tat-tat* jackhammered street blacktop.

Miss Smith pushed open her screen door as she said: 'Come on in.'

Their teacher wore a denim blue shirt, faded gray slacks, black slippers.

Books were stacked like towers in the brown house's living room. Lucas spotted a battered record player and a mountain of record albums. Through an open archway waited a kitchen with white appliances.

That black piano stood waiting. Old-fashioned. Like in a cowboy movie saloon. What Laura called an *upright*. A tall box with black and white keys jutting out at waist level, two brass pedals. The bench was flat with a worn cushion.

'You guys are on the dot.' Miss Smith motioned for them to sit on a couch while she took the piano bench. 'Let's figure out our lessons together, OK?'

Both children on the sofa nodded.

'We leave school stuff where it belongs. We keep *here* out of school. OK?'

Bobbi Jean and Lucas nodded.

'Do we need to talk about horseplay?'

The kids shook their heads.

'Good. Each lesson is a half hour. I have a lot of things happening now, so you're my only piano partners. Who can come on Thursdays, starting tomorrow?'

'Me!' cried Lucas.

Bobbi Jean trumped him. 'I can come any day!'

'Looks like you're first, Lucas. Bobbi Jean, I'll schedule with your folks.

'So,' said the teacher, 'Lucas: Besides practicing, what do you hate about piano lessons?'

'Huh?'

'There's no wrong answer. So what bugs you about all this?'

'Dumb songs!' He held out the magazine-like red Palmer Method book passed down from his sister Laura. '"The Volga Boatman." What's a Volga? "Afternoon in the Gazebo." I've never seen a gazebo! How come we have to learn stuff that's got nothing to do with our life?'

'It's our secret plan to torture kids.'

Bobbi Jean's jaw dropped—

—then she and Lucas laughed.

'Sometimes you don't realize what you should learn until you need to know it,' said Miss Smith. 'So you have to find people to trust who can teach you. Learn the keys and the notes. Chords. How to read music. Tempo. But I get your point. After the basics, there's a million songs, but true music has only two heartbeats: the music inside you and the music you're inside.'

'What?' said Bobbi Jean.

'The music you are inside of is the roar of what's going on around you. The way everything flows. Individual moments like notes. Bone-shaking chords like... like when you kids run out of class for recess. Rhythm like when you're strutting down the street and everything feels in sync with you. Melodies like how you brush your hair. Lyrics that feel true down to your own bones.

'The music inside of you is how you truly sound. Sometimes a lone key. Sometimes as a chord. Part of a song or tinkling off in your own direction.'

'We're not about that,' said Bobbi Jean. 'We're here to have piano lessons.'

'What good is a music lesson if it doesn't harmonize with your life?'

The two kids looked at each other. Shrugged.

'Lucas, sit on the bench.' Miss Smith rummaged in a cardboard box stuffed with papers as he settled in front of the row of hungry black and white keys.

'Don't mind Bobbi Jean,' said Miss Smith as she sat beside him. 'She's gonna just sit there quietly like you will when it's her turn.'

Lucas felt the brush of Jordan Smith's arm. The heat of her leg near his.

'Life's hard lesson is to match up the music you're inside of with the music inside of you,' she said. 'Few people get that chance, but when it comes...'

Her hands stroked the black and white keys into a grand chord.

'Magic,' she said.

'*Wow,*' whispered Bobbi Jean.

'It makes sense to get our piano lessons from the music we're inside of so we can harmonize with the music inside of us – right?'

'Yes,' whispered the boy.

'You're not inside music about a Volga boatman, are you? Or a gazebo?'

'No.'

Miss Smith put a sheaf of paper on the piano stand.

His glasses filled with the music's black-lettered title:

SMOKE GETS IN YOUR EYES
Words by Otto Harbach
Music by Jerome Kern

'That's the song—'

'From the radio when we were in the car,' said Miss Smith.

'I can't play this!' he said. 'It's too old for me. I don't know how!'

'But it's out there and you're in it, so you better start learning. Just use your right hand, the easy hand. Put yourself in position, play the notes you can.'

His right hand moved by itself. His thumb rested on middle C. An itch of electricity filled his middle finger on the ivory E key, the song's first real note.

'*Someone's on the porch!*' yelled Bobbi Jean.

A hulk of a man dodged out of view beyond the window glass.

'Stay put, kids!' Miss Smith was two steps from her front door before Lucas could whirl on the piano bench, before he could stop her, *protect her.*

She opened the door.

'Oh, good,' she said. 'It's you. Come in.

'It's OK,' Jordan Smith told the man on her front porch. 'It's safe.'

His winter cap jammed on tight, flaps folded over his ears. Filth smudged his coat. His pants were torn. Black tape held his faded army boots together. He took three baby steps into the house. His bloodshot eyes flicked anywhere but to the beating hearts staring at him.

'How are you, Garth?' said Miss Smith. 'I expected you to drop by earlier.'

'Saw people.' His eyes flicked toward the floor near Lucas. 'See people.'

'They're OK. This is Bobbi Jean Warren. And Lucas Ross. Lucas, shake Mr Jones's hand.'

I have to touch—!

'You'll have to excuse Lucas,' said Jordan Smith. 'He's shy.'

A rough, scaled red hand jerked on the end of Garth's coat sleeve. Lucas felt his own hand twitch. Snap up closer to that scaly paw.

They did it! Touched. Let go *damn* quick.

'Garth is thinking about helping me,' said Miss Smith, talking more to him than to her two pupils and Lucas knew it. 'With some painting.'

She nodded toward the nervous man. 'Remember Neal Dylan?'

'Marine,' said Garth.

'Neal introduced us, remember, Garth? He has leftover house paint from his last summer's work. Isn't it nice of him to let us use it to spruce up this place?'

'Can't. Noise.'

'You mean the piano. A piano is just a piano. And it's not playing now.'

'Hear it.'

'That's because your ears are stronger than mine. I don't hear it now. But when I do hear it, it's not noise, it's music.

'We'll show you,' she said. 'Lucas: put your hands on the keys. Very softly, play the first note of your song.'

Lucas's nervous thumb stroked middle C.

Garth twitched.

'There,' she said. 'That wasn't noise. Not that hurts. That was music.'

No one replied.

'Now, Lucas: play the *other* first note, then the first three measures.'

What he played sounded nothing like the song on the radio.

'See? Didn't hurt you, Garth. You're OK. Because it wasn't noise. It was music and the piano and your friend Lucas.'

'Heard it.'

'Me, too. See Bobbi Jean? Another friend of yours. She heard it, too. And she's just sitting there, nodding OK. So it must not be bad noise. Must be music.

'Lucas, for tomorrow, bring that song sheet with you. Come at four o'clock.'

'Come at four o'clock,' said Garth.

'Ah... Fine, Garth. If four o'clock is good for you, it's good for us. Lucas will be here. He'll be playing piano, but you'll be fine because it's him and it's music.'

'How know?'

Miss Smith looked around her house. 'We'll show you. Lucas: Do you mind waiting while Bobbi Jean has her lesson? Walking her to her dad's office?'

'I'll wait as long as you want me to!'

'Garth, you and Lucas wait on the front porch. Out there where it's safe. Where you're not alone. Then you can hear what's in here. Know for yourself.'

Bobbi Jean's eyes were silver dollars as Lucas edged his way out the door.

The black piano made a sly ebony and ivory grin.

A slatted swing dangled from chains screwed into the porch roof. Lucas sat on the swing's far half, his sneakers dangling above the porch floor.

The porch swing groaned. A great settling weight rocked the swing.

Ever so slowly, Lucas turned his head.

Garth sat beside him, cap jammed on his head, earflaps snapped, black-taped boots flat on the porch floor that Lucas's sneakers barely reached. Some distant horizon trapped Garth's eyes.

The porch swing creaked. From inside the house came the riffed tinkle of the eight-note scale, the one-handed warm-up exercise of a girl's fingers.

Garth twitched.

'It's OK!' said Lucas. 'That's music. Just music.'

The sound of a right hand playing Chopin.

Garth stayed still as a rock.

Lucas sat beside him. *Change the topic.* 'Windy out here today.'

Garth took a beat. ''S always windy.'

They sat side by side. The black piano tinkled. The wind of always blew.

The music stopped. The screen door flew open.

Bobbi Jean balleted onto the porch, called back into the house: 'Bye!'

Lucas. Bobbi Jean. Garth.

Their trio walked in rhythm on the same Vernon sidewalk. In the distance up the street, two men loaded tools into a white pickup.

Garth vanished.

'How'd he do that?' whispered Lucas.

'Maybe he learned that in the war,' said Bobbi Jean. 'Do you ever think about the war?'

'Which one? WWII or Korea or—'

'The one we're in now. Like Mr Olsen was talking about. Communists. Do you ever think about them? Worry about them?'

'Well, *yeah*, but I never thought you did, or any, *um*, what I mean is…'

'You mean 'cause I'm a girl I can't think about things? *Hah* to you, Lucas Ross. *Hah* to you. I think about things all the time. Wonder.'

'Like about Garth,' said Lucas. 'I never thought I'd even talk to him. But now… I'll walk you to your dad's office.'

'Or do you want me to walk you to your house? You live by that lawyer guy. He said so when he was out to the refinery talking geology with Dad. That's about rocks. My dad knows everything about rocks.'

'*You kids!*' yelled the driver of the city crew's white pickup near them.

Harley Anderson leaned out of the pickup. 'Crazy Garth! He hurt you?'

'What?' said Bobbi Jean.

'That crazy guy! He touch either one of you?'

'He didn't do nothing,' bad grammar'd Lucas so he wouldn't have to lie about the handshake.

Bobbi Jean said: 'He's just been with us at Miss Smith's house. He's painting for her tomorrow after school when Lucas comes.'

Harley blinked. '*What?*'

'Nothing!' said Lucas.

'That crazy loon's painting for that... *Hey*: you two in school with my kid Ralph? Isn't she his teacher?'

'Yes, sir,' said Bobbi Jean.

'I'll be damned.' Harley's eyes burned with the sinking sun he faced beyond the two kids to one brown house. 'You say it's on for tomorrow?'

'After...' Bobbi Jean stopped.

Noticed that adult's eyes.

Gears ground in the white pickup. Harley Anderson, father of Ralph, said: 'You be careful with guys like Garth. Can't never trust people who are strange.'

He drove off and left two kids standing alone on the sidewalk.

THE COLOR OF BLOOD

Today is going to be great! thought Lucas when he woke up the next morning. He smelled fresh grass and crisp air outside his sunlit bedroom window. *Only one more day of school left after today, and this afternoon…!*

He rode his bike to school. Hooked his handlebars around the bike rack.

Ralph Anderson whirled him around. 'What're you telling my dad? He said you told him stuff yesterday! I told him you weren't no liar an' you better not be!'

Ralph speared Lucas's ribs with his steel forefinger. Stalked away.

First Bell rang.

Miss Smith separated her class into their research project groups.

Kurt, Wayne, Marin, and Lucas huddled around his back-of-the-room desk.

Lucas handed Kurt two pages on how American spies helped the French Resistance kill the Nazis who ran the death camps for Jews. That matched Kurt's two pages on the after-WWII history of the country that was now fighting a war to keep its colony Algeria after losing the war to keep its Asian colony five years ago, someplace now called Viet Nam.

Marin dropped a black portfolio on Lucas's desk.

'*Marin!* You did like… *SIX PAGES* on great French stories like… You've got *The Count of Monte Cristo!* And *The Three Musketeers!* You even cut up the Classic Comics versions of them. Scotch-taped parts of them into your report!'

Wayne shook his head. 'I got two pages about their farms and factories, but your stuff gets us way over the page count!'

'This is great!' Kurt gave Lucas the *you were right* look.

Dismissal Bell rang.

'Kurt,' said Lucas, 'put everything together and turn it in. I gotta go.'

He hurried down the hall. Blasted out of the front doors.

Bobbi Jean waved to him as she stood beside Donna.

Then Bobbi Jean hurried to catch her bus.

Waved to Anna, who stood laughing with the coolest sixth grade girls.

Donna'd fallen behind Bobbi Jean's scamper. Stood there. Watching.

Lucas saw Anna raise her hand to her forehead. Might have been a wave back to Bobbi Jean. Maybe to Donna, too. Or Anna might have been just brushing her golden hair out of her sapphire eyes. Who could tell?

The bus carrying Bobbi Jean drove away.

Donna stood on the playground.

Anna and the sixth grade girls went wherever cool girls go.

The wind fought Lucas as he biked to the truck shop. Hurried into the Office. Out of Dad's private room bounced the company's owner, his hands jingling coins in his pants pockets as he said: 'Hey, now it's really father-son day!'

'Hi, Mr Marshall.'

'Call me Alec and come on in here, Lucas. Got somebody you gotta meet.'

Dad stood in front of his own desk. Locked his eyes on a young man who wore a striped shirt and a smile that bragged he had lots he could say.

Call me Alec said: 'This is Ben Owens, married my Fran.'

'How you doin', Lucas. You don't have to call me Mr Owens, Ben's fine.'

Alec smiled at Lucas. 'Ben's on board now to help out.'

'As soon as Fran and I get all settled in.'

'Oh, sure.' Alec jiggled the coins in his pocket. 'Sure. You know, Ben, Lucas here works for us, too. He's a damn fine helper and cleaner-upper in the shop.'

'Always good to meet one of our men.' *Call me Ben* flicked his gaze from the Ross son to the father. 'Don't worry about Lucas. I'll keep an eye on him.'

'Nobody's ever had to worry about Lucas,' said Dad. 'He knows what to do.'

'Then we'll get along great.' Ben nodded. 'This is good for him. Like I was saying, this place has got lots of opportunity. I see lots of possibilities here.'

Alec jiggled his coins. 'Got that right. Good business. Don runs a tight ship.'

Ben smiled.

Dad didn't take his eyes off that smile. 'What do you want, Lucas?'

'Mom told me to get a check after school for—'

'Right, yes.' Dad slid his middle desk drawer open.

'Kids,' said Ben Owens, who was more than twice Lucas's ten years. 'Always gotta keep the checkbook handy for 'em.'

'So I hear,' said Dad.

The young man fresh from college found nothing to say.

Dad signed a check. 'Here, have her fill it out. Now go. You'll be late.'

'I've got until four—'

'Go now.'

So Lucas didn't risk visiting The Secret. Biked over the viaduct across the railroad tracks. Past the Catholic church at the end of Main Street. Past the city crew with their white pickup hitched to an air compressor for jackhammering up pavement. Past the sandstone-brick high school. Pumped his legs to where Neal Dylan climbed out of his old green car parked in her driveway.

'You're early,' said that sixth grade teacher. 'You can help.'

'Help what?' Jordan Smith strolled down her front porch steps. The wind mussed her midnight hair as she gave them a smile.

'Hey, you,' said Neal as she stepped closer, ever closer.

'Hey, yourself.'

'I brought every can of paint I've got,' Neal told her. Lucas waved to get her attention. 'Hi, Miss Smith!'

'How you doing, Lucas?' she said, not taking her eyes off the other teacher. 'You sure you brought every can?'

'I even grabbed up stuff I probably shouldn't have.' He opened the green car's trunk. 'Since he's here, Lucas can help me carry it all in.'

'I got two strong arms.' She unfolded them from across her chest.

'I'm real strong!' insisted Lucas.

He made them load his arms with a mountain of tarps. Staggered up her porch steps. Into her house. Dropped them on her couch. Headed back outside where she stood beside that sixth grade teacher.

Look at me, thought Lucas. *See? I'm working!*

Then so was Mr Dylan, carrying two paint cans with each hand.

Lucas grabbed a can in each hand. Raced from the car to the pyramid of supplies in her living room. The black piano watched with its ivory and ebony grin.

Miss Smith grabbed paint, too. The glistening metal cans stretched her arms like rubber bands. The buttons of her white blouse strained into a line from the V of her pale throat. Lucas bounded down the porch stairs, grabbed two cans, staggered back to the house as fast as his sneakers could go.

'*Oh-oh!*' said ex-Marine Neal Dylan as he watched Lucas. 'Double time!'

The man ran past the staggering boy.

'You two are crazy!' she yelled from the front porch.

Then she charged down the steps, laughing as Lucas hustled

past her, infecting Neal with that laugh as he lumbered past her, his hands full of cans.

So they worked. Running. Laughing.

'Done!' yelled Neal Dylan as he clunked a bucket of brushes and tools on the living room floor amidst the sprawling pyramid of paint cans.

'Good,' said the woman with tousled ebony hair. 'Because Lucas is scheduled to get here in five minutes for his lesson.'

'And I'm due at the jail,' said Neal Dylan.

Two adults stared at each other.

Then he was gone. Out the door. Down the porch. Driving away.

Jordan Smith led Lucas to the black piano. Sat beside him on the bench. 'Thanks for—'

Creak! The screen door – opening.

A visitor stood in that portal to warm sunlight. His cap's flaps snapped over his ears. He stared into the brown house without looking at the two people it held.

'Garth,' she said. 'Yes, right on time, four o'clock. Just like the plan.'

Garth rocked in his duct-taped work boots.

She pointed to the pyramid of paint cans, the mountain of tarps. 'I haven't picked what colors we'll use. Don't even know what we've got.'

'Open cans.'

'Great idea. Why don't you—'

Garth snatched a screwdriver from the tool bucket. Stabbed the blade into the rim of a paint can and popped it off, catching the lid and laying it face up to make a red circle on the pyramid. The screwdriver popped open another can.

'Wait!' said Miss Smith in her schoolteacher voice.

Garth froze, screwdriver poised to open a third paint-smeared can.

'Good job, Garth. But there's a basement through the kitchen.

That's the best place to open all the cans and check them, don't you think?'

'Basement.'

'That's right. You can carry the cans down there. Paint test streaks on the walls. We know what's in the two cans you've opened. Looks like Neal must have painted a barn. But let's work on the others down there. Isn't that a good idea?'

'Lights on?'

'Yes. Absolutely. Lights on.'

'Alone. Quiet.'

'But you'll hear music, Garth. Remember music?'

Wind blew.

'Lucas,' she said, 'show music to our friend Garth again.'

Garth blinked as Lucas played one lone note of middle C.

'See?' said Miss Smith. 'Music. Music doesn't hurt. Music is fine. Safe.'

Garth didn't run.

'So you're OK to start in the basement?'

Garth quick-sealed the two opened cans. Left them. Grabbed the tarps. Virgin cans. Bolted down basement stairs. Shook the house with pounding boots as he raced back. Grabbed buckets of brushes. Clumped back down the stairs.

'Dang!' said Lucas.

'At least *dang*,' whispered his teacher as footsteps thundered upstairs.

She shot up her hand as the dervish charged into the living room. 'Garth!'

He froze like a statue.

'Why don't you start with the ones you've got? We can do more later.'

Boots rumbled downstairs to where work waited, lights glowed, and quiet reigned. Lucas imagined the sounds of lids popping off paint cans commandeered off the pyramid still waiting behind him on the living room floor.

Jordan Smith rejoined Lucas on the piano bench. Somewhere outside a motor whined. The wind blew. Her hand brushed the sheet music as she said: 'What do you like most about your song "Smoke Gets in Your Eyes"?'

Lucas shrugged. 'It's true.'

'How so?'

'The guy – or girl. I guess it doesn't have to be a guy.'

'No, it doesn't.'

'Well, he – let's call him "he"—'

'Yes, let's not make this another song about a woman being sad.'

'So for him... *there it is.* He loves this woman, and that's that. Then she's gone, and he has to just... *take it.* Tell the truth and lie at the same time. Say it's the smoke getting in his eyes that makes him, *well*, you know, cry.'

Jordan's face seemed far away.

'The words are dopey,' continued Lucas. 'I mean, *true*, but... dopey.'

'Sentimental. Trite. Common. Ridiculously silly and juvenile.'

'*Ahhh*... Well, OK. But still true, right?'

'Oh yes.'

Lucas took a deep breath. *Have to tell her the truth.*

'Um, Miss Smith? My big sister Laura? She helped me practice last night, and she said – it was my idea, too! – maybe the song is about more than just a guy losing the woman. Maybe it's about everything that's gone. Lost.'

Wind blew.

Lids popped off paint cans. Brushes stroked basement walls.

'Thought I was supposed to be the teacher,' said the woman beside Lucas.

'Did I say something wrong?'

'No. Not wrong. Not you.'

Then she said: 'Put your hands in position. That's right, just a light touch on the keys. Sensitive. Now let's hear—'

DAT!-DAT!-DAT!-DAT!-DAT!-DAT!-DAT!

Machine-gunned metal massacred blacktopped road outside the house.

DAT!-DAT!-DAT!-DAT!-DAT!

Paint cans rattled in the pyramid on the living room floor.

DAT!-DAT!-DAT!-DAT!

Lucas and Miss Smith jumped to their feet.

DAT!-DAT!-DAT!-DAT!-DAT!

Echoes boomed up through the house from the basement: A crash. A slip-sliding fall. A man's guttural scream. Boots pounded up basement stairs.

DAT!-DAT!-DAT!-DAT!

The basement door flew open and bounced off the wall as a collision with the refrigerator knocked off a vase of flowers to shatter on the kitchen floor.

Garth slipped/sprawled/fell into the living room – smeared yellow and green and blue from cans he'd opened in the basement.

DAT!-DAT!-DAT!-DAT!

'Machine guns!' screamed Sergeant Garth. 'Get down! Get down!'

'No!' yelled Jordan, her arms spread wide to catch Garth's charge.

'It's—'

He swept her white-bloused form into his wet rainbow embrace. Scooped in the boy. Threw them down with his tackle. He flopped on top of them. Offered up his own flesh to save them from the bullets of war.

DAT!-DAT!-DAT!-DAT!

Lucas and Jordan got to their knees. Their feet—

Garth yanked his hysterical comrades back to safety.

The three of them crashed into the pyramid of paint cans.

Lucas flew through the air. Jordan tumbled beside him. Garth's thrashing knocked a minutes-before opened paint can skyward.

The lid popped off the can of red paint as it flew above the chaos. Spun end over end spewing crimson waves. Splattered the ceiling. The pale wall. Furniture. Books. Crimson rain hit Lucas. The black piano wept scarlet tears.

DAT!-DAT!-DAT!-DAT!

'*No!*' moaned Jordan Smith as her protector held her down. '*No!*'

Garth waved his hand covered in crimson. 'Medic! Medic!'

Lucas flung himself off the floor. Hit the white wall and left his red smear as he threw open the screen door. Charged outside. The grass he crashed onto cushioned his pain as through scarlet-smeared glasses he saw…

White pickup. White doors black-lettered CITY CREW. Rusted air compressor hitched to it. A man hunched over a clattering jackhammer.

'Stop!' yelled Lucas. 'Stop!'

Can't hear me, won't – like in Dad's truck shop!

Lucas ran to the air compressor hitched to the white pickup.

Slammed his palm onto the red emergency shutoff button.

DAT!-DAT! Compressed air hissed. The whine down of the compressor motor. The jackhammer died. The big man bent over it turned around…

'Hey, boy!' grinned Harley Anderson. 'You got a problem?'

'Stop it! The noise!'

'Hell yes, lots of noise. But I'm just doing my job. Ask my foreman.'

'Don't do any more!' pleaded Lucas.

'You think a man like me takes orders from a kid, you got another think coming.' Harley shrugged. 'But hey: I don't mean to bother anybody. I'll shut down for the day. Almost quitting time anyway.'

Paint-smeared Garth exploded through the screen door and ran away.

'Looks like there's a problem!' yelled Harley. 'Can I help?'

Laughter chased Lucas inside the brown house.

She lay flat on her back in a scarlet lake, her hands out to her sides, palms up to crimson rain dripping from her ceiling. A scarlet smear claimed her once-white blouse. Lucas heard only her quiet sobs.

'It's OK now!' he whispered, crying too.

He grabbed rags from the debris. He grabbed a dish towel from the kitchen. Knelt on the bloody lake in his new jeans. Touched the white cloth to her red-paint-spattered forehead, to the goopy rouge tangle of her hair.

The screen door slammed.

Neal Dylan yelled: 'Oh my God! Jordan! Jordan!'

Then he was kneeling in the crimson slop surrounding the woman and the boy. Lifting her up with Lucas and cradling her in his arms.

'I should have been here!' cried Neal. 'I should have been here!'

She turned her face to his chest. Sobbed.

Neal checked to be sure Lucas wasn't hurt.

'Tell your parents I'll call them tonight,' said the sixth grade teacher. 'Tell them I'll explain then. Go home now.'

So Lucas did. Walking his bike as far away from his stiffening sticky clothes and his crusting, paint-stinking self as his grip allowed. He felt numb.

A pickup idled at the corner. Not a white pickup for the city crew that quit work at five. A pickup Lucas recognized as he and his bike drew closer.

Harley leaned out of the pickup's driver's window. 'Hey, kid, you OK?'

Say nothing! Lucas ordered himself. *Keep on walking. Ignore him.*

'Yeah, you're all right,' drawled Harley as Lucas walked past. ''Spect nobody's got no real hurts on 'em. Whether they should have or not, that ain't my say-so. Just the way things work out. An accident here, a being-stupid there.'

Lucas crossed the street. Harley's words hit his back as he walked on.

'Missy teacher. That's what she gets for messing with a crazy. Her own damn fault. Hell, she ain't got no complaint. Nothing for her to be no letter writer about like certain old bitties. Teacher lady got off easy for being dumb. Ain't like somebody went and sugared her gas tank.'

MONSTER

Jordan Smith stood in front of the stunned faces of her 5A class.

She'd scissor-chopped her midnight hair until it was a soldier's buzz cut.

'So this is our last day of school,' she told her wide-eyed fifth graders.

'*I don't know what she's going to do,*' Dad'd told Lucas after The Important Phone Call the night before. '*I just know what's changed for you.*'

The woman who'd chopped her hair stared at children she'd shepherded. 'Things start. Things end. We got to figure out how to live with that.'

Brrring! clanged the last bell on that last day.

Joyous chaos ruled Blackhawk Elementary—

—except in Miss Smith's 5A classroom. That cropped teacher's twenty-eight students strained to hear her as the last bell died.

'Promise me something,' said Miss Smith. 'Promise me you'll think about our time together and remember one true thing.'

Everyone held their breath.

'*Now go!*' she told them.

Cheers erupted around Lucas.

His classmates swept Lucas out the door, past Miss Smith's wistful eyes.

Donna shuffled next to him.

'*Um,*' he said, 'thanks for the blackboard help.'

'Yeah. Sure.'

'Maybe we'll be in the same class next year. And if the alphabet works out, maybe you'll be behind me.'

'Behind you.' She *humphed*. 'That's the desk I always get.'

'What desk do you want?'

She said nothing. Limped away.

He found his three buddies on the playground.

Marin had his arms spread wide and his face arched to the clear blue sky.

Kurt said: 'What was she talking about? "*One true thing*"?'

'Doesn't matter,' said Wayne. 'School's over!'

Marin grinned. 'Who wants to see a monster?'

Kurt shrugged. 'We don't have any around here.'

Far enough away to *not* be with Lucas's crew but near enough to hear them stood Bobbi Jean. Habit kept Anna in Lucas's vision, so he knew Bobbi Jean was eyeing her too as Anna laughed for ex-sixth grade girls Jane and Kay and Bonnie, who were officially cool *plus* now promoted to grown-up seventh grade.

Bobbi Jean wavered between her best friend Anna and the four boys. Told *the guys*: 'My dad says that if people saw the dinosaurs who'd lived here, they'd think they were monsters and we got their genes inside us just like monkeys!'

Watch out for monkey shit, thought Lucas.

Wayne glared at Bobbi Jean. 'Don't you have to catch a bus?'

'Mom said that on the last day of school, I don't have to go right home.'

'Well, go somewhere.'

Wayne led his buddies away from her.

Bobbi Jean saw the newly promoted seventh grade girls surf away from this schoolyard for 'little kids.' Her best friend Anna rode their flow.

Bobbi Jean stood alone as those girls sailed off.

As those four boys drifted across the playground.

As brakes hissed and the last orange school bus pulled away.

As wind stung her bare legs with grains of sand.

'I don't have to go anywhere!' she yelled to the boys' backs.

Lucas started to turn back to her…

… but again Marin said: 'So who wants to go see a monster?'

Lucas shouted: 'Who wouldn't?'

'No such thing,' said Wayne. 'I'm not going looking for some no-such-thing.'

'Before we do stuff like that, our folks should say it's OK,' said Kurt.

That's right, thought Lucas. But something woke up inside him on this last day of school and he said: 'What monster?'

'You have to come see to find out,' said Marin. 'That's just the way it is.'

Wayne argued: 'You don't know what you're talking about.'

'Then why are you scared?'

'I ain't scared.' Wayne pitched a rock through the chain-link fence surrounding the town's cement tennis court. 'I'm not stupid. I won't be a sucker.'

'What about you, Lucas?' said Marin.

'It's the last day, so I suppose if I get home a little late…'

'So there's you and me.' Marin looked at the other boys. 'Come on, guys! It's our chance.'

'Just because you get a chance doesn't mean you should take it,' said Kurt.

Lucas remembered Laura and the trial: *You lose something either way.*

Wayne glared at Lucas, who he'd known since kindergarten, a whole five years longer than Marin had been around. 'I'm with Kurt. You coming?'

'I'm going with Marin,' said Lucas.

'Suit yourself.' Wayne shook his head. '*Monster.* Hah!'

Kurt and Wayne trudged off.

Kurt turned around when they were half a block away. Waved.

Wayne kept his face pointed the same direction as his toes.

'Come on,' said Marin. 'This way.'

We're together! thought Lucas. *Going somewhere!*

The *where* didn't matter as much as the *going.* The sidewalk under his shoes stretched forever smooth.

Three cars sat in the bright afternoon parking lot for the Buttrey's grocery store three blocks away where his mom never shopped *because.*

Because, why? wondered Lucas. *And why all the other becauses?*

'Come on,' said Marin.

The grocery store's glass doors slid open. Sucked them into its aisles of multicolored boxes and canned goods. The chill of machined air goose-bumped Lucas's arms. His glasses carried his vision back to the refrigerated counter where the white-aproned man swung a cleaver into a child-sized slab of beef.

Thunk went the steel blade as it chopped through flesh and bone. *Thunk.*

The lone cashier had long black hair, copper skin, a red-lipstick smile, and gave off the kind of sly sass Lucas felt in his aunts, the Conner sisters.

Marin said: 'Hi, Mom. You doing OK?'

'Honey,' she said, 'stop worrying about me.'

The man who stood first in her line of customers drawled a leer.

'So, Ruby, this your kid?' He wore a fancy tan shirt and brown pants. Wore a sports jacket like a boss. Every strand in his slick hair was placed just so. 'You're a fine-looking cuss, boy. You a ballplayer?'

'No,' answered Marin, who starred in every playground game.

In line behind the fancy man, Mrs Sweeny clung to the handle of her shopping cart, said: 'Decent folks don't hold up the line with jawing!'

'Hell,' said Mr Fancy. 'I didn't know you was back there.'

'The sum total of what men don't know would flood this store.'

'Come around me.' Mr Fancy stepped aside so she could squeak her cart forward. 'I'm just here considering switching cigarettes.'

He grinned at the cashier he called Ruby, not Mrs Larson or ma'am.

'I ain't particular about brands,' he told the world, his eyes on Ruby. 'Old Gold, Chesterfield, Pall Malls, Lucky Strike, Winstons: They all got the same burn inside their papers. You just got to know how to light 'em up. And appreciate the taste. I ain't so proud I won't go with a good switch when I find one.'

'That's mighty white of you.'

Those words from Marin's Indian mom cut flat and cold with an edge Lucas couldn't name. Somehow, he knew she didn't mean whatever it was those words were supposed to mean. He'd never understood the 'white of you' phrase when people used it in movies or books. Or said it in town. Made him feel… *yucky.*

And he realized Mr Fancy also didn't get whatever Marin's mom meant because he said: 'That's the kind of guy I am. Hell, I'll show you.'

He swaggered away from the cashier toward the back of the store.

Mrs Sweeny put three cans of peas from her cart onto the checkout counter for the cashier to pull along past her like they were supposed to go.

Ruby rang up Mrs Sweeny's four cans of sardines.

In her mom voice, Ruby said: 'You boys going to have fun?'

Her widowed customer frowned.

'Children's fun can be ruin and damnation.' Mrs Sweeny squinted at Ruby. 'As I recollect, people 'round here don't know about your boy's father.'

'Really.' Ruby rang up a can of prunes.

'Seems like he's never around.'

Ruby totaled the price of three cans of tomatoes.

'So did he die in the war? Korea or such?'

Ruby snapped open a fresh brown paper sack. 'Not as I know.'

'So if he didn't die in the war, then… you're… ?'

Steady tan hands sculpted the paper sack into the perfect shape. 'I'm your cashier. I total up your bill.'

Mrs Sweeny's talons plucked a white paper packet from the cart. 'If totaling is your lot, then you're blessed to have it. God gives us what we deserve.

'Which is more than we can say for your butcher.' The crone waved the white packet. 'This meat is thirty-three cents a pound, but he marked it forty-one cents.'

'That thirty-three was last week's sale price.'

'This is just hamburger! My car needed gas last week. It's not my fault I couldn't get here, so you should fix the price.'

'Would you like me to ring for Zeb?'

'Thought you could total things yourself.' The crone gave a sigh for all the martyrs of her Lord. 'Don't bother. I won't pinch pennies.'

'No, ma'am,' said Ruby as she rang up the meat doomed to sizzle in Mrs Sweeny's black frying pan. 'Not if you can get me to do it for you.'

The grocery store's glass doors slid shut after Mrs Sweeny's departure.

Mr Fancy boomed: 'Here you go, boys!'

He stood in the cashier's line, a cold can of soda pop in each fist, his eyes on Ruby. He winked. 'A real man knows kids.'

Put coins for the cans on the counter.

'My boy knows not to take anything from strangers. Or handouts.'

'We ought to fix that "stranger" thing.'

Marin grabbed the two cold cans from the counter in front of Mr Fancy.

'Wow!' he said. 'Gosh, thanks!'

That's not your real voice, thought Lucas.

'Here.' Marin turned to give an orange soda to his buddy. His other hand gripped a grape soda near his chest so the adults behind him couldn't see him violently shaking the can. He hooked a finger under the newfangled pull tab. 'You want some, mister?'

Marin whirled so the grape soda was inches from that gift giver.

Popped the tab.

Purple mist sprayed the fancy man like a blast from a shotgun.

'You son-of-a—'

'Sorry, mister!' yelled Marin. 'Must be something wrong with the can!'

'Something wrong with you! Somebody needs to learn you what—'

Ruby snapped: '*The boy said his polites.*'

She scooped the two coins off the counter. *Dinged!* them into the cash register. Looked at Mr Fancy with eyes like rifle barrels.

Mr Fancy glared at his purple-spotted tan shirt. Stormed from the store.

Ruby's eyes drilled her son. 'That's a new one.'

'It was an accident, Mom!'

'Oh yeah.'

She turned a smile to her son's friend.

'You must be Lucas. Marin talks about you.'

A grin stretched Lucas's face. *He talks about me!*

'You two better get going,' said Marin's mom. 'Zeb's a decent man, but boys hanging around having "accidents" aren't good for his business or my job.'

In the safety of outside sunlight, Lucas said: 'Why'd you do that?'

Marin trash-canned the unopened orange pop. 'He was just another jerk.'

'All he wanted was to buy some cigarettes.'

'No he didn't.'

Marin led them west through blocks of homes.

Lucas saw the housewife who used to be Fran Marshall. She wore her white blouse outside black slacks as she rolled a chaise lounge into the shade of her front yard tree. Fran waved at the boy she'd known since he was born.

Lucas waved back.

Spotted Fran's new husband sitting on the front porch.

Ben Owens held a beer bottle in his hand. Held the bespectacled kid across the street in his unblinking eyes. Ben Owens tilted his beer bottle for a drink.

How come, middle of the day, you're here drinking beer, not working at Dad's office? thought Lucas.

Marin said: 'Who are they?'

'Her father owns the trucking business my dad runs. That guy, her husband, he works there now. I used to, but Dad doesn't think it's best for me to be around his office anymore, so after last night's trouble—'

'What trouble?'

As they walked, Lucas told Marin about Why Jordan Smith Cut Her Hair.

'Will Garth go to jail?' said Marin.

'He didn't do anything wrong. He just *is* wrong.'

Lucas flashed on what Gramma Meg liked to tell the world about him.

'So nothing's going to happen to anybody?' said Marin.

'Except me. I got a new job. One besides passing out flyers every couple of weeks for the Roxy. Since it's not a good idea for me to work at the truck shop anymore, when Mr Dylan called to explain about the trouble, Dad got him to use me on his summer painting jobs. Plus, he needs help watching his baby Rachel. Plus help him and Miss Smith with teaching Hal at the jail.'

A dog panted at them from the lawn beyond a chain-link fence.

'I leave for the ranch after the fair,' said Marin. 'I run with kids on the rez. Feed the chickens. Gather eggs. The hen house is an oven. Itchy straw. And, *man*, those chickens peck when you slide your hand under them! I weed the garden. Shovel horse stalls. The brown bay is who I get to use, so I ride him lots.'

Lucas frowned. 'What's the rez?'

'The reservation. The Rocky Boy. You know. For us Gros Ventres.'

'Oh. Yeah.' Lucas took a step. 'Those kids, are they, *um*, your best friends?'

'About like here. *Hey!* I got a great idea!' Marin took off running, three steps gone before Lucas realized it. 'This is better than the monster!'

'Wait up!' Half a block and Lucas felt his wind start to go. 'Where are—'

'You said her house was trashed!' Marin darted into a graveled alley. 'Let's help her clean it up. And we can see what Garth did.'

'I already saw.' Lucas slowed his pace.

Marin stayed beside Lucas as they walked down the alley.

An old green car nestled between a shed and a garage, tucked out of sight of passing traffic. Lucas had unloaded a million cans of paint from that car. And if you punched the dashboard…

'What's the matter?' said Marin.

'Nothing.'

'Come on, then. Just up ahead there: Isn't that her brown house?'

'*Shh!*' hissed Lucas. 'This isn't a good idea.'

'Sure it is. We can see monsters anytime.'

Lucas grabbed Marin's shoulder to stop him. They saw the back of the brown house. The wooden door inside the screen closed with a quiet *clunk*.

'Let's go!' whispered Lucas.

'Around to the front door?' said Marin.

But Lucas hurried down the alley. 'You said we'd see a monster.'

'Yeah, but she was good to us.' Marin stopped. 'She could use our help.'

'Yeah, but… not now. Feels like a bad time.' *Change the topic!* 'That guy you sprayed in the store: Why didn't he want cigarettes?'

Marin snapped: 'You want to see a monster?'

'Ah, yeah, I—'

'Then come on!'

Marin stormed out of the alley. Turned right to where a slope of a vacant lot rose toward blue sky from a dead-end street. Scrambled up the scrub hill.

'Wait up!' Lucas slipped on a rock. 'Slow down, Marin!'

Who whirled like a boxer.

'Another guy, that son-of-a-bitch, he didn't want cigarettes!' Marin leaned so close Lucas felt his hot breath. 'He… he wanted to sex my mother!'

'*No!*'

'Don't you tell anybody!'

Lucas expected fire in his friend's eyes, but Marin's gaze was soft, pleading.

'Promise me you won't tell anybody!'

'I won't! I promise!'

Marin nodded. Trudged up the hill.

'Sorry, Marin. I didn't know.' Lucas sensed the other boy's forgiving shrug as prairie grass crunched under their sneakers. 'I swear I won't tell anyone.'

Three steps later, he said: '*Um*, Marin: Does your mom know?'

'Yeah.'

'Can I help?'

'No.' Marin looked at the horizon. Said: 'Thanks.'

They had ten yards of hill left to climb when Lucas said: 'What's sex?'

Marin stopped.

Looked out over the dozens of square blocks of trees and towns spread out in the dusty valley below them. The cobalt peaks of the Three Buffaloes poked up from the northern horizon. White clouds sailed the breeze across deep blue sky.

Marin said: 'You don't know what sex is?'

Lucas shrugged.

'Don't you think about my mother!'

'I won't! I swear!'

'And don't tell your folks that I told you. They might get mad.'

'Why? It can't be like the secret to the atom bomb.'

'You can never figure grown-ups.' Marin looked left. Looked right. Whispered: 'Sex is what men and women do!'

'When?'

'Whenever!' Marin whispered to Lucas. 'The man sticks his dick in where the woman goes pee and she lets him!'

'*Nuh-unh!*'

'*Un-huh!*'

'That's… so weird.'

'I know. But that's what it is.'

'Why do they do that?'

'That's how you make babies.'

'That guy wanted to make a baby with—'

'You promised you wouldn't!'

'I wasn't!' swore Lucas. 'It just slipped out!'

And then it hit him:

The man puts his dick in a woman.

Gramma Meg says my dick needs to be cut. Is broken. Ugly.

Why would any woman want my ugly broken dick in her?

Marin said: 'Let's just not talk about it, OK?'

'Yeah,' mumbled Lucas.

'My mother, I mean.'

'Nobody's mother,' said Lucas. 'Nothing is about nobody's mother.'

Marin ran up the hill. Lucas hurried after him. The two boys charged over the crest. Bulled through a tangle of bushes.

Lucas pushed his glasses back up his nose. Blinked.

An army of stone slabs surrounded the two boys.

'Cemetery!' hissed Lucas. 'We're in the—'

A motor rumbled closer. Tires crunched gravel. A rusted station wagon spewed a cloud of dust behind it as it roared into the cemetery.

Marin and Lucas scrambled behind a marble slab.

'Is it the monster?' whispered Lucas.

'Don't be stupid! Monsters don't drive!'

The rusted vehicle's engine shut off.

Lucas and Marin peered around the gravestone.

A woman loomed ten graves beyond where the boys hid. Her rusted ride waited for her. A bird sang. A freshly grassed mound of earth trapped her eyes.

'Mrs Klise!' hissed Lucas. 'That grave must be…'

The boys retreated behind the marble slab.

The grass around them smelled of summer.

Metal clinked.

Lucas spotted the chain slapping the white metal flagpole of the Veterans' Memorial – a white stone pedestal supporting a painted-black, tripod machine gun from World War I. He'd stood there on Memorial Day with his Cub Scout pack. Saluted with two fingers pressed against his forehead as the high school band teacher raised his trumpet and played Taps.

'Marin!' he whispered. 'The sex thing: How do they do it?'

'They get on top of each other.'

'Who's on top – the man or the woman?'

'How should I know!'

A seagull gliding above them blinked away the sun.

'We gotta get out of here,' said Marin. 'This place gives me the creeps.'

Marin led Lucas through a gap in the windbreak row of bushes.

'Did she see us?' said Marin.

'I don't think she sees anything,' said Lucas.

They slid down the long ditch of the barrow pit. Marched up the other side and across a county gravel road. Crossed the next barrow pit…

… and were over the border. Out of town.

Brown earth stretched in front of them. Parched grass. Tumbleweeds. The boys moved toward where the blue sky curved down to meet the shadowed land. They grinned because they knew they weren't scared.

'It's OK,' said Marin. 'Long as we can see houses behind us.'

'How far?'

'Just a little ways. Getting stuck in the cemetery is why we aren't already there. Course, we could turn back now, if you want to.'

'I'm OK if you are.' Lucas shrugged. 'Wish we'd kept that orange soda.'

They walked maybe twenty steps.

Marin said: 'There's one more thing about sex.'

'What?' asked Lucas.

'People don't just do it to make babies.'

'Why else would you do something like that?'

'Beats me. Somebody said for fun. Or 'cause you're love crazy.'

'Love won't ever make me that crazy!'

Marin walked backward to watch Lucas as they walked, which kept his eyes on the town. Marin told Lucas 'bout *one time* on the ranch when a black stallion got loose. 'Bout *one time* drivin' in a blizzard when the world outside his mom's car swirled up in a whiteout. How cool it was that when they came back to school next fall, there'd be an "experiment" to let sixth grade boys play football.

Came the *buzz* of the first fly.

Marin was saying: '... probably hunkered down in its cave while we were stuck in the cemetery. We might as well head home so you'll make it to dinner—'

Lucas froze.

'—even if we didn't see a monster.'

'Too late.'

Marin turned – jumped back shoulder to shoulder with his friend.

'I just said all that about a monster to see who'd follow me!' whispered Marin. 'I've never been out here before. I only wanted you guys to not leave me.'

Lucas couldn't turn his eyes away from what they saw.

Whoever strung up the coyote on the barbwire fence did a damn fine job.

The animal's rear legs were spread wide. Bound to the fence's bottom strand of barbwire with scraps of the same. On the top wire, barbwire bent from the fence post held the coyote's forepaws out like a crucifixion. A red and white bandana knotted under the coyote's jaw kept his rigor-bared grin level and locked his fly-emptied eye sockets straight at Lucas and Marin.

They knew what hung on this fence. Knew it for a gunman's trophy. A warning to any other lone runners and vermin who challenged civilization.

And as they ran home, Lucas knew one true thing:

We got monsters.

CINNAMON MOON

Inside the Martin County Sheriff's Department. Cop radio chatter. Highway Patrol check-ins. Loose cow reports. WANTED posters. A rack of shotguns.

The deputy on desk duty put harsh eyes on the kid who'd tiptoed into this gray cement blockhouse behind Main Street on a fine summer morning.

'Got any knives or guns?' asked the lawman.

Lucas blurted: 'I've got a .22 rifle for gophers, a knife like Jim Bowie's my mom didn't want me to have. Dad said it was OK!'

'Ain't talkin' 'bout what everybody's got t' home. You bring stuff in here?'

'No, sir!'

'Go up those stairs.'

'*Wait*: I forgot my Cub Scout jackknife but I left it at home, too!'

The deputy laughed so hard he fell to coughing.

'Second floor. If he ain't up there, holler.'

The deputy shook a white 'coffin nail' from a pack behind his badge.

Lucas heard the rasp of a match as he climbed the stairs to the second floor where a narrow path of gray cement ran through a forest of black steel bars.

'Come closer,' said a male voice amidst the jail cells. 'Don't be scared.'

Too late, thought Lucas.

The voice in the shadows said: 'I can smell paint on you.'

Lucas called out to who he couldn't see:

'Mr Dylan – *Neal*, he says when we're working, I should call him *Neal* – we mixed the colors for Dix's house before Mrs Dix came out to get him for the phone call to go home, which worked out OK because I got to know his baby Rachel. She was sitting up in her playpen holding on to the b-b-bars…'

Lucas swallowed the rest of his words.

The shadow voice came from a bench bolted to the far wall. The cell opposite the bench stood open. 'Where was the kid's mom?'

'Neal said she had to lay down again. That's why she called Mrs Dix.'

The shape on the bench became a teenager in a white T-shirt with his bare feet on the cement floor. 'So is it just you and me?'

Each step brought Lucas closer to the barefooted teenager. *How come he's wearing blue jeans without a belt?*

'Where's Miss Smith?' said the prisoner.

'She had a shift at her summer job at the phone company.'

The prisoner nodded at the books Lucas clutched. 'What'd they send?'

The prisoner stretched his neck to look, but took nothing from the kid who wore black and white sneakers with laces.

'History, huh?' said the prisoner. 'When do you figure history started?'

'Nobody's told me yet.'

'You know when history starts? When it's too late to do anything about it.'

'*Ready, set, go!*' Gramma'd said as the hospital elevator doors slid open.

'What else you got?' said the prisoner.

Lucas held out both of the textbooks.

When the specter on the bench took them, he became *just Hal*.

'Damn, *algebra*.' Hal flipped through the textbook's pages. 'See what you got ahead of you being one of the smart kids?'

'Just because Laura's my sister doesn't mean we're the same.'

'Maybe. Can't help who we are. I told those two teachers I was general math. They said long as I was in probation, I might as well get as much as I can.'

Pale light filtered to the bench as they stared at shiny textbook pages.

'Look here,' said Hal. '"*X equals the unknown.*" If X is the unknown, then what equals the known?'

Hal's gaze roamed the forest of black steel bars. 'I guess right here.'

Lucas looked around.

Hal said: 'What do you think of jail?'

'Once they lock your cell, can you get out?'

'Nope.'

'Can anybody else get in?'

'Never thought of that.' Hal stared at him. 'Until now.'

Steel bars rising from the jailhouse floor trembled laughter.

Stone walls pressed against Lucas. 'What can you do here?'

Hal shrugged. 'Days, they unlock it so I can wander around. Nights, I'm all alone. "*Free, white, and twenty-one*" is what they say out there. In jail, it's who can say no to what. The deputies, Sheriff Wood, they say I'm lucky to be here. That I didn't get *the big time*. The prison in Deer Lodge. Or hell.'

'You have to be dead to go there,' popped out of Lucas.

A teenager and a boy sat surrounded by silence and time.

Until Lucas said: 'Do you want me to bring you some comic books?'

'Superman and Batman? Green Lantern? Thanks, but don't bring me any stuff where bad guys end up in jail. I'm already here.'

'You're not a bad guy!'

'So this is just a way to spend summer vacation before my senior year?'

Lucas had no answer.

Hal nodded to beyond the walls. 'What are they doing out there?'

'Everybody says it's going to be hot today. Farmers need rain. The fair is soon. I don't know what's going on. I just go to work and come home.'

'Regular life.' Hal ran his hand along the jail's wall of stones.

Risk it. 'Are you mad at Laura?'

'Your sister? Why?'

'Because she told stuff at the trial.'

'I was headed here no matter what. She did what she had to do. Maybe she erased some Xs. She should be mad at me. I put her in a jam. Tell her I'm sorry.'

'OK.'

'Hell, tell everybody I'm sorry. They don't hear it no more when I say it.'

Lucas's heart hammered.

'How long you supposed to stick around?' asked Hal.

'I'm supposed to bring you the books. See what else you need.'

'So you could go anytime. Now.'

'If you think, if you're sure it's OK.'

'I can feel you itchin'. Go on. Get on out of here.'

But on the stairs' landing, Lucas looked back. The teenager slumped against the far wall in a shaft of steel-bars-scarred dusty sunlight.

'It's OK to go,' said Hal. 'I'm where I belong.'

After dinner that night – before Lucas rescued Anna – he sat in the backseat of the Ross family car parked on Main Street. Imagined Hal in his cell.

'We just have to wait,' said Gramma Meg from the car's front passenger seat. She'd ordered Laura to park near the Roxy two doors away from the Alibi Club with its window of black and white photos of a sequined woman.

Laura pulled the car to that curb. Killed the engine.

Chris Harvie rumbled his family's car alongside Laura's door.

Claudia sat beside him, thigh to thigh. She called over for Laura to come riding with them. Lucas heard their radio playing some song with a guy singing: '*Put your head on my shoulder...*'

'We're going home as soon as I get back,' said Laura as she stepped out of her family's car and opened the door to her friends' growling machine. 'No arguments, Gramma. When Mom told me to take you and Lucas driving, she didn't say anything about us having to sit here to wait to see somebody like...'

'What your mother don't know won't bug her and she likes it that way,' said Gramma. 'You go on now, honey. Have fun. Don't get caught this time.'

'Lucas!' said Laura as she slid beside Claudia. 'Don't let her make trouble.'

Chris punched it and the Dodge surged away.

'Look over there across the street!' hissed Gramma.

Over there Uncle Orville curled his thick oil-driller arms across his chest to light a cigarette. He wore his steel-wool hair buzzed short. Kept his narrow eyes aimed at the lawyer. Falk talked and talked. Lucas couldn't hear any of those words. When the lawyer waved his hands, Lucas spotted a glint of gold.

Gramma said: 'He better watch himself.'

Lucas didn't know who she meant as those two men shook hands.

What Lucas was paying attention to was Anna.

She stood across the street in front of the huge picture window for the Cinderella Shop. Her sapphire eyes stared through the glass to three mannequins in fancy dresses. Blonde hair curled around her shoulders.

A heavy adult hand dropped on her shoulder.

Anna stepped sideways so that grasp naturally fell away.

The big woman who lost her grip on Anna wore a purple circus tent.

'Hell's bells!' whispered Gramma as the giant woman said something to Anna, then stepped off the curb. 'Here comes Jenny Mason.'

That purple dress trembled with the fat woman's every step. She leaned on the open driver's window. 'Megan, whatchya up to?'

'Got us a show happening here.'

'Hi, Lucas. You out with your grandmother tonight is nice, real nice. Me and Anna are going for ice cream.'

'Your daughter's sure a pretty thing,' said Gramma.

'Smart, too,' said her mother. 'Nobody ever says that, though.'

Anna's mother settled her weight on the car. She hid Lucas's view of Anna.

'Ice cream sounds like a great idea,' said Gramma. 'Lucas: You got money in your jeans. Get us treats at the Whitehouse.'

Lucas's eyes widened. *I get ice cream AND a chance to be with Anna!*

He scooted out of the car as Mrs Mason said:

'What show are you talking about, Megan?'

'Don't you know?' said Gramma. 'The Alibi Club's hired a stripper!'

Anna stood across the street facing the Cinderella Shop window.

Two cars of teenagers *dragging Main* passed in the street between Lucas and the blonde girl. The cars honked at each other. Drove on.

'Pity's sake, Megan Conner!' said Anna's mom. 'You parked on Main Street just for a chance to see some stripper woman walk inside a bar to go to work?'

'It ain't just her,' Lucas heard Gramma answer. 'Look at all these grown men down here. They're a bunch of dogs dragging their tongues on the sidewalk. It's pure entertainment to watch them pretend otherwise.'

Lucas stared at Anna's back. Her gaze seemed glued to the

window. He wondered if she saw his reflection in the glass she faced.

He ran past Main Street offices. Ran past the bookstore owned by Mrs Marple with her gothic dresses and giant goiter that scared him every time he went into her musty lair to buy comic books or paperback books for his mother – "historical romances," she called them, pictures of strong men and swooning bare-shouldered women on their covers.

Lucas jerked open the tinkling-belled glass door of the Whitehouse Café.

The counter stools were empty. Only Mr Wells sat at the tiny tables. He looked up from the evening newspaper when the bell above his café door *dinged*.

'Hey, Lucas.' Mr Wells pointed to the ceiling's metal grids over fluorescent tubes. 'Is it dark enough out there yet that we need to snap on the electrics?'

'I don't think so.'

'Good, I like my light real.' Mr Wells leaned on his newspaper. 'Do me a favor? Watch the place while I do my business in back. You're in charge.'

'Ah, OK,' the ten-year-old boy told the shuffling-away middle-aged man.

People went to the Whitehouse for coffee, for fountain drinks, for newspapers and magazines and the town's second-best selection of comic books. They went there for hot chocolate and ice cream.

Ding! went the bell above the glass door.

Anna sailed into the café. Her sapphire eyes widened when she saw the scrawny boy in glasses as the door closed behind her to trap them alone together.

'I thought you went home!' said blonde-locked Anna.

'So you did see me.'

'Well, I… I was waiting for my mom to finish, but she's still—' Anna turned to look back through the glass door. '*Oh no!*'

On the other side of Main Street, behind the car where Gramma Meg sat watching for whatever a stripper was, Lucas saw what Anna spotted:

Her overweight mother in that purple tent dress only twenty lumbering steps from the shelter that promised ice cream…

… as beyond Anna's mother, new seventh grade stars Jane and Kay and Bonnie emerged like triplets from the Roxy's early show of *North by Northwest.* They turned their lockstep parade toward the Whitehouse.

'This can't be happening!' Anna's blue eyes pleaded to Lucas. 'The movie's long, so it was OK to go out with Mom because we left home in time. Mom saw your car or we'd be gone. But now… She's my mom, but she's… They're going to all be here *together* and they'll all see me and *I'll just die*!'

Her blue eyes shimmered like lakes and for a moment—

—*if only for a moment*—

—the only person in the whole world she saw was Lucas.

'What am I going to do?' she whispered.

'Hide!' He scooted her with him behind the counter. Had her scrunch down on the floor out of sight. He stood there, a sentry pretending to be a soda jerk.

Ding! went the bell above the door.

'Hey, Lucas.' Mrs Mason caught her breath. 'Anna in here?'

Lucas licked his lips. Looked around. Put his eyes straight on the mother.

Honestly said: 'I don't see her now.'

Mr Wells sauntered out of the back room.

'Looks like I got back just in time,' he said. 'Evening, Jenny. I'll get around the counter, fix up Lucas, then—'

'*No!*' said Lucas. 'Aren't I in charge? Let me do it.'

The two adults shared a puzzled smile.

'Please?' said Lucas. 'Let me try?'

'Hell, take your shot.' Mr Wells swept his arm toward his table against the wall opposite the counter. 'Jenny, join me for a spell.'

Ding! went the bell above the door.

JaneKayBonnie bubbled in and spun onto stools at the counter.

Mr Wells called out to Lucas: 'Take care of the real customers first.'

Anna huddled beneath the counter by the ice cream bins.

Lucas's sneaker crunched her fingers.

Anna strangled a scream.

Jerked and bumped her head on the underside of the counter.

JaneKayBonnie blinked.

BAM! Lucas hit the counter.

Whispered: 'Bug.'

'*Eeeww!*' went JaneKayBonnie.

But he held his finger to his lips. Nodded at the grown-ups at their table.

These cool girls ordered dime Cokes with lots – *and we mean lots* – of ice.

'One second,' said Lucas.

Ran around the counter to the table as Mr Wells asked Anna's mom: 'How's the dressmaking?'

'Keeps me busy.' She frowned. 'I expected Anna to be here. She must have gone home, so... I'll have a one-scoop dish of strawberry – *no* – cinnamon.'

'Can you handle that, Lucas?' said Mr Wells. 'Want me to get up and—'

'No! I got it!'

Mr Wells told Lucas to bring him a coffee, let the boy get two steps gone before he called him back for the empty mug on the table.

'You clean the counter for your customers?' said Mr Wells.

Rag, where – in the sink. Squeeze the water out.

Lucas pivoted, his foot—

Anna jerked her hand off the floor before Lucas's sneaker landed.

He wiped the rag in front of the cool girls.

Bonnie said: 'You guys are *so* lucky your hair is great.'

'No way,' said Jane. 'Yours is so, you know.'

Lucas filled three paper cups with crushed ice.

Pulled the soda machine lever like he'd seen Mr Wells do.

As Lucas put icy Cokes in front of the girls, Kay said: 'I wish my mom would let me wear lipstick.'

'Tell her that pink is OK because it keeps your lips from getting chapped,' said Jane, 'so it's, you know, healthy.'

Lucas shuffled the scalding coffee mug to the table.

The café owner nodded to the girls at his counter. Smiled at Jenny Mason. 'Won't be long before your Anna's fitting right in with the likes of them.'

The purple-tented woman sighed. 'It's so important to be a pretty girl.'

'Well… it's nice,' mumbled the man sitting across from her.

'It's more than nice.' Anna's mom smiled at Mr Wells. 'It used to be me.'

'Hey,' said the ice-cream parlor owner. 'Hey now, Jenny, you're… you're…'

'Kind of like that white whale in that movie with Gregory Peck?' She laughed. 'When I used to think I could be a movie star, I had in mind like Marilyn Monroe in that funny movie about gangsters and jazz.'

'I ain't much for movies,' said Mr Wells as the boy eased the coffee mug down to the table. 'I have a hard enough time figuring out the story I'm in.'

'Well, least you ain't a whale.' She shook her head. 'But in mine, even if Al up and left, least I got a swell daughter.'

Lucas hurried back behind the counter where words from the adults drifted into one ear while chatter from JaneKayBonnie filled his other.

Grab that metal scoop. Flip open the first cold metal cooler.

The ice cream tub down there is chocolate.

Jane loudly asked her friends: ‘So do I look fat? I don’t want to be like…’

Oh! My! God! flashed the three girls’ faces as they realized *what* Jane almost said. And *when*. And *where*. In front of *who*. They tightened their huddle on the stools. Burst out laughing so hard Kay blew Coke out her nose.

The faces of the two grown-ups claimed they hadn’t heard the girls.

Lucas slammed down the cooler lid above the tub of chocolate. Stepped down the aisle closer to the counter space ruled by three princesses.

Spotted Anna huddled under the marble counter. She could hear everything. If she made a sound, everyone would hear her. She hugged her knees against her chest. Tears scarred her cheeks.

Lucas found the tub of cinnamon ice cream. Pushed the scoop—

Hit a frozen slab. The metal scoop didn’t pierce the ice cream.

Kay told her two friends: ‘Do you know what, like, everybody says?’

Lucas used both hands to push the metal scoop into the ice cream. It barely made a dent. He spotted a wooden mallet by the spigots for syrup toppings.

Tapped the mallet on the scoop to wedge it deeper in the ice cream.

Across the counter from him, the three girls knew only the world of them.

Mr Wells and Anna’s mom paid attention only to the world of their table.

Anna hid her face.

Kay hissed: ‘Out back of the junior high last night, Sue Saklin let Warren Iverson, *well*, she let him do more than just, *you know*, kiss her.’

Lucas couldn’t pull the scoop handle free from the tub of cinnamon ice cream.

'*Nuh-unh!*' said Bonnie.

'*Yuh-hun!*' said Kay.

Lucas grabbed the mallet. Cocked it high. Rose up on his tiptoes.

'Oh my God!' said Jane.

The mallet slammed down on the scoop handle.

Cinnamon ice cream cannonballed above the oblivious teenage girls.

The ice cream cannonball slammed into the metal grid over the dark fluorescent lights above the table where Mr Wells and Anna's mom sat as unaware as they had been the Sunday morning of Pearl Harbor.

Hung there on the ceiling like a cinnamon moon.

Waiting, just waiting to drop. To melt. To drip creamy cinnamon tears.

Oh shit! screamed through Lucas. *Gotta get Anna and get out before!*

He plopped a chunk of cinnamon ice cream in a glass bowl.

'Oh my lord, Lucas!' said Anna's mom as he dashed to the table. 'Even I can't eat all this. I'll just have a couple spoonfuls.'

'Lucas,' said Mr Wells, 'fix what you want for you. On the house.'

Lucas ran behind the counter. Prayed to the cinnamon moon: *Don't fall!*

Kay slurped the last of her Coke, said: 'Wasn't Cal Westlake so cute in his parents' car?'

'Cal's not so cute,' said Bonnie.

'Is too,' said Jane as they all slid off their stools.

'Is not,' said Kay.

'Well,' said Bonnie.

As to obey Mr Wells, Lucas poured two cups of Coke.

'Oh my God!' Jane said to Bonnie. 'Do you *so* like him?'

The girls plunked coins on the marble.

Jane's coin rolled toward the back of the counter. She lunged to catch it—

Lucas hurled himself in front of Jane to block her seeing over the counter as his hand dove down—

—Anna caught the falling dime. Slid the coin into Lucas's empty hand.

He clinked the errant dime onto the marble counter.

Bonnie asked her friends: 'What day are you guys going to the fair?'

'Not the first afternoon,' said Jane as the trio headed toward the door. 'Not with the little kids. Go that night. Everyone cool does. Mom will let me this year.'

At the table, a purple-tented whale struggled out of her chair.

Mr Wells waved away her offer to pay. 'You didn't even finish.'

Mrs Mason shuffled to the door that had closed behind JaneKayBonnie. Said: 'Lucas, if you see Anna, tell her I walked on home.'

Ding! went the bell as the door opened and she lumbered out to the world.

'Looks like it's just us now, Lucas.' Mr Wells frowned when the boy didn't come out from behind the counter. 'You did good.'

'Umm... Do you, while I'm still here... want to go out back again?'

Mr Wells laughed. 'My plumbing ain't that old yet.'

'I mean, *right now* would be a good time to do... something. If you need to.'

'Suppose I could lock up the back.'

Mr Wells disappeared down the dark hall.

'*Anna, now!*' hissed Lucas.

Her blonde hair streamed behind her as she charged out from behind the counter. Ran to Lucas and the escape door to Main Street—

Stopped.

Stared at him.

'Our secret,' he said because he knew that was important to her.

Her lips quivered. Her blue eyes went soft. She said: 'OK.'

Ding! went the door and she was gone.

Mr Wells walked into the front of his café.

Reached the table where his newspaper lay.

Where there was a dish and a coffee cup to be cleaned up.

Where he stood under a cinnamon moon.

'Do me a favor?' he said to Lucas. 'Hit the lights on your way out.'

That hurrying-out, empty-handed boy flipped the wall switch.

Fluorescent tubes warmed the ceiling's metal grid with its cinnamon moon.

The door *dinged!* closed behind Lucas to seal in the sound of any scream.

Across Main Street, Laura opened the car door to hear Gramma say: 'You kids missed it. She just went right in like it was nothing.'

Lucas saw Anna running away, her blonde hair flying.

But in that twilight moment as the streetlights winked on, it seemed to Lucas that her running didn't matter, for in all her coltish golden beauty and grace, Anna looked already caught.

THE PARADE

Lucas sat at the breakfast table trying to make sense of the front page of the newspaper that hid his father behind Friday, July 10's stories about 1959.

'Terrorists' in South Viet Nam bombed a movie theater like the Roxy and killed two American soldiers in the first lethal attack on US military advisors in that country that – like Lucas's school report said – used to belong to France.

Cops in Montreal seized $8 million worth of heroin from Chicago mobsters.

Robert Kennedy planned to resign as chief counsel for the Senate Rackets Committee so he could work on his older brother's campaign to be president.

Nobel Prize-winning diplomat Dr Ralph Bunche was denied membership in a New York City tennis club because he was a 'Negro.'

The club also refused to let in Jews.

How come no Jews or Negroes live here in Vernon? wondered Lucas.

'Don't you have to go to work today?' said Dad from behind the newspaper.

'Neal's taking his baby girl to the parade.' Lucas *harumphed.* 'So I could—'

Standing at the kitchen sink, Mom said: 'I told you, *we'll see.*'

Truth was, Lucas didn't know what he wanted Mom to see.

If Mom took him out to the Grady River's Four Counties Fair and Rodeo that afternoon, the carnival rides only cost a nickel.

There'd be hordes of kids running wild over the oil-packed earth of the midway.

If Mom took him out there after dinner, the rides would cost a dime, but JaneKayBonnie said all the cool guys walked the fairgrounds on the first night.

'I'm going to the parade this morning,' said Lucas. 'Mom said Main Street's too crowded, Laura's working at the phone company, but you could come, Dad.'

'I've got to work,' said Dad from behind the newspaper.

'But you're the boss.'

Dad laid the newspaper on the kitchen table. Blinked. 'You're damn right I am. And I take my son to the parade.'

First they drove across the tracks to Dad's office for him 'to do a few things,' which was fine by Lucas. The parade didn't start for two hours and it had been forever since he'd last seen *Her.*

But what Lucas saw as their black station wagon drew near the company buildings was a new white convertible parked in front of the garage bays. Maroon and gold lettered banners on the convertible read:

MARSHALL TRUCKING & THE CIVIC LEAGUE

The second thing Lucas saw was a burly truck driver wrestling one end of a metal desk stuck in the doorway to the Office.

Dad gunned the station wagon to where the trucker struggled. Jumped out. Grabbed the desk just as that teamster lost his grip and fell on his butt.

'Got it!' said Dad to whoever gripped the desk inside the house. 'In or out?'

'Out damn here,' muttered the trucker as he struggled to his feet.

'Turn it on its side!' ordered Dad to partners he couldn't see.

Then that man of fifty who'd carved prairie sod with a horse-drawn plow...

That man who had as a boy ran the family homestead when the Spanish Flu epidemic laid his brothers and parents low...

That once-a-boy who'd survived that flu when a country doctor chopped holes in his rib cage and stuck in hoses so he could breathe...

That man who at thirty-four had made it through WWII Army basic training...

That man who now was a boss, a pencil pusher, a keyboard tapper, a desk jockey who wore a sports jacket and who was only *Dad*...

That man gripped the steel desk with no more visible strain than he used to turn the steering wheel of the company station wagon.

The steel desk stood on its edge in midair.

'Bring it out!' yelled Dad.

The desk emerged from the house in McNamer's slipping grip.

The trucker rushed to help him. The two of them strained to handle one end of the desk while Dad carried the other end alone.

'God-damn, Don!' said McNamer as they set the desk on the sidewalk. 'Wish you'd shown up sooner!'

A man's voice said: 'Seems like he got here just in time.'

Ben Owens stood in the doorway of the Office. He wore his wedding suit and call-it-a-smile. No sheen of sweat glistened on his golf-course-tanned forehead.

'Don't know what we'd have done if you hadn't shown up,' he said to Dad.

McNamer said: '*We?*'

'What's all this?' said Dad.

'You'll be glad to know I got us a hell of a deal,' said Ben as he strolled down the steps. 'A frat buddy of mine works for a furniture outfit in Great Falls.'

Dad said: 'If we need something, we buy from Mark's Furniture downtown.'

Ben's smile didn't change. 'Yeah, but this way, we saved a bunch of dollars.'

'And sent a bunch more out of our town.' Dad nodded to the desk. 'I don't remember knowing about this.'

'*Didn't I tell you?*' said Ben. 'The chief and I figure to get modern. When I found a deal on the new desk I needed, we up and seized the moment.'

McNamer leaned on his good leg. 'Me and Jake got to seize something, too.'

'Thanks, guys,' said Dad. 'If we need you again, I'll ring over to the shop.'

The trucker followed the mechanic to the garage bays.

Dad told Ben: 'Those guys aren't a couple of yard mules.'

'They work for us,' said Ben.

'They work for the company. Like us.'

'How do you get them to do anything if you don't tell 'em what to do?'

'Treat a man right and all you have to do is ask, not tell.'

'Whatever. We got the desk out, didn't we?'

'Somebody did.'

Dad strolled over to the white convertible. 'And what's this?'

Ben said: 'This is my new car. Seeing as how this is a company car—'

'Alec mentioned he was writing some vehicle for you two into the company books, but I figured it was some kind of family car.'

'And this deal makes it perfect! We're clear on your station wagon 'cause it's got MARSHALL TRUCKING painted on its doors and the guys haul parts in it, but for this beauty, we need to prove it's really a "company car" to the tax boys. So we use it for advertising and civic promotion. Drive it in the parade. Get pictures. So what can they say?'

'We better hope they say nothing.'

'Damn right they got nothing. Plus, we're sponsoring the Civic League—'

'We are?'

'*Didn't I tell you?* Alec thinks it's a great idea, 'specially 'cause it ties in with the tax angle and gets Falk on board for that. He's a lawyer, so there you go.'

'Where am I going?'

'Well… come ride in the parade! We figured on just me and Falk, but hell, you're a part of Marshall Trucking Company. A big damn part.'

Dad stared at the white convertible. 'Three of us bunched in there would look like monkeys.'

'Huh?'

'Plus, I don't want to spoil that for you and Falk. Besides, I can't make the parade. I'm a man with work to do. But you go on. Have a good time.'

Ben reached for the white convertible's door.

'By the way,' said Dad, 'the phone company will have you fixed up soon.'

'What?'

Dad smiled: '*Didn't I tell you?* Alec and I been figuring on what you need to do besides getting a new company car in all the parades. *Didn't he tell you?*'

'Ah, no, he—'

'Figures. He's the owner but I'm the manager, so he likes me to run things. Along with your everyday paperwork, you get to be off-hours dispatcher. That's why Alec brought you in, isn't it? To help out? All you got to do is sit at home or your new desk from five in the evening until I take over come nine in the morning. Plus on weekends. Our secretary Adele and I have been splitting that, Alec, too. We'll spell you when we can, but it's your shift.

'The phone company will rig a dispatch line in your new house. You take customers' orders. Check with the refinery out west. The pumping rigs up north. Dispatch trucks. Somebody's always got to answer the phone. Now that's you. You're having a baby, so you won't be going anywhere anyway, plus you get to learn the business sitting at home. That'll make Fran happy. When she's happy, Alec glows like this new car.'

Ben stood there with his hand on the convertible's door.

'Have a good parade.' Dad steered Lucas past the deserted steel desk on the sidewalk to the Office. As soon as the Office screen door shut behind them, Dad raced down the hall to the room with his desk.

Lucas glanced back through the screen.

Ben stood beside the convertible. Frowning.

Lucas walked in on Dad talking on his desk's black phone. 'This is Don Ross. My Laura's working a shift there now. I need to – Thanks a lot.'

Outside the Office, Ben slammed shut the convertible's door.

'Laura?' said Dad into the phone. 'Can you adjust paperwork there so a new phone order gets processed like it came in *before* today?... Just tell me... You can! I'll call you back with the *what's whats*.'

Dad hung up and spun the dial on the phone to make another call:

'Hi, Alec, I wanted to let you know I've taken care of Ben as off-hours dispatcher... You remember. We talked about how to let him learn the business like you and I did, from the ground up. How he fits perfectly, busy as we're getting. How this way, your Fran will have him home more to help with the little one. When's the baby due?'

Dad said good-bye. Held on to the black receiver. Saw his son.

'Lucas, I, *ah*...'

'I know.'

Lucas walked out of the Office.

Walked into the garage past mechanic McNamer like everything was OK.

She whispered from the softly lit wall: "*Remember me?*" Lucas walked by himself through northside streets to the viaduct over the train tracks to squeeze into the wall of boisterous spectators lining Main Street. Walked until he found a place in the crowd standing in front of the Roxy.

A police car siren wailed way down at the far west end of Main Street.

Sheriff Wood led the parade in that rolling black cruiser with gold stars on its front doors and a cherry light spinning on its roof.

Five cowboys on saddled horses pranced behind the cruiser. The middle rider carried the American flag, its pole set in the stirrup while the banner fluttered proud and free above the brown horse's neck.

Lucas snapped to attention, right hand over his heart. He kept his face from showing embarrassment for the adults around him who merely stood a little straighter, or worse, didn't stop chattering as their flag passed by.

Then came three high school twirlers tossing batons up toward Christmas lights still strung across July's Main Street. One twirler caught her baton.

Behind the twirlers marched the high school band torturing a brassy song.

There! Across the street:

Wayne lunged toward the motoring-past volunteer fire department truck.

Lucas knew all the men in blue shirts who rode the fire truck and threw handfuls of penny candy toward Wayne and the crowd.

They were Sam, who careened his car through town every time the fire whistle blew. Archie, who seldom bathed and had a tooth-free grin. Pete from the furniture store Ben Owens hadn't gone to. They were everybody's neighbors.

The parade rolled on.

Mayor Nelson waved from the backseat of an Army jeep leading a uniformed and shouldered-rifle marching squad of local National Guard guys.

Across the street from Lucas stood Neal Dylan. Baby Rachel straddled his shoulders. Cooed to her father and pointed toward what was coming.

Rolling between them and Lucas came a flatbed truck bearing bales of hay and a black Angus steer bred by the science of evolution. Green fourleaf clover signs emblazoned with '4-H' hung on the truck doors. The smiling driver was bald farmer Herbst, who'd rescued Lucas from Mrs Sweeny on Easter.

Farmer Herbst saw Lucas. Grinned.

Neal Dylan looked away from the parade float for the Masonic Temple with its women's auxiliary of the Order of the Eastern Star and its youth groups, Rainbow Girls and boys-only DeMolay – a national group whose ranks included the first president of the United States to come from Lucas's generation. With his child riding his shoulders, Neal's gaze searched the crowd on Main Street.

The float for Our Fair Queen rumbled past. A high school girl wore the sash, her prom dress, and someone else's smile as her arm fluttered that special wave.

There! spotted Lucas. *Across the street on that sidewalk.*

Short black hair. Tan slacks. A soft dawn blouse. Fighter pilot's sunglasses.

Don't wave! Lucas ordered himself. *Don't jump up and down yelling: "Here! Miss Smith! It's me, Lucas! I'm standing across the street way down over here!"*

The truck carrying the high school basketball team rolled past her. Chris Harvie waved their Second Place, North Central 'B' District trophy.

A circus truck painted with red and yellow swirls rolled past Lucas blaring calliope music. Its sign for the fair proclaimed:

'THE MOST ASTOUNDING RIDES IN THE KNOWN UNIVERSE – AND BEYOND!'

Kurt's missing all this, thought Lucas. Every summer Kurt went away to Lutheran camp near Glacier Park. Didn't have to get a summer job, but still: "*The most astounding rides in the known universe – and beyond!*"

Lucas scanned the crowd for Marin. *He's not supposed to leave for the ranch on his rez until after the fair. Where is he?*

A tractor molded with white napkin-stuffed chicken wire float for the Benevolent and Protective Order of Elks rolled by as the little girl on Neal Dylan's shoulders bounced up and down, pointed to the coming float for the Moose Club.

Across Main Street, Lucas shook his head.

Masons, Elks, Moose, Lions. What do all these men's clubs do?

Lucas saw Neal Dylan beckon Tap Room bar owners Barb and Gary Harmon to join him and Rachel.

The white convertible paraded down Main Street.

Ben Owens drove while lawyer Falk waved to the crowd.

Lucas felt cold inside.

Sunglassed Jordan Smith walked the sidewalk behind the spectators.

Neal motioned her to where he stood with his daughter and the Harmons.

A red combine for harvesting wheat rumbled between them and Lucas. Such a machine held spinning blades across its front and towered more than twice as tall as any family car with a glass-windowed high cab for its driver.

Jordan Smith smiled at Barb Harmon. Shook Gary's hand.

A flatbed truck bearing a ten-foot-tall model of an oil-drilling derrick filled Lucas's view as it drove past. The signs on its side cited sponsorship from the oil refinery west of town and proclaimed: 'We Fuel America's Future!'

Neal glanced across the street. Saw Lucas standing there. Pointed toward the end of the parade. Beckoned that when it had passed, Lucas should join him.

A kindergarten boy beside Lucas whined: 'Is that all there is?'

'Hush!' said his mother. 'Just wait.'

Lucas heard the blare of the high school band reach the east end of Main Street. Turn to go up the hill and toward his house, where Mom stood inside her front screen door. She'd watch the marchers and floats pass by to detour around the nursing home where Gramma and other survivors of her generation sat parked on the sidewalk in wheelchairs or gray metal folding chairs so they could see the parade they couldn't go to come instead to them.

A truck chugging past Lucas carried a dozen women wearing the same blue dresses, odd smiles, and dots of gold pinned to their chests. Some of the women were as young as Lucas's mother. Most seemed as old as Gramma.

'Let's go!' whined the kindergarten boy. 'Who are they?'

'The Gold Star Mothers,' whispered the woman who bore him. 'Wave.'

'How come they don't put you up in the parade? You're the best mom! How come they don't give you a blue dress and a gold star thingy and let you ride in—'

That mother jerked her son's arm. *'Don't say that!'*

The boy wrinkled his face to cry. The mother dropped to sit on her heels and comfort him. Her face burned with shame as the Gold Star winners rolled by.

'No! Don't cry, honey! It's OK! Mommy's sorry! I didn't mean to scare you. You're all right. Here, you're all right and safe here with Mommy.'

A trembling lip showed Mommy and Lucas that the boy wasn't convinced.

'No, it's OK. Really. See, those mommies, they aren't like me. I won't be – Those mothers, their sons went to wars. Fought and didn't come back home.'

'Wh-why?'

'Because they died. And I won't ever ride in that truck. OK?'

The boy nodded. If his mother said it was so…

'Look!' She smiled and pointed back to the parade. 'Look at the horses!'

A posse of horsemen clattered past, iron horseshoes on a city street.

Four of the riders wore dusty leather chaps and drover's shirts, scuffed cowboy boots and weather-beaten Stetsons.

Real cowboys, thought Lucas. *Grampa Conner must have looked like that.*

But most of the riders wore shined boots. Fancy snap-button shirts. Bolo ties and spotless ten-gallon hats. Shiny spurs that jingle-jangled.

Three women riders wore calico cowgirl dresses.

Five Blackfeet Indians off their nearby reservation rode using saddle blankets. They wore buckskin pants, beaded shirts. Two sported eagle feather headdresses. None of the Indians smiled as they rode proud: *We're Still Here.*

'It's over now,' the mother told her son. 'The posse comes last because—'

A horse lifted his tail to drop a football of brown shit on Main Street.

The son and much of the crowd laughed.

The crowd became people going their separate ways.

Lucas hurried to where Neal Dylan held baby Rachel and stood with the Harmons in front of the radio repair—

There! Beyond the teacher and his baby. On the other side of the window, inside the radio repair shop.

Donna from his class. She stared out at the parade of regular walkers who she'd never be. Saw the first kid she knew in this new town where she'd thought things would be different. Saw him stare at her through his glasses that let him not need her anymore. Stare at her through the glass wall between her and him and the rest of the world. She limped away into the shadows of her father's shop.

Baby Rachel spotted Lucas. Memories of when Daddy brought that big boy to the house to play with her when Mommy was gone or lying down made Rachel smile. She reached toward Lucas.

Lucas used all his strength to pull the not-yet-walking baby into his arms. She squealed and tried to pull his glasses off.

Neal said: 'Glad we spotted you, Lucas. I need to know when you're going out to the fair.'

Lucas shrugged. 'Mom said *we'll see.*'

Neal turned to the Harmons.

'You probably know that Hal's ninety days ended two days ago,' he said. 'We – Jordan and I – we're still teaching him. He went from being locked up in the jail to hiding at home. His mom, Jordan and me, Sheriff Wood and Judge Guthrie, plus the doc are worried that if he doesn't go out into the real world...'

'That poor kid,' said Barb. 'He's gotta take that first step.'

'We came up with a plan—

'—and maybe it'll include you, too, Lucas. You're on Team Hal.

'Tonight his mom, Jordan, me – we're taking Hal out to the fair. Never let him be alone. Let him feel that—'

Gary said: 'That he's one of us and we give a shit about him.'

'Walk him 'round the midway,' said Barb. 'Let folks see him. Let him see them. Let people come up and say hi, show him they don't...'

'What can we do to help?' said Gary.

Neal said: 'Get busy telling folks about the plan. How Doc, Judge Guthrie, and Sheriff Wood are all backing it. We got a few hours. Spread the word through town. People gotta know what they're seeing to appreciate it right.'

'I'll work the phone,' said Barb. 'Gary'll be on Main Street, stepping outside if he ain't tending bar and telling folks there.'

'That'll be great,' said Neal. 'Thanks.'

Lucas strained to hold the squiggly infant girl in his arms.

Rachel grabbed toward Jordan and got swept up in that woman's care.

'Lucas,' said Neal, 'I'm going to call your folks and a couple of your aunts about the plan. If anybody can get the word out, it's the Conner sisters.

'And if it's OK with you, I'm gonna ask your folks to have you help us out with the fair tonight. You're good with both Rachel and Hal. We'll pick you up.'

He smiled. 'Safety in numbers.'

Jordan Smith told Lucas: 'You don't have to do this.'

'Are you kidding? *Sure!*'

'Don't worry,' said Neal. 'All we'll do is have a good time.'

CARNIVAL LIGHTS

The car door *whunked* closed.

'Everybody ready?' said Neal Dylan from the driver's seat.

Jordan Smith rode shotgun. She wore her sunglasses. Rachel rode in her lap, her baby arms flapping in the warm breeze through the car's open windows.

Lucas got the backdoor seat behind them.

Hal filled the middle of the backseat beside Lucas while his mother Pauline rode beside the other back door into or out of the green car.

Lucas frowned. *The littlest kid is supposed to sit in the middle where there's no door to lean on. Why did they put Hal there instead of me?*

The setting sun reddened Neal's mirror as he drove the blacktop highway toward gray grain elevators rising like prairie skyscrapers by the train tracks. A mile out of town, the car nosed off the highway to a dirt road leading past livestock pens jammed with mooing cattle. A man with a flashlight waved them to a spot in a field of parked cars.

Neal led the way from the parking lot. Carried baby Rachel in his arms.

Hal shuffled behind the sixth grade teacher.

Hal's mom Pauline walked beside her son's heart.

Sunglassed Jordan rear-guarded Hal.

And I'm Hal's right-hand man, realized Lucas as he walked that way.

The fairgrounds spread out before them.

To their left rose the white wooden wall of the grandstands. With Superman's X-ray vision, Lucas could have seen through that wall to displays of garden roses, huckleberry pies, and homemade bread, home-sewn clothes, arts and crafts competing for a blue ribbon. The grandstand cradled fumes of beer and sloped tiers of wooden benches for daytime rodeos and horse races, for the night show with bands and stage dancers from as far back east as St Paul.

To Lucas's right, low barns held calves, pigs, horses, sheep, and barnyard fowl in stalls pungent with straw and manure. Beyond the livestock barns was Machinery Row, ranks of new grain trucks, red combines, and the latest tractors.

Lucas ached to run straight ahead toward razzle-dazzle game stalls run by chanting carnies: '*Easy money! Everybody a winner! Hey-ya, hey-ya, hey-ya!*'

Straight ahead to where shacks for the town's clubs sold burgers, barbecue.

Straight ahead to the rides.

To the merry-go-round of steeds for cautious riders.

To the Ferris wheel that lifted your rocking box seat so high you could see all the way back to the lights of town.

To the Tilt-A-Whirl that spun you in the palm of a giant hand.

Every year at the fair meant a new special ride.

This summer, when he was ten, the jewel of the midway was the Hammer.

High school graduation summer in 1967 meant the Tunnel Of Love.

The summer of 1970 when he was twenty-one, *the* ride was the Wall Of Death.

'Lucas!' cried a girl's voice.

Bobbi Jean waved as she ran toward the Science & Industry building. 'I gotta see if my flowers won a ribbon! See you later!'

Neal joked: 'Let's go see a horse about a man.'

'*Oh*.' Lucas shrugged. 'Sure.'

He knew then that they would not be seeing just one horse swishing its tail. They'd be seeing them all. Plus sheep and pigs and a lot of mooing cows in wooden stalls filled with pungent hay. Every sight ticking away valuable seconds.

The fifth stall in the first barn caged a black stallion.

Lucas wondered if the midnight animal had been cut from stud to gelding.

Fixed, he told himself. *Gramma'd say "fixed."*

Neal kept staring at the black stallion pacing the straw-filled pen.

Jordan Smith said: 'He's beautiful. But he's not ours.'

They left that barn for the sinking sun.

Jordan said: 'What do you say we go see the sheep?'

But the little girl in her arms wouldn't have any of *that* nonsense. She bounced and jiggled, whined and waved her tiny white hands toward the glow of the oil-packed earth's midway.

'We just got outvoted,' said Neal.

The five of them reached the midway as the carousel near them slowed and stopped to let kids younger than Lucas scurry off.

Neal sat Lucas and Rachel on a merry-go-round bench facing forward with the wooden horses and stepped off their ride.

Calliope music turned louder. The bench pushed Rachel and Lucas forward. The horses on shiny metal poles rode up and down. Circled forward around and around, going somewhere and nowhere at the same time.

Rachel squealed, bounced, and watched them go.

Lucas kept his loose but protective arm around her.

The circling horses ahead of him rode up and down and past where Hal and his mother stood talking with two smiling adults.

The horses ahead of him rode up and down past where Neal Dylan and Jordan Smith stood shoulder to shoulder, their not-touching hands side by side.

Calliope music played and the horses rode up and down and around and around until the music… slowed. The merry-go-round eased into a full stop.

Neal took his daughter from Lucas and they stepped off the merry-go-round. Hal and his mother joined them. So did Jordan.

Hal cleared his throat. 'Would it be OK if Lucas went off on his own? Most kids get one shot at coming out to the fair. You can't waste your one shot.'

Neal made a show of frowning. Told Lucas:

'Stick to the midway. Don't do anything your folks wouldn't want you to. You've got a watch. Nine thirty sharp, meet us outside the grandstands.'

Lucas's sneakers ached to fly, but he pressed them into the oil-packed earth until Hal looked at him so the teenager couldn't miss Lucas saying:

'Thanks!'

'Forget about it. Nobody wants to hang around with a kid. Now get.'

Lucas ran.

Which way to go? Kids everywhere. Moms and dads and Main Street guys. Farmers. High schoolers. Laura is coming out later with Claudia and—

A cable tripped his left sneaker into his right. He stumbled. Flapped like a goose. Stopped smack in front of the startled faces of JaneKayBonnie.

With Anna.

'Oh my God!' said Jane, who like all the other girls wore phone-call-decided shorts, a dark top, and bleached sneakers. 'Like, what's wrong with you?'

'You should see your face!' said Bonnie. 'It's redder than a fire hydrant!'

The girl trio laughed. Anna laughed. Calliope music played.

'What's the matter?' said Kay. 'Are you going to cry?'

'Momma's boy!' said Jane.

'Four eyes!' said Bonnie.

Anna said nothing.

Kay led a chant: '*Four-eyes – Loo-cas! Four-eyes – Loo-cas!*'

And Anna… joined *in* but *not*.

Or so she told herself, a decision written on her face that only the boy in glasses standing on a carnival midway could see.

Four girls glided away into the carnival. JaneKayBonnie with seventh grade sashay, a year younger Anna with her blonde hair and desperate eyes.

Colored bulbs and yellow spotlights outlined him in that hard night.

Tap on his left shoulder!

'*Hah!*' said Marin. '*Gotchya!* How come you're just standing here?'

'Um… Nothing else to do.'

'Are you *crazy*? Wait a minute,' said his buddy. 'Are you broke?' Marin pulled coins out of his jeans. 'I got two dollars fourteen cents. Plus three ride tickets! Mom's working the Elks booth. With what I got, we can do lots.'

'I got money, but…'

'But what?'

'I just kind of feel like a doofus.'

Marin frowned. Thought about it. Waved his arms and shouted:

'*Of course we're doofuses!* We're at the fair! Everybody here's a doofus. That's what makes it *fair!*'

Lucas burst out laughing.

'We got money,' said Marin. 'We got time. What are we waiting for?'

They ran.

Dodged a high school couple sneaking a kiss in the crowd.

At the shooting gallery, plopped down twenty cents each for two air rifles to crack off BBs that won them nothing.

On the roller coaster, they snagged the first car. Hollered the whole ride.

Their bumper boat war became a global legend. They bounced off each other. Allied to swamp an eighth grader. Fled before he could get his buddies.

They scored a Tilt-A-Whirl tub all to themselves. Spun round and round, centrifugal force pushing their skulls into the cupping wall. The lights of the carnival against the night's blackness became wavy lines of purple, blue, and red.

They ran down the Tilt-A-Whirl's ramp as Marin said: 'What's next?'

The Hammer rose from the far end of the midway. A forty-foot steel spoke with each end fastened to a football-shaped car for passengers. A fat man on a stool pushed a control lever. The spoke arced up into the sky. The fat man stopped the spoke pointed straight up so the second car waited at the loading platform. Six teenagers laughed to show how cool they were while a carnie belted and locked them into that steel can. The carnie gave the fat man a thumbs-up.

Lights in the two cars snapped off. Screams hammered inside those metal cans. A motor whined to a roar. The spoke windmilled as the cars on each end spun horizontal circles around their own axes. Pulsing light bulbs made the Hammer a spinning circle of light mirrored in the lenses covering Lucas's eyes.

He hid his fear with the truth:

'If I go on that and lose my glasses, I'll get in big trouble.'

Marin said: 'If I go on that, I'll barf my guts out.'

He frowned. 'What's that?'

On the border between the midway and the night stood cottage-sized tents tied to a wooden stage, and above it all hung a banner:

THE BEAST & THE BEAUTY!

Adults crowded near the tent as a man in a black vest over a white shirt, a straw hat, and a pencil mustache climbed onto the stage.

'Here we go!' cried the mustached man. 'Gather 'round! Tonight, right here in Vernon, Montana – or as your local police have informed me, right *outside* and *beyond* the city limits…'

Knowing chuckles in the crowd pulled Lucas and Marin closer.

'You have the opportunity of a lifetime! For your entertainment *and* education, we will show you a freak beyond nature and science. Tonight, you can personally see the legendary half-man, half-beast known as… The Geek!

'But wait!' The mustached barker thrust his palm toward the crowd. 'If the Geek were all we had to show you, then this would be a bargain for fifty cents.'

The barker wagged his finger. 'But this is the Beast *and* the Beauty.

'I know what you're thinking. You've got fine-looking women here, so why pay small change to see Fatima, the most exotic beauty to ever flee a harem?'

The barker winked. 'It ain't what you got, it's what you can *do* with it.'

Chuckles floated through the crowd.

'I'm not the kind to sell a pig in a poke. So to give you a taste of what she will reveal tonight when inside this very tent, she performs the sacred Dance of the Seven Veils, without further ado… *Fatima!*'

Invisible metal jangled.

A tambourine in a woman's red-nailed hand thrust through the curtains.

Onto the stage whirled Fatima, wrapped head to foot in colored cloths. Her ringed hands snaked poses. Below the turban hiding her hair and above her veil, Fatima showed her dark eyes. Out from her dress flicked one *way* naked leg.

Then she whirled behind the curtain. Gone.

'Ladies and gentlemen,' said the barker, 'for fifty cents, you get them both: the horrifying Geek plus the incomparable Fatima. Beast and Beauty. She is something every bachelor needs to see and every husband wants *his wife* to see.'

The crowd chuckled.

'Only ladies and gentlemen will be admitted. And despite the educational value, no kids. That includes you two sawed-off guys at the back of the crowd.'

Lucas felt his face catch on fire. Knew Marin burned, too.

'Yeah, I see you. Come around when you grow up. But now… One… Two… Three… *Run!*'

Lucas took off like a lightning bolt. Marin raced past him between two games of chance stalls to the surrounding prairie darkness.

'Wait!' said Lucas. 'We don't have to run just because somebody told us to!'

'Thought you're the do-what-you're-told guy,' said Marin.

'I'm more than one kind of guy. *And I'm not a momma's boy!*'

'Never said you were.'

Dusty prairie sod crunched under their sneakers as they walked in the shimmering shadowed borderland between the midway and the warm night.

'Man,' said Marin, 'I'd love to see that Geek.'

'We won't get another chance, and something like that… It's not fair.'

'Nope,' said Marin. 'It's *the fair.*'

Lucas heard an engine humming. Marin spotted the vibrating metal box parked on the prairie. 'It's the generator transformer booster thingamajig.'

A dozen black cables snaked from the thingamajig.

'Look!' whispered Marin. 'That one goes into the Geek's show tent.'

The tent with its stage facing the midway was wide. A smaller tent jutted out from the main tent. A flap hung where the tents met.

'The padlock on that flap!' hissed Lucas. 'It's just hanging there!'

The glowing hands on Lucas's watch showed 8:11. *Plenty of time.*

He lifted the padlock from its canvas loop. Ducked past the flap. Marin crowded behind him. Lucas wiggled his hand back outside to hook the unlatched padlock through its loops so no one would miss it and then they were *in*.

The hiding boys peered over a pile of wooden crates at the gathered crowd.

Those people who paid fifty cents entered and found a chain-link fence as tall as a man's heart curving out toward them to make a C-shaped pen closed against the wall of a wooden stage. No chairs.

The barker glided through the shuffling crowd. Stepped into the pen. Made a great fuss of padlocking the pen's gate shut.

Walked to the prairie sod center of the pen. Faced his customers.

'Step right up to the fence, though management accepts no responsibility for any excitements you receive from standing too close.'

The barker reached toward a black box of electric switches.

'As you know, Geeks are sensitive to bright light.'

The lights dimmed in the pen. Brightened on the faces of the gawkers.

Lucas saw men squint. A woman held up her hand to shade her eyes.

Whoosh!

The flapped rear wall of the tent exploded and a human figure landed in a crouch to snarl at the illuminated faces beyond the chain-link fence.

The Geek had wild black hair. Unshaven puffed-out cheeks, and a jawbone too big for his face. Bare feet. Torn army surplus pants.

Lucas recognized what else the Geek wore: a buckles-up-the-back, arms-tied-across-the-chest straitjacket designed for insane killers who creep through the night to jerk open the car doors of teenage couples parked on the lonely prairie for kissing and grab them out to meet his hungry knife.

The barker pulled the Geek to his feet. Unbuckled the straitjacket.

The Geek roared free, a bare-chested fiend who used his long arms as a second pair of legs to scurry back and forth in the pen. He ripped dirt from the earth. Tossed it in the air and ran under its rain. He did a somersault that left him sprawled on his back. He snarled. Drooled. Rolled his eyes.

'Is that all there is?' hissed Lucas. 'Just a really ugly guy acting weird?'

'What a gyp,' whispered Marin.

The looks on the faces of the paying customers agreed.

Then the barker brought out the chicken.

The white-feathered bird flapped its wings and pawed the air with talon feet. The barker held the bird out to the crowd. The chicken clucked. Spotted the Geek. And went berserk.

The barker tossed the chicken into the air.

The chicken crashed to the ground. Scurried squawking and flapping along the earth floor of the tent's chain-link pen.

The Geek scrambled on his hands and bare feet like a chimpanzee. The chicken ran. Round and round they went while the crowd cheered and the chicken squawked. The Geek roared. *Finally* he had to stand erect like a man, use a hip fake to cut off the chicken's flight, trap him against the chain-link fence.

Out snapped those Geek paws. Caught the chicken.

The chicken twisted in the Geek's grasp. Barnyard talons slashed. Scarlet lines striped the naked flesh over the Geek's heart.

The Geek's scream sounded positively human. Muscles corded his arms as he shook the bird. The chicken lolled, dazed as the Geek wrapped one hand around the bird's neck and with the other guided the chicken's head…

… into his mouth. The Geek bit down, his lips closing around feathers. The chicken flapped its wings. The crowd gasped.

Bright red glop squirted from the Geek's mouth. Drooled

down his chest. Splattered the white feathers of the trapped bird. He threw his prey away.

The chicken hit the ground running.

And headless.

A wet crimson stump rose at its neck. The white-feathered, crimson-stained, wing-flapping chicken bounced madly around the chain-link-fenced pen.

Running around like a chicken with its head cut off! thought Lucas.

'*Ummmn!*' The Geek slumped to the floor of earth. Chewed the cut-off chicken head in his mouth. Swallowed. Burped.

The barker grabbed the flopping headless bird.

Scurried out the back to dispose of the corpse.

The Geek sat cross-legged. A red smear covered his lips like a calendar beauty's crimson kiss gone horribly wrong. The Geek lifted a white feather in pinched fingers. Pursed his gory lips, blew a soft breeze.

The feather sailed all alone in the caged night air.

Snap!

The sound of a padlock closing behind Lucas and Marin.

Lucas reached through the tent flap. Found the padlock locked. By a carnie with sharp eyes. By the trickster Old Coyote Marin's grandmother warned him about. Didn't matter. The padlock trapped them inside the tent.

'Submit, Geek!' yelled the barker inside the pen.

Lucas and Marin whirled from the locked exit to see the Geek march toward the mustached barker. The Geek walked stiff-legged with his arms straight out like a movie Frankenstein monster.

The barker pulled a black cylinder from his pocket. Aimed it at the Geek.

The flashlight beam hit the Geek in the eyes. He threw his hands up to block the dreaded glow. The barker advanced with the straitjacket.

'Dress, Geek!' yelled the barker. 'Dress!'

The barker half-forced, half-helped the mesmerized creature into the straitjacket. Whirled the Geek to face the audience.

'Let's hear a round of applause for my amazing Geek!'

The crowd clapped.

The barker pushed the Geek behind the curtain. 'Go where you belong!'

Flipped switches to leave the crowd in shadows and light the stage.

Murmurs and the snaps of matches. Cigarette smoke filled the tent.

'What are we going to do?' hissed Marin.

'We got to get out of here!' said Lucas. 'The show can't last for—'

The barker yelled: 'Ladies and gentlemen! *Apres le* Beast... *La* Beauty!'

A phonograph needle crackled a record. Eerie flute and tambourine music wafted through the tent, the kind of music Lucas knew from the Roxy's movies about Bombay street wizards charming swaying cobras.

Onto the stage whirled the gossamer-wrapped Fatima.

She spun across the stage. Whipped the turban off her head. Curly black hair flowed free to her shoulders. She bowed to the audience. A tremor moved up her spine to her shoulders, her neck. Her black hair flicked from side to side. She snapped straight up, hair whipping back over her head as she tore off her veil.

Her face was a pink moon with a slash of red lipstick, purple-rimmed eyes.

'That's two veils out of seven!' hissed Marin.

We can escape later, thought Lucas.

Fatima swayed with the eerie music. Spun out of the full body veil. She wore a purple top and a black skirt. An ankle bracelet with golden bells tinkled as stomping bare feet carried her down the stage's three steps to the chain-link fence. Her red-tipped fingers brushed those metal links as she danced past faces pressed so close they could smell her perfume.

Back on the stage, she whirled. The purple shirt flew from her hand to the waiting barker. She wore a bulging halter top covered in gold glitter.

Fatima stretched her palms to the eyes watching her from beyond the chain-link fence. Her thumbs snaked into the waistband of the black skirt. Her blood-tipped fingers caressed swaying loins.

'*Hah!*' cried Fatima as she ripped off her black outer skirt.

There on the stage she swayed, a wispy veil skirt covering her down to her thick knees. She wore a belt of jangling gold circles under a roll of pale flesh.

Fatima shimmered. Bare flesh trembled on her arms. Her golden belt jingled. She danced to center stage, whirled so her back was to the audience.

Froze. Locked there. Hands splayed out below her hips as if to ward off evil rising from the depths of Hell. The music played on. And on. And on. And on.

The scurrying barker jerked the needle arm off the spinning black phonograph record. Flipped a switch. The spinning colored lights snapped off.

None of the customers could see Fatima's face.

Hiding in the dark corner, Marin and Lucas watched her yawn.

'Ladies and gentlemen,' said the barker, 'as you know, the Dance of the Seven Veils for sacred and legal reasons is rarely performed beyond five veils. We'd like to thank you, and—'

'*Nebbish!*' cried Fatima in a foreign language no one in that Montana small town crowd knew. '*Gib zich a traisel!*'

Silence grabbed the audience.

'One moment please!' cried the barker. 'Though she speaks American, Fatima now commands me to speak in her own ancient desert infidel tongue.'

The barker turned to Fatima: '*Makooba buluka seemota koy?*'

Fatima kept her back to the crowd as she replied: '*Gai kakhen afenyam.*'

The barker shook his head. Thrust his denying hand toward the woman who wasn't looking at him. '*Keenawhacka mos o dodo lakameeta*, and I mean *no*.'

'*Oi, vai. Gai zich a traisel. Gai tren zich, mamzer schmuck.*'

The barker shook his head. Faced the crowd:

'Ladies and gentlemen, despite my warning, moved by your warmth, Fatima wants to invoke the Holy Dispensation of the Last Two Veils, which allows her, under certain special circumstances, to go beyond the rules. As promised, you've seen the dance within the sacred tradition. But to go beyond that, Fatima needs the honest encouragement of a freewill offering.'

The barker held out his straw hat as he walked along the chain-link fence. Lucas saw someone toss a silver dollar. Heard someone else do the same. A woman pitched in a handful of pennies, proclaiming: '*I know what it's like to work for that!*' She got a few laughs. The barker stepped away from the fence.

'Your fans have been kind, Fatima.'

'*A shaynem dank di rim putznik.*'

'Your wish is my command.'

The barker flipped switches. Colored lights spun. He changed the phonograph record. Lowered the needle.

This pounding drums and blaring saxophone record sounded more like *waa-waa* jazz than mysterious Arab music to Lucas, but what did he know.

Fatima threw off the gossamer skirt. Her bare legs trembled. A gold thong barely covered the crack of her bumping butt. She shuffled in a jiggling circle.

Shook her butt at the crowd. Fingered the knot tied on her gilded halter under the black hair draping her neck.

Suddenly her back was bare.

A great inhale from the crowd sliced through the music. Fatima flung her halter top to the barker. No eyes left her naked back as she danced.

She whirled around and everybody saw them:

Tear-shaped breasts that were *totally naked*—

—except for gold tassels covering those magical mysterious tips.

The tassels swung from side to side as Fatima danced.

Drums beat. The saxophone blared.

Blackout darkness filled the tent.

Offstage near them, Lucas and Marin heard the clump of a tent wall colliding with flesh. A woman whispered: 'Shit!'

The music died. Lights snapped on. In the glow of the pen stood the barker.

'Thank you, ladies and gentlemen! Next show is in an hour! Come back!'

The barker guarded the ring and the exit as the crowd shuffled outside.

'What are we going to do?' whispered Lucas.

Marin grabbed the tent wall near where the Geek had gone. Forced a gap big enough to crawl through. Lucas wriggled after him…

… to crouch behind a backstage tent's giant wardrobe trunk standing open on its end. The top hinge holding the lid to the chest was broken. Lucas pressed against Marin as they stared through that crack.

Fatima sat in front of a mirror braced on a folding table. Her back was bare. Dangling below the arms that were powdering her face, Lucas saw gold tassels.

On a stool near her sat the bare-chested Geek – but now he wore a straw-colored wig that made him look like just some ugly guy.

A wire cage filled with a shifting whiteness waited on a wardrobe chest.

The barker walked into view.

The Geek said: 'We gotta get a new chicken.'

'He's spry enough to keep you chasing him around,' said the barker.

'That's the problem. He knows what's coming, so he runs like hell. He fought like a banshee. I barely got the condom sneaked over his head with him in my mouth. Near made me swallow the goop capsule before I could pop it.'

The Geek pointed to his scratched chest: 'Look at the blood he drew.'

'You got trouble choking the chicken, ask our Yid princess here for pointers,' said the barker. 'She was famous for that back in Jersey.'

Fatima powdered her nose. 'Least I had a rep. So fuck off.'

'Yeah, well, lucky me, not anymore, right *Fat*-ima?'

'My dumb days are done.'

'Huh,' said the barker. 'I talked to the guy you got to talk to around here. He ain't got no never mind to any side action you get, long as he gets a taste.'

'Of the action or the cash?' she said.

'He ain't one you mess with. He takes cash. Not that there'll be any. I got no notes or *let-me-talk-to-you*s after the show. The damn John Laws let 'em open a full-time house here, and they just had a stripper working Main Street.'

'I should have gone that route.' Fatima stared into the mirror. 'I could have been a star on the Block in Baltimore.'

The barker pinched the roll of flesh hanging over Fatima's gold belt. 'You'd never be no star with a donut like this.'

She slapped his hand away. Never took her eyes out of the mirror.

'Leave her be!' hissed the Geek.

'Or what?' The barker jerked his black vest flat over his white shirt. 'You'll find somebody else who'll let you be their freak?'

Fatima leered at the barker's reflection in her mirror as she said: 'Why don't you pick on a real man? Oh, that's right, *I forgot*: it takes one to know one.'

The Geek trembled on his stool.

Fatima stared into the mirror. 'Why is every town so rube?'

'Rube is as rube does,' said the Geek. 'Besides, you don't want that.'

'You're always smarter than you look,' she told him.

'Yeah,' said the barker. 'And so unselfish.'

Fatima turned on her chair so she faced the broken wardrobe and the boys hidden behind it as she plucked the gold tassel off her right breast.

'Remember,' she said, pulling the gold tassel off her left breast. 'Get some eyelash stickum at the drugstore or the rubes will get a real show for free.'

Oh. My. God. Lucas trembled. *There. They. Are.* Truth dotting the middle of each of her bare-naked teardrop breasts. Two tiny pink eyes. His mouth went dry. His heart stopped. The luminous hands on his watch froze.

Fatima sighed. 'How come my show never gets any nice guys?'

'You don't want a nice guy,' muttered the Geek.

The chicken in the cage clucked.

Fatima grabbed a robe. 'I'm going to the trailer!' At the flap, she turned to the two men. 'Are you going to make me walk there alone for the rubes to grab a free one?'

The Geek hurried after her as Fatima stepped out into the night.

'Hey!' said the barker, following them. 'No running off! We got shows.'

Then the three of them were gone.

The caged chicken clucked.

Marin raced to the wall opposite the flap used by the carnies. 'Come on!'

They scrambled under the tent…

… into the safety of the night air's neon glow.

Steel jaws caught Lucas by the back of his neck.

He saw Marin trapped in the grip of the man's other hand.

'Look what we got here!' growled a nasty voice Lucas recognized.

The two boys whipped from side to side. Their captor held them out to a line of four men – town guys Lucas had seen near the rough bars. The eyes of the four men glowed like the red sockets of junkyard dogs.

Their captor tossed them toward the snickering men, who backed farther onto the prairie, deeper into the darkness, farther from the midway's lights.

Lucas and Marin whirled to face their captor:

Harley Anderson, his fedora jammed above nasty eyes.

'Well, I'll be damned.' Harley chuckled. 'Piano boy. What were you doing in there? Looking for your crazy-ass buddy Garth?'

'N-n-no, sir!'

'What we got here is a situation,' said Harley to the junkyard dogs. 'Caught us some sneak thieves. Lawbreakers.'

Junkyard dogs laughed. 'We got 'em, Harley! Let's string 'em up!'

'Hear that?' Harley stepped closer. 'We could throw you to the carnies. They'd nail your nuts to the wall. We could haul you to the sheriff, but he's got to wrangle outsiders. Shouldn't have to worry about locking up your shit.'

Junkyard dogs howled and laughed.

'And I bet you don't want us to drag your parents out here. Make them see their brats sneaking into hoochie-coochie shows.

'No,' said Harley, 'it's up to us to take care of this mess you made. That's what this country is about. A man taking care of what a man's got to do. Like the boys in Mississippi with the niggers. You two got to take it. You know you do. For your own good. Ain't something we *want* to do. But tell you what: it's fair we give you a choice for your smart-ass butts. You want belts or the flat of—'

Like a cold whisper blew through the night.

They all felt the chill and froze.

Lucas blinked at the dark shape in the tent's indigo glow.

Just a man. Shadowed hands by his sides. Moonlight glistening on his slick black hair. Standing there as a carnival-lit silhouette. Watching.

Marin edged closer to Lucas.

Four junkyard dogs shrank into their skins.

Harley turned and saw *who* was behind him. Sank into his leaden shoes.

The night breeze carried carnival smells of machine oil. Cotton candy. Caramel apples. Popcorn. Just a running scream away spun the Hammer. Children laughed. Teenagers kissed at the top of the Ferris wheel.

But here in the indigo shadows, *he* ruled. He skimmed the earth to the huddle of boys and men and they all heard him say: '*Kid*.'

Lucas swallowed. 'Hi, Uncle Johnny.'

Oh, he was a handsome man! All Aunt Beryl's sisters admitted that. "*Handsome as the devil,*" Gramma Conner always said. As the devil.

Johnny Russo's *noir* eyes nailed Harley. 'You put hands on my nephew.'

'Hey, now look—'

'Don't "*hey*" me. You think I'm a horse? You think I deal in horseshit?' Uncle Johnny kept his eyes on Harley but sent his words to the four junkyard dogs who were easing away. 'Where you guys going? Stick around.'

Harley sputtered: 'Nothing happened here 'ceptin' your – forgot him and you – Him and his breed buddy was tent sneaking! That's flat-out wrong. I mean, *dangerous*. For him! So we got a 'sponsibility to – And nobody hurt nobody!'

'Yet.'

'Them boys are lucky was guys like us who come around!'

'Ain't the kids who's lucky, Harley. It's you.'

'M-m-me?'

'You're the crapped-out SOB standing here who put hands on my nephew. But hey: nobody hurt nobody. Is that right, Lucas? You or your buddy get hurt?'

'We're OK, Uncle Johnny.'

'Well then, Harley, it damn straight is your lucky day. You know why?'

Harley shook his head.

'Nobody got hurt. Not tonight. Not *ever.* Me. My nephew and kin. This other kid and his momma. No flat tires. No car trouble. No coots going loco. No rat phone calls or letter to no bosses or John Laws. Not even a lightning bolt. Nobody gets hurt 'cause Harley's gonna keep them safe. If hurting happens, I know who screwed up. You figured out yet how that makes this your lucky day, Harley?'

Again Harley shook his head.

'Because now you know *what's what.*'

Johnny Russo wrapped a smile that would charm a church choir around Harley and the junkyard dogs.

'Go beer up at the Elks booth. They're running it for the orphans' fund. You can do some good instead of jerking off here in the dark.'

The five men flew away like bullets shot from a gun.

'Thanks, Uncle Johnny!'

He shook his head. 'Don't go risking it for some cheap carnie show.'

'Yes, sir!' chorused Lucas and Marin.

'I figure telling your folks is your call, but my advice?' The handsome man shrugged his shoulders. 'No hurt, no need to say nothing.'

'No, sir!' said the boys.

'You need a ride, Lucas? Your buddy, too? I got the taxi.'

'We're fine, Uncle Johnny.'

'Really.'

He melted into the night.

Lucas checked his watch. 'We got eleven minutes! If—'

Marin grabbed his friend's arm. 'Lucas! *Your new glasses!* They're gone!'

Lucas's hands felt his bare face. 'That's why backstage looked fuzzy!'

'You must have dropped them in the tent!'

Crackling electricity and delighted screams cut through the night.

'What are we going to do?' said Marin.

'You go on, your mom—'

Marin stood tall. 'What are *WE* gonna do?'

This time they snuck through the front flap.

Inside the empty show tent, Lucas fished his only dollar bill from his jeans and wedged it in the chain-link fence. He nodded to Marin. 'We aren't thieves.'

They scanned the ground by the walls of the tent—

'You looking for these?'

Out of the shadows came the Geek, bare-chested and without his wig.

He held up Lucas's glasses.

Lucas swallowed. 'Please, Mr Geek—'

'Please?' The Geek took a step toward Lucas.

Lucas took a step to the side. Just like the chicken.

'You think *please* is a magic word? That it makes what you want happen? Just because you mean it? You still that dumb, rube?'

'I'm not dumb!'

'You're trapped in here with "*Mister*" Geek. And he's got these of yours.' The Geek wiggled the glasses in the air. 'How "not dumb" is that?'

'I just want to get them and—'

'Go? Escape? What makes you think there's an escape?'

Marin yelled: 'Leave him alone! I'll—'

'You'll what? If you run, it'll be over before you can get back here with some hero.' The Geek let a smile curve his long jaw. He stepped closer to Lucas.

'You snuck in here. Watched the show. Got in at the flap by the stage wall where I found these. Being where you ain't supposed to be and getting what you ain't supposed to have. For free. Nobody gets nothing for free.'

'We didn't steal!' cried Lucas. 'We paid. Look over there, stuck in the fence! See? That's our dollar. Fifty cents apiece. We paid!'

The Geek saw the bill crammed in the chain-link fence.

'Well, I'll be damned.' The Geek smiled. 'Oh yeah, that's right: *I already am.*'

Marin yelled: 'If you nail his nuts to the wall, I'll get you no matter what!'

'*Nail his nuts to the wall*?' The Geek shrugged. 'Hadn't thought of that.'

The Geek feinted a lunge that made Lucas jump back.

'*Bwack bwack bwack bwack!*' clucked the Geek.

Lucas blurted: 'The chicken is alive! You're not a real Geek!'

'Is that right?' said the creature. 'Is that the truth?'

Lucas held his ground.

The Geek stalked to him. Crouched down so they were eye level.

'Truth is,' said the man-thing, 'I was born looking like a hay wagon ran over my face. Truth is, this pen is where I am. So if that doesn't make me a real Geek, then what does, huh? What's the truth?'

The man-thing unfolded Lucas's glasses. Slid them onto Lucas's face, over his ears, pushed them snug against his nose.

'You see what I mean?'

The Geek reached to the three crimson scratches on his naked chest. Rubbed his finger in the blood. Smeared red goo on Lucas's forehead.

'Now you're a Geek, too.'

He jerked his head toward the tent's front flap.

The two boys raced out to the carnival night. Blasted past the Tilt-A-Whirl. Lucas spit-rubbed his forehead clean.

Marked the time as 9:32, Friday night, July 10, 1959.

'I'll help you tell them why you're late!' yelled Marin.

'No! Your mom! Go! This is mine!'

Marin cut left toward the food booths. 'See you!'

A great screaming tore across the night sky as Lucas raced to the grandstands.

There stood Miss Smith, holding Rachel in her sheltering arms.

Mr Dylan shuffled in front of Hal and his clinging mother as Sheriff Wood pushed his hand toward Mrs Klise, who was grabbing at the teenage boy.

Fireworks ripped into the air. Burst blues and reds and magnesium-burning shimmers above the fairgrounds. Lucas knew his mom would be watching the fireworks from their front porch. Knew him being late didn't matter anymore.

'It's OK, Ruth!' the sheriff yelled to Mrs Klise as she tried to dart around the sheriff to get to Hal and his mother.

'No it's not! It's never gonna be OK! Look at him!'

Hal's face twisted in horror as his dead friend's mother stabbed her finger at him.

'That's not OK!' yelled Ruth Klise.

Two red flares streaked across the black sky. Burnt gunpowder rained.

Sheriff Wood said: 'He's done his jail time. He's on probation. He's in the teachers' supervision. It's all legal!'

'Legal?' screamed Ruth Klise. 'My boy is dead an' he gets to go to the fair?'

Pheww! went a purple skyrocket that made Lucas think, *Wow.*

Ruth Klise shook her fist at the two teachers. At Pauline, who was a mother, too, and had once been a friend. At the still-alive teenage boy Hal.

'No! Not fair! Not right! *Legal*, I'll show you *legal*! I'll get you!' she yelled. 'I'll get him if it takes forever! He won't get away with this! The hell with all of you. I'm gonna make it be justice!'

A giant booming crimson starburst lit the night sky above them all like a rosy dawn that glowed – sparkled – winked out into the black void.

RADIO DAZE

'So, kid,' said the woman in the pink bathrobe to Lucas that next Monday morning as they sat at her kitchen table, 'how's your summer been?'

She lit her cigarette.

'Kind of different, Mrs Dylan.'

'You call my husband *Neal*, so call me *Rita*.'

She plowed fingers through her mussed hair. Scanned the kitchen. The white stove. The humming refrigerator. The sink with dirty dishes.

'Different. Huh. Looks pretty damn much the same to me.'

The cigarette waved in the air.

'But what do I know? I'm not the smart one.'

Lucas sniffed. 'Is coffee supposed to smell like that?'

'Shit!' Rita lunged to the stove. Twisted a white knob. Killed the ring of blue flame beneath a rumbling coffeepot. 'God-damn it! Now it's boiled to…'

She flicked her eyes to the boy at the kitchen table.

Brushed the hair off her face. Swept her scowl into a sweet smile.

'Oh well, coffee is coffee. You want some?'

'I'm not old enough.'

'Who is?' Her smile was a grin Lucas believed. 'Any sugar in that bowl?'

Lucas lifted the lid off the table's brown bowl. 'Not much.'

'Behind you on that shelf,' she said as she got a green mug off a hook. 'Can you reach the sugar bin? Fill the bowl?'

With his back to her, Lucas fetched that metal cylinder of white crystals.

Turned back to the table.

Across the kitchen, Rita pushed a brown paper sack into a cupboard's shadows. Turned to face Lucas. Held her green mug steady. Walked to the stove and poured coffee into the mug.

Lucas filled the sugar bowl. Returned the bin to its place.

While he did, she eased back down into the chair at the table, saying: 'Thanks. Sit down. She's doing fine in there.'

Baby Rachel sat on the living room floor stacking wooden alphabet cubes. She'd been in there, *doing fine*, since Neal had left for his painting job and Rita had shuffled out of the bedroom to find Lucas watching the toddler.

Rita'd kissed her, ambled to the kitchen, told Lucas: 'Come talk to me.'

Now she spooned sugar into her green mug. Stirred the mix. Took a sip.

'Nothing like that first cup of coffee,' she told Lucas. Rita sipped from the cup. 'I'm not a bad sort, no matter what you've heard.'

'I haven't heard anything.'

'Maybe your family never says nothing in front of the kids. My mom never shut up. Never stopped letting you know who you were and *damn sure* who you weren't. She's still the queen of all that, let me tell you.'

'*Ah*, OK, but shouldn't I be taking Rachel to the park like Neal—'

'Forget about Neal. Talk to me. That's not too much to ask.'

'What should I talk about?'

'Anything but the damn weather: "*Hey, hot enough for you?*" And don't tell me what's in the newspaper or some book and then get all mopey when I don't give a shit, or what you learned in law school before you quit 'cause it was the right thing to do.'

'My dad wants me to go to law school.'

'Yeah? What do you say?'

Lucas shrugged. 'I just got out of fifth grade.'

'You know any lawyers? Want to be like them?'

Falk's ghost breezed through the kitchen, a glint of gold on its wrist.

Lucas shook his head *no*.

Rita said: 'Parents try to stick you in a picture of who they want you to—'

BAM! BAM! BAM!

Knocks on the front door.

Rita clutched the lapels of her robe. Jerked her head at Lucas. 'You get it!'

Lucas stepped past the toddler on the living room floor.

Rita whispered: 'If it's Mormon missionaries, couple o' young guys in black ties and white shirts, tell 'em nobody's home!'

Coincidentally, that was also the only lie allowed in Lucas's own house.

He swung open the front door.

'Oh!' said the woman standing on the stoop. 'I didn't know you were here.'

From the kitchen came: 'Who is it?'

'Mrs Klise,' answered Lucas. Thought: *Did you see me standing there at the fairgrounds when you were yelling?*

'Ruth Klise?' Rita edged into her living room. 'What are you doing here?'

'Why, I was just driving by. Thought I should stop in for a visit.'

Rita clutched her robe shut and fluffed her hair. 'Come in! I've been, *ah*, under the weather.'

Mrs Klise stepped into the younger woman's house.

'So I see,' she said. 'How are you feeling now?'

'Been worse. You know Lucas? He's kind of babysitting. For Rachel.'

'Yes, that's what he's doing,' said Mrs Klise. 'What a beautiful baby. You don't know how lucky you are.'

'You never know about luck, right? I never expected you to drop by, but – *Coffee!* We should sit around the kitchen table and have some fresh coffee!'

Rita rushed into the kitchen, the older woman trailing her.

'I'm sorry I look such a mess,' said Rita, 'but you know: the baby. Had to get up early and take care of her. Plus get Neal off to work.'

'He's painting the Mallettes' today,' said the woman who'd dropped by.

'Who can keep track of what he does.'

Rita grabbed the coffeepot off the stove. Filled the pot with fresh water. Found the spindle and basket in the sink. Fumbled them into the pot. Coffee grounds rained on the counter when she shook their red can. Rita put the pot on the stove's burner and turned the knob.

Nothing happened.

'Damn it!' Rita twisted the burner knob off. 'The pilot light went out again. Landlord is supposed to fix it, but all he gets around to is his rent check.

'Lucas!' she yelled.

He ran to the kitchen as Rita pushed up the stove's white top.

Rita told the boy: 'Hand me the matches.'

Mrs Klise said: 'Here, dear, let me—'

'No! I can do it. I mean: Lucas is doing just fine.'

Rita held the stove top up with her shoulder. Pushed in and turned the stove's big knob. Tore a match from the pack Lucas gave her. Lowered its flame toward the pencil-thick, chimney-like pipe centering the guts of the stove top.

Poof! A blue flame shot up from the pipe to meet the match.

Rita turned a burner knob – a ring of blue flame filled the burner. She struck a victory pose with her hands out from her sides.

'*Ta-dah!* Fresh coffee, coming up!'

'That's wonderful, dear. Let's sit down and chat.'

Ruth Klise settled into someone else's kitchen chair.

Gestured for Rita to sit across from her.

Rita obeyed her guest.

Who smiled. 'And I'm sure Lucas is fine to watch the baby.'

'Hell,' said Rita, 'sometimes he's better with her than – Lucas! Be sure Rachel's OK while Mrs Klise and I have some coffee. And… *chat.*'

As Lucas left the two women at the kitchen table, he heard Rita say: 'So, Ruth… Hot enough for you?'

Baby Rachel crawled over to Lucas. She grinned. Widened her blue eyes. Went: '*Ah gah ga!*' and held out a colored block.

Lucas leaned closer to take it…

Smelled what couldn't be denied.

He walked back to the kitchen just as Rita was telling her visitor: 'Sometimes getting up in the morning is about all the getting you can do.'

Coffee percolated in the pot on the stove, a rich, warm scent.

'*Um*,' said Lucas, 'Rachel… Her diaper…'

Rita glared at him. 'You know what to do.'

Mrs Klise frowned. 'Never mind, Lucas. You're just a boy, and this is a woman's thing. You go on, and, Rita, you just sit right—'

'Don't leave! Neal – we taught Lucas how.'

'Neal helps with the baby?'

'I do most of it.' Rita's eyes begged Lucas: 'Take care of her? Please?'

This house on Knob Hill was small. The scent of percolating coffee and the women's voices drifted from the kitchen as Lucas picked up the stinky child.

Ruth Klise's voice said: 'Such a nice place you have here.'

Rita's voice answered: 'Yeah, well, not quite like I imagined it would be way back when. Jesus, look at me: I already got a "way back when"!'

'*Ooo-cus!*' Rachel put her tiny hand on the big boy's cheek as he carried her upstairs. '*Ooo-cus!*'

'Yeah, Ooo-cus, that's right. Hold on.'

Rachel shifted in his arms and a fresh shit smog wafted over him.

'No problem, huh, little girl. We'll just walk down the hall. No, don't squirm like – Oh, man! *Phew.* Here's where that goes: this is a bathroom.'

That white room held a shelf stacked with diapers beside the sink, a toilet, a brown rubber pail for dirty diapers, and a bathtub saddled with a blue mat.

'Hold on, Rachel.' Lucas toed the blue bath mat off the tub to the floor.

'*Ay da yah Ooo-cus!*' She clapped his face between her tiny hands.

'Big help, keep me from watching what I'm doing.' Lucas knelt on the blue mat. Lowered the squiggly toddler so she lay looking up. 'How easy was that.'

'*Oony gah.*'

Lucas pushed Rachel's yellow T-shirt above her pink belly. Her bulging cloth diaper knocked him back with its pungent aroma.

He pulled a red washcloth off the tub spigot. Kept his right hand on the kid while he stretched his left to turn on the sink's hot faucet.

Voices trickled into the bathroom like the water from that faucet.

'*... hard you have to work. You. And Neal.*'

'*Got that right. Like there's always somebody keeping score.*'

Lucas paid attention to what he had to do: Take two safety pins out from the cloth diaper. Set them on the sink. Take off the diaper.

Holding Rachel's feet in the air with one hand, Lucas folded the soiled diaper beside the toddler. She cooed at the sight of her toes above her face. He soaked the washcloth until it was warm. Wiped the baby clean.

Rachel kicked her legs and waved her arms and laughed.

'Oh, you think so? Is it so funny? What are we going to do with this?' Lucas lifted the heavy cloth diaper. 'It's not like we can just throw out a dirty diaper.'

'*Your Neal is so busy. Working. Like with that new teacher.*'

'*I hear enough about her. "Jordan this" or "Jordan that." Least since school's let out, he don't keep going on 'bout her. Hell, now he don't go on 'bout nothing.*'

Lucas stepped over the toddler on the blue bath mat. He held the folded cloth diaper above the toilet water. Released one side so that the cloth unfolded its burden into the toilet a blink *after* Lucas depressed the flush handle.

Whoosh! went the water as the waste flushed away.

Ta-dah!

He held the toilet handle down as he lowered the diaper's soiled surface to the cleansing rushing water with wonderful results—

—right up until the dangling end of the diaper swirled into a water-soaked corkscrew and got sucked down the toilet drain.

He jerked the diaper. *Stuck! And the toilet won't stop running!*

Rachel pushed herself up like she never had before to stand on pudgy bare legs. She wobbled. Swayed. Her arms flapped. The twin lenses of Lucas's glasses reflected her wide-eyed grin as she heard Mommy's voice:

'*... never got a chance to tell you sorry about your boy. Him and Hal hit high school when I left for the U. Riding back and forth to Missoula, fixed it so Mom paid part of the gas so Neal would... him back from the Marines itchin' to – And law school! Both starting out, even if he was seven years older. Seven years ain't what it's cracked up to be. Not when you're riding for hours alone together.*'

Mommy's out there! thought Rachel. *Go see Mommy!*

Rachel's bare left foot popped up from the bathroom floor. Hung motionless in the air. She stared at its awesome magnificence. *So many little piggies!* Down went her left foot. Rachel toppled forward. Before she knew what was happening, her right foot threw itself out in front of its partner on the cool bathroom tiles.

And she didn't fall down! Rachel waved her arms. *This is great!*

Lucas twisted the diaper around his right wrist so it couldn't be wrenched from his grasp by the Toilet Monster. Grabbed Rachel's shirt just as she took the third solo step of her life.

'*Yeah, Neal could have gone back, but college people stare at you. Least here, you know the lookers and you can either strut your stuff or wave them off.*'

'*And here Neal can…?*'

'*A man does what he's supposed to. Heard that more than once, let me tell you. Hell, he should be grateful he gets to be a damn grade school teacher.*'

Lucas crouched in the bathroom.

One hand fought the Toilet Monster for the diaper.

The other hand held on to the fleeing toddler.

Lucas's glasses slipped down his nose. *No, not that, too! Not now!* He wiggled his ears. Tugged on Rachel's shirt. Down she plopped.

She giggled as Lucas pulled her across the bathroom tiles on her bare butt.

In the kitchen, Rita called out: '*How's it going, Lucas?*'

'Moving right along!' yelled Lucas as he pulled Rachel to his sneakers.

She rolled onto her back.

Lifted her feet into the air to ponder those piggies.

The gurgling Toilet Monster shook the ten-year-old boy's aching arm.

Lucas held on to the straining diaper with his right hand.

His left hand wiggled in his jeans pocket to get his Cub Scout jackknife.

He held the knife handle in his teeth so that free hand could open the blade.

The Toilet Monster swirled the diaper-bound boy back and forth.

Lucas plunged his knife hand into the toilet's whirlpooling cold water as close to the Toilet Monster's gurgling maw as he could get. Sawed on the diaper.

Rachel crawled up the side of the toilet to watch Lucas.

The Toilet Monster rock 'n' rolled the boy sawing the diaper they both held.

Cloth ripped – snapped free!

Lucas stumbled backward.

Rachel's naked butt plopped down on the tiled floor.

Lucas watched the sawed-off tail end of the diaper twisting in the swirling water at the drain opening – *not* being sucked down.

The water in the toilet began to rise.

'Uh-oh,' whispered Lucas.

'*Ho-ho!*' mimicked Rachel.

She grabbed the lip of the toilet bowl, pulled herself up. *This is fun!*

From the kitchen, Rita said: '*Lucas! Aren't you done yet?*'

'Um… Close!' said Lucas.

A chair scraped the kitchen floor as Rita yelled: '*Let me come help—*'

'*No!*' snapped Ruth Klise. '*I mean, I'm sure he's doing just fine. Sit down, sit down, that's right. We'll finish our coffee. And what we were talking about.*'

Water rose to the toilet bowl's rim an inch from overflow.

The vision of a car radio that wouldn't turn on grabbed Lucas.

He kicked the toilet.

Water rose to half an inch from the rim.

Rachel slammed both her palms against the toilet.

A great slurping filled the bathroom. The whirlpool in the toilet bowl sucked everything – water, diaper, drool from Rachel – down, gone, vanished.

The toilet filled its tank. Shut off.

Lucas washed his hands as he yelled to the kitchen: 'Almost done!'

He dropped the sopping remnant in the brown pail. Grabbed a clean diaper. Laid Rachel on the blue bath mat to slide that unfolded white cloth rectangle under her bare bottom. Reached onto the sink's ledge for the two safety pins—

Found only one.

Lucas folded two diaper corners around her leg. Tied them in a Cub Scout square knot. Did the same on the other side. Realized the loincloth would slide off the baby the moment she stood up.

Unless…

He safety-pinned the diaper to the front bottom of Rachel's yellow shirt.

Stood up with Rachel in his arms.

She nuzzled her face into his shirt.

Couldn't help it, he had to nuzzle her back.

Lucas carried Rachel into the kitchen just as Rita set her green mug on the table across from Ruth Klise's sword smile.

Rita shook a cigarette from her pack on the table. Struck a match.

'Listen to me carrying on.' Rita exhaled a smoke cloud toward the older woman. 'Guess it comes from being cooped up with just a kid and a baby. Or maybe not enough coffee. Something like that. Something like this, you must think I'm real stupid.'

'Why, dear, what makes you—'

'What makes me?' Rita took a drag on her cigarette. 'Hell, if I knew what makes me – but I do know better than to just be stupid. You never came here before. You never came to the coffee social Neal's mom threw after we got married and she still liked me. You was nobody special to my folks, so I never thought about that then. But this is now. In my own damn kitchen. There you sit, and it ain't about me or just dropping by.'

'There is no call for you to get—'

'You don't care how I get. You're here 'cause you don't like Neal helping poor Hal.'

'My son is dead!'

'And I'm sorry. Everybody is. Ask around the joints. You can always find somebody at the bar saying "*poor Ruth.*" Life's shit, and I'm sorry about that, but don't sit here shitting me.'

'Don't you care about what your husband is doing? *All* that he's doing?'

'I never know what my husband's doing. Ain't that a kick in the head? But he's my damn husband. *Mine!* So you screw with him, you screw with me, and that's why you're here.'

'All I want is justice!'

"Just-*who*? Just *me*, or just *you*?'

'You've got to help me stop your husband—'

'I'm not so good at the *got-to*s. Sure as shit ain't gonna work them *just* for you.'

'You're sitting here, half-dressed, middle of the morning. With that boy who's helping them, too. His sister who wouldn't do her duty, and you're not—'

'Nobody's sitting here anymore.' The kitchen chair scraped as Rita stood.

Ruth Klise rose to her feet. Glared at the younger woman.

Got hit with an exhale of Rita's cigarette smoke.

Stormed to the living room, past where Lucas held Rachel.

The door slammed shut behind Ruth's exit and made Rachel cry.

'*Shh.*' Rita stroked the cheek of the child Lucas held. Rachel reached for Mommy. Rita didn't take her. "S OK, better 'n OK. Mommy made that sneaky lady go away, *yes she did*. Daddy will be so proud of me. So happy for somethin' I done.

'You know what?' Rita leaned back as Lucas bounced her child in his arms. Rachel stopped crying. 'It's Mommy's turn to get cleaned up. Let's have a party!

'Lucas,' she said: 'How 'bout you two go run a bathtub for me.'

Lucas carried Rachel into the bathroom. Filled the tub. Carried the baby girl back to the living room.

Green-mugged Rita stood at the front window. Stared out at the street.

Lucas heard her whisper: 'All that big *out there*.'

She saw two children watching her.

'Go ahead 'n' set her on the floor. She gets heavy. Still feels like if I sneeze, she'll break. And she cries. Jangles my nerves. But no crying today for us!'

Rita drank from the green mug.

Switched on the radio in the brown wooden floor cabinet.

Vernon's radio station filled the house with Marty Robbins singing 'El Paso,' about a man whose love for a woman got him gunned down.

'Do us a favor, Lucas? Get rid of that cowboy crap. Find the Great Falls station all the high school kids listen to.'

The upstairs bathroom door shut behind her.

Rachel crawled to the blocks on the living room floor.

Lucas remembered the numbers he'd heard Chris Harvie tell Laura. His tuning fingers summoned the sound of a steady beat and whisking cymbals.

From beyond the closed bathroom door came a splash as Rita yelled: 'That's perfect! Turn it up! *Do-doh dote-doh* shark *hey*, has *dum* teeth, *yeah*!'

Rachel waved her arms as Mommy sang.

Lucas rubbed Rachel's head while Bobby Darin, who, like most male singers in 1959, tried to sell himself to Laura's generation as their Chairman of the Board like the star of their parents' generation, a suit and tie Jersey guy named Frank Sinatra. On the radio that morning, Bobby Darin finger-snapped 'Mack the Knife' about someone sneaking around the corner to do something rash.

Through the bathroom door, Rita yelled: 'Feels like we're in a movie and they're singing that song in the background. You ever feel like you're in a movie?'

'Who doesn't?'

'And wherever you are after that, if you hear that song, you're right back in the old then 'n' there.'

The radio sang about the crazy magic of Kansas City.

'This is better,' said Rita as she bustled through the living room, a white blouse tucked in the waist of lime pants. Strode into the kitchen. Reappeared, steaming mug in her hand. She leaned on the kitchen doorway. Her auburn hair was brushed. Her cheeks were pink. The green mug rose to her lips slick with a sly crimson smile. 'You want a party, you dress up.'

Rachel leaned forward to put her hands on the carpet, her bare feet flat on the floor. Stood straight – fell back on her rump, a puzzled look on her face. *Worked before!* Rachel fingered the safety pin fastening her shirt to the diaper.

'Hey, there's my precious, precious baby!'

Rita set her mug on the radio as the man inside that brown box read news about steel mills on strike back east in Ohio. She scooped Rachel off the floor. The child laughed as Mommy swooped her round and round.

From the radio came a song with the haunting plea of one man asking—

No, thought Lucas, "*commanding*" *us to come with him to the sea of love.*

Rita whirled with her child and sang with the radio: '… want to tell you, just how much *da-dah da…*'

'This is dancing, baby girl! Have to know how to dance. Smell Mommy's perfume? Always helps. *Da-da da.* Can't say nothing yet, can you? 'S OK. Just let his words bounce off your lips so he's just *dying* to kiss 'em. Mommy will teach you an'—

'*Ooops!* Gotta be careful an' not fall. *And* be careful to not be too careful. They always go for it. Can get 'em even when they think they wanna walk away. Little drinky never hurts neither.

'Damn, baby girl, you're getting heavy! Here, you like it when Lucas holds you. You go for those older guys with glasses. Your daddy, I knew he was smart even without 'em.'

The child in Lucas's arms reached for her mother as that woman retrieved the coffee mug from on top of the radio, drained it, said: 'Dancing is thirsty work.'

She left Rachel bouncing on Lucas's lap and headed into the kitchen.

The radio played.

'Mrs – I mean Rita, I can take Rachel outside in the front yard.'

'It's hot out there,' said Rita over the sound of a spoon clinking her mug.

Rita stood in the doorway to the kitchen. Smiled as she gestured with her green mug. 'Besides, look at me. I just got all dressed up. Don't I look nice?'

'Well *sure*, but she's a kid and you don't have to, I could—'

'No.' Rita sipped her mug. 'First thing when Neal comes home, he checks on the baby. I could wrap my bathrobe belt around my neck and be hanging from the ceiling and he'd check on Rachel. So when he walks through the front door, she's gotta be here so he can see she's OK. Then he's going to see me all dolled-up and I'll tell him about Ruth Klise. How I did good. You can tell him, too!'

'I guess so.'

'You guess right. And today, we did everything right, you and me.'

Lucas sat absolutely still and said nothing about the Toilet Monster.

'Gonna be perfect.' Rita took a long drink from the green mug. 'Just like it should be. *Then'll* be a good idea for you to get Rachel out. Be out of the house while Neal and I are here, my *husband* and me, you know what I mean? The town wading pool. You take her there an' I'll take care of business here.'

Baby Rachel put her hands on the floor, pushed herself up—

—the jerk of her clothes toppled Rachel back down to her rump.

'Do me a favor?' said the baby's mother. 'Check in the bathroom, make sure I didn't make a mess.'

'What?'

'Diapers, maybe. Make sure I didn't knock them over.'

Lucas found the bathroom looking no worse than when he'd left it.

Found his boss stirring sugar from the bowl on the table into her mug when he came back into the kitchen.

'One last cup,' she said. 'Top it all off.'

She left the brown paper sack on the table. Drifted toward the living room.

Rachel sat on the living room floor, her face scrunched in frustration.

Her mother leaned on the brown box as *again* it played Bobby Darin singing, only this time the crooner wondered, '*Dream lover, where are you?*'

'Yeah,' said Rita. 'Where the hell?'

She took a drink from the green mug. Peered out the living room window.

'Just got to sit here and wait,' she told the street outside. 'He'll come. It'll happen. Just got to wait. He'll remember how it was and we'll go back to that.'

Rachel cried. Whimpered. Like a freight train coming, her whimper built to a whine, to a full-throttled, window-rattling, hurricane tears, exploding bomb of crying.

Lucas sank to the floor. 'Rache! What's the matter? It's OK.'

Rita dropped her gaze from the window. Shut her eyes. Cupped her brow with her hand that wasn't holding the green mug. Shrank as small as she could.

She leaned on the brown radio as the baby screamed and Lucas did nothing to stop it. Rita kept her hand over her face. Blindly groped the mug to her lips. Drained it without spilling a drop, and if she could do that, why couldn't he make the baby stop, *just stop*, crying?

'Come on, Rach-e,' said Lucas as he lifted the crying girl off the floor.

The noon whistle blew over the town of Vernon.

Neal Dylan stepped through the front door of his rented house.

Saw his Rachel crying in the arms of spectacled Lucas.

Saw his red-lipsticked wife in lime green pants perched on the brown radio.

She jerked her face from behind her right hand. Flinched at the sight of him. Thrust a green coffee mug behind her. Set it down on nothing.

The mug crashed on the living room floor. Shattered.

The explosion startled Rita. She slid off the radio. Her lime hips plopped on the floor. Her right palm slammed down on a jagged piece of broken mug.

Rita howled.

Stared at the red stream in her palm.

Neal ran to help his wounded wife wobble to her feet as Lucas set their wailing baby on the floor and raced to help her parents.

'Honey!' said Rita. 'Welcome home!'

'Lucas!' yelled Neal. 'Take care of Rachel!'

'Guess what I did!' crowed Rita.

'Take this!' Neal tied a clean handkerchief around her gouged hand.

'Doesn't really go with my outfit.' Rita smiled so he'd know she was joking.

Neal sniffed her words so loudly Lucas heard him above Rachel's wails.

Turned to Lucas. 'There's a baby bottle of milk in the fridge!'

'Should I heat it in a pan of water? Or wait! I could pour the coffee that might still be hot over it.'

Rita said: 'None for me, thanks. I've had plenty of coffee.'

Her husband led her toward the couch. Didn't resist when she held on to him so he had to sit beside her.

'Lucas, just give her a bottle. It's OK, Rita. You're going to be fine.'

'Fine, hell. Did great. You should have seen me. Ask Lucas.'

'First—'

'First lemme tell how I showed that Ruth Klise when she came over.'

'Ruth Klise came here? Came to… She told you… What did she tell you?'

'Wasn' what she told me, was what I told her. *Oww!* Your handkerchief, why you wrap it so tight? Just a cut, won't stop us from doing anythin' you—'

'*Ruth Klise!*' said Neal as Lucas guided a cold baby bottle toward the crying Rachel's bright red face. 'Tell me!'

'Supposed to say "*pleazze*."' Neal's wife pressed her forefinger to his lips. 'She would've if I asked. She wanted t' worm secrets out of me.'

'Out of you? Secrets… "*out*" *of you*?'

''S all about what you're doing with Hal. Wouldn' tell her a damn thing. She sat at our kitchen table. Smiled at me like I was still a dumb kid.'

Rachel grabbed the baby bottle of milk. Sucked like this was the world's last best bottle. Shuddered in Lucas's arms.

'Is that true, Lucas?' Neal caught the nod from the boy standing in the kitchen doorway holding his daughter. 'What the hell is she… She must be crazy!'

Neal checked the crusting handkerchief on his wife's hand. 'That's drying. Lucas: go put Rachel in her crib. She probably needs a nap.'

'What about me?' said Rita from the couch. 'Or do you wanna talk 'bout what else you're doing that Ruth Klise wanted to tell me about?'

'Lucas,' said Neal in a cold voice. 'Get Rachel into her crib *now*!'

Lucas made himself go deaf as he hurried to the bedroom, laid Rachel on her back in the crib. Made himself go back downstairs.

Rita stood in the living room, her eyes blazing toward her husband.

As the radio played.

For the rest of his life, whenever Lucas heard the song about Stagger Lee shooting Billy, Lucas tumbled back into the then and there of that clapboard house.

'So you got no words?' Rita shouted to her husband. 'All them first damn talky months, now nothin' you got to say. Doesn't matter you got nothing to say. I know what's what. I know what's mine. So you can play Mister Big Shot Hero. You can... But don't you forget. Don't you forget. I got what I got and that's you.'

'Lucas,' whispered Neal, his eyes never leaving his wife. 'Go home. I'll call you about tomorrow, about... *Go!*'

Lucas blasted out of that house to his waiting bike.

Let the screen door slam behind him.

Didn't look back as the radio told how Stagger Lee's bullet tore through Billy to break the bartender's glass.

THE DEVIL'S TOOLS

Lunch two days later for Lucas meant bologna and catsup white bread sandwiches with his family around their kitchen table before his big heat ride.

Laura was home after working a half-day shift.

Mom and Dad didn't talk about much before he went back to work.

He rode his bike to the Mallettes' house. The aluminum ladder lay flat in the driveway. Still-sealed cans of white paint sat beside the house's scraped wall.

A screen door creaked. Mrs Mallette yelled: 'Neal's not here, Lucas! Phoned that something came up. You're supposed to take the rest of the day off.'

Lucas waved. Pedaled away like he knew where he was going.

Marin was a million miles away on a ranch. Kurt's camp in the mountains didn't get out for weeks. Wayne was helping out his dad at the rebuilding hardware store. If Lucas went home, he'd have to keep out of Mom's sight.

'Idle hands are the devil's tools,' she'd quote from Gramma Meg.

Or she'd storm into his bedroom where he'd be happily *imagining* in his chair. She'd – *kind of like a joke* – shout: 'Quit thinking on my time!'

You gotta go somewhere, Lucas told himself. The only breeze was the *whoosh* he made.

Lucas turned the corner at the Methodist church.

Across the street, Mrs Sweeny lifted the red flag on her mailbox. Saw him.

'You! The Ross boy! I got something for you!'

Stop. He had to stop. 'Yes, ma'am?'

She fished an envelope from her mailbox. Scraped off its stamp. 'Waste not, want not. Now you can personally take this where it has to go.'

'But I'm on my way to—'

'Are you going where your mother wants or are you looking for trouble?'

Lucas knew Mrs Sweeny had a phone. "*Hello? Lucas's mom?*"

Lucas sighed. 'What is it you want me to do?'

'What you're supposed to. Supposed to help your kin. And your elders. Won't be no trouble for you to pedal out to your Uncle Orville's shop.'

'That's way west of town along the highway and—'

'*And* you got to do what you got to do. Just like the rest of us. Unless you're special, in which case, why, pardon me: I didn't know Megan Conner's people up and got special.'

'No, ma'am.'

'Good. Tell your Uncle Orville now that I know he's not a thief. I appreciate what he thinks. I prayed on it. Wrote those letters in that envelope like we talked about. And I'm going to sign that other deal my lawyer worked out for us.'

'Ma'am, I don't understand what—'

'You just tell Orville that Mrs Sweeny's gonna get what's hers. *Finally.*'

She told Lucas to drink from her garden hose so he wouldn't parch out.

When he turned on that water, she said he might as well give her marigolds and peonies a good dose. The crone disappeared behind her shut door.

He rode through town. Biked past the Tastee-Freez and crossed over the highway to pedal with the flow of traffic. Passed the sign that read CITY LIMITS. Biked and biked more. Crossed the highway to a gravel road leading across a flat stretch of prairie that held a distant Quonset building that looked like a giant metal tube. Pedaled past a peeling black and white sign: DIXON DRILLING.

Off to his left waited two flatbed trucks with wrinkled tires. Stacks of long pipes made windbreaks for a buildup of tumbleweeds. He smelled grease and gas. Saw Uncle Orville's blue pickup parked by the Quonset's open door.

But where is everybody? thought Lucas as he climbed off his bike. Once when he'd been riding with the Conner sisters, Aunt Iona brought mail out here to her husband. Then, this place had been a beehive with men loading trucks, revving engines. Now all Lucas heard was one hammer banging *Ding! Ding! Ding!*

Lucas rolled his bike into the Quonset's shaded cavern where metal walls trembled every time a bull of a man hammered a steel rod cinched in a vise.

Between sledgehammer strokes, Lucas yelled: 'Hi, Uncle Orville!'

The big man stared at the flush-faced boy in the sweat-soaked T-shirt.

'Lucas! You bike all the way out here? Get some water in you!'

Lucas followed the big man to an iron sink. Water gushed out of the spigot. His uncle made him drink gulps. 'Now stick your head under there.'

Arctic water rushed over Lucas's baked skull. Felt wonderful.

He shut off the water. Put his glasses back on.

His uncle pointed at a small bathroom. 'Now go pee. Get the flow going.'

And *oh* did he flow.

Looked around as he came out of the bathroom.

Coffin-sized clothes lockers filled this rear wall of the Quonset. A folding chair leaned against the lockers near a cluttered desk and a torn office chair.

'Why'd you come out here?' asked Uncle Orville.

Lucas handed him Mrs Sweeny's envelope. Said she wanted

Uncle Orville told *yes* to a deal. But Lucas didn't say anything about anybody being a thief.

The big man grinned as he tossed the envelope on his desk.

'She's so cheap she makes a kid carry her load. Come on. We'll throw your bike in the pickup. Ride you home so—'

A car crunched to a stop outside on the gravel road. A car door slammed. An invisible man shouted: 'Orville! You in there?'

Uncle Orville propelled Lucas to the shop's back wall. Swung open a locker. 'Get the hell in there and don't make a God-damn peep!'

Lucas scrambled into the locker. Metal walls pinched his shoulders. He scrunched. Couldn't sit down. Swore to himself that he wasn't scared.

Uncle Orville leaned the folding chair so it propped the locker door open.

'There you are!' called out the visitor – Lucas's ex-neighbor Mr Falk. 'What are you doing?'

Uncle Orville replied: 'Catching up on paperwork.'

Lucas heard a desk drawer open and close.

'But it's hot as hell out here,' said Uncle Orville. 'We should go into town and grab a cold beer. Talk there. You drive on ahead. I'll—'

'You know people shouldn't see us together, though when the dust clears, why, me and the wife sure want to have you and yours over for dinner.'

Lucas shrank as small as he could. Took slow, quiet breaths.

Falk said: 'Fine place you got here. A real working stiff's palace.'

Uncle Orville said nothing, but Lucas imagined his uncle's blockish face going as hard as hammered steel. He smelled oil, the metal walls pressing him.

Falk said: 'I'm dying to know. Did you make up with old lady Sweeny?'

'Must have. She got word to me that she's gonna sign your deal.'

'Hot damn *yes!*'

'So we're done here now. We—'

'I still don't know why she had to talk to you. I proved to her that McDewel couldn't have slanted her land.'

'We don't need to talk about this now. I got work to do. You do, too. You should probably get ready so things can move quick once you call her.'

'You should never be too eager. You got to know how to play things.'

'Yeah.'

'Will you relax? I'm on top of everything.'

'So let's have a beer to celebrate. We can meet in Shelby. Nobody'll see us.'

'You're acting squirrely all of a sudden. When a man's partner is anxious to walk him out the door, a man's got to wonder.'

'I just want to finish up here and get the hell out of the heat an' to home.'

'*Home* isn't exactly where guys like us like to go, now is it.' Falk laughed. 'But you're right about the damn heat. Take a load off your feet. Relax.'

Through his shaft of light, Lucas saw a hand, a man's arm in a white shirt, a fancy watch with a gold trinket. The hand pulled the folding chair away.

The locker door clicked shut.

Only a high-up slotted grill of sunlight and fresh air connected Lucas's metal coffin of darkness to the outside world.

Uncle Orville grunted. 'Guess we gotta go through it quick and get it done.'

Falk said: 'I still don't know why she had to talk to you.'

'She only trusts Jesus whispers and the right kind of people from around here. She figured that since it turns out I'm not a thief, maybe she can trust me.'

'What did you tell her?'

'The truth. She called me up to her house to clear up her

thinking I worked for a thief who slanted her land. So I let her know that the numbers you showed her were the numbers McDewel logged to the well I drilled next to her parcel.'

'She ask you anything else?'

'After she got that from me, she let out there was a deal on her table. Asked if I thought she should lease her land for drilling. I told her it was free money, whether they found oil there or not, and only a fool turns down free money.'

'Does she know I own a chunk of the leasing company?'

'Not from me.'

The locker's metal walls are getting slick. Pushing in.

'Good. As her lawyer, I advised her that Kaimin Oil's contract is solid. Didn't tell her it was a lowball fee, but if we can wrap this up tight, she won't have time to shop it around and find out. And believe me, that's an ironclad contract.'

'You're gonna have to hammer one more bolt to it.'

'Huh?'

'When me and her were talking, the idea came up that I know the oil field her land sits on. She's worried that I might hustle up a drilling deal on her neighbor's place. Suck up oil there before it could soak over to her well. She doesn't want to take that chance. Wants to tie me up – and pay me back for branding me a thief all these years. "*Atone for her misunderstanding,*" she said. You know her: she likes to write letters, so she penned up letters of agreement between her and me that say if there's any oil drilling done on her land, I gotta be the driller who does it.'

'What letters? I'm her lawyer and she never showed me—'

'Oh, I got 'em. I figure she'll show you her signed copy, same as mine.'

Heavy silence and air getting heavy.

'You sly wildcatting son-of-a-bitch! You got her to… Our deal was… You know I'm gonna take care of you for helping out!'

'Now I really, *really* know it.'

'Those letters might not be legally binding. You two aren't lawyers.'

'Yeah, but if we get to arguing about that out in the open, who knows what's going to come out as legal and what's not.'

Slow, thought Lucas. *If I just breathe very, very slowly...*

'She's getting a paid-each-month lease! If it wasn't for this deal, she'd keep getting nothing and you wouldn't be getting a ton of work!'

'I'll do the drilling work, fair and square.'

Lucas heard Falk take a deep breath.

'We're all businessmen here,' said Falk. 'We'll make a provision that ironclads you as the driller. Only fair. This is the perfect deal for all of us. Me and my old law partners in Missoula have a big investment in this.'

'Good for you,' said Uncle Orville.

'Good for everybody. Even old lady Sweeny. All you and your men gotta do is work your job. Drill until you hit the gushers. Leave the thinking to me.'

'If that's the way you want it.'

'That's the way it is. Hell, if it wasn't for me thinking, we wouldn't be here.'

'That's a fact,' said Orville. 'But now we each got work to—'

'There I was,' said Falk. 'Sitting in front of a coffee cup in the Chat & Chew. I heard somebody laugh about Mrs Sweeny and her slanted land.'

Spy. Just think about being a spy. Not getting tighter, burning in here.

'When I heard that,' said Falk, 'I reeled her in as a client because I saw it in a flash: What if your ex-boss never slanted her land and all that oil she thought he stole was still there?

'I got damn dusty in the back rooms of the courthouse looking up lease records and checking them against the production reports on file with the Oil & Gas Commission.

'Then like the French say, *Voilà*: the well drilled next to her property, the well you worked back in high school, that well came in with oil – but not so much that it was off-average with other wells in that field.

'Which means McDewel couldn't have slanted her. If he'd been stealing from her, the volume of that would have shown up in the reports through the Oil & Commission. His oil *plus* her oil would have equaled a great well, but that well you worked on logged in as average, so he wasn't robbing her. Numbers don't lie.'

'No, lying is a lawyer's job.'

Somewhere far away, Lucas heard Falk laugh.

'Lawyers don't lie, we make motions. As long as you keep moving, *what is* and *what ain't* don't matter.'

'So you say. You're the smart city guy who came to town. I'm the dumb country wildcatter.'

'Not as dumb as anybody figured. But from now on, let me do the thinking. Why, one time down in Missoula, I had this tort action that was going to…'

'LUCAS!'

What? Hot. Sticky. Legs cramped. Uncle Orville lifting me out of the locker.

'Come on, Lucas! You OK? You're OK, right? You're OK.'

'Must have fell asleep.'

'Yeah! That's what you did. You fell asleep. But you're OK now, right?'

Lucas nodded. Blinked. Pushed his glasses back up his nose. Looked around the Quonset. 'Where's Mr Falk?'

'Mr Big Wheel finally rolled away. Come on. Let's go soak your head.'

They did. Uncle Orville made him drink more water. Wash his arms. Lucas swore to Uncle Orville that he felt fine. Uncle Orville loaded the bike into the back of his blue pickup. Kept one eye on Lucas and the other on the highway as they motored to town. Dry hot air blew on Lucas's face from the open window.

Uncle Orville steered the pickup into the drive-up lane at the Tastee-Freez. A high school girl passed Lucas a large Coke through the drive-up window. Orville paid the girl with a silver dollar. Put the three quarters in change on the dashboard. Drove away.

He parked the pickup in front of Lucas's house. Shut off the engine. Lit a cigarette. Asked his nephew beside him: 'What do you figure that was about?'

Lucas gave the safest answer he could. 'You and Mr Falk's business.'

'You got that right. But what do you think about it? You're a smart kid, Lucas. Tell me what was going on before you… fell asleep.'

'I don't want to get in trouble!'

'Me either. So we best put all our cards on the table, right?'

July's late afternoon sun beat down on the pickup that held them.

Lucas swallowed. Whispered:

'Are you… Did you and Mr Falk snooker Mrs Sweeny?'

Uncle Orville laughed out cigarette smoke. '*Snooker*: that's a funny word.'

'I'm just a kid!'

'Maybe, but you know that Falk, me, and Mrs Sweeny are dancing in some deal about drilling for oil. You worried that your Uncle Orville is a crook?'

Lucas couldn't say anything. Shrugged.

'Answer me this,' said the big man crammed behind the wheel of a pickup truck. 'If there's nothing to steal, can you be a thief?'

'Huh? But… Mr Falk said the numbers prove—'

'Numbers are just numbers. They aren't *what's what*. Numbers that get written don't have to be real numbers for that well or for any slanting that well did. They might be numbers of oil counted off another slant far away.'

'But if that… I don't…'

'If Mrs Sweeny had no oil, then how could anyone steal it from her?'

'How could anybody know she never had any oil to steal?'

Orville ground out his cigarette on the pickup door. Tossed the butt outside to the street where Mother Nature would take care of it. Told his nephew:

'You could work for somebody who *tried* to steal from her, slanted her, but found out there was nothing there to take.'

'But Mr Falk thinks—'.

'Let him think what he wants. Guy like me should leave the thinking to him. I'm just along to get paid to do the job he thought up. Mrs Sweeny, she'll get paid for what he thought up too.

'So,' said his uncle, 'if anybody's getting snookered... It ain't me. Ain't you. Ain't even Mrs Sweeny. And the man whose idea it was to snooker... Since he's in charge, you could figure what he gets is what he earned.'

Uncle Orville frowned.

'Did Mrs Sweeny pay you for busting your butt for her in this heat?'

'No.'

'Figures.' Uncle Orville dropped the three shiny quarters off the dashboard into Lucas's hand. 'Shame a tight-ass like her'll come out ahead on this.'

Lucas stared at the pieces of silver on his palm.

'You earned it,' said Orville. 'You give a man what he earns.'

'I didn't ask for it!'

'So it's your luck.' Uncle Orville sighed. 'You want to tell your folks how you helped out, go ahead. Just be sure you get it right. And keep it in our family.' The big man nodded toward the hospital across the street. 'Look there.'

Lucas whirled. 'That's your car.'

'Likely, your Aunt Iona's visiting Gramma Meg. Do me a favor? Go over there, tell her I'm fixin' to need dinner early.'

They unloaded his bike. Lucas wheeled it to its place by the garage. Uncle Orville drove away. Lucas found no one home.

Walked across the street to the hospital. On the way, he glanced at the house where Mr Falk once lived.

And smiled.

Wipe that grin off your face! Lucas told himself as the elevator doors slid open to let him out on the second floor of the nursing home.

Old-people smell welcomed Lucas. No one sat at the nurses' station.

A plaintive wail sliced the hallway air: '*I-o-na. Ber-yl.*'

From around the corner came Gramma Meg's voice: 'Come closer. *Please!*'

Lucas hurried into Gramma Meg's room in time to see his aunts Iona and Beryl draw close to the white-haired woman lying in the bed against the wall.

Lucas spotted his mom rearranging framed photographs on the cramped room's chest of drawers as her two sisters leaned closer to Gramma Meg.

Who whimpered: 'Beryl… Iona…'

'What's wrong, Ma?' said Beryl. 'We're right—'

Wham!

Gramma Meg grabbed Beryl and Iona by their wrists. Her expression went from pitiful sorrow to pure glee as her two daughters fought her lumberjack grip.

'*Gotcha!*' yelled Gramma.

Beryl and Iona twisted and jerked and pulled.

Gramma Meg shook her daughters like they were rag dolls.

'*For Christ's sakes, Cora!*' Beryl yelled to Lucas's mom. '*Do something!*'

Mom said: 'Like what?'

Restraining bolts held this hospital bed on wheels to the wall. The women's battle banged the bed against that plaster. The bolts pinged free.

The hospital bed flew away from the wall.

Iona and Beryl tumbled over the bed's side rail. Fell on top of their mother. Rode the runaway bed as it careened across the room. Cora/Mom yelped as the runaway bed crashed her into the bureau, knocked over the framed photographs.

For a moment, there was silence.

A bolt fell out from its ripped hole in the wall. Tinkled on the tile floor.

Iona whispered: 'Oh shit, not again.'

'You girls climb off of me,' said Gramma Meg, as proper as could be. 'Getting in bed with your mother. Aren't you a little old for this?'

Iona and Beryl slid off the bed. Rearranged their clothing as Mom joined them to glare at the white-haired grandmother who lay propped on her pillows, serenely staring back at her children with eyes that twinkled.

Beryl snapped: 'What the hell did you do that for?'

'Felt like it. Doing something makes you feel like somebody.'

'That makes about as much sense as flying pigs,' said Mom.

'Or flying monkeys? Don't worry, you'll get it someday. What good is this world of pain if you can't get a little laugh?'

Beryl said: 'You broke the bed. Pulled it right out of the wall.'

'Wasn't just me.'

Lucas helped his aunts push the bed back into its official position.

Gramma put her arms up like she was on a roller coaster. '*Whee!*'

Mom told Lucas to crawl around on the floor and find the bolts.

Gramma wanted to buzz for the nurse, complain about shoddy nursing home walls, but Mom told the room: 'We don't need any more trouble.'

'I'll go make sure the coast is clear,' said Iona.

Beryl snorted as her sister fled the room. 'Is that what you're going to do?'

Gotta tell Iona what Uncle Orville said, thought Lucas.

He told Mom: 'I can't find the fourth bolt. I'll go help Aunt Iona.'

He found her smoking in the dining room.

And talking to three old people in chairs: a wispy woman who wore a pink sweater over her nightgown, two liver-spotted men – one with teeth.

Iona was saying: 'You remember me, don't you, Sue? Orville and I lived around the corner from you after we got married.'

Wispy woman Sue's head bobbed like a sparrow pecking for food.

'So, how's it going?' said Iona, taking a drag on her sneaked cigarette.

The wispy woman bobbed her head.

'Look,' Iona told Lucas. 'They use dish towels to tie 'em in the chairs.'

Belts of twisted white cloth circled the laps of the three senior citizens.

'Tying people up sure as hell ain't right,' said Iona.

Took a last drag on her cigarette. Walked over to the ashtray stand near the couch and buried the butt in the sand. Craned her neck to look down first one corridor, then the other. Stared at the empty nurses' station.

Hurried back to her nephew, leaned close to whisper: 'Lucas! Get down there on the floor and crawl around behind the chairs and untie them!'

'I can't do that!'

'You already got your jeans dirty crawling around on Gramma's floor. You know it ain't right that they're all tied up. Let's just let 'em walk around a little.'

'We'll get in trouble!'

'We're already there, so we might as well do some good while we're at it.'

'Why can't we just untie the top knots?'

'Hell, kid, I gotta keep lookout, and if you're crawling under the chairs, nobody's likely to see you.' Her laugh was quick and quiet. 'Come on. It'll be fun. Better 'n going back there to let Gramma knock us around.'

So while Iona guarded the dining room entrance, Lucas got down on his back to crawl under the chairs looped with knotted dishtowels.

By the time Lucas crawled out from under the last chair, wispy Sue was shuffling away. Lucas pushed himself off the tile floor. Grabbed a hand reaching toward him. The hand was thin. Frail. Lucas's pull launched the old man with teeth straight out of his chair. He steadied himself. Careened toward the light from the window at the end of the long hall.

'Attaboy, Mr Pellet!' said Aunt Iona. 'You're doing great.'

Wispy Sue shuffled into the kitchen nook.

The liberated toothless old man stood wobbling by his chair. His eyes filled with other horizons. White tape on his shirt above his heart read: *Cody.*

Elevator doors whirred open, and out marched polar bear Nurse Kesey.

Who took the scene in with wide-eyed horror.

'Well, hi there!' said Iona. 'Want a Lifesaver?'

Nurse Kesey bustled past Aunt Iona to the swaying toothless old man.

'Cody!' Nurse Kesey wrapped her paws gently around his arms.

Lucas helped the nurse lower the staring man into his chair.

'Cody,' she told him. 'It's OK. Everything's OK. You're right here.'

No he's not, thought Lucas, but he said nothing.

'Oh my God, *Sue*: put that down!' The nurse charged into the kitchen nook. Plucked the bread knife from the wispy woman's fluttering hand. Led Sue out of the nook as fast as the wispy woman's shuffling slippers could go.

'Where's Mr Pellet?' yelled the nurse.

'We'll help you look,' said Iona. '*Hey, Beryl! Cora!* We need some help. Mr Pellet's gone a-walking.'

'Yeah,' muttered Nurse Kesey. 'And how the hell did he manage that?'

'Ain't these old folks something, though.' Iona turned to face her sisters Beryl and Cora hurrying to her from Gramma Meg's room. 'And if anybody done anything, why, had to be just trying to do a good thing for folks who deserve it.'

'You Conners are nothing but trouble!' snapped Nurse Kesey.

Beryl glared at Iona. 'You told her about the bed?'

Mom beckoned for her son to come a-running. 'Lucas has to go home!'

She swept him away from everyone else to ride the sinking elevator.

They stared at their blurred reflections in the sealed silver doors.

His mom told those images, told him, told herself and the whole damn world: 'I just want to make it all safe for you kids. Why can't it all be like that?'

JAILHOUSE ROCK

Lucas finished painting with Neal *way* early the next afternoon.

Biked home.

And for the first time in his whole life found that front door locked.

Spotted his family's gray Dodge parked across the street by the hospital.

Where it didn't belong. Not when this house had no cars parked at its curb, an empty driveway, and the garage he and Dad had cleared out last Halloween.

His watch read 3:07.

Lucas wheeled his bike along the west side of his house. Closed Venetian blinds. Cowboy curtains in his bedroom were pulled shut. All the house's windows on that hot July Friday afternoon were closed.

Nobody's home, thought Lucas.

The locked door made him feel like he didn't want to be there either.

But you have to make sure the house and Mom are OK.

Lucas kickstanded his bike on the back lawn. Closed blinds filled the kitchen's picture window. The screen door to the back porch looked latched. The storm door behind it was shut tight.

Nothing covered the garage windows.

The blue taxi! Uncle Johnny's cab! Why is it in our garage?

Lucas looked at his watch: 3:13.

Tiptoed up the back porch steps. Knocked on the latched screen door. Knocked so softly sparrows perched in the Dentons' trees didn't take wing. So softly maybe no one inside his house heard the knock. Knocked harder.

A woman glared out through the slats over the kitchen's picture window.

'For Christ's sakes!' came her voice muffled by the glass. 'It's just Lucas!'

He pounded five heartbeats before the back doors swung open.

Aunt Beryl pulled the boy inside the house. Locked the doors.

'Your mom said you wouldn't be home till five.'

'Neal made a phone call at the Leavitts',' said Lucas as he followed his aunt into the kitchen. *What is that smell?* 'Then we quit early.'

'What time is it?' said Beryl as she stood below the kitchen clock.

Lucas told her.

'An hour until four thirty,' she said.

With his glasses' good vision, Lucas corrected her: 'Seventy-two minutes.'

Mom stood in the living room. 'Lucas! Come right here!'

That smell grew as Lucas stepped toward the living room. A cigarette smoke smog from the ceiling brushed his head. The alien smell was sticky sweet like the flowers sent to the nursing home when Mrs Turner died. The bouquet that Gramma had Lucas take from the nurses' counter and put in her room because *what the hell*, Mrs Turner had been a friend of hers.

That smell is orchids, remembered Lucas as he entered the living room.

'Oh my God!' cried a woman Lucas didn't know who sat across from where Mom stood. 'This can't be your son. You told me he was a little boy.'

Mom pulled him close. 'He is!'

'No, I'm ten!' insisted Lucas.

Beryl said: 'For Christ's sakes, he is what he is.'

'What a handsome young man,' said the woman. 'Don't you just love men at that age when they're harmless?'

She sat in the Ross family chair like a foreign queen. A green dress clung to her. Her straw hair was dark near her scalp. *Dyed*, thought Lucas. *She's trying to belong on a calendar.* Her face glistened pink. She had eyes like pebbles. Fire-red lipstick matched her fingernails that waved her smoldering cigarette.

'It's Lucas, right? Sorry, names tend to slide past me.'

''S OK.' His inhale carried the sticky-sweet odor of her perfume: *orchids*.

'My name is Marilyn. Your wonderful mother and aunt are saving my life.'

Mom said: 'She's waiting here until she catches the train. That's all!'

'At four thirty.' Marilyn stubbed out her cigarette in an ashtray. 'Is it time?'

'Must be!' said Mom.

'No,' said Beryl. 'We leave too soon, Johnny spots us, there's hell to pay.'

Marilyn said: 'I already paid.'

Shrugged. 'Somebody's got to get away. Why not me?'

Her ruby smile curled around Lucas. 'Want to sit over here?'

Mom pulled Lucas down beside her on the couch.

Marilyn's smile went away.

The boy said: 'Are you going all the way to Chicago on the train?'

'Honey, I'm going straight out of here into the rising sun.'

'Elvis rode the train the other way,' said Lucas. 'He didn't get off here.'

'Makes him smarter than me. Probably rode to Seattle. That ain't always a town you wanna go to. I came from there, so I know what I'm talking about.

'You get on a train,' she said. 'Seems like the thing to do 'cause a girl has to travel and it's a gyp trip, so you might as well go that way, too. And men, you can't never find a good one and the bad ones are a dime a dozen, so why not just take the damn dimes?

'Cause the real ones, the wild ones, they just break your heart or your jaw, put you out, and walk off.'

Lucas nodded like he knew what she was talking about.

Silence squeezed all four of them in that room.

Lucas knew he'd burst if somebody didn't say something.

So he asked what he'd heard adults say: 'Do you work around here?'

She laughed. Beryl fumbled a cigarette from her pack. Handed the pack to Mom's reaching hand.

Lucas gambled: 'Do you work at the bank?'

'That's a good one! Me and the bank. I see the money all right. Kind of like a teller. In it comes and away it goes.'

'Do you know my dad?' asked Lucas. 'He goes to the bank.'

Mum lunged forward on the couch. 'You don't know him! She doesn't!'

'Oh no, Lucas,' said Marilyn, her pebble eyes talking not to the boy but to his trembling mother. 'I've never met your dad.' She shrugged. 'Not a lot of guys around this town you can say that about.'

Mom and Aunt Beryl looked at the walls. At the ceiling. At anything *not Lucas.*

Marilyn drummed her ruby fingernails on the green dress over her knee.

What's going on? swirled Lucas. Uncle Johnny's blue taxi hiding in the garage. A woman he'd never seen before who worked in this town where he knew everyone or everyone knew him. Fingernails painted as red as the house on… *Oh.*

But he still didn't know more than *oh.*

Mom said: 'It's almost a quarter to four.'

'I ain't figured the ticket yet,' said Beryl.

'Me either,' said Marilyn. 'When you said you'd help, save me, take me to the train instead of to the doc for my VD checkup, I didn't want to wait two more weeks until my turn rolled around again. Take a chance that it wouldn't be you driving the taxi. That it would be—'

'We know who I ain't,' said Beryl. 'I just drive the cab. You ask, I go.'

'And you'll tell everybody you dropped me off at the clinic. Always takes longer sitting in the doctor's office than you think it will. That buys us this time. When I don't call the cab, when it's after four thirty, then you say what you gotta say.'

'Usually do.' Beryl shook her head. 'Never done this before.'

'But how are we going to do the ticket?' said Marilyn. 'He knows you're at your sister's. He's on the cab call phone. He'll ring you here if there's a customer. Cora will say whatever works, but how are we going to get the ticket? If I go in the depot, somebody might call somebody. Last minute, I can jump on the train. Be gone with the whistle before anybody can see me. But buying the ticket…

'*Beryl!* You can call the depot! Say you got a tourist who you're going to pick up the ticket for and – *No*: you'd have to leave the cab with me alone in it. The cops or somebody might spot me. Us. But if someone else got—'

'Not me!' said Mom. 'I'm no good at stuff out there. Plus, we need me to stay here. If Johnny calls and nobody answers my phone…'

Marilyn's ruby lips curled around her words. 'What about the boy?'

Lucas's heart pounded so hard he thought his chest might explode.

His watch read forty-two minutes to the train's good-bye whistle.

'No!' yelled Mom. 'Don't you touch him! You can't have him!'

'I'm only thinking out loud,' said Marilyn.

'Stop thinking! That's not going to do you any good. I should never have let you two in here. Trouble comes in if you open your door.'

'Easy, Cora,' said her older sister. 'We're not in trouble yet.'

'Yes we are! We're always in trouble and it's always your fault!'

'*Always my fault?* You're the one who *always* wants to stay inside. Always says *no*. Hell, the only fun you ever had as a kid was when Iona or Dory or me tricked you out to where it was happening. And *now* you *always* talk about how wild and great being a Conner was.'

'That was then and it's over so it's OK, but this is now and it's my house!'

'Where else was I supposed to go? I figured my sister would give me a hand. Would help me do the right thing like she preaches and help some gal who needs it by just letting us hide out in her damn house for an hour or so.'

'Now she wants Lucas!'

'He just showed up when he wasn't supposed to. She just wants a ticket.'

Lucas watched Marilyn's eyes flick between the two quarreling sisters.

'Don's going to find out!' said Mom.

'Don finding out isn't who to worry about.'

'You married him!'

'So I'm not as lucky as you got with Don. So what do I do? I got a family, too. And him. Sure, he's why we're here, the son-of-a-bitch, but—'

'*Oh my God!* Did you do this to piss off Johnny? Show him that you—'

'*Why* doesn't matter, it's done. Now we gotta figure out *how*.'

Marilyn stifled a sob like she was in the movies.

'All I wanted was to be gone and forgotten by tomorrow! I don't want you two to get in trouble with Johnny – *I know about that!* You've got to be a saint, Beryl. And, Cora, I never had a sister. Now look what I've done to you two.' Then her words floated: 'Maybe I should just walk out of here.'

The second hand swept around Lucas's watch.

'You can't do that,' muttered Beryl. 'Walking around town,

some friend of Johnny's will call him, or the cops will roll you up and that'll end up the same.'

'There's another train,' said Marilyn. 'In the morning. Going west.'

Lucas said: 'That's the train Elvis rode!'

Marilyn said: 'I could stay out of sight until…'

Mom yelled: 'You can't stay here. Don comes home at five and Laura – You can't, Laura, not her, not *ever* her and you can't stay here. Not even till dinner.'

'Gee, then what are we going to do?' said Marilyn. 'Isn't it getting late?'

Lucas said: 'It's five minutes to four.'

Beryl said: 'Cora, all Lucas has to do is ride with us to the depot. Run in and pick up the ticket. Run it back out to the taxi. He'll be OK and I'll ride him back here before Don comes home. Then it's over. Done. That's what we all want.

'Otherwise… If she doesn't go, she's gotta stay. Who wants that?'

'Somebody's gotta get away,' repeated Marilyn. 'Why not me?'

Mom's wet eyes drilled into Lucas.

'Don't you do anything else! Don't you get hurt! Don't you… Just don't. And let me tell your father. Don't you say anything to anyone about this ever *ever*!'

Beryl scurried to the kitchen and the *order a ticket* phone on the wall.

Across the room in her chair, Marilyn smiled a ruby smile.

Lucas had to grin, too. *This is all so wild and cool!*

Beryl backed the blue taxi out of the garage with Lucas watching.

His aunt said: 'You ride up front.'

Marilyn lay flat on the backseat, a big purse on the floor beside her.

Beryl told Lucas: 'We gotta show me riding you around town.'

Lucas rode in the front seat of a blue taxi cruising through the streets of Vernon. KRIP radio played an old Elvis song.

Aunt Beryl randomly drove past Hal's house. Parked across from that teenager's home was a rusty station wagon. Lucas saw Mrs Ruth Klise behind that car's steering wheel. Just sitting there. Watching Hal's house.

Aunt Beryl skirted the edge of Main Street to drive over the viaduct's arch bridging fifty feet above the railroad tracks.

'Look out west,' she told Lucas. 'You see the train coming?'

Steel rails stretched across the prairie to Vernon. Box cars waited on side spurs. But the tracks that ran through town toward tomorrow were empty.

'Good,' said Beryl. 'We still got time.'

She drove past the white-walled depot to the adjoining red gravel lot. Parked facing the steel rails at the spot just before where the engineer would stop his locomotive, though most of his passengers would get off or board from the farther-away white depot's weathered gray-planked platform.

Lying on the backseat, Marilyn slid her green dress up her leg to the top of her garter-belted stocking. Greenback bills bulged between the top of her nylon stocking and the flesh of her thigh. Marilyn slid a wad free. Held it toward Lucas.

He swallowed. Filled his shaking hand with the cash.

The painted smile of the woman on the car's backseat said: "*I trust you.*"

Somebody's gotta get away, thought Lucas. *Why not her?*

Beryl said: 'Do it simple. Say nothing you don't have to. And hurry.'

He ran to the depot's door handle, pulled – *wrong way* – pushed and was *in* with the overhead tinkle of a bell.

The depot waiting room was a box of sounds. The whir of the ceiling fan. From beyond a wooden counter came the *clickety-click* of a telegraph key and the clatter of a typewriter. From a brown bench came the muffled cough of a white-haired old man in a black suit, his chin on his cane. '*Shh,*' said a young woman as she paced the wood floor cradling a baby. '*Shh.*'

The big clock on the wall declared official train time as 4:14, only sixteen minutes *until*.

Mrs Sweeny clung to the ticket window bars caging a green-visored clerk.

'You're not listening to me, young man!' Mrs Sweeny told the clerk.

'We all hear what you're saying, ma'am,' answered the stony-faced clerk.

The old man leaning on his cane smiled.

'*Shh*,' said the mother to her baby. '*Shh*.'

The big clock on the wall read 4:15.

Hunchbacked Mrs Sweeny gripped the ticket cage bar. 'Do I understand you to mean something by that?'

'Probably not. All I'm trying to do is help if'n you're here to buy a ticket.'

'What I'm here for is due respect. Proper treatment.'

'Yes, ma'am. Respect is something that's due.'

'Respect is something you earn. Like a ticket.'

'You're the customer.'

'And the customer is always right.'

'If you're a customer, I've got tickets to sell, and time—'

'Time is money,' snapped Mrs Sweeny. 'My money. Coming into a batch of it that's long overdue. Buying a ticket to Minneapolis. Going to my cousin's daughter and her family. Told them their prayers were answered. That I can finally afford to visit them for Thanksgiving. Wrote them. Won't phone. Long distance phone calls are priced almost as much of a scandal as your tickets.'

Lucas trembled. *The clock says the train will be here in fourteen minutes!*

'The price is the price,' said the clerk in his cage.

Mrs Sweeny *humphed*. 'I won't pay that.'

'Your choice, ma'am. But now if you'll excuse—'

'What are you going to do about that?'

Lucas shook like he had to go pee.

'My job is to sell tickets, not change the fares.'

'I might have to write a letter about this.'

'Great idea. If you step over to the counter there, Mr Poirer'll give you the address of the home office. And I'll help my other customers.'

'Other customers?' Her claw tightened on the window cage. She cranked her hunchbacked frame around. Saw Lucas behind her. 'He's just a child!'

Twelve minutes!

The clerk grabbed a silver microphone. Flipped its switch that amplified his voice through the train station.

'*Your attention please!*'

The old man in the black suit. A mother with a babe in her arms. Lucas. Mrs Sweeny. Only five members of the public stood in Vernon, Montana's, small train depot as the clerk's voice boomed out like New York City's Grand Central Station.

'*Now selling tickets for today's train. Today's train only, please.*'

The clerk turned the mic away from his face and his normal-toned voice said: 'Mrs Sweeny, are you buying a ticket for this train?'

'What?'

'Then I'm afraid I have to ask you to step aside.' He smiled. 'You heard the official announcement.'

The whistle blast of a barreling-close train tore through the depot.

Mrs Sweeny stepped away from the ticket cage. Her eyes blazed at Lucas.

The wooden floor shook and the room rumbled.

The ticket clerk fanned the stack of dollar bills Lucas thrust to him.

'Beryl called,' said the clerk.

Handed Lucas two dollars' change and a stiff paper ticket inked CHICAGO.

Lucas jerked the station door open, the *ding* of its bell lost beneath the blare of a coming-fast train whistle.

A roaring orange passenger train chased the running boy. He ran alongside the tracks. Ran with arms pumping, hand clutching a ticket.

The engineer blew the train whistle.

The kid raced toward the parked blue taxi with the orange steel train monster on his heels. Lucas leapt into that blue car. Flung himself into the shotgun seat, where Aunt Beryl sat behind the wheel staring at the windshield as the orange locomotive squealed to a halt in front of the blue taxi. Air brakes hissed. Passenger cars clunked together. The train shuddered still and silent.

Lucas let his eyes close as his head hit the back of the car seat. His left hand triumphantly held up $2.00 in change and the get-out-of-town ticket.

A man's voice in the backseat said: '*Kid*.'

The backseat man plucked the ticket from Lucas's hand.

'Chicago,' read the man in the back of the blue taxi. 'Ice pick city.'

He balanced the ticket on the ridge of the cab's front seat.

The rearview mirror caught it all: a handsome black-haired, dark-eyed man sat in the backseat right behind driver Beryl and beside the rigid woman in the green dress and lipstick colored like the blood drained from her face.

Lucas whispered: 'Uncle Johnny.'

'What is this, the summer you keep stepping in the shit?'

'Guess so.'

'Guessin' don't make it. Ya gotta know. Or do it so tough that it don't matter.'

Outside the blue taxi, a uniformed attendant climbed down from the train. Put a stepstool on the ground by an open door into a waiting passenger car.

'What's the two dollars you got in your hand?' said Uncle Johnny.

'Ch-change. Marilyn's change.'

'*Marilyn*?' Uncle Johnny whirled to the green-dress woman. 'You told them your name was *Marilyn*? You tricked out my family like they was johns?'

'Honest, I didn't—'

'You callin' my nephew a liar?'

The woman in the green dress sat absolutely still. Silent.

'You wanted to meet my family, shoulda asked,' drawled Uncle Johnny. 'Sitting there behind the steering wheel, not saying nothing, trying to figure out what game to play next: that's my wife Beryl. And beside her, the always-stepping-in-shit boy: that's my nephew Lucas.

'*Hey, family*: this liar in the green dress sitting beside me is *Arlene*.'

The train attendant looked at the blue taxi. Looked away.

'Ain't nobody going to say: "*How you doing?*"' asked Uncle Johnny. In the rearview mirror, he shook his head. 'Whatever happened to polite society?'

The train ticket wobbled on the top of the taxi's front seat.

'The two bucks is your vig,' Uncle Johnny told Lucas. 'You earned it.'

Lucas's hand had been stuck up in the air with the money in it ever since Uncle Johnny grabbed the ticket. Lucas let his arm fall. Dropped the money.

'I said put them bucks in your pocket.'

Lucas crammed the bills in his jeans.

His jostling shook the car seat, but the ticket didn't fall.

'Leave him alone, Johnny,' said Beryl.

'He ain't alone though, is he?' said her husband. With a smile. 'Whose doing is that, do you figure? Who's going to pick up the chit for that?'

'Nobody owes you nothing. Not him. Not me. I drive your damn cab.'

'How much you figure this trip costs?'

No one answered him.

Far off down at the depot, the old man in the black suit got on the train.

'Speaking of what's worth what and who owes who, *Arlene…*'

'Johnny, don't be like this, you gotta under—'

'I be like *I* want and I *understand* how if somebody cops money, then makes a deal to pay it back with interest, but then tries to get on a train like she promised she wouldn't—'

'It's just luck, Johnny!' said Arlene. 'I had busted luck.'

'Nobody gives a shit what you had. What you got now is a stone promise to be-right people and your fat ass on the backseat of my taxi.

'But looky here,' said Uncle Johnny. 'Balancing right there on the seat: a train ticket. Just sitting there. Waiting for somebody to grab it.'

A soldier hurried off the train.

Swept the woman with the baby into his arms.

Uncle Johnny said: 'Hey, Arlene. Do you think you can make it? Get on the train? An' if you did, you think there's any phone lines from here to wherever?'

Arlene whispered: 'Give me a break, Johnny!'

'Sure. All you gotta do is grab the ticket. Get out of the cab. Walk the walk.'

The blue-uniformed attendant on the platform checked his pocket watch.

In the rearview mirror, Uncle Johnny smiled like a knife.

The train whistle blew.

'*Kid*: get the fuck gone. You got nothing to say to nobody. Not here. Not uptown. Nowhere. Never. Not even good-bye. And remember,' said Uncle Johnny, 'I'll see you later.'

The attendant waiting on the platform saw a boy rocket out of the blue taxi, run in front of the locomotive, and disappear on the other side of the train.

Made it! thought Lucas when he reached a backstreet parking lot separated from the depot by a half dozen rails and the hissing passenger train.

Main Street waited behind Lucas.

The orange passenger train stretched out in front of him.

The train whistle blasted.

The passenger cars *clunked* like links of a chain suddenly pulled tight.

A scream cut the air.

Just the whistle, thought Lucas. The train whistle.

Steel wheels rolled.

Lucas pulled the two green bills out of his pocket. *Two dollars!* That's twenty Cokes at the Whitehouse or four Special Edition Batman or Green Lantern comic books, all gotten without smelling like Neal's painting jobs.

The train surged eastward. Picked up speed and added its *whoosh* to the July wind brushing Lucas's bare arms.

Orchids.

The heavy *sticky* smell of orchids perfuming this day from the bills he held.

He remembered Laura on the highway saying *no* to getting stuck there.

If he kept the money, that orchid smell would stick to him.

He opened his grip.

Watched two green dollars flutter into the wake of the orange passenger train. The caboose flew past him, *clickety-clacking* toward the border of town. Nothing blocked Lucas's view across the tracks.

Mrs Sweeny stood on the platform, scowling in the afternoon sun.

The soldier walked away with his arm around his wife and baby.

Farther down the tracks stood no blue taxi.

Lucas knew that on that going-*gone* train was no one named Marilyn or Arlene or Elvis.

… AND THE LIVING IS EASY

August brings the big heat to the northern high plains where Lucas lived.

Oh sure, you hang up your jean jacket in June. And July's sun can zap your energy. But the big heat, the thick baking heat, *that* comes in August.

Nobody wants rain. Not in August when the big heat needs to ripen fields of wheat tall and golden for red harvest machines with spinning blades. Farmers drive those combines. Guillotine acres of wheat. Trucks haul the grain to skyscraper gray elevators for storage before trains carry the crops off to feed the world.

From the day school let out until after July's fair, Lucas heard people say: 'Hot enough for you?' or 'Wish it would rain.'

But come August, what folks around Vernon ask is: 'Think it'll rain?'

The answer is a prayer: 'Hope not!'

Rain stops wheat from ripening. Turns fields into bogs. Mildews crops. Delays harvest until something worse than rain comes along, like a lightning fire. Or swarms of grasshoppers who chew waving fields down to stubble.

Or the Dream Killer.

The Dream Killer stalks on hot August days.

Wispy gray threads swirl overhead. Then come thunderhead clouds that billow a mile high. The air goes from baking dry to steamy hot. Goes still.

Too still.

'*Watch the sky!*' warned Lucas's favorite horror movie *The Thing.*

Clouds warn of a coming Dream Killer.

Indigo monsters full of rain and rumbles and jagged lightning are bad enough. But when those clouds turn black on top of gray, murder is in the air.

Out of the stillness blasts the Dream Killer's wind.

Dust whirls on the streets. Trees sway. Traffic lights on Main Street herky-jerky on their cables. The corner stop sign shakes, rattles, and rolls.

Wham! Crashing down come a billion ice pellets the size of peas. The size of marbles. Ice chunks the size of *golf balls!*

Hailstorms are crazy. One farmer's fields are untouched. His neighbor's crop is wiped out. Gone, a whole year's mortgaged work. A whole crop. A whole dream murdered in the time it takes to hard-boil an egg.

Lucas rode in the backseat of Neal's green car on that August Tuesday.

Stuck his head out the car window and looked up.

Nothing but blue sky.

'Careful your glasses don't fall off,' said Jordan Smith from the front seat.

She was right – *of course she was right.* His glasses flew off as he jerked his head back inside the car, but Lucas caught them.

He looked out the rear window with his bare eyes. Saw the endlessly receding highway. The farther back Lucas focused, the blurrier his vision became. But he knew the dark dot behind their car was not a hailstorm on the horizon.

He put his glasses on. Looked to the front seat where Neal Dylan drove. Where Jordan Smith sat in the passenger's seat. Where the windshield filled with the highway leading out of town under a clear blue sky of the big heat.

Hal rode in the backseat beside Lucas. *Click!* went the baby-shit-yellow pen Hal held, over and over again. Lucas ached to throw it out the car window like you did with hamburger wrappers and Coke cups to watch them bounce across the prairie because there's endless land where the trash just fades way.

Lucas hated that damn clicking baby-shit-yellow pen.

Wish I'd never gotten it in the first place!

Last night.

Dad came home from work.

Mom said: 'It's too hot to cook.'

So the family went out to dinner at the newly air-conditioned Dixie Inn.

White-uniformed waitress Mrs Fisher padded menus to their table.

Laura sighed while Mom was explaining to Lucas how a slab of beef could be a '*chicken* fried steak' when a man's voice called out:

'Well, looky here! It's the whole Ross clan!'

Walking into the dining room came Dad's boss Alec and his wife.

And their daughter! Fran's blouse stretched over her basketball belly.

'Hey, Laura!' said Fran. 'How you doing?'

'Ah... OK. How are—'

'Me? Pregnant!' Fran led everyone in laughter. 'But not for much longer!'

Alec Marshall's hands jiggled coins in his pockets. 'We figured we better get these kids out for dinner while they still got the chance.'

Dad said: 'So I see.'

But his eyes were only on the leer of the man behind Alec. On Ben Owens.

Who held a shiny *Big City* black briefcase.

'Evening, Don,' Ben told the man who was his boss, who worked for his father-in-law. 'Hey, Lucas. Haven't seen you around much.'

'I got other jobs. Painting. Door-to-door handbills for the Roxy.'

Coins jiggled in Alec's pocket. 'Good for you, Lucas. Good for you. That's just what a young man's gotta be, isn't it, Don? Ambitious.'

'That's part of it.' Dad stared at Briefcase Ben: 'Thought you were on dispatch phone.'

Alec said: 'See, Ben? A good man always has his eye on the ball.'

'Or on me.' Ben chuckled like he meant some kind of a joke.

No one laughed.

'Don't worry, Don,' said Alec. 'When the missus came up with taking the kids out, I called Adele. She's on the phone. So relax. Everything's jim-dandy.'

'Glad to hear that.'

Alec told his wife: 'Hey, hon, take Fran over to that table, get the load off her feet.'

His *women folk* mumbled "See you!" to the Rosses. Walked to that faraway table. Left Alec and Briefcase Ben standing beside Dad.

'You gotta see this, Don,' said Alec. 'You too, Cora, kids. Show 'em, Ben.'

The son-in-law put the briefcase on the table.

That Important Work Papers bag gaped open like an alligator mouth.

Ben lifted a wall calendar for two years ago out of the briefcase.

'Different pictures for each month,' he said.

The calendar showed January. Above the sheet for the days and dates hung a picture of two dogs romping in a green field. Above that were huge black words: YOUR BUSINESS NAME HERE!

'You got your choice of themes,' said Ben. 'Regular animals. Or lions, tigers, other African stuff. Mountains. The ocean. I like the one that has monkeys dressed up like people playing poker.'

I know the perfect picture for a calendar! thought Lucas.

Alec chimed in: 'Ordered a bunch of those chimp ones for us to send out to our customers. "Marshall Trucking" with our phone number. Next year, they'll hang 'em on the walls of the gas stations, the refineries, think of us first.'

'Nobody else to think of for petro hauling around here,' said Dad.

'But a man's gotta be prepared for competition.' Ben grinned. 'You never know about the future.'

'No,' said Dad. 'You never do.'

'That's not all.' Ben handed Dad a baby-shit-yellow ballpoint pen that was lettered in red. 'Check this out.'

Dad read the pen's words out loud: 'Montana Madison Avenue Adverts.'

'And see?' said Ben. 'Got my name, phone number, and address. Not only a sample of pens we can make for customers, it's my *remember-me* calling card.'

'Are you quitting us to—'

Alec jiggled coins: 'Oh no! Can't let the guy do that with a little one about to pop out. Plus, we gotta have somebody on board to help you, Don.

'No,' said the man who owned Marshall Trucking. 'Way Ben here figures it, and sounds solid to me, this advertising gig is his outside line. Works out great with what you got him doing. Days, he's not handlin' much anyway. That wouldn't be fair, working full days plus being the nights and weekends dispatch guy.'

'I've worked running things all day *and* the nights plus weekend stuff all these years,' said Dad.

'There you go,' said Alec. 'Then you know how much it is for one guy. Plus, he doesn't have your experience at juggling things.'

'Seems to be juggling real well.'

Lucas saw Ben's smile slip. Saw it curl back.

'Anyway,' said Alec, 'now that you're freed up with him on board, you got more time to do the big stuff. He can take his advertising orders from home. When he goes on the road – day trips only, he won't be leaving Fran and the little one alone, plus there's our dispatch phone – when he goes out to make deliveries, scout sales prospects in towns around here, he'll check in on our customers.'

'He's going to show up at our customers? Wearing two hats? Will he try to sell them this… his… promotional stuff?'

'Oh yeah,' said Alec. 'He's smart enough to work that, too.'

'Guess he is,' said Dad.

'We're lucky there,' said Alec. 'Like Falk explained, him doing that traveling to see our customers squares us with the tax boys for his car and such.'

'When you look at it,' said Ben, 'you see the smart moves.'

'Is that what you see?' Dad's voice was flat.

Ben nodded. 'That's a good pen. Let me know how you like it.'

'No thanks,' said Dad, handing it back. 'I already got one.'

Ben yelled: 'Lucas!'

Tossed the pen into the air in front of the boy.

Caught it! thought Lucas. *I actually caught it!*

The smart moves man said: 'A guy can always use a good clicker.'

'Thanks!' said Lucas. Because saying that was The Right Thing To Do.

'Come on, Ben,' said Alec as he led the young man away. 'Let's get fed.'

The waitress lumbered over to the Rosses. 'You guys know what you want?'

Dad whispered: 'Order something now! Right now!'

Jukebox music from the bar drifted into the dining room. A new guy named Johnny Cash sang: 'Don't Take Your Guns to Town.'

A diner called over to Alec: 'Think it'll rain?'

The waitress brought the Rosses' dinners.

Dad shoveled food into him before she'd finished passing out the plates. Mom snatched her fork to spear a bite twice the size she normally took. Laura shot her eyes at Lucas, and it was like he could hear her scream: '*Go! Eat fast!*'

The waitress sashayed over when Dad beckoned.

Frowned at their plates. 'That was quick. Y'all must have been starved.'

Dad said: 'Yes, well, we gotta hit the road now, so if you've got the check…'

'It's your lucky night.' The waitress grinned. 'Alec already picked it up. Tip, too, so don't go leavin' nothing on the table, you hear?'

She leaned over the table. Winked. Whispered: 'Wish I had a boss like that.'

Padded away.

Dad didn't watch her go. Didn't look over to the table from which came murmurs of a story Fran was telling about her college sorority. Didn't look at Mom. At Laura. At Lucas. At anything Lucas could see.

Whoosh as Dad stood. Chairs scraped as Mom, Laura, and Lucas rocketed to their feet with him. He stared to the table in the back corner.

Called out: 'Thank you, Alec.'

Mom and Laura and Lucas chorused: 'Thank you!'

Alec had a mouth full of steak, waved his hand. 'Don't mention it.'

'Well,' said Dad, 'thank you again.'

They drove away from that diner in the company's black station wagon.

'Lucas!' said Dad. 'Get rid of that damn pen.'

But he couldn't just throw it out the car window as they drove home. That would be a waste. And like Mom said, with babies starving in China, wasting is wrong. So the next morning when Neal called him with the work surprise, Lucas took the baby-shit-yellow pen and gave it to Hal.

Who took it with them in the green car.

Who sat beside him in the backseat.

Who wouldn't stop *clicking*.

Driver Neal pointed across the road. 'Look over there.'

The pyramid skeleton of an oil drilling rig rose toward the arching sky from farmland dirt. Lucas spotted a blue pickup parked next to a stack of pipes.

And just *knew*.

'Think they'll hit oil?' said Neal as the rig receded behind them.

Lucas grinned. '*Naw*.'

'Hal,' said Jordan, 'let's listen to the radio instead of you clicking.'

She turned the radio knob.

Hammered her fist on the dashboard.

In the rearview mirror, Lucas saw Neal's reflection wink at him.

The radio blared on with the disk jockey from KRIP radio.

'… just got a call from Dan Moldea, who says the weather is still looking good east of town. Looking good all around our four-county listening area.

'And that reminds me. I'm wondering if you folks saw the picture in the newspaper yesterday. The first picture of earth taken from outer space. *Man, that's something!* And if they can do it again in a few weeks, that picture will show that we got a new state for America. After Alaska joined up with us back in January of this year, Hawaii about to join in gives us fifty – Five Oh – states. We're going places, folks, and it's looking good.

'All of which kinda leads me up to a song I'm gonna play for you. That singer Billie Holiday died a couple weeks ago back in New York, but all the good news we got going on today reminds me of my favorite song by her, a classic tune that you gotta admit she does a fine job with for a colored gal.'

The radio scratched as a needle dropped into a groove on

a black record spinning on a turntable in Vernon, Montana, America, with soon-to-be fifty states.

Then came *that voice*:

'Summer-time, and the livin' is e-asy…'

Lucas, Hal, and two teachers peered out their car windows.

'Hey,' said Lucas. 'Do you guys know that Miss – I mean *Jordan* – did you know that she for real got to see that Billie Holiday?'

'No!' said the driver, but the sly look he shot to the woman sitting near him made Lucas wonder. 'I didn't know that. You two been keeping secrets from me?'

'If we tell you,' said Jordan, 'they won't be secrets.'

Neal's eyes in the rearview mirror watched Lucas. 'What do you think about Jordan getting to see somebody famous and important like Billie Holiday?'

'Cool.' Lucas frowned. 'Miss – *Jordan*: I didn't get it when they said it, but… the radio said she was colored. What color was she?'

Car wheels hummed over the highway.

Jordan said: 'Blue. A woman, the songs she sang, she's blue.'

Car wheels hummed on a two-lane black highway in August 1959.

'Lucas,' said Neal. 'Do you think it matters what color somebody is?'

The youngest boy in the backseat shrugged. 'Only if they're sick.'

'That's right,' said the driver. 'That's right.'

Polka music played on the radio as they drove toward the river hills.

Neal waved to a man driving a tractor along the barbwire fence beside the highway. The tractor pulled a duck-foot plow scraping dark furrows in the tan field near neighboring fields where ripening wheat waved in the breeze.

The tractor jockey lifted his cap off his bald head to return Neal's wave.

Jordan smiled at Neal. 'You know everybody around here, Hometown?'

Lucas blurted: 'I know him, too! I'm just as hometown!'

'Lou Herbst is a good man, isn't he, Lucas?' said Neal.

'Sure,' said Lucas.

'Is he related to you like the rest of the town?' asked Jordan.

'No, he goes to the same church as we do. When we got to go. He, with Mrs Sweeny, Mr Herbst rescued me on Easter Sunday.'

Car seat springs creaked beside Lucas.

Horror shook Lucas. *Easter Sunday, Mrs Sweeny, who had the car 'fore it got gas tank sugared, Hal and Earl… and I had to go and say EASTER SUNDAY!*

The car crawled over the big heat highway.

The radio broadcast hog reports.

Jordan finally said: 'Think it'll rain?'

As their car reached the crest of the river hill, Neal said: 'I hope not.'

The highway sloped down the river breaks toward a bridge. Chessboard farm fields gave way to uncultivated slopes and a wide valley floor. Unlike the prairie, the river valley grew thick with trees. Cottonwoods. Ash. Weeping willows drooping over flowing water called the Grady River.

Neal put on the left turn blinker. Steered off the highway to a gravel road. When Lucas looked back, all he saw was their dust cloud.

They drove past the sign reading: MUNICIPAL PICNIC GROUNDS.

Neal hadn't told Lucas exactly where they were all going when he phoned him that morning with the change of plans.

'Hal's mom is worried. Doc and Sheriff Wood, too. And us, Jordan. After that… dustup at the fair, Hal hasn't stepped foot out of his house.

'One thing we agree on is he's gotta go back down to the river. It's always going to be there. And it will get harder to face the longer he takes to see it again. And we could use your help.'

Now all four of them drove a graveled road between the valley hills and the wall of trees bordering the river.

No one else is out here, thought Lucas. Not on a big heat workday.

The tire track trail led into a grove of trees. Shaded river air cooled the big heat. The car engine shut off. The four of them climbed out. Neal opened the trunk. Lifted out an ice chest. Jordan grabbed the picnic basket and blankets. Hal put the library books, his notebook, and that damn baby-shit-yellow pen in a cardboard box. Lucas slammed the trunk.

Neal led them through the trees. The car vanished behind them. Sounds of the gurgling river grew louder. The light of the day flickered greens and browns and dappled blue sky. They walked through perfumes of tree bark and leaves. Reached the open glade center of a U bend in the river. Where the river came from and where it was going curved around them.

Jordan spread blankets on shaded ground where rainbowed gravel bordered the forty-foot-wide silver river.

Tuna fish sandwiches from Lucas's mother. Jordan brought a flat of fresh cherries. Neal handed out green Coke bottles. Hal passed around the tin of homemade chocolate chip cookies from his mom.

'Here's the deal, Hal,' Neal told him. 'Mr Dart says you can make up the classes you missed if you do projects for both biology and earth science. You need to get them done before school starts, or you won't be caught up with the others in your class who will all be seniors.'

'I don't do good in science,' said Hal.

'Me either,' said Jordan. 'But learning it helps us figure out other stuff.'

Neal said: 'Mr Dart's plan. You've got to do the work. Today. Now. Science is a two-parter,' he said. 'From right here, collect thirty rocks. Take that white tape. Number each rock. Sketch out the land. Note on the sketch where you found the rock. We'll take the rocks back in that box. Hammer a few open so the library book on geology will help you figure out what kind they are.'

'Bustin' up rocks,' said Hal. 'Kind of like those chain gang movies.'

'Choosing these rocks is about you getting free,' said Neal.

Hal sent his eyes to the river flowing behind the teachers.

'Jordan came up with the biology project,' said Neal.

'It's not just biology,' she said. 'Nothing in life ever is. And it's not so original.' Jordan gave the boys a half-smile. 'Nothing in life ever is. Everything in every moment is new and unique but still the same as.'

'That doesn't make much sense,' said Hal.

'Don't worry: you don't need to figure out the universe to make it through high school. I got the idea for your project from Thoreau. You know who he was?'

'Some weird guy who went out and lived alone.'

'Close enough for now,' said Jordan. 'We're adapting his method. Instead of a pond called Walden, we've got this bend in the Grady River, and instead of two years, we've got a slice of today.

'Pick a spot to be. After you do the rocks, choose a certain amount of time.'

'Say a full hour,' said Neal. 'It's what we've got.'

Jordan focused on Hal.

'Make a journal of all the life you see from your spot. Bugs. Ants that come for picnic crumbs. Fish jumping in the river. Don't just use your eyes. If you hear a frog, that counts. Count the birds. List the plants and trees. That book on trees has pictures. Even if you don't know what to call something, write it down. Maybe you won't figure out its real name, but you can't ignore what's there.'

'Lucas,' said Neal, 'you've got a watch. You'll be Hal's timer.'

'Can I help him spot stuff?'

'No, but you can help him collect the rocks.'

'What about when I'm timing him just sitting there? For a whole hour!'

Jordan said: 'Did you bring that new book I got you from the library?'

'Yeah.' Lucas wouldn't say *Dandelion Wine*, a title about drinking, in front of Hal. *I'm not going to screw up like that again.* 'By that berry-something guy.'

Jordan laughed.

'Nobody remembers authors, but that's OK. It's the story that matters.'

Lucas said: 'What about you guys?'

'We'll take a walk by the river,' said Neal. 'You guys will be fine here. Stay right here, Hal. That'll take care of Mr Dart's worry that we'd do too much of the work for you. Can't do it if we're not here.'

'See you later,' said Jordan as the teachers left the boys standing on the river shore, Lucas by the cardboard box, Hal with pen and notebook in hand.

'Yell if you need us,' said Neal as they walked away into the trees.

When they were gone, Lucas told Hal: 'Point to a rock and I'll get it.'

As Lucas taped the fourth rock, Hal said: 'Do you think I'll pass the test?'

'What test?' Lucas dropped rock #4 into the cardboard box.

'You think coming out here is about rocks and birds and trees?' Hal shook his head. 'This is a test to see if I'll run off or go crazy or wild or bad.'

'Will you?'

'Who knows?' Hal shook his head. 'Nobody knows nothing about nothing.'

'That's why Jordan and Neal are teaching you.'

'Is *teaching* what's going on around here? With them?' Hal stared at the ten-year-old boy standing by the river. 'You really are just a kid. A good kid.

'Look at all this "out here" I'm supposed to write down in my notebook,' said Hal. 'It all looks like… like a blurry dream.'

'Looks like that when I don't wear my glasses,' said Lucas. 'Maybe you need to go see Dr Bond on Main Street.'

'They got no doctor for me.'

Lucas pointed to a blue rock in the shallow water. Hal said nothing. Lucas fetched the blue rock. Rubbed it dry on his white T-shirt. Stuck a piece of white tape on it. Took the baby-shit-yellow pen from Hal to write #5 on the tape. Put the rock in the cardboard box. Showed Hal where to write #5 on the sketch and gave him that damn pen.

Just get it done, thought Lucas. *Help him get through doing it*.

Lucas picked out rock #6. Rock #7. Stone #8.

When Lucas brought him rock #9, a slab of quartz crystal, Hal said:

'I miss Earl. Do you remember how he always laughed?'

'Yes,' said Lucas.

The river gurgled over stones.

What Lucas said about remembering Earl's laugh was a lie. Lies are wrong. The lie filled Lucas's mouth and stomach and heart with acid. But Lucas didn't know how else to get Hal on to the next rock. And the next. And the next.

'Enough,' said Hal.

'We've only got six to go!'

'You think one stone more or less makes any difference?'

'Yes!'

'Like I said, just a kid.'

'So are you! Sure, you're older and can toss me in the river, but you're no grown-up! You don't know.'

'School doesn't help anything.'

'Come on,' said Lucas after he'd picked, labeled, sketched, and stored thirty rocks. 'Sit on the blanket. I'll start timing and you look for life. You gotta.'

'Why? Because that will change the world? Because it'll fix what happened?'

'I don't know why. I'm a kid! But I know it's true and—

'*And you got to do it for me!*' yelled Lucas. 'Because working with you, making it all work, *that's my job* and that's what should be. I promised to help you and I want to and can't let bad happen 'cause I promised. Took the job. I can't *not* do my job. That's not right. That's wrong. Don't make me do wrong!'

The river tumbled over a billion trillion rocks they'd left out of the box.

Hal stared at the just-a-kid in the scuffed sneakers, blue jeans, dirt-streaked white T-shirt. Stared into those eyes behind thick-lensed glasses.

Said: 'I don't have the stomach for making somebody do wrong.'

'So then you'll do it. Do it all.'

'Guess that's our new deal. The *real* deal. Guess I gotta do this for you. But one thing,' said Hal. 'Do I gotta do it with you sitting there staring at me? We're friends and got a deal, but to have even your eyes on me like… like a cop waiting to catch me, lock me up, and no way is that our deal.'

'All I'm gonna do is say "ready, set, go." And tell you when to stop, but by then Jordan and Neal will be back. I got a book. I won't be watching you.'

'Feels like it. If it feels like it, then it is. Or might as well be.'

'OK, I'll go off and poke around. It's cool down here.'

Hal let his eyes scan the green walls surrounding them.

'Go the way they did, downstream. Be careful. If you mess up, find the river. Follow it upstream. If they show up and you're not here—'

'I'll tell them I had to go pee. Heck, it's true.'

'Yeah,' said Hal. '*True* really matters.'

Lucas waited until Hal sat on the blanket, notebook on his lap, that baby-shit-yellow pen in his hand, his eyes on the gurgling silver river.

Lucas checked his watch: 2:09 on a big heat day.

Announced: '*Ready… Set… Go!*'

Walked into the stand of trees along the river.

Above Lucas hung a patchwork of dark leaves and blue sky. He climbed over a log. Walked around twisted deadfall. The river was maybe twenty yards through the thick growth off to his right. He could hear it, so he wasn't lost.

A sudden sense of joy swept him up.

This is a cool place! Wish I was down here with Marin and Kurt and Wayne. Running around screaming. Leaping over logs. We could play soldier! War!

Lucas sighted an imaginary rifle. Swept his aims across the ranks of white-barked aspens. Thought: *Here could be the place in Dad's newspaper where Bad Guys killed our soldiers in a movie theater! The place in our school report.*

This is Viet Nam and we're the good guys!

Lucas hurdled a log. Ran zigzag. Jumped behind a big tree. Shapes flitted in shadows. Bullets zipped past Lucas's tree. He ripped a blast from his machine gun.

Crept forward. Parted branches. Eased saplings aside. Stayed silent as he moved through the green veil between him and the shimmering river.

Voices. Somewhere beyond the leaves.

Real voices, Lucas told himself as he strained to hear them.

Slowly, oh so slowly, Lucas pushed his face into a web of branches between him and the river where the voices flowed. Leaves brushed his cheeks, tickled his nose. He refused to sneeze. A twig pressed a line on his forehead.

The lenses of his glasses emerged from the underbrush and let him see:

Jordan Smith and Neal Dylan stood on a swirl of gravel at the river's edge.

Stood close together. Face to face.

Neal held her hands by their sides.

Light shimmered off the rippling river.

Lucas heard their murmurs, not their words.

Jordan's black hair had grown over the summer. She needed to brush it off her face. Yet when her hand floated up from Neal's grasp, it went not to brush her own cheeks, but to caress his.

Lava roared through Lucas.

Neal leaned forward.

And Jordan, *oh Jordan*, she tilted her perfect face up for that kiss.

A mute howl tore through the trees along the Grady River.

A stubble-cheeked enemy soldier charged Lucas. Speared his bayonet into Lucas's chest. Pinned the limp boy on his rifle bayonet. The evil soldier squeezed the rifle's trigger. BLAM! Point blank. The bullet knocked Lucas off the bayonet. Slammed him flat on his back on the jungle floor. Heaven laughed.

Blink and they were still there.

Jordan and Neal by the river. Pressed together. Her hands held his face to their kiss. His hands cupped her ebony-tressed skull.

I'm so small, thought Lucas. *A dopey kid hiding in the bushes. With glasses. Seeing what I wouldn't see before.* The closed back door on a brown house. A green car hidden in the alley. This look and that laugh. A pissed-off, coffee-drinking wife. *Everybody knows. Everybody knew. But me.*

Back, Lucas eased back. The veil of leaves covered his glasses. He tiptoed back the way he'd come. Quietly moved under the sound of the tumbling river.

Sexing. They're sexing each other here by the river and how could she! Neal, of course, any guy who could get so lucky to… How could she? Didn't she know? Neal's married! Rita. Baby Rachel. The *Thou Shalt Not*. He's going to hell. But Jordan. Not her fault. Must not be her fault.

My fault.

Lucas walked out of the underbrush to the garden of trees.

My fault. If I wasn't so me. Just a dopey little kid. If I was somebody bigger. Better. Older. Smarter. Cooler. Tougher. For her. Then, oh, only if-then!

But there is no *if-then.*

Not a kid anymore, he thought:

Walk on. Through the trees. Be a soldier. You're a soldier.

Lucas lifted his glasses off his face. Wiped away his dopey tears. Jammed those damn glasses back on tight. Focused on the dusty trail in front of him.

Saw the earth move.

First it looked like a rope flicking in the dust of the trail.

And close, real close.

But not a rope. Thicker than a rope. Sinewy like a whip curling into an *S* that spiraled closer, spinning into a coil of circles. A mound rose out of the dust right in front of him with one tip swaying shin-high off the ground and the other tip vibrating that bone-certain buzzing sound like sand shaking in a can.

Rattlesnake.

Lucas's mouth went dry as the dust where the rattlesnake coiled.

Don't move.

Everyone who grew up in Montana knew Do Not Move.

What Lucas saw was worse than what he'd expected.

On those high plains, what slid through the yellow scrub grass, what ambushed mice and gophers and even rabbits, what ate beetles and fed hawks, what dropped into deep badger holes for the winter and curled into balls with a hundred of its own kind to hibernate until robins sang, what Lucas had expected to see *if-and-when* he heard that sand-in-a-can rattle was the prairie rattlesnake, a dusky serpent not much thicker than a broomstick and seldom longer than a yardstick. With venom sacs that could drop a cow or buy a man's coffin, *sure,* but especially in these modern times of hospitals stocked with anti-venoms, even a bad snake bite left you with a good chance of getting up and going on.

If it was a common prairie rattlesnake.

DO NOT MOVE.

Bzzzzztt!

Because nothing was common about this snake.

Instead of a yardstick long, he was longer than most men. Coil upon coil of muscle and bone that was thicker than Lucas's calf in his thin jeans no more than one *Mother-May-I* step from that serpent swaying off the ground. Forget about dusky. Call the serpent reddish-brown, scaled skin patterned with interlocked point-to-point shapes that gave this snake its name.

Diamondback.

Maps in library books shaded the Western Diamondback's original domain from Mexico to Canada, west to the Rockies and east to the Mississippi where gamblers floated on paddle-wheeled steamboats.

But, said those books, since government investigators Lewis and Clark tramped that earth for the Louisiana Purchase, since the slaughter of the buffaloes and the *reservationing* of the Indians, since cars and towns took over that territory, since atom bomb tests blasted the deserts of Nevada, the turf ruled by Diamondbacks had shrunk, dwindled, pulled away from even remote outposts of civilization like Vernon, Montana, and the Grady River valley.

That probably pissed off this snake, thought Lucas.

DON'T MOVE!

Because a Diamondback is big-time death. Poison sacs behind that wedge-shaped head carry a toxin stronger than the Diamondback's prairie cousin and squirt more of it through inch-long fangs. A Diamondback strikes like a boxer's jab, forty pounds of coiled snake ramming into you, injecting a double dose of nerve-frying juice that burns through your blood to your heart, to your brain.

If he bites my leg, I've got a chance, thought Lucas. Scream. Hal/Neal/Jordan will charge to the rescue. Scoop him up and rush him to the hospital in Vernon. They'd yell at him to KEEP CALM. Carry him to keep his heart from pumping faster, from pumping the poison deeper in him.

But if the snake struck high, if it bit him in the chest, the neck, his face, slammed into his groin and hung there like… If the snake did that, struck him two, three times or more, nailing him with multiple big doses…

I'll die. Today. Now.

Though it was a dumb thing to think of then and there, Lucas wondered if Jordan would lean over his dying body and cry, knowing she'd been wrong.

Click!

Don't flinch! Don't move. Don't look to those trees, that sound, that click.

Bzzztt!

Do snakes hear? No: vibrations, they pick up vibrations. Did that click vibrate enough to get the snake's attention? Is that why it rattled? Or was it me?

The snake's head swayed. Black marble-sized eyes. Flicking red tongue.

Branches crunched off to Lucas's left.

The Diamondback swung its flicking-tongue head to that crunching.

When the snake looked, so did Lucas. But only with his eyes.

There! Through a stand of trees, a dark shape in the forest shade:

A person crouched in those trees. That shape became a woman. She stepped over a log. Raised something, pointed it toward where Hal would be. Pointed it away from where Lucas stood frozen in front of a killer.

Here! Lucas ached to scream. *Look over here!*

But he made no sound. Sounds are vibrations. And snakes…

Click!

The snake's head swayed between Lucas and the distant rustling shape.

Mrs Klise! That's Mrs Klise! She's taking pictures with a camera!

Click!

Look over here! willed Lucas. *Not toward those trees and Hal.*

But Mrs Klise raised the camera to her face. *Clicked* off another picture. Crept through the woods toward the river bend beach where Hal would be recording signs of life. Four creeping steps and she vanished in the trees.

The Diamondback rattlesnake thought about it. Curled away from Lucas. Uncoiled like a fluid *S* flowing through the dust. Going, going, *gone.*

Lucas charged through the brush. Branches scraped his arms. Crashing through trees. Out of the woods. Onto the packed beach. Staggering five steps to where Hal sat on the blanket, notebook in his lap.

'*Lucas!* You see a damn ghost or—'

Laughing, they heard people laughing.

Around the bend in the river came Jordan and Neal wading in the water. They held their shoes in their hands.

Neal frowned at Lucas's frantic face. 'What's going on?'

'Snake! And Mrs Klise! Hiding in the trees. Taking pictures.'

Jordan whispered: 'Taking pictures of what?'

Of you breaking my heart! Lucas wanted to scream.

But he told the truth: 'Of Hal.'

Five minutes to pack up the car. They raced through the gravel wasteland in a ball of dust, teachers in the front seat, younger souls in the back.

Neal steered his bucking auto over the rough road. 'What do you see?'

'Nothing!' Jordan told him. 'Nobody's there. She's not there.'

They roared past the MUNICIPAL PICNIC GROUNDS sign. Rolled onto the oiled highway and raced north toward home.

Halfway up the river hill, Jordan looked behind them.

'There! She was on the other side of the bridge. That rusted station wagon. It's hers. Following us.'

'Me,' whispered Hal. 'Not *us*. She's following me.'

'Don't worry.' Neal's rearview mirror captured the trembling teenager. 'Don't look at her. Don't pay any attention to her. You're OK. Nobody look.'

But as they roared home through the big heat afternoon *not* looking, all that their minds' eyes could see was a rusted station wagon rolling after them.

As their green car hummed over the highway, they didn't see the workers on the oil derrick.

Nor did they notice the empty tractor parked in a field that whizzed past.

Even if they had noticed that chugging red machine, they couldn't have seen behind it to the figure sprawled on the ground. The figure of bald farmer Lou Herbst as he lay there, face up to the clear blue sky, stone dead.

HOW MAGIC WORKS

Minutes before she became the first person to slap Lucas, the woman who answered his morning knock on her front door frowned.

Said: 'Why are you here?'

She wore a black dress. Her feet were bare. Her nose was red.

Standing on her front stoop, Lucas sneezed.

Then so did she.

'Listen to us,' said Rita as she shuffled into her living room. 'Summer colds are the worst. An' we both got it. People will talk.'

Lucas stepped inside the house. The door shut behind him.

'Did I call you?' she said as she scooped a pack of cigarettes off a table.

'No.'

'Sorry about that. Should have called you, said you didn' need to come.'

'Yes, but Mrs – Rita.' Lucas sneezed.

Conjured up his rehearsal. Started *the speech*:

'You know, it's August now. Summer vacation is almost over, and—'

'Vacation?' Rita shook her head. 'You ever had one? A place where you get away? No matter where I am, it's always the same old crap. You got a match?'

'*Ooo-cus!*' Rachel toddled into the living room on pudgy bare feet. She wore a light blue, egg-stained shirt, a white diaper, and a drooly grin.

'Look at her,' said her mother. 'Walking and talking. How'd that happen?'

Lucas couldn't help himself. Met Rachel's grasping hands.

She wrapped herself around his leg. Laughed.

'What about a match?' said the mother in the room.

'I don't have any.'

'Now we got a problem.' Rita stared at the pack of cigarettes. 'While we're at it, check Miss Poopy Drawers. I can't smell nothing with this cold.'

Lucas pulled the diaper away from the toddler. Saw snow dust on her smooth pink bottom. *Good thing I looked. I can't even smell the baby powder.*

'She's clean,' he said. Cleared his throat. 'You know, it's August and summer vaca – *Achoo!*'

'You sound like me. Thought I'd go to the deal, but don't want to sneeze on ever'body.'

'Guess not.' Lucas eased Rachel away.

Rita shook a cigarette out of the pack.

Gestured like a symphony conductor with it held between two fingers.

Said: 'How come you didn't go to the funeral?'

Rachel looked way up. *Mommy's hand goes whoosh whoosh in the air!*

Lucas said: 'My parents said I didn't have to.'

'So we both lucked out. I hate funerals. Always sit in the back. On a pew behind someone tall so you can't see the coffin.'

Ooo-cus no play! Rachel pouted.

'Laying dead and waxy in a coffin's not how you want to see somebody for the last time.' Rita stabbed her unlit cigarette at the boy. 'Trust me on that.'

Picked a mug up from the coffee table.

'Best thing for what ails you,' she told Lucas. 'Now if I can just find a match so I can soothe my lungs and stop my skin itchin', we'll be doing fine.'

'I'll check the kitchen,' sighed Lucas.

The pale kitchen housed a wooden highchair. The white gas stove with its black meal-burner rings and round knobs. Sunlight streamed through the closed window above the sink. On the counter stood a brown-paper-sacked bottle.

Lucas turned from the counter—

—spotted Rachel toddling into the kitchen.

'Hey, Rache! Where you going?'

She waved her arms. Reached toward a brown box atop the refrigerator.

'You want a graham cracker?' Lucas yelled: 'Can I give her a—'

'Whatever,' said Rita in the living room. 'Find any matches?'

'Not yet.'

Rita *humphed*. 'What's a gal gotta do to get lit up?'

That woman of the house marched over to the silent brown box rising up from the living room floor like a stood-on-its-end child's coffin.

Came the *Click!* of the sparked-on radio.

Lucas handed a cracker to the bouncing girl. He had an urge to take one for himself. Taste the graham crunchiness his cold refused to let him smell.

But he had to launch The Plan.

'Look in the silverware drawer!' yelled Rita. 'Check in the cupboards!'

The radio played Hank Williams's twangy guitar singing 'Hey, Good Lookin'.'

Lucas checked the drawer. Stared into the cupboard. 'Don't see any!'

Rita yelled: 'There's gotta be matches somewhere in this God-damned house! *Umm*, when you come back in here, would you bring that sack on the counter with a bottle of medicine in it?'

Lucas knew what she meant.

Rachel sat on the kitchen floor, a chewed graham cracker

clutched in both hands as Lucas took the brown paper bottle off the counter. Held it along his side.

Even if Rachel sees it, she won't know what it is, he thought. *Not now.*

'Thanks, kid.' Rita took the sack from the boy who wouldn't meet her eyes.

'Home remedy,' she told him as she unscrewed the bottle's cap and filled half her mug. 'The kind of thing your Gramma *wha's-her-name*—'

'Meg,' said Lucas as he kept his eyes on Hank playing in the radio.

'Yeah, old people: turns out they know a thing or two after all.'

She raised the mug between them like for a toast, a motion that pulled the skinny boy's eyes up so she could see her reflection in his glasses.

In the kitchen, Rachel heard Mommy say: 'Everybody needs something.'

Then Ooo-cus said: 'Guess so.'

Gone! G'aym cracker all gone!

Mommy said: 'Poor Lou Herbst. He sure didn't deserve what he got.'

There's the oven where Daddy warms up my milk bottles jus' like I like.

Mommy's voice: 'Neal says you all drove right past the field where Herbst had his heart attack. Drove right past without knowing a thing.'

Rachel toddled until *slap*, her hands smacked on painted white metal.

Look: my fingers on the oven. Ooo-cus read me 'bout Hansel and Gretel and Wicked Witch who baked a cake in an oven.

Rachel patted her hands on the oven.

You in there, Hansel and Gretel? You want gayam crackers?

Mommy said: 'Shame about Herbst. Goes to show, get it while you got it.'

Rachel saw a line of white knobs on the oven.

Ooo-cus cleared his throat. '*Um*, it's August and summer vacation is—'

'I already said I'm sorry I didn't call before you showed up.'

Rachel closed her fingers around the nearest white knob.

Turned it.

Ooo-cus said: 'What I'm trying—'

'We're both trying,' said Mommy, 'but it ain't getting us nowhere.'

What's that? Rachel frowned. A sound from the oven. Kind of like... like a hiss. *Like when Mommy presses her finger against her lips and says: 'Shhh!'*

Hansel and Gretel? Is that you?

Rachel went up on her tippy-toes. Turned the white knob beside the first one. More hiss. Sometimes when Daddy turned a knob, *poof!* went blue flame. Sometimes he made LOUD WORDS and jerked the oven's stovetop open like the crocodile mouth in Peter Pan.

Rachel frowned as the hiss sound came at her.

No blue flames.

She tried to turn the big knob: too hard. But one knob on the other side of it turned as easily as the first two.

Now the oven made even louder hissings.

And if Hansel and Gretel are in there, boy, were they in trouble! Now they're making a big stinky-poo.

'All we're doing is standing here,' Rita told Lucas, holding her cigarette up between them, 'when what we need to be doing is finding a match.'

The radio played Dion singing 'Who Knows Where or When.'

Rachel toddled toward the radio.

Rita waved the cigarette. 'Match? Me? Add it all up: I need this before my nerves jump out of my skin. Do any of us want to be here when that happens?'

Lucas sighed. *The speech* can wait. 'Where should I look?'

'You try the bedroom. I'll take the bathroom.'

They left Rachel bouncing up and down as she danced to the radio.

Like Sherlock Holmes, Lucas knew which side of the unmade bed was hers. Her bedside tabletop held a gold leaf earring. An ashtray with cigarette butts. But no matchbook waited there.

Books sat on Neal's bed table: *U.S.A. Trilogy* under *As I Lay Dying.*

Lucas pictured the cemetery today. Pictured the farm field where he'd seen nothing. He wanted to run out of this room. Run out of this house. Run away from this whole chunk of time pressing on him.

But you're not a little kid, he told himself. So he did his job. Let his eyes roam over the bureau dresser with its framed pictures of baby Rachel. Of a somber Neal and a grinning Rita as she clutched a wedding bouquet.

But he found no matches.

Found Rita pacing in the living room.

Gave her a shake of his head.

'This is nuts!' She closed her eyes and rubbed her nose with her hand that held the unlit cigarette. 'I don't know whether to scream or sneeze my head off.'

Rachel sat on the floor in front of the radio. Studied her bare toes.

'Think about it,' said Rita. 'If you were a match, where would you be?'

Lucas shrugged. *Feels like the house is pressing in on my head.*

'Here's how magic works,' said Rita. 'If you want something, think like it.'

She filled the mug with medicine from the brown sack. Swayed as she put the mug on the coffee table. Exploded into a smile: 'The coat closet!'

Rita turned toward that cubicle by the front door – whirled back to Lucas.

'The cupboard above the refrigerator. Neal stashes matches up there for when that damn pilot light on the stove goes out. Check there. Hurry!'

Lucas headed toward the kitchen. Rita wobbled to the coat closet.

Lucas glanced down as he walked past Rachel. Saw her yawn.

Not even nap time, he thought. Pulled a chair away from the kitchen table. Stepped up on the chair. Swung open the cupboard.

Lucas grabbed the matchbook painted with a woman's face and the words DRAW ME! He stepped off the chair. Looked into the living room. 'Got it!'

'Beat you!' Rita grinned at him with pure triumph. Held up a match pack of her own. 'My old cheerleader coat! You're too late!'

She stuck the cigarette between her lips.

Lucas glanced toward a faint *hissing* sound he heard under a radio ad.

In the living room, Rita opened her matchbook.

Luças saw the oven, the stove: five white knobs, three of them...

Rita tore a match free from the book she'd found in her trophy coat.

Like magic, Lucas *saw* and *heard* and through his clogged nose *smelled* Rita close the cover of the matchbook in compliance with safety rules.

'*NO!*' screamed Lucas.

Rita blinked. Looked up—

—saw Lucas charging her.

Couldn't stop him as he swatted her hands. *Hit her!* Knocked the matches all the way across the room. The cigarette fell from her lips.

Rita slapped Lucas and knocked him backward, his glasses spinning off as he crashed to the floor beside Rachel.

'You little shit!' yelled Rita. 'What the hell do you think you're—'

The crazy kid scrambled to his feet. Charged into the kitchen. Frantically spun the white knobs on the oven back like they should be as he yelled: '*GAS!*' Lucas threw Rachel's wooden highchair through the window above the kitchen sink in an explosion of shattered glass.

Get out of here! screamed through him. *Grab Rachel!*

'Whee,' she said. 'Whee!'

Catch the woman trembling in the living room. Pull her with you and the baby to the door. Knock a chair down so the door stays propped open. GET OUT!

Thirty-one minutes later, Rita sat hunched against the front lawn's picket fence as their green family car drove into sight.

Through his windshield, Neal saw her there with his daughter and Lucas. Saw the shattered kitchen window with the wooden highchair wedged in its gap.

Neal screeched the green car to a stop. Ran into the front yard.

Tears flowed down his wife's cheeks as she looked up to him and screamed: ''S not my fault! Not my fault!'

'Daddy!' cried Rachel as she hurled herself into his scooping-up arms.

Lucas squinted at the blurry image of a man wearing a black suit.

'I think it's OK,' said Lucas. 'I turned off the gas, and with the door open, the window I broke... Might be OK.'

'*Gas?*' Neal whirled to his wife.

'Not my fault.' She sniffed. Looked away.

Neal closed his eyes as he kissed his little girl now safe in his arms.

To Lucas, Neal said: 'Tell me.'

So *that* was the speech Lucas got to deliver, a story about a hunt for matches when Rachel turned on the gas that neither he nor her mother could smell because of their colds. And him bustin' glass made sense with one of the hundreds of 'in case' instructions his dad gave his kids.

Lucas held Rachel while Neal gingerly entered the house. Raised windows. Radio music drifted out to the lawn with murmurs of Neal talking on the phone.

Neal walked out of the house.

Squatted in front of the woman against the fence.

She wouldn't look at him.

'Rita,' said her husband. 'Come inside now.'

'Wouldn't let Lucas bother the neighbors. Made him wait until you came home. Not tell anybody. Wasn't my fault. Ask Lucas, he'll tell you!'

Lucas couldn't read the expression on her husband's blurred face.

'Rita, I called our landlord. Gas company. Everybody's still getting home from the funeral, but they'll come over today. Fix the stove. I'm sorry I wasn't here. I left the cemetery. Had to detour because I promised to help out, but—'

'*Help!* You're always helping somethin'! What about helping me? Not tryin' make me go to see Dr Horn or those damn meeting people. I won't do that, told you over 'n' over again, I won't do none of that damn shit. I'm your wife, you damn son-of-a-bitch! You won't, all you wanna do is with *her*, that damn *her*, and you think I'm going to let you dump me and get away with—'

'RITA!'

Neal bellowed his wife's name. Grabbed her arm. Shook her as she sat against the white picket fence.

Rita whispered: 'You never done nothing like that before.'

'Sorry,' said Neal. 'I'm sorry, but you're out here in the front yard. This isn't the time or the place, and you're in no condition to… to…'

'I didn't get hurt! Honest, honey, I didn't get hurt and look: See Rachel? She's not hurt. It's all OK, just ask Lucas, and it's not, it's *not* my fault!'

'Come on.' Neal eased her to her feet. 'Let's get you inside. It's safe now. Get you laying down before everybody shows up. You've got a cold, remember?'

'Can't smell shit.' Rita wobbled. 'That's why this all happened. Because I have a cold and can't smell shit and Lucas has one, too, so it's not his fault he busted a window and it's not my fault. It's this damn cold.'

She swayed as Neal led her to their front door. 'Makes you lightheaded.'

'Daddy!' said Rachel as he led Mommy into the house. Ooocus held her.

Seven minutes passed on Lucas's watch before Neal came outside. He'd ripped his black tie off, unbuttoned the collar of his white shirt that Rachel drooled on as he lifted her away from Lucas.

'You have to stay,' said Neal. '*Please,* Lucas: *stay.*'

Then the dad carried his daughter into the house.

Nine minutes later, Neal walked out of the house. Walked to Lucas. Gave him the glasses he'd found on the living room floor.

Told him: 'Thank you! *Thank you!* a million times, but that's not enough, not nearly enough. You saved my little girl. Saved Rita. You—'

'Did it for me, too.' Lucas shrugged. 'I was in the house.'

'But you were there for me. And for Rachel. Not for you.' Neal shook his head. 'She said she hit you. When I laid her on the bed, she told me she hit you.'

Lucas shrugged.

'I knew she'd been drinking "*for her cold*" before I left, but I thought, only going to be gone for a while. If you hadn't knocked the matches out of her hand...

'I'm telling your folks. They've got to know you're a hero, that you saved... *Jesus,* I want to tell the world! If you hadn't been there—'

'I just broke a window.'

Neal slumped beside the boy. The blue sky arced over them. The big heat filled the dusty streets. No smells of gas. Baked grass, a whiff of the prairie surrounding the town. A white car drove past. The driver waved.

'I want to tell the world,' whispered Neal. 'So much I want to tell the world. I wanted to grow up to be a good man. If you're a good man, the least that happens is that you got that. So you can be happy with just that.

'One mistake. I've made a million mistakes, but only one… defining mess. Not what I intended. Those things aren't about sin or God. One bad luck twist, but I took it. Did the right thing. Only, turns out that the man I am isn't good enough.

'You get stuck in so much *doing,* you become somebody you're not. You follow rules because you want to do right or because you're scared not to. Maybe all that plays out the same, but never mind *why* when you're stuck with *what.*

'Then one day, suddenly there's blue sky.

'Only you can't fly because you're the "you" who you already made. Even if it means a wonderful miracle like Rachel. You're you. Stuck in a life that's not you. And all you can do is cause people pain and get windows broken.'

Down the block, a neighbor turned on her lawn sprinkler.

'Saw your folks at the funeral,' said Neal. 'Now I get to tell them… Thank you, Lucas, *oh man*, thank—'

'OK,' said Lucas, his face on fire. 'OK.'

'Your dad found me at the funeral to tell me you want to quit,' said Neal. 'Told me you wouldn't say why, but you didn't want to work painting with me anymore. Or helping with Rachel. That you were nervous because you're going to keep helping Hal. Your dad said his rule was that you had to tell me in person. He said you've been rehearsing the speech to give me.'

Lucas sent his eyes to the horizon past the edge of town.

'So I lied,' said Neal. 'I stood there at Lou Herbst's funeral, looked your father straight in the eyes, and lied. "*Nothing's wrong,*" I lied. Told him the truth about you being a great worker. How much help you are. How I depend on you, not just for the painting, but for Rachel. How much she likes you. How Rita…

'Maybe he knew. Maybe the whole town does. You know, don't you? You know what's wrong. What's so damn right and so damn wrong. With me. With—'

'OK! I know. I didn't tell anybody, I won't and…'

'Yeah,' said Neal. '*And.*'

The adult shook his head.

Stood in front of the boy and made their eyes meet.

'There's nothing right about me doing this,' said Neal. 'But you saw what happened today. What would have happened if you weren't here to save Rachel and Rita. She won't be so… sick for a while. Something happens, she gets scared or guilty and tries hard to do better. For a while. So for now, if she can just have a little help, if I can just keep it all together…

'Plus, Hal's life is on the line. Mrs Klise. Nobody knows what we're going to do. Hell, Lucas, she was at the funeral. Not for Lou Herbst or his family, but to see if I brought Hal. Now she's parked outside his house. Waiting. Like a one-woman lynch mob. I've got to figure this all out. Get it to…'

'Where?' whispered Lucas.

'I don't know. But I need your help. Don't leave us. Work like you have been. Just until school. Just a couple more weeks. For Rachel. For Hal. Hell, for Rita. She needs what I don't have and all I've got is you.'

A man and a boy stood on the front lawn of a house.

Lucas raised his eyes to the arcing blue sky. Looked for a sign. An omen. Some magic signal from Heaven or God or the cosmic forces that moved the stars.

Nothing. Not one damn thing. Not even enough *nothing* to be 'nothing' so that *that* would be a sign. Nothing but ordinary sky.

Dad's not here to say something. Or Mom. They're under this ordinary sky. With Laura and my friends. Gramma Meg and this whole town where a rusty station wagon is parked outside a barely-making-it family's house. Hal's in there holding the promise I gave him. In the house behind me, Rachel's in her crib and the woman who slapped me lays on the bed she shares *with.* And Jordan…

The wind blew over Lucas's bare arms. Always blew. Bone-cracking blizzard or big heat day like today, always is the wind.

Lucas said: 'What time should I be here tomorrow?'

SUNSET MILES

Sleep, thought Lucas. *I'm asleep. Shaking me, who's—*

'Come on,' said Dad. 'There's something you need to see.' Lucas sat up in his bed. His bedroom was dark. He rubbed his eyes.

'What time is it?'

'Three A.M.'

'Three – That's like… *way dark out.* I don't have to be to work until nine!'

'You're not going to your job today. Now hurry up, Mom's fixing breakfast.'

Bacon! smelled Lucas. *We never have bacon on regular weekdays!*

'Get dressed,' said Dad as he stood in the open bedroom door.

'What is it?' said Lucas. 'What am I supposed to see?'

Pale light silhouetted his father. 'You'll tell me when you know.'

Scrambled eggs, bacon, toast, and orange juice. More than Lucas wanted when he sat down at the kitchen table with Dad, yet they ate everything Mom put in front of them. She wore her bathrobe and floppy slippers.

Dad wore the old shoes, shirt, and pants he used for yard work.

Mom filled a thermos with steaming coffee.

Said: 'Be careful.'

Dad shrugged into his torn windbreaker. Made sure Lucas wore his jean jacket as he led him out to the company station wagon.

'How come it's just us?' asked Lucas.

'Your mom's busy.' Dad ground the station wagon to life. 'Laura's working a double shift at the phone company to free up some women to help. Besides, this is a two-man job.'

Blue-black, decided Lucas. That was the color of this time. The color of the air enveloping this town like an ocean. Ivory mist coned down from streetlamps to empty streets. No other vehicles motored through the town.

The traffic signal above Main Street flashed GREEN to RED.

Dad braked to a halt in front of its glow.

Five passed-out parked cars lined Main Street's row of stores, cafés, bars, offices for who knows what. Phone and electric wires swayed in the night breeze.

Not night, decided Lucas. Not morning either. A kind of in-between *now*.

GREEN flashed the traffic light. Go.

But where? Through streets Lucas'd known all his life. Streets that now felt like another world. Another dimension. Dad rode beside him in the rattling company station wagon. They clattered over railroad tracks. Drove past blocks of dark houses. Someone had a kitchen light on in that house. As small as Vernon was, Lucas realized he didn't know who lived there.

Tired as he was, Lucas swelled with delicious awe. As though he alone in the entire universe was really there. Lucas envisioned screaming out the car window at the top of his lungs as they drove through the silent streets. Though that notion intrigued him, he felt more the power of *not* doing that. Of not screaming. Of letting this strange, chilly, ghost mirror world sleep.

Dad drove the station wagon to the trucking company. In the glow of watch lights over the oiled dirt in front of the garage bays, mechanic McNamer waited beside a hulking tanker truck.

''Bout time you got here,' joked McNamer.

'Enjoyed the extra sleep,' said Dad with a smile as he led Lucas to the slumbering tanker truck.

McNamer slapped the truck's gleaming silver tank. A hollow *Thonk!* 'She's fueled and ready to go.

'Where's your gloves, Lucas?' said McNamer. 'Come prepared so you won't let the job down. And so you won't rip the shit out of yourself. Here, take mine.'

The crusted rawhide gloves McNamer passed Lucas were too big for a boy.

Lucas mumbled: 'Thanks.'

'Don't lose 'em. Don't wanna work 'em out of your hide.' McNamer winked at his boss. 'There's a pair on the console for you. Did you talk to Alec last night?'

'No.'

'He said to do us proud.' McNamer grinned. 'His heart's in the right place, even if it is all busted up.'

'Yeah,' said Dad.

McNamer limped Lucas around to the truck's passenger door.

Reached high to jerk open the passenger door: 'Get in.'

So Lucas did.

Wondered if She knew he'd been there.

And found Dad sitting behind the truck's huge steering wheel.

'What are you doing?' said Lucas. 'You're the manager. Not a driver.'

Dad grinned. Keyed the engine to life. A rumble shook Lucas. Dad fumbled with switches. Headlights blasted out through the darkness.

'You ready?' said Dad.

Moved the two gear shifts. Eased his left foot up off a pedal.

Clang-runk, grinding metal, whining engine… The truck lurched forward.

Died.

Dad keyed the engine back to roaring life. Again let out the clutch.

Going! thought Lucas. *We're going straight ahead! Driving away from the shop. Bouncing behind the steering wheel, shifting gears, Dad is driving truck!*

Dad said: 'There are a few things you don't know about your old man.'

Barreling over the viaduct. Onto the westward highway.

Lucas glanced in his outside mirror vibrating on the truck door.

Saw the lights of Vernon shrink away until the truck rounded a curve and the mirror held blackness. A pair of yellow-eyed headlights came toward them in the other lane. Dad flicked the truck beams to low. A car zoomed past them.

They drove west through the night. The engine rumbled Lucas's bones. This steel shaft racing him over the two-lane highway smelled like grease and oil. Night air whistled around the loose windows. He smelled prairie stretching out past the glow of their headlights. Smelled September a-coming.

Dad nodded to the darkness outside Lucas's window. 'Northern lights.'

Shimmering fans of green and pink undulated across that dark horizon.

Father told son: 'If you're out of town where it's quiet and dark, sometimes you can hear them whisper, crackle. Long as we got the Arctic snow to reflect them down here, they'll keep trying to tell us what they got to say.'

Lucas rolled down his window. Rumbling air rushed his face. A million billion sparkling white stars sailed the black ocean above the road he rode.

On they drove, westward through the darkness.

White slash marks and yellow stripes flowed past their wheels.

Won't ask! thought Lucas. *But where the hell are we going in a truck?*

The windshield filled with a coming-closer distant orange flame dancing like the flicker of a candle high above ground.

'Gas fire of the refinery,' said Dad. 'They burn it off at the top of the stack.'

Lucas inhaled a whiff of oil smoke and sulfur.

Memories of Bobbi Jean filled him. A girl on a sidewalk leaning close with a promise, a plea, a prayer.

Lucas wrinkled his nose. *Now I know why she worried.*

A bubble of yellow light emerged below bursts of the orange flame. A bubble that became spotlights and porch lights. They drove toward those fortresses surrounded by chain-link fences. Toward houses set as close to the highway and as far away from the stinky buildings as allowed by corporate efficiency.

The truck engine whined as Dad steered the tanker into the refinery yard. A man with a flashlight directed the truck to a mountainous cylindrical tank. Dad cut the engine.

'Take the flashlight from the jockey box,' he told his son. 'Hop up on top.'

'What?'

'Climb up the ladder rungs on your side of the truck. Work the hatch.'

'I've never done that before!'

'Yeah.' Dad stepped down from the truck's cab to the man holding a clipboard and flashlight.

Gotta do it, Lucas told himself. *Stick the flashlight down the back of your jeans so hands are free. Cram McNamer's gloves into your jean jacket pockets.*

Lucas stepped out to the running board. Grabbed a metal rung on the side of the truck, and stretched his left leg up to an iron ledge.

Don't drop nothing. Don't let go. Don't fall. Don't slip. Don't hang on the side of the truck like a goofy little kid. Push off and go!

Made it! Standing on top of the truck in the dark. In the whipping wind. *But I got my balance. Flashlight out and…*

Uh-oh.

The hatch is way, way down there at the back of the truck. A yardstick-wide catwalk ran along the truck's curved top.

Fall off and they'll laugh at your corpse.

Don't close your eyes. One foot in front of the other. Step only where the flashlight shines on catwalk metal – not on the giant curved silver tube below it.

Nineteen paces – and he'd made it! Suddenly the catwalk was twice as wide. The wind pushed on him half as hard. The fall down was no more than double Dad's height. Up here, standing in the night, the stars made him tingle.

'Boy!' yelled a man on the ground. 'Pop the hatch!'

Lucas lifted the heavy hatch open to free a black hole to the night.

'Now heads up!'

Swinging toward him through the dark came a pipe with a spout. Lucas pressed his gloved hands against the sticky steel spout. Worked with a boom operator on a platform fifty feet away to guide the spout into the hatch hole.

'Now, boy, step back! Don't breathe the fumes more 'n you have to!'

Men on the ground chuckled as Lucas catwalked to the front of the truck.

A great *whoosh* gushed out of the spout stuck into the truck hatch. The tank vibrated beneath Lucas's sneakers. Gasoline stenched the dark air.

Not '*boy,*' thought Lucas. He stood in a million billion stars as they sailed a night wind. This wasn't babysitting. This wasn't stirring paint or dabbing up drips or cleaning brushes. This wasn't working as a soda jerk or sweeping a mechanic shop. This wasn't delivering handbills for the Roxy. This was muscle work. Climbing up, scary work. Screw up and bad things will *dead-certain* happen. Standing on top of a truck in that chilly wind darkness made him no *boy*.

'Lucas!' yelled a girl.

Down on the night-dim ground: Dad, flashlight man, and some other guy.

And Bobbi Jean.

She waved. Excitedly bounced up and down in her white sneakers.

Bobbi Jean yelled: 'This is so cool!'

Lucas saw his dad whisper to her. She laughed.

Yelled orders sent Lucas to the hatch. He guided the boom pipe out of the hole. Felt it crank away from his hand. He shut the hatch with a clang.

Don't want to climb down. When I get off the truck, I'm back to just me.

But you have to do what you have to do, and he did.

Bobbi Jean ran to where he stood on the truck's running board. Handed him brown paper grocery bags soaked with the greasy perfume of hot dough.

'Mom and I baked these for you guys to take to – for the thing. I know what it is and it's *so cool*! I wish I could go with you. You're so lucky!'

Lucas put the wonderful-smelling bags on the truck seat.

Dad climbed in. Fired up the engine and, with a blast of the horn, circled the truck back the way they'd come.

As the truck rolled away, three men and one girl waved.

The fully loaded truck rode like a quarrelsome dinosaur.

When it was just them, the truck, the highway, the night, the ride, Dad said: 'What's her name?'

'She's a girl from school. Just a girl.'

'But she's got a name.'

'Bobbi Jean. Don't call her just Bobbi. She wants to be her whole name.'

'Nobody wants to be a *just*,' said Dad. 'We all want to pick who we are.'

They drove in heartbeats of dark silence.

Until Dad said: 'What did she give us?'

Lucas opened one of the greasy paper sacks.

Out rushed a cloud of dough and sugary cinnamon.

'Donuts!' he cried. 'All these sacks! I've never had homemade donuts!'

'We should sample a few,' said Dad. 'They sent that carton of cold milk. Wouldn't've done that if they hadn't meant for you to wash down a donut or two.'

Or three. Even after Lucas's huge breakfast. First a chocolate one. Then a cinnamon one. Finally, a plain one to 'clean the palate,' said Dad, his eyes on the road and his hands gripping the steering wheel.

Lucas poured him coffee from Mom's thermos.

Drank the cold milk.

The smells of cargo fuel and truck grease. The bouncing seat. Scary/cool man's work. Not knowing where or why they were going. And those donuts tasted better than anything he'd ever had. Ever imagined!

Or, thought Lucas, *maybe 'all that' was part of it, the doing and the being here in the truck with Dad.* Maybe that's what made the donuts taste like heaven.

As they drove through darkness.

'Dad? The headlights don't go way out even on high beams. You can't know which way the road turns or if there's a loose cow or some guy coming at you over the center line with his lights burned out.'

'You drive beyond your headlights. Sense what's out there you can't see.'

'What if something's out there that you can't sense?'

'Then you better be riding safe and smart.'

The road rumbled beneath their wheels.

Through the windshield came the glow of Vernon.

We're going home, thought Lucas.

But Dad turned the truck south on the highway toward the river.

Lucas opened his mouth. Closed it. *I won't ask where.*

Security poles lit the missile silo construction.

'Still got a lot of stars.' Dad shifted gears. 'Think it'll rain?'

Lucas shrugged.

'Hope not,' said Dad. 'Hope to hell not.'

Dad eased off the accelerator. The engine clattered back. He down-shifted. Pressed the foot brake. Lucas felt tons of fuel in the tank behind them surge forward – slosh back. Dad flicked on the right turn signal, a clicking sound that made red lights blink outside on the night highway.

Called out: 'The Butwin Motel billboard should be – on the right!'

The truck whined and lumbered as Dad muscled the wheel to steer off the highway and onto a gravel road. Twelve truck tires kicked up a storm of dust. Lucas closed his window as the road bounced him on his seat.

A jackrabbit hopped through the headlights' glow.

Dad said: 'Keep your eyes peeled to the left for an old building.'

But Dad spotted that shape beside the road before Lucas. The tanker crawled to a stop off the road by a deserted shack. Dad killed the engine.

The gravel cloud they'd kicked up swirled and settled.

Dad rolled down his window, so Lucas did, too.

His father said: 'Look there.'

'There' meant two football fields dead ahead in the grayness. A farmyard beside this county road. A house with a glowing porch light.

'Do you know who lives there?' asked Dad.

'No.'

Night melted. Crickets fell silent as stars faded. Lucas smelled the donuts. The gravel road. Grain fields and clear morning air.

Dad climbed out of the truck. 'Going to stretch my legs.'

Lucas watched his father walk onto a field facing that farm. Saw a wink of flame in the darkness. The breeze floated cigarette smoke into the truck.

Dad came back. Left the truck door dangling open as he climbed behind the steering wheel. He poured steaming coffee into the thermos cup.

Lucas's father stared through the windshield.

Whispered: 'Being alive is more than just not being dead.'

A meadowlark whistled.

A rooster crowed.

'Look!' Dad nodded to the rectangle mirror mounted outside Lucas's door.

A burning yellow dot shimmered in that reflecting glass. That yellow ball became a chain of lights snaking closer across the land.

Lucas jumped outside the truck to stand on the running board and look.

He saw the ball of the rising sun.

And coming toward him out of that dawn on the gravel road from the highway flowed a dragon line of lights-on vehicles – ten, twenty, no: an army of yellow-eyed machines driving closer, a convoy churning a dust cloud that billowed over shadowed fields of golden wheat.

The truck beneath Lucas roared and shook to life.

'Let's go!' said Dad.

Lucas scrambled into his seat.

The convoy rolled past them, a rumble so loud Lucas couldn't hear the growl of the tanker engine under the hood outside his windshield.

A pickup truck drove point. Then another. Another.

Grain trucks – five, six, fifteen.

Family cars, a dozen of them driving through the gravel dust.

Last came the twelve-foot-tall combines. Ten, twenty, fifty grasshopper-like red harvest machines with front-mounted horizontal blades.

The lead pickup drove into the farmyard as Lucas and his dad sat in their idling fuel truck.

The final combine rolled by.

Dad motored the truck onto the gravel road like a caboose for the convoy.

The combines drove past the farmyard now filled with cars and pickups. Followed the gravel road. One after another turned down paths to fields of waving grain. Parked side by side at the edge of the fields.

Waiting.

Grain trucks parked on the road near those fields.

Waiting.

By the time Dad parked the tanker in the farmyard, men and women swarmed over that packed earth. Setting up tables from the Methodist church. Unfolding metal chairs stamped ELKS CLUB. Lifting boxes, picnic baskets, and barbecues from pickups and the trunks of cars. Everyone chattering. Obeying whatever made sense. Car radios played the Vernon station's country songs.

'Go help set up,' said Dad after he and Lucas climbed out of their truck. 'But come back soon. We got work here, too.'

Lucas wandered through a swirl of Martin County residents as they built a cross between a community picnic and a Marine Corps bivouac. There was pharmacist Mr Shook setting up tables. Those two women unpacking baskets of food on a table were farm wives. There's a furniture store clerk carrying a box. A volunteer fireman with a bag of charcoal. The Catholic priest carried a clinking box of silverware. The librarian ferried napkins.

'Hey, Lucas!' Hal said, carrying two gray metal folding chairs in each hand.

Sheriff Wood sat in his police cruiser talking on the two-way radio.

Over there helping a housewife unfold a tablecloth: Jordan Smith.

Haven't seen her or talked to her since the river, thought Lucas.

Jordan looked up. Saw Lucas. Her smile was soft. Sad.

'Well there you are!' said Aunt Dory to Lucas as she bustled through the crowd, laughing, answering questions about where to set a barbecue, encouraging a woman worried about ice around the watermelons. 'Good day for it, huh?'

The door of the farmhouse flew open.

Out hurried a woman in a thrown-on dress. Behind her came a boy near Lucas's age in jeans and a T-shirt but barefoot. He held the hand of a girl not yet out of what her one-room country schoolhouse called kindergarten. Stunned awe strained the face of that mother of the house.

Mrs Herbst! Lucas recognized her from Easter Sunday. *She's Mrs Herbst. This is her farm, her family and… And her bald husband Lou. Just buried.*

'What's happening?' cried Mrs Herbst as she stared out at the crowd of neighbors and townspeople setting up tables in her front yard. 'What… ?'

'Well, hi there,' said Dory, motioning to two other women at the same time she beamed her smile to Deborah Herbst. 'We're putting ice cream in your freezer. Edna over there's got coffee ready. And you kids go on now with Lucas, get some donuts. Eat a bunch and bring them back to that table by Mrs Harvie.'

'Dory? These people. I… What are you doing?'

Dory'd already turned away to help a woman with a bowl of corn cobs.

Deborah Herbst closed her eyes. Swayed. Lucas took a step toward her. Saw two women move toward her, too – ready, waiting, but not grabbing. Deborah opened her eyes and those two women magically diverted their reach.

'Come on,' Lucas told the son of the farm. 'We got a job.'

'What are you doing?' said Deborah Herbst, turning this way and that amongst faces she knew, faces who smiled but gave her no answers. 'What are you doing?'

Lucas fetched the donut sacks from the truck. Gave them to the Herbst boy. Gave him a smile he'd never used before.

'Take the sacks over there,' said Lucas. 'Then go get your shoes on.'

The son of this land barefooted away to do what he should. Could. His sister trailed him. Turned back to give Lucas a shy wave. They walked past their mother, who stood in the bustling crowd, a stranger in her own front yard.

'Hey, Lucas!' yelled Neal Dylan as he leaned out of the passenger window of a pickup driven by a man Lucas couldn't name. 'Hop in back. Give us a hand.'

Lucas charged to the pickup. Scrambled into the open back end. The driver stomped on the gas. A dozen cardboard boxes shared the pickup cargo box with Lucas, all stamped DUMAS SOIL SERVICE. Lucas counted twenty handheld grease guns on the cargo box floor. He lifted the flap of one box: more grease tubes.

The pickup bounced on the gravel road. Bounced Lucas like a bronc rider. The driver slammed on the brakes at the first field. Neal was out the door before inertia let Lucas stand. Neal scooped up half a dozen grease guns. Trotted out to the line of combines at the field's edge. At this one, at that, farmers' hands reached down from the combine cabs to grab a grease gun, store it under the seat.

Neal ran back to the pickup. Vaulted into the cargo box beside Lucas, slapped: 'Let's go!' on the cab's roof. The pickup rocketed over the gravel road.

Neal's smile was serious as he looked Lucas straight-on.

Said: 'Rachel's with her grandmother.'

The pickup bounced over the gravel road.

Farmers stood waiting at the next line of combines. Neal and Lucas passed half of them grease guns they took to their idle and silent machines.

So it went, line after line of farmers and combines. Giving out grease guns, grease tubes. Neal and the ten-year-old boy ran grease guns out to the line, jogged back, vaulted into the pickup's cargo box.

But Lucas got to be the one who pounded the roof of the cab. The one who gave the signal to GO! After the pass-out, the pickup's driver roared back to the first field with its troop of deployed combines.

Dusty gravel wind blew in Lucas's face as he stood beside Neal while they held on to the roof of the pickup cab. As Lucas rode like a lookout on a ship at sea.

The pickup crunched to a halt. The driver shut off his engine.

Red combines lined the borders of golden fields where boy-high golden wheat swayed in the breeze. Those giant red machines made a line like a troop of cavalry soldiers just waiting to charge through the prairie's morning air.

Only a hint of a breeze gave this scene sound.

Lucas felt like he was in church.

Whispered: 'Why are we all waiting?'

Neal said: 'Crops turned yesterday, but you can't cut wet and there's dew.'

'How do you know when it's OK?'

Neal nodded toward the first field.

A farmer wearing a billed cap climbed down from his combine. He ambled away from the line of waiting red machines. Walked into the sea of waving wheat with his hands held out at his sides to brush the fruity-heave stalks.

'That's Uncle Paul!'

'Figures.' Neal gave a benedictory nod. 'Your uncle, he knows.'

Uncle Paul stood in the center of a waving gold field. The red sun above the horizon made him squint. He broke the top off a wheat stalk. Rubbed grain heads between his palms. Put a few kernels in his mouth to work them with his teeth. Paul danced the stalk in his bite like a long toothpick. Looked at white clouds floating closer like scouts for a raiding party. Stood alone and quiet until he became part of that field.

A meadowlark whistled. Fell silent.

Uncle Paul whipped his cap around in an electric circle above his head.

'*YEE-HAW!*' yelled the pickup truck driver.

Came rumbles and roars, the lurch of the universe's machines.

Fifty harvest red combines spun their blades and moved out in a slow-motion charge to mow fields of gold.

'Look at that,' whispered Neal. 'You'll never see it again – I hope. Even if you're around when the custom cutter outfits come up from Kansas. Even if there's more combines, machines from horizon to horizon, it won't be like this. All they'll be doing is making money, but these people...' He shook his head. 'These people.'

Then Lucas saw the first gray cloud.

Nudged Neal. 'Look.'

'Yeah.'

'It doesn't even have to hail! All it has to do is rain!'

'Yeah.'

The combines rolled, staggered lines mowing up a crop at three miles per hour.

'These are Lou Herbst's fields,' said Lucas. 'His last crop. His family's only... All these people. Farmers from all over the county. Have they finished their own cutting?'

'Haven't started it. Wasn't ready around here until now.'

'The weather might turn! Or their machines could break here and then they couldn't harvest their own crops, *their whole year*, they... Today they...'

'Yeah,' said Neal. 'Look at what they're doing. Look at them go.'

Red combines chugged across wheat fields. Grain trucks rolled alongside the rolling combines while the harvest machines sprayed clouds of wheat kernels into the truck's cargo boxes to be hauled into Vernon's grain elevators.

The pickup ferried Lucas back to the farmyard.

Where Hal needed help scattering charcoal through five barbecues.

Where a three-year-old boy toddled into a wheat field. Lucas ran him down. Led him back to where Mommy was buttering rolls.

Where volunteers from Main Street swarmed over combines parked in the fields, greasing and lubing them while pickups ferried their farmer drivers to the Herbst yard and women who served them lemonade with platters of barbecued steak and potatoes and corn on the cob and homemade apple or cherry pie and in the big heat of that place, hotter still coffee.

Where before Lucas could take his place in the food line, Dad needed him to help fill a pickup truck's cargo box tank with gas to ferry out to the fields.

Where Mrs Herbst saw her children set to working that chore, then this one. Where she drifted, always greeted, never ignored and never, *never* given the chance to stammer, to sob, to break down or cry and say: '*Thank you!*'

Because there was no need, knew Lucas. Because this all was just what was supposed to be. What 'we're' supposed to do. So to take – or worse – to encourage a thank-you was small.

Gray clouds laced the sky by noon. Dad and Lucas scrambled into the tanker. Pulled it behind Sheriff Wood, who turned on the cruiser's spinning red lights to escort them to the refinery. Bobbi Jean used a soapy water bucket to wash the tanker's windshield while Lucas worked up top. Dad and Lucas drove the tanker behind the sheriff's spinning red lights back to the farm.

Midafternoon.

The gray spider web lace overhead became a dark shroud that veiled the big heat sun. The Ross 'men' filled portable tanks on pickups, one after the other racing away to feed the combines in the fields. Filled gas cans for town men who'd race their family cars out to the fields to fuel grain trucks. Pumped gallon after gallon of donated dead dinosaurs through a truck provided by Dad's boss Alec Marshall, who showed up to see and jiggle coins in his pocket and who had to be stopped from doing any work that might rip his paper-thin heart.

The first lightning flashed the gray sky at 4:21 by Lucas's watch.

Uncle Paul was in the farmyard while a mechanic from the implement store replaced a leaking fuel hose on Paul's combine. He shuffled over to say hi to his brother-in-law and nephew. Saw the boy flinch at the flash in the sky.

'Believe it's just heat lightning,' he told Lucas.

'What if you're wrong?'

'Could be a hell of a deal.'

Uncle Paul went back to work.

Thunder, thought Lucas. *There's no thunder. So it's far off. Maybe OK.*

Maybe, maybe, maybe as the clouds laced the reddening sky.

A screech of brakes in gravel as a grain truck slammed into the farmyard.

A wild-eyed, gasping man staggered from the truck.

Hollered: 'We got 'er done!'

Lucas checked his watch: 5:49.

Flame-doused barbecues dropped into pickup trucks. Piles of trash crammed a grain truck to go to the city dump. Tables collapsed themselves as men who'd worked in the fields drove their machines homeward over the gravel roads. Lots of them shuffled over to a panel truck where the Harmon's Tap Room handed out cold beers.

Gave one even to Lucas, a tall bottle filled with the same gold of the fields. Nobody, not even Sheriff Wood, said a thing as Lucas took a long drink.

Bitter cold with a yucky tang.

His face scrunched as he handed the bottle to his dad, who took it with a grin, went back to talking to a farmer as someone passed Lucas a cold Coke.

Hal stood next to Sheriff Wood, also with a bottle of Coke in his hand.

Neal stacked folding chairs in the cargo of a borrowed pickup.

Jordan sat on the hood of her red coupe. She wore a denim shirt. Black pants ending at her slim calves. White sneakers. Like down at the river. Her hand curved around a bottle of beer. Some horizon filled her eyes.

What does she see? thought Lucas.

Then he thought: *Maybe what I saw, what I know… Maybe it's… complicated.*

'You ready to go?' said Dad.

Because of where they'd parked the tanker truck after the second run, because the farmers had to get home to get ready for their own harvests in the morning, because of sentiment Lucas sensed deep inside Dad, they waited as all the other vehicles pulled out of the farmyard in the evening's orange light.

First to come, last to go, thought Lucas as they sat in the tanker. *Fits.*

'How do you feel?' asked Dad.

His eyes burned. Soreness throbbed through him. He'd stubbed his toe on the tanker rung. Even with McNamer's gloves, calluses chafed his hands. Wheat chaff and gravel dust clotted the sweat painted on his face and bare arms. The evening air was turning cool, but he was too stiff to put on his jean jacket.

'I feel great,' said Lucas.

Not just great, he felt… big. Certainly bigger than before, than last spring, than even this morning when Bobbi Jean had yelled: 'This is so cool!'

Bobbi Jean. She fights to get to be her whole name. To pick her own name.

To be her own self.

He sat with his father in the truck that would ride him home.

'Dad?' said Lucas.

'Yeah?'

'Can I change my name?'

'Huh?'

'Not really, but I've been "Lucas" since I was a little kid.'

'What are you now?'

Lucas saw the cruiser carrying Hal pull out of the farmyard. Saw the pickup truck of chairs drive toward town. Saw Jordan's red coupe rumbling away on the gravel road.

'I'm not grown-up. Or even a teenager. But I'm not "*that Lucas*" anymore.' He shrugged. 'And I'm not *Ooo-cus* or *Loo-cus*.'

Knew Dad didn't get what those sounds meant.

Knew neither of them wanted Lucas to explain.

Instead he said: 'All the stuff I've done this year. Seen. I even got glasses.'

A father saw his son shrug. Look away.

'So who are you?' said Dad.

Sundown reddened the sky and the big heat eased toward night.

'Luc,' said the boy. 'Call me Luc.'

'OK, *Luc*. Let's go home.' Dad gunned the truck engine. 'So, now do you know what I woke you up this morning to see?'

The truck pulled onto the gravel road.

Luc said: 'Yeah.'

Glanced into his side mirror of where they'd been.

Saw the rose-lit image of a woman watching them go as she stood on her front porch, her dress flapping in the sunset's breeze, her arms draped around the two children, her face aglow and her eyes shining like silver lakes.

DRACULA

Hal shoved his chair away from his mother's kitchen table. 'No more!'

'What?' said Luc, who sat at the table with new notebooks and pencils from the dime store. He felt the house close in around him. *We're here all alone.*

'I can't do this!' Hal's hands pushed back a tidal wave.

'All we're doing is getting ready for school. In a few more days—'

'A few more days! A few more years! Doesn't matter!'

Hal stalked across the room that held him.

Stared at the sink window filled with morning sunlight.

'What did you see?' snapped the teenager as he paced.

'What?' said Luc.

'When you biked here. What did you see?'

'Nothing.'

'Nothing? Outside these damn walls it's all a big *nothing*?'

Luc's glasses reflected flames dancing in Hal's eyes.

'She's out there,' said Hal.

Luc burned. *Don't say nothing!*

'Isn't she? Out there.'

Hal angled his head toward the window above the sink.

'I don't need to look to see her. But if you really didn't see her, then you must think I'm crazy. Like I believe in movie monsters. So go on. You look.'

'I don't want to look.'

'Ain't that your job? To look out for me?'

Lucas shrugged.

'Go look. See if I'm right. See if she's there.'

'Doesn't matter.'

'I'm either wrong or right. Don't right and wrong matter?'

Luc shuffled to the sink. Through the window he saw trees dotted by gold leaves. Scruffy lawn. The graveled street. Parked at the opposite curb with a shadow hunched over its steering wheel waited a rusted station wagon.

Lucas retreated to his chair at the kitchen table. 'She's there.'

'She's been there since the fair. Follows Mom and me to the grocery store. When Neal takes me anywhere. She's there when we wake up. There in the night if I get up to go pee. She must go home, but whenever I look, there she is.'

Hal paced.

'She's always going to be there. Come winter, I'll be sitting in government class watching Mr Pulaski drone on 'bout things that don't matter. Outside there'll be snow covering everything. And parked across the street from the high school will be that damn rusted station wagon.'

'Why?'

'So she can catch me.'

'Catch you what?'

'Doing one wrong thing. Busting my probation.'

'She can't do that forever! I mean she'll... she'll...'

'Forget about it? Be wrong for her to forget. Wrong for me to forget. So she's parked out there, I'm parked in here, and we're both stuck not doing wrong.'

'All you have to do is get through this year to graduate!'

'So you wear a black robe and a funny square hat, they give you a piece of paper, and *presto*: you're free?' Hal shook his head. 'While I'm in the high school gym getting a diploma, that station wagon will be parked outside.'

Hal paced. Luc watched Hal *not* look at the window. He knew it was there. Knew what was beyond it. Hal walked back and forth, back and forth.

'You know what this year was going to be?' said Hal. 'For me and Earl? Senior year was going to be the year we were finally cool. We kept planning how we'd divvy up using the car, because we were both going to have a girlfriend.

'God, I miss him.' Hal's hand lingered on the refrigerator door. 'He was the only one who knew I had it bone deep for Claudia.'

'Claudia my sister's friend?'

'There's only one Claudia.'

'But she's—'

'Chris Harvie's girl. Of course she's his girl. Hell, if I was a girl, I'd want to be his girlfriend.' Hal shook his head. 'I'm glad she's got Chris.'

Hal's eyes burned holes into Lucas's chest like Superman's X-ray vision.

'When you got it bad for a girl who likes someone else, you want him to be an asshole. If he's an asshole, maybe you got a chance. Unless she's a girl who likes assholes. Wouldn't that be a sad joke. But when you're out of chances, if you never had one to begin with, be glad she's got a good guy.'

Hal said: 'I used to tell Earl he should go after your sister because that would be swell, me and Claudia, him and her best friend.'

'*Laura?*'

'Earl thought she was too "honor roll" for him. And too pretty.' Hal shrugged. 'Don't freak out about your sister and Earl. He's dead.'

'Oh.'

'Yeah: *oh*. Doesn't seem real. Feels like I've been asleep. Seeing somebody else's movie. Feels like a horn is going to honk and he'll be out there in our car. But it ain't him out there. It's his mother and she's never going away.'

Hal's hands gripped the kitchen counter.

His head hung between his arms.

He told the floor:

'I never meant for any of this to happen! I rebuilt Mrs Sweeny's car with him. Got drunk with him. But this... This "*what happened then!*" He's dead and I'm here 'n' not fair and... How can I make anything right when I've done something wrong?'

'Wait! I forgot!' blurted Luc. *Lied* Luc. 'I'm supposed to call somebody.'

Taped beside the phone on the kitchen wall was a list of phone numbers. Blue ink showed the hospital number. Red ink linked to 'jail payphone.' The blue 'Miss Smith' matched a number Luc had never called, though he'd looked it up in the phone book, learned those digits by heart. 'Lucas' and his family's phone number were penciled at the bottom of the sheet. Red inked near the brown-suited lawyer's name was the number for Neal Dylan.

Luc spun four spins of the dial to make his call. The black receiver buzzed in his ear. He moved as far away from Hal as the phone cord allowed – one step into the living room. He stared at the ironing board Mrs Hemmer used to press her waitress uniform as the phone buzzed. Hal paced the kitchen floor.

Fifth buzz – interrupted by the answer of a woman's slurred voice: 'Yeah?'

A child wailed in the phone's tunnel of sound as her mother slouched against the wall. The phone receiver tucked into the crook of her neck while she struck a match to a cigarette. Exhaled cancerous smoke with her second: 'Yeah?'

Luc wondered if the pacing Hal heard him whisper: 'Rita?'

'That you, Falk?'

'*Ah*, no. This is Luc.'

'You used to sound different. Thought you was someone else.'

'Mr Falk used to be my neighbor, but—'

'Seems like I know a lot of "used to be" guys.'

'Is, *ah*, is Neal there?'

'He's supposed to be working with you.'

'We're painting a garage on the northside, but he's starting without me while I'm up here with Hal and… I really need to talk to him. So he's left?'

'Soon as he could. But he won't get far. You can count on that, buster.'

'But he's not there now?'

'You deaf or something, kid? *For Christ's sakes, Rachel! Shut up when Mommy's on the God-damned phone!*'

'It's OK! I can hear you fine.'

'Does that do me any good?'

'I… don't know.'

'When you going to find out?'

'*Um*, well, if you talk to Neal, have him come right up to Hal's.'

'I'm through being his secretary.'

Luc held the phone. His mind burned. Was empty of words to say.

Rita's voice in his ear said: 'Why don't you call your girlfriend and see if he's there? You need that number?'

'*Ah*… no.' Then because he could think of nothing else: 'Thank you.'

The phone hummed Lost Connection.

Hal paced the kitchen.

'You get to a point,' said Hal. 'You get to a point.'

Luc swallowed. 'We're OK. And it's all OK.'

'Never figured you for the lying kind. Must be just 'cause you're a kid.' Hal faced the shorter boy. 'You been good to me. Like a friend.'

'I am your friend!'

'That's not a smart thing to be.'

Hal looked at dishes in the drying rack.

Picked up a clean glass.

Filled it with tap water from the river.

Took only one sip before he poured the water down the drain.

Turned away from the sink.

Held the drinking glass out in front of his chest.

'Hal? Are you—'

Hal opened his grasp—

—caught the falling glass with a blur of his other hand.

'That's all it takes,' he said in a voice as flat as the kitchen floor. 'Hold on—

'—let go.'

The glass dropped through thin air into Hal's grip.

He whispered: 'I can do that.'

'Don't!' pleaded Luc.

Hal said: 'Should I just…'

Fingers flick open, the glass drops a blur, *caught!*

His other hand holds the glass as Hal says, 'Let go?'

'No, you'll bust it all over the floor!' Luc caught his breath.

'And it'll be all done. Sweep up the busted glass. Dump it in the trash. The garbage truck'll haul it away, all gone and done.'

'But it isn't just yours! It's your mom's!'

Hal gazed through the empty glass.

'Don't want to keep making messes for her.'

'That's right.' Luc sighed with relief. 'You're right.'

'Clean it up myself.'

Those words chilled Lucas.

Hal said: 'A glass gets cracked, just a question of time before it busts.'

'Wait a minute!' *Lying gets easier*, thought Luc as he said: 'I got to make another phone call. Just wait one minute.'

Hal stood in the middle of the kitchen floor. Holding the glass.

Luc spun the dial of the phone on the wall. Stayed in the kitchen. Hal stared at the glass. The phone buzzed. Buzzed again. And again.

Answer your phone, Jordan! Please, Miss Smith! Answer the phone!

The glass moved through the air in Hal's hand.

Luc slammed the phone down on its hang-up hook.

Hal set the glass on the kitchen table by his new notebooks for school.

'I can't do that.'

'Sure you can,' said Luc. 'You can do anything.'

'You still believe that. So I guess you *are* lucky.'

Hal grabbed his head with both hands to keep from exploding.

'She's still out there! I can't just stand here!'

'Wait!' yelled Luc. 'Wait a minute!'

'Waiting is tearing me apart!'

'Phone call! Remember? I still gotta make that phone call. No one was home, nobody there, *and just let me make one phone call!*

'Here I go!' said Luc. 'See? I'm dialing the number.'

Truck shop, middle of the morning, he's gotta be there! If Dad's not in the office, the ringing phone has an extension in the shop garage and somebody will—

A raspy male voice whispered in Luc's ear: 'Hello?'

'I gotta talk to my dad!'

Through the phone, in the truck stop, probably standing not far from the phone by the open garage bay door, came the sounds of voices.

Dad yelling: '*What are you saying?*'

The man who answered the phone whispered: 'Hey, it's McNamer.'

'I got to talk to my dad right away!'

Dad yelled: 'If you stop working dispatch calls until after ten at night, the only time you're earning your pay is when you're asleep!'

McNamer whispered: 'This ain't a good time.'

From the phone came the sound of Ben Owens's voice:

'Don, don't get all high horse mad at me! Since the baby, Alec's come to think freeing me up to help is best. Plus, me staying off days here where you're doing just fine keeps things smooth. Plus, it doesn't make sense to pull me away from customer relations and the advertising biz. And Adele's always talking 'bout how she needs to stay close to home because of her laid-up husband but still have hours, so this works out for everybody.'

Dad yelled: 'This isn't how things should run!'

'Well,' said Ben Owens, 'this is a family-run business.'

McNamer whispered: 'Kid, whatever it is, you gotta handle it yourself.'

The phone clicked as McNamer hung up.

'OK,' Luc told the dead connection's hum. 'That's fine. We'll do it.'

He hung up the phone. Gave Hal a big smile.

'Hear that?' said Luc. 'Everything's OK.'

'Is that why you're here?' said Hal. 'Because everything's OK?'

'Ah…'

'You're here because my mom's at work, our two teachers are somewhere, and school's not for three more days. You're here because they don't want to leave me alone. You're here to be sure nothing happens.'

'Don't be crazy. Something always has to happen.'

'So let's make something happen now.'

'We're supposed to—'

'*Supposed to* doesn't beat *has to.* How do you stop what has to happen?'

'We can watch the TV that Mr Applegate lent your mom for you to watch! The channels, they come on – OK, not until four, but that gives us time to… to…'

'Nothing's on TV that matters. You turn it on. You turn it off. That's all.' Hal nodded to the kitchen window. 'Are you going to turn that off? Come on,' said Hal. 'Something's happening.'

'No it's not! We're going to stay right here, right in here, and… and…'

'And what? Wait for that station wagon to rust to dust?'

Luc grabbed Hal's arm. 'You can't do anything or you'll get in trouble! Besides, she'd yell right through you. Or do something worse.'

'Now do you get it? I can't do nothing and everything is coming at me.'

'I'm sorry nobody was there when I phoned!'

'Nobody's ever there. What difference would it make if they were? *Now* still turns into *later.* They can't do nothing about that and it's all happening to me.'

Luc swallowed. 'Wait.'

'For what? Another phone call to somebody who can't?'

'Wait for me.'

Hal looked at the boy. And saw him. Luc felt it. Hal really saw him.

Luc marched from the kitchen through the living room to the front door.

Went outside.

Walked past two battered chairs on Hal's front porch. Stepped down the concrete steps. His legs trembled. But they kept moving. Carried him across the dusty street. Closer, ever closer, to the rusted station wagon.

Luc saw a human shape behind the car's steering wheel. Two hands pressed around a black box held in front of where a face should be.

Click!

He knew she'd snapped a picture of him.

Luc stood beside the rusted station wagon.

Watched her lower the camera.

Her hair was twisted and clumpy, streaked with gray born after Easter. Ugly stains dotted the dark smock she wore. But what scared Luc was her skin.

Wrinkles wrapped her skull. Ropes of flesh snaked over her shape. Hung loosely around her arms. Those cords of flesh shrank in on themselves. Were pale, as if Dracula had vampired out her blood.

Luc said: 'Please.'

'Is that all you got to tell me? I heard that already. Plenty.'

'Honest, he won't do anything. Won't go anywhere.'

'I'm not going anywhere either. Until.'

'You can't do this.'

'Law says I can. Ask the sheriff. I told him. So did the county prosecutor. This is America. I got rights. The law gave him a slap on the wrist. But the law also hung a rope on him. Put the other end in my hands.'

'You don't have to do this.'

'You got something else we can do? Can you raise the dead?'

'Can you?'

She glared right through him.

'I want to help,' said Luc.

'You people who want to "help." My husband shuffles off to work. Sits and stares. Father Louis drives up here to preach about forgiveness. You forgive when the debt is paid. And Lord Jesus, I got nothing to confess. I'm not the one who sinned. Who murdered. Who's getting away with it. I don't need schoolteachers or sheriffs or doctors or priests lecturing me. My Earl didn't deserve to die. I don't deserve this. And the law says I got a chance to make the guilty pay.'

'What if Hal wasn't driving the car?'

'He's alive and free. You call that fair?'

'You call this fair?'

'Won't be fair even *when*.' She leaned out the window. 'You want to do what's right? Help me pull the rope on him.'

Luc ran back into the house.

She screamed at his back: 'You can't run from a guilty conscience!'

Luc found Hal sitting at the kitchen table. Staring nowhere.

Hal said: 'Is she still there?'

Luc had to nod *yes*.

'Sure she is.' Hal's mouth looked like the smile painted on Rachel's toy jack-in-the-box. 'That's just the way it is.'

He whirled toward his guardian with a leer that ripped Luc's heart.

'Make the most of it, right?' said Hal. 'That's what we're supposed to do.'

The chair clattered back from the kitchen table as Hal surged to his feet.

'No, Hal! Don't do anything!'

'Isn't that impossible?' said the teenager. 'I mean, hey, no matter what, I'm doing something. Even if I just sit there breathing, that's something. Even if I don't get to pick the air I get.' Hal grinned at Luc. 'Am I right or am I right?'

'I don't know! I don't care!'

'*Don't care.* How's that working out for you? Maybe I'll give it a try.'

'What are you talking about?'

'Doing what I can with what I got.'

Hal marched into the living room. Pulled Luc with his wake.

'Let me help!' yelled Luc.

'You already done what you could.'

Hal pulled open the door to the dirt-floored cellar.

Clumped down those stairs.

Luc stood in that doorway. Up from that bare-bulb-lit crypt floated a rotten earth cloud carrying Hal's chatter.

'Mom used to hide the one thing she got me for Christmas down here. Every year I'd sneak down, find it, and she never knew. Have to stand on that box, reach up in the floor beams, the crawlspace – fucking spider, get – *Yes!*'

Hal marched up the wooden steps *proud*.

With what he held.

Luc knew but had to whisper: 'What's that?'

'She'd never get rid of the bottle of whiskey Dad bought when he was home on leave in the war. They only drank a little of it before he went back. They were saving the rest of the bottle for when he got home. But he never made it.'

Hal picked up the glass from before.

'OK, this is bad,' he confessed. 'But hey: the booze was

evaporating anyway. Earl and me, we poured off a glass. Earl put water back in the bottle to the same line so she'd never know. Burned like hell when we drank it. I'll never be a whiskey man. But I'm glad I did that. Glad I got to drink my dad's.'

He reached in the freezer. Pulled out a metal tray of ice. Slammed it into the sink to pop out half a dozen ice cubes. He dropped three into the glass.

'And now lucky me, I get to drink my best friend's brew *and* my dad's.'

All Luc could say was: '*Please!*'

Hal smiled softly as he rubbed Luc's brush-cut hair.

Said: 'Remember when we helped harvest?'

Yes, nodded Luc, his tongue too thick to speak. *Yes*.

'That was one good day. Don't ever forget it.'

Whiskey and glass in hand, Hal marched to the front door.

Luc tackled Hal around the waist. His sneaker toes plowed the living room carpet as Hal dragged him past the ironing board, past the yellow chair.

Hal gyrated his hips like Elvis.

The clinging boy cracked like a whip. Luc's grip broke. He hit the floor.

Hal stepped out his front door.

Luc charged from the house. Stumbled down the concrete porch's three steps. Staggered onto the yellow lawn before he realized what he was not seeing.

Turned around…

Hal sat on the porch. Raised the whiskey bottle high and poured a long river of its brown into the ice-filled glass in his hand. Smiled.

'No!' yelled Luc.

Click! came a sound from the street behind Luc.

'I got you!' bellowed a voice from the rusted station wagon. 'I've got you!'

Hal took a long drink from his glass.

Click!

'Got you! Damn you, I got you!'

Click!

He frowned. Turned the frown to a soft smile for Luc.

Then he took another drink.

Click!

Luc whirled toward the street.

Mrs Klise crouched beside the gaping-door station wagon. She held the camera in front of her face. Made it click and whir as moans ripped from her.

Luc exploded:

Can't stop it! Got to, got to – GET HELP!

He charged to his bicycle waiting on the lawn.

Click!

He created a perfect picture: a buzz-cut boy in glasses and a white T-shirt, blue jeans, and sneakers. A blur with his knee high like a sprinter across the lawn while behind him, a teenager sat on his front porch holding a whiskey bottle.

'I've got you!' screamed Mrs Klise as Luc jumped on his bike, whirled past her. 'A minor drinking whiskey! Probationer drinking alcohol! I got you!'

Luc leaned over the handlebars. Wind rushed past him. His elbows jammed up like wings. His knees pumped so furiously his sneakers slipped off the pedals. He craned his neck. Peered through bouncing glasses.

The crest of Knob Hill rushed toward him.

Beyond it waited blue sky, the distant horizon with the Three Buffaloes.

Luc raced down potholed oiled road bouncing under his whirring tires. An invisible hand pushed him ever forward, ever faster down the road's screaming slope until Luc had to jerk his sneakers off the spinning pedals' blur.

Two blocks ahead. The high school corner, turning to drive up the hill:

The blue taxi.

Luc waved, screamed: 'Aunt Beryl!'

His bike's front tire bounced over a rock. The bike flipped up in a wheelie. Skidded down Knob Hill's slope on its rear tire and flew out from under Luc.

He hit the ground running downhill. He tumbled. Tripped. Pavement slammed up to stab his outstretched hands as he rolled into the first somersault when a rock gouged a jagged canyon into his right shin as he rolled into the second somersault and somehow his glasses didn't fly off as he flipped upright, back on his feet, his hands coming down – BAM! – smack onto the hood of the screaming-brakes, shuddering, stopped blue taxi.

'Jesus Christ, Lucas!' Aunt Beryl threw open the taxi door. 'Are you—'

'*Help me gotta get Neal northside painting Mrs Klise is kill Hal!*'

Beryl saw her crazed nephew with her Conner eyes that knew *trouble.*

'Get the hell in!' she yelled.

Luc dove into the backseat.

The cab careened into a sliding-tires circle turn.

Beryl yelled: 'Where?'

'Over behind the Totem Motel!'

She floor-boarded the gas. Inertia threw Luc against the backseat cushions.

The high school flew past. The Catholic school. A cranking right hand skid turn onto Main Street bounced Luc off the inside of the taxi's door.

Words machine-gunned out of him. The station wagon. Mrs Klise. The boy with whiskey. The clicking camera.

They roared across the viaduct bridge. Beryl swerved over a double-yellow road stripe to pass a slowpoke car. Zoomed down an alley. The blue taxi slid through a graveled canyon of backyard fences. Their dust cloud slammed to a stop near a garage where Neal Dylan was opening the trunk of his green car.

Luc screamed out the taxi window: 'Mrs Klise! Up at Hal's house!'

Neal scrambled into his car as Beryl ground the taxi into reverse and shot backward so Neal could race out of the alley.

'Go!' yelled Luc. 'We gotta go!'

Beryl drove into Neal's dust cloud. But not bullet fast.

'We've got to get there!'

'Yeah,' she told her nephew. 'But he should get there first.'

'*Please*,' whispered Luc, but that wasn't just about how much faster Aunt Beryl should go and she knew it. '*Please*.'

They drove over the viaduct at a quarter of the speed they'd come. No blaring horns. No swerving over yellow stripes. Stopped for the stop sign.

The taxi motored up Knob Hill. Luc's hands reached for something to grab onto. His fingers pushed into the crack between the seat cushions. Touched something metal, flat, small. The blue taxi crawled past the high school as he pulled the found thing out of the seats' crack.

What lay on Luc's palm looked like a tiny gold book scarred with weird letters: *Gamma Delta Zeta*. That metal didn't belong to Luc. He hadn't gone to law school so he could wear it on his watchband where it might slip off into the crack of the backseat in a taxi that during daylight hours ferried old ladies on errands and at night ferried men to the red cathouse.

Aunt Beryl hit a pothole, a collision that knocked Luc's eyes off what he held so he saw his bike as they sped past where it lay on the road. Luc shoved the gold tablet into his jeans' front pocket.

Red lights spun on the block of Hal's house.

Aunt Beryl stopped the taxi. Her eyes in the rearview mirror found Luc's.

'Whatever's going on,' she said, 'it ain't about you.'

Luc realized he was standing on the sidewalk. And seeing:

The Hemmer house. A brown whiskey bottle on its front porch.

Neal stood in the road. Pleading with Sheriff Wood.

The rusted station wagon, its driver's door gaping open.

Mrs Klise prancing on the street, the camera swinging at her side.

The police cruiser, its cherry dome light spinning out blats of red light.

Through the window of the cruiser's back door, the blank face of Hal.

'I got him!' yelled Mrs Klise. 'I got him! Fair and square!'

'It's the law,' muttered Sheriff Wood. 'That's all it is. It's the law.'

Then he watched his boots march toward the driver's door of the cruiser.

'Nobody can do nothing but what's right!' yelled Mrs Klise. She shook the camera at the cruiser. 'I got him fair and square and all wrapped up in law!'

Neal roared away in his green coupe. To a brown-suited lawyer's office. To the judge. To the café where Hal's mom worked to tell her and not catch the plate she'd drop on the floor. To a brown cottage.

Doesn't matter where Neal goes, thought Luc. *He'll get there too late.*

The cruiser pulled away from the curb. Sheriff Wood drove with his eyes fixed on the windshield. He didn't see a boy on the sidewalk as he drove past. Hal sat in the cruiser's rear seat. He stared somewhere beyond Luc.

Luc knew it didn't matter where Hal went, he was already gone.

But then…

Oh then!

Aunt Beryl. The toughest of the Conner sisters. Still stiff from some 'accident' after the train left town without fake Marilyn. Beryl, just back from staying out at her sister Dory's farm until the accident's bruises faded. Beryl, who'd come back to live with

Uncle Johnny like she always did after her leavings. Beryl, who'd been given the keys to the blue taxi like Luc had heard her tell her sister/his mom: "*cause the son-of-a-bitch can't make it work on his own 'n' needs me 'n' what the hell else am I gonna do, huh? Still got my ring on him.*'

That Beryl grabbed Ruth Klise's arm.

'You happy now?' yelled Beryl.

Ruth Klise struggled to break free.

'You know what you done?' yelled Beryl.

Fear shook Ruth Klise's wrinkled-skin face.

'You know who you are now?' yelled Beryl.

Ruth Klise broke free of the crazy Conner sister's grip.

Scurried to her open-driver's-door rusted station wagon. Her camera swung wildly at her side as she flung herself behind the steering wheel.

Beryl grabbed the driver's open door.

Wouldn't let Ruth pull it shut.

'Where you gonna go?' shouted Beryl. 'Where you gonna run to?'

Beryl slammed the car door shut.

Rocked Ruth Klise in her driver's seat.

Luc stood in the street three steps away from Ruth's slammed door. His face was level with hers.

Aunt Beryl yelled through the car's open window.

'Do you think you've won something?' yelled Beryl.

The woman trapped behind her steering wheel.

The woman screaming on that street.

They'd known each other their whole lives.

'Life fucked you!' yelled Beryl. 'So what did you do? You went for revenge. And you took it out on that poor boy who'd been fucked, too!'

Ruth Klise frantically ground the ignition key.

Got only *rrr rrr rrr* as her rusted machine tried to spark itself to life.

'Didn't you learn nothing in this damn town?' yelled Beryl. 'Everybody from the high school to your damn church to the bars on Main Street knows if'n you set out for revenge, you dig two graves.'

Vroom!

Ruth's station wagon roared to life.

Yet Mrs Klise and Luc still heard Beryl's whisper:

'*Hey, Ruth: Where you going?*'

Ruth stared out her driver's window to the street where she was.

Luc saw her quivering face.

Saw the wrinkles of flesh drained of lifeblood by some Dracula.

Saw her eyes – *Oh, her eyes!*

Her eyes were two empty black holes.

Beryl turned her back on the rumbling station wagon.

Beckoned Luc to follow her.

'Come on,' said Beryl. 'We're out of here.'

This time he rode in the front seat.

'None of it is your fault,' she said as the taxi rumbled through streets of homes. 'You tried as hard as you could. We all know that. Especially Hal.'

She rode the brake down the hill that had thrown Luc. 'There's your bike.'

The bike stood upright, placed safely on the sidewalk. Some Vernon citizen did the neighborly thing. The right thing. No credit asked or expected. Because that's the kind of place the town was.

Aunt Beryl pulled the taxi to the curb.

'Let's put your bike in the trunk. Ride you home.'

Luc shook his head.

And her eyes told him she'd respect that choice she didn't prefer.

He got out of the taxi. Closed the door. Watched her drive away.

His jeans stuck to his sore leg as he biked home. He knew that meant blood.

The first thing he saw as the bike rode him ever closer to the block where he lived was the house where lawyer Falk once lived.

Luc wheeled his bike up that driveway. The blinds on those windows were gone. Those rooms were empty. The girl he was supposed to marry didn't live there anymore with her mother and her father *who.* Luc rolled his bike from that ghost house to his own home. His leg burned as he walked the bike around back to park it on the patio where the rules, *oh the rules,* said it belonged. He glanced at the kitchen picture window. Didn't see Mom inside. No *Marilyn*, no *Arlene.* Walked to the lilac hedge that made the border between their grass and the shale hill dropping down to the alley. Again he looked into the picture window: no one.

Mom was in there somewhere. She'd fix his leg wound. Paint it with iodine that made him want to scream. But he wouldn't. What good would screaming do? She'd tell him to forget about today, because it just goes to show that you can't do much about much. That the only thing to do is get safe inside your own house and keep absolutely everything there exactly like it should be.

'I tell your father you can't do what you can't do,' she'd tell Luc while painting his leg with fire. 'Don't go looking for trouble. Don't go getting ideas because everything will come crashing down. That's the way things are.'

Luc would say nothing.

Wouldn't tattletale on Dad being in some kind of trouble fight at work.

But before he went inside, he clumped down the back steps on the shale hill sloping down from the lilac hedge border of their backyard. The alley waited there. Another gentle slope led down to Main Street's level. No buildings blocked Luc's view of that artery of commerce and community.

He looked across the alley to Main Street where the cars drove by.

A storekeeper waved to a banker.

A mom pushed a baby carriage past a shop.

The gold medal came out of his jeans pocket. You got it for being A Man of the Law like his parents told him he was gonna be.

Luc threw the medal as far away as he could.

PERMANENT RECORD

'First day of school feels tingly,' said Kurt as he, Wayne, and Luc watched the herd of special-occasion-dressed kids play on the schoolyard.

'Sixth grade!' said Wayne. 'We're on top.'

Kurt nodded to the next block where the brown-brick high school rose beside the gray-castle junior high. 'Not over there.'

'There's always some over there,' said Marin as he walked up.

'Hey,' said Wayne. 'Hey,' said Kurt. Luc nodded *Hey*. Marin made *them* official when he said, 'Hey.'

Here we are, thought Luc. Our gang. Ready to go. Their crew joined the other kids surging up the school steps like cattle into boxcars.

Wayne said: 'We're all going out for the football "experiment," right?'

Luc and Marin shrugged *of course*.

'Nah,' said Kurt.

And *like that*, Luc saw Kurt... standing on the other side of a border.

Inside the crowded hallways of their school, the four boys jostled their way to read the sixth grade class assignments taped on the hall wall.

'Yes!' said Kurt. 'I'm in 6A with Mr Dylan and Luc and Wayne and... ah...'

Marin said: 'What about me?'

Everyone knew what the look on Kurt's face meant.

'6B,' said Marin. 'Old Mrs Wilcox with her chin hair.'

'And other great kids!' said Kurt.

But they all knew.

They knew Principal Olsen had sat at his summer desk and judged all the ten-year-olds' pasts and futures, shuffled still-growing children into two groups.

'Good' students were in 6A. Science freak Fred was in there, plus Bobbi Jean. Kids who could be counted on to be and counted on to do so they would create the honor rolls of tomorrow. Sorted and selected because he said so.

6B was made up of 'regular' kids. Plus kids whose history, income, oddities, or independence implied trouble – if not trouble now, certainly trouble to come.

Like Ralph, whose dad had clashed with the school superintendent.

Nick with his twitching arm.

And Anna, who was dangerously pretty and thus *obviously* couldn't be as smart as she seemed. She got a desk in 6B's dictatorial matriculation to protect boys from diversions that would be totally her fault because of her beauty.

Marin and those kids had been shepherded into the care of Mrs Wilcox, who swung a yardstick and had stayed faithful to the same *sit still and shut up* lesson plan for the twenty-nine years that tenure had cemented her in Vernon's schools.

'Don't worry!' Luc told Marin. 'You can switch!'

Marin nodded to the list. 'Can't you see it's written in ink?'

Then he turned away. Walked down the long telescoping hall. Alone.

Donna's voice behind Luc: 'Think you can handle the blackboard?'

Kurt and Wayne hurried into their new classroom to leave Luc with her.

Luc stared at her with questions he didn't know how to ask: Were you in the radio repair shop during the parade? Where were you all summer?

She seemed taller, her dusty hair scissored short.

'Um… hi,' said Luc.

'*Um, HI!*' she repeated and he knew it was a tease. 'I'm in the B class.'

'But you got higher grades than me last year!'

'I'm not A class material,' she said. 'Like I didn't already know.' Donna nodded at him with an expression Luc couldn't understand. Gave him a faint smile. 'Your glasses going to be able to read the writing on the wall?'

'I'll be OK,' said Luc.

'You were born OK. You'll always have OK.'

She limped away before he could say anything.

Remember to call him Mr Dylan, not Neal, thought Luc as he entered the classroom where a blank-faced man sat behind the 6A teacher's desk.

I don't want any favors, thought Luc. *Not from him*.

Bobbi Jean popped up right in front of him. 'Lucas!'

'*Um*… Bobbi Jean, please call me—'

'Are you taking piano lessons again? My mom phoned Miss Smith and she said to wait. Aren't you glad we got Mr Dylan? He's supposed to be great so it'll be cool to have him, 'specially since this is our last year as just kids.'

'I think it's already been that,' said Luc.

'Not everybody's like Anna.'

'I wasn't talking about her.'

Bobbi Jean rolled her eyes. 'Since when?'

Last Bell killed anything Luc might have thought to say.

He plopped into a desk.

Silence. Sunshine. Twenty-nine sixth graders. One empty-faced teacher.

Neal Dylan finally said: 'Do you know who I am?'

Huh? thought Luc. He met Kurt's glance. Saw Wayne frown. *What?*

'Let's pretend that you do,' droned the teacher behind the big desk. 'Let's pretend that all we have to do is get through sixth grade. We can do that.'

Then he picked up a book. Turned pages. Read them aloud like a robot.

When the noon bell rang and the kids exploded out of the school, Luc passed Jordan – *Miss Smith* – in the hall. Her eyes watched her moving shoes.

Shuffling home for lunch took Luc past the side street to the city jail.

'Hal's gone,' Dad had told him the night before. 'The sheriff drove him to the state boys' home.'

'Then when he turns eighteen, he goes to prison,' said Luc.

Dad shrugged. 'There's always a chance.'

'There's no chance,' mumbled Luc. 'It's the law.'

Laura was eating lunch with Mom and Dad by the time Luc got home. He sat in front of his tuna fish sandwich and glass of milk, said: '6A, Mr Dylan.'

Laura said: 'Thank God you didn't get Mrs Wilcox!'

Their parents shared a look that made Luc wonder what credit God deserved.

'And OK, Dad,' said Laura, 'you were right. The guidance counselor stopped me in the hall. Since I resigned from Honor Society before they kicked me out, last year's grades count toward eligibility this year. If I keep B+s… No promises, he said. *But.* And that means I'd be eligible for the scholarship.'

'That's the way things are supposed to work,' said Dad. 'You're supposed to make them work out.'

'Just don't make trouble,' said Mom. 'Making trouble makes trouble.'

Luc prayed his dad was right, not his mom.

He swore he'd come right home after football. Pretended that was why he took his bike as he hurried outside, saying: 'I gotta go back to school early!'

Few kids were on the playground when Luc wrapped his hand

around the brass handle of the school's front door. Took a deep breath. Stepped inside.

Luc stood alone in the long, quiet hall. Sunlight lit the gray tiles. The green hall telescoped toward the exit he'd used last spring when he thought he could run away from having to see better.

You can't run away, he told himself. *Couldn't then. Can't now.*

If things aren't the way they're supposed to be, you make them right.

One step at a time, Luc followed the sunlit hall past classrooms.

Stopped outside the portal labeled office.

Nobody sat at the secretary's desk.

Luc knocked on the inner door. Coughed. 'Hello?'

From the inner office came Principal Olsen's bellow: 'Get in here!'

Principal Olsen crouched on his office chair like a tiger. File folders stacked like mountains covered his desk. Whiffs of coffee and a vanished chicken sandwich floated in the office's air with scents of dust, mimeo ink, and paper.

'What's your problem?' snapped the principal. 'It's ten minutes before you're supposed to be in the building. Unless you have lunch detention.'

'No, I—'

'Didn't think so. You're not one of those kids.'

'That's what I'm here about. There's – I think there's been a mistake.'

Principal Olsen frowned.

'See, Kurt, Wayne, and I, and Marin Larson, he was new last year, but we're a team for class projects and he's smart as any of the kids in 6A except Fred and nobody's as smart as him and so the mistake is that Marin kind of got put in 6B – not that those kids aren't – but he's not with us like he's supposed to be.'

Luc swallowed. 'So I came to ask you to please switch him to—'

'You got nerve, Mr Lucas Ross. But you're not as smart as you think.'

'I don't think I'm smart!'

'This bonehead move proves you're right about that. Seems your buddy Marin is more of a problem than I thought. He put you up to this.'

'No he didn't! Honest!'

Principal Olsen rolled his eyes.

'I'll let that fib go because you've got a good record and it's only the first day of school, so thank your lucky stars.'

The tiger leaned closer to the boy trembling in front of him.

'I wasn't sure about that smart-aleck Injun kid. You never know, he's got a hard-working mom. I'd have respected him if he'd had the guts to march in here himself. But sending you to do his dirty work for him...'

'He—'

'One more word out of you and we have to rethink *your* situation!' Principal Olsen shook his head. 'Didn't you learn anything this summer? What happened to Hal Hemmer when he didn't take the chance he got?'

Olsen tapped the stack of file folders.

'Screw up or shape up, it all – *everything*, and I mean *everything* you do – it all goes into your Permanent Record.

'And that, *young man*, means *everything*, because your Permanent Record decides your whole life. Now stop being a stooge for your friends. Get better ones.'

The stab of the principal's finger thrust Luc back into the hall.

Left him dazed.

A daze that lasted until the last bell when fourth grade teacher/coach Cox presided over a melee of thirty-one sixth grade boys in the lunchroom where they grabbed football gear as old as their parents.

None of the helmets had a faceguard. Luc's eggshell-white dome and leather side straps made a tight fit over his glasses. His shoulder pads were too big. So were the football pants. His strap-on hip pads were missing a flap. Like everyone else, he wore his own sneakers.

'What position are you going for?' asked Wayne as they buckled up.

'I can't throw worth crap. I can't catch the ball. Everybody is faster than me.' Luc shrugged. 'Guess I'll be a guard. Sounds easier than a ball hiker and cooler than a tackle.'

Coach Cox blew his whistle.

'What are you going out for?' Luc asked Wayne as they ran outside.

Wayne said: 'Guess I'll be a guard, too. I'll be right side, you be left.'

The difference between right and left occupied much of their first practice on the shale lot across the street from their school by the junior high. Coach Cox barked the sixth graders through jumping jacks, push-ups, sit-ups, wind sprints where Luc always came in last while Marin always glided in first.

The coach divided the boys into two teams. He had to stage races among the nineteen boys who'd insisted on being halfbacks, fullbacks, or quarterbacks, with the slowest ones suddenly discovering they were to be anonymous linemen instead of ball-carrying stars. Luc and Wayne's *from-the-get-go* choice of grunt work over glory meant they landed first string on the maroon jerseys.

Marin became a maroon halfback without having to gasp for breath.

Stinky blue ink memo sheets with plays and defenses waited on a metal folding chair when they trudged back to the gym. As he changed into his street clothes beside Marin, Luc wondered if he should tell him about what he'd done in the principal's office.

Better not get him in trouble, too, thought Luc. *Besides, what if he thinks I shouldn't poke my nose into his business? Please don't let him get mad at me!*

So it went for three days. Sixth grade taught from textbooks by a robot. Football practice on the shale field. Home for dinner at six.

Until Friday.

Regular school days, the high school team ruled the town's gridiron while the junior high squad worked out on whichever end of that field the high school's team let them use.

Game-night Fridays meant only the junior high team practiced at the grass field on the northside, so that afternoon, the 'football experiment' elementary school team traded their dirt lot for real grass and goalposts.

'Grab your gear,' Coach Cox told the sixth graders. 'Dress-out on the bus!'

A roaring stampede of boys exploded out of the elementary school. The bus door *whooshed* closed. The yellow machine rumbled away from the school while the boys in it wrestled off blue jeans, struggled into pads.

'Honk the horn!' yelled somebody.

'Let them know we're coming!' yelled somebody else.

Dave Maynard stuck his butt against the window to moon three Catholic school girls. *OK*, his underpants were still on, but *man*, how funny! Luc got his jersey stuck halfway over his shoulder pads. Marin and Wayne wrestled it down.

'Who farted?'

Laughter drowned out accusations and boasts.

September sunlight stretched a golden glow across a perfect blue sky arcing above the town's emerald field. The yellow school bus rolled through the chain-link fence's gate, tires crunching as it followed the gray cinder oval track around the field, past the white goalpost where junior high giants hurled themselves at canvas blocking dummies. The bus rumbled to the other goalpost. Luc and his buddies charged out of the bus. Stampeded past the high school football coach as he striped white hash marks on the green grass.

'One back, one lineman!' yelled their coach. 'Marin! Lucas! Lead 'em!'

Oh. My. God.

Suddenly there Luc was: standing beside Marin in front of their classmates, *the team* who wore faded jerseys, floppy pads, helmets, and grins.

'Jumping jacks!' bellowed Marin. 'Ready!'

Every muscle in Luc tensed. His legs coiled with burning springs.

'One!' yelled Marin as his arms flew up and his legs scissored out.

And I'm with him! knew Luc. *In time together! Everybody following us!*

'Two! Three! Four! One! Two! Three! Four!'

Luc felt himself soaring against the sky for the world to see he wasn't a four-eyed teacher's pet, Momma's boy, bookworm, no-muscled, uncut, uncool, girls-laugh-at geek. *That's not me. I'm here. With my friends. In this glorious moment.*

Fifteen minutes of leading exercises changed to a half hour of being just another jersey running drills to Coach's yells. Of not falling over in the three-point stance – right knuckles digging into the grass, helmet-heavy head craned up to look at the horizon beyond the distant goalpost, butt stuck high on spread and bent legs. Coach set two squads on a scrimmage line. Luc's squad practiced offensive plays while the second squad dug in on defense.

'Look,' Marin told his teammates as they pulled each other up from the dogpile following a quarterback sneak that only gained a yard.

Coming through the distant chain-link fence gate. Tires rolling over the cinder track to stop at the parked yellow bus. A brown sedan.

'Principal Olsen!' said Wayne. 'What's he doing here?'

Coach yelled: 'Offense! Huddle up!'

Principal Olsen climbed out of his car.

Yelled: 'Coach Cox! I need to see you!'

The coach nodded, leaned into the huddle, whispered: 'Run Give-33.'

Coach Cox walked toward his boss as quarterback Jesse whispered: 'On two. Give-33 on two. Break!'

Give-33: The number 3 man running through the number 3 hole. Left guard Luc had to block a defensive lineman out of the way of the charging halfback. Who was Marin.

The huddle broke. Luc and his squad trotted toward the ball waiting on the grass where eleven kids on the other squad tensed to stop the coming play.

Luc glanced to the sideline.

Principal Olsen held Coach Cox by the arm as if to steady the teacher.

Quarterback Jesse loomed behind the center.

Luc sank into ready stance: knees bent, head up, forearms on his thighs.

'Ready!' yelled Jesse. 'Down!'

Luc and Wayne and the other offensive linemen dropped into their three-point stance. The center cocked the football pressed into the ground.

'Set!' yelled Jesse. 'Hut one! Hut two!'

Boom!

Luc rammed his shoulder pad into the kid across from him. Shouts. Grunts. Thuds. A blur of jerseys and waving arms. Luc staggered…

… saw Marin stiff-arm a linebacker. Throw a hip fake at two defensive backs who collided with each other. Dash past them toward the open swath of green grass stretching toward the distant goalpost and practicing junior high team. Jog back toward his teammates.

The brown sedan drove away with Coach Cox.

Principal Olsen stood in front of the team. Twirled the coach's whistle.

'Listen up!' yelled the principal. 'Coach's wife broke her arm. She'll be OK. But no need for you guys to waste your chance here.

'Now,' he said to the sixth graders, 'what the hell do you call that?'

Jesse cleared his throat. 'Um... We ran Give-33. Just like Coach said.'

Olsen glared at the kids playing defense. Squinted at the kids on offense.

'Marin: you carried the ball on that play? And nobody stopped you?' Olsen shook his head. Told the whole team: 'You can't make it in life with bad defense!

'Run that play again!' he called over to Jesse.

Then Principal Olsen blew the whistle. Clearly liked that sound.

The center yelled: 'Huddle up!'

Ten boys on the offensive team circled quarterback Jesse.

'The other guys know what we're going to do!' whispered Pete Nasset.

Wayne said: 'Marin'll get creamed!'

'Listen up,' said Jesse. 'Give-33 like we got to, but... Pettigrew, you're fullback. Blast off and go through the hole first. Knock guys down. Marin, hang back, take the handoff late. But make it look like it did before, OK? On two.'

Break the huddle. Clap. Ready, down, set, hut one, hut two—

BAM!

The defensive lineman tore into Luc's block. Would have pushed him over but Pettigrew slammed into them and blew a gap in the line of battling boys. Marin charged behind him. Spun around the tumbling bodies and grabbing hands and surged three steps down the open field before the blast of a coach's whistle.

'What the hell!' yelled Principal Olsen.

'Marin!' Olsen's bellow froze him. His teammates prayed for invisibility. 'You think you're pretty good, getting away with that. You got lucky. Luck and other guys carrying your weight won't get you by on this field. Or anywhere else.'

Olsen whirled to the boys playing defense. 'And you guys! What would Coach Cox think, you slacking off. Guess we need some *educational assistance*.'

He whirled, marched up the middle of the grassy field.

Walked past the high school coach striping the fifty-yard line.

'Where is he going?' said Luc.

Principal Olsen walked to where the junior high team was practicing in helmets with face masks and pads that fit. Talked to the junior high coach.

The crowd of junior high players split into two groups.

Group One resumed attacking canvas dummies.

Group Two marched down the field with Principal Olsen.

'Uh-oh,' whispered Jesse.

Eleven junior high knights crossed the fifty-yard line, armored adolescents clapping their hands, slapping each other's pads. Those seventh and eighth graders were bigger than any of Luc's team except center Bill Woon.

'Sixth grade defense!' yelled Olsen. 'On the sidelines. Watch and learn.'

'Yeah!' yelled a junior high giant. His teammates positioned themselves as defenders on the chalk line.

'Run it again!' Olsen yelled. '*What you call it*, Give-33.'

He whirled to the junior high squad. 'Show my boys how to stop a run.'

Quarterback Jesse chewed his lip as his team circled around him.

'They'll murderate us!' whispered Wayne.

Pettigrew said: 'And they know what—'

'But they don't know *when*.' Jesse looked at his halfback. 'Sorry, Marin. We gotta surprise 'em,' Jesse told the team. 'Quick snap. I'll go "Ready, down" – then on "Set," we blast off. They think we won't go until at least one. *Marin, Luc*: there's no time to send Pettigrew through to help. Sorry.'

They clapped.

Broke the huddle.

Moved toward a football waiting on a chalk line.

The high school coach walked closer to watch.

Luc sank into Ready's crouch. Turned his helmet up to see…

A giant crouched across the white line from him: Clayton Schenck, eighth grader. Luc knew if they stood up, Luc's helmet would only reach Clayton's eyes – eyes that now stabbed steel spears at Luc. Luc swallowed.

'Ready… Down… Set!'

BAM! Luc sprang forward, elbows out and fists pressed to his chest as he crashed into Clayton, moved the surprised bigger boy back a whole two inches.

King Kong rammed Luc. Rocketed him backward, stumbling—

A blur of football gear shot between blasted-backward Luc as his teammate Bill Woon whirled to slam into Clayton.

Luc's back crashed onto the emerald field.

Blue sky filled the lenses of his glasses.

Flicking past his vision came Marin's sneakers.

Marin leapt over the jam of grabbing hands and shoulder pads, helmets, and backs. Landed on his feet, the football wrapped in his arms as he sprang forward.

He gained five more yards before the linebacker and two safeties tackled him. Marin crashed, buried under a pile of adolescent knights.

Junior high giants climbed off the pile.

Left a sixth grader lying on the grass as they walked away.

Get up! pleaded Luc. *Please Oh God Marin don't be – Get up!*

He did. Slowly. Standing. Walking. Coming back to his team.

Principal Olsen stood with his hands on his hips. The whistle dangled on his chest. Something like a smile lined his face.

'So, Marin,' he said. 'You learn anything yet?'

Marin gingerly bent over to put the football on the white chalk line where it started. Walked ever so carefully back to where his team should huddle.

Olsen whirled to the junior high squad.

'And what is it with you girls? You call that tough? You call that football? You knew he was coming and he still damn near got a first down!'

'Come on!' yelled an eighth grade linebacker. 'Hold 'em! Kill 'em!'

Principal Olsen yelled: 'Last chance!'

The junior high giants dug into position on the white line.

'Marin!' yelled Olsen. 'You're running it again. Huddle 'em up, Jesse!'

A cool September wind waved through the white-striped grass as Luc huddled with his ten teammates who smelled like smeared earth, like sweat. Luc knew he bled where his glasses had gouged his cheekbone. Wayne's jersey was torn. Marin's left jaw was scraped, his left eye puffy. His nose trickled blood.

'I'm sorry!' blurted Luc. 'I'm sorry!'

'Hey,' Marin kindly lied, 'you made a good block. No sorry.'

Not about that! Luc wanted to scream. *This isn't about that! This is about…*

Tried to tell himself this *wasn't* about what he'd done going to the office.

Jesse leaned into the huddle.

He was the quarterback. He was in sixth grade. Just like the ten boys facing him in this huddle, all of them sentenced to Blackhawk Elementary School in Vernon, Montana, September 1959, where the buzz-cut, husky man standing on the sidelines wore something like a smile and a coach's whistle.

'OK,' said Jesse. 'He said "*last chance.*" Let's do it. But do it our way.'

Jesse looked at Bill Woon. Bill shrugged his shoulder pads. Wayne made a smile. Luc caught Jesse's glance, nodded *yes.* One by one, the other boys voted with nods, with grimaces, with their beating hearts. Marin nodded *yes.*

'Forget Give-33,' said Jesse. 'That pitchout sweep? They think we're coming up the left middle. We'll go outside right. Pettigrew, you lead and, Maynard, you're the other halfback, you cover our butts. Marin, run like hell. Pitchout, Sweep Right. On one. Ready… Break!'

Eleven sets of hands clapped.

Eleven soldiers moved toward the line of battle.

'You're all dead dead dead!' yelled a junior high knight.

Jesse yelled: '*Ready!*'

The giant eighth grader Clayton snarled as he settled into his defense stance to crush the grade school dweeb named Luc across from him.

'*Set!*'

Luc felt himself float through this clock-stopped moment. Speared his right knuckles into the grass. Craned his neck up to see Clayton through his glasses.

'*Hut one!*'

Fury crashed Luc into Clayton. The world went white light. He spun in a sea of shouts and thuds. Slammed down to the emerald hard earth.

'Go!' bellowed some boy. 'Go!'

Luc realized he was on his feet, standing with a crowd of junior high and sixth grade players whose parts were over, done, all of them turned to watch.

To see the race of a lifetime streaking down that afternoon football field.

Two defensive backs chased Marin, certain they'd catch him.

'Go!' yelled Wayne and Bill Woon.

Luc pushed his way through the crowd: 'Run!'

Marin crossed the fifty-yard line dead even with the two eighth grade pursuers. They angled their charge. Their outstretched hands grabbed air.

'They'll catch him!' said a junior high giant beside Luc. 'Has to happen!'

At the twenty-yard line, one eighth grader drove through the air, crashed face first and empty-handed onto the grass.

Junior high coach Littlejohn turned from explaining pass blocking to his boys to see a sixth grader streak across the goal line and circle the white goal post while a wheezing star from Littlejohn's team stumbled at the boy's heels.

The sixth grader nodded to Littlejohn. Loped back the way he'd come.

His eighth grade pursuer shrugged at his coach. Jogged to follow the kid to the other end of the field.

The junior high player who'd missed his desperation tackle stood waiting for Marin. The older boy slapped "*good job*" on Marin's back. Marin kept going.

Going all the way to the other goal post where the whole sixth grade team jumped up and down, clapped and whistled and cheered. Where Principal Olsen stood on the sidelines a few feet from the applauding bus driver. Where the high school coach stood, his eyes squinting in light from the sun near the horizon.

Marin flicked the football toward the adults.

And the high school coach intercepted it.

'Whoa, guy!' said that man who everyone knew as the emperor of this field and a prince of the town. 'You've got some speed on you. What's your name?'

'Marin Larson.'

'Marin, when you get to high school, we got some good times ahead of us.'

The high school coach *pressed* the football into Principal Olsen's chest.

'Looks like you've got yourself a winner,' said the emperor of this field. 'Give the horse a rest. He burns out, that's no good for anybody.'

Principal Olsen watched the high school coach walk away.

The junior high coach came close, loudly told his fellow tenured educator:

'Your guys should take a break. I'll walk my squad through a few things to give them pointers. You know, on how this game is supposed to be played.'

The whistle dangling around Principal Olsen's neck tethered him to the grass where was. He said nothing. Did nothing more than stand there.

Luc edged through his teammates to Marin. 'That was so great!'

Marin let Luc fill his hardened eyes.

Said: 'Take care of my gear.'

Walked away.

They all watched him go.

Luc.

His teammates and the junior high squad.

The high school coach who was putting the striper back into its shed.

Principal Olsen and his whistle standing rooted in the grass he'd claimed.

Wayne shuffled to Luc's side, whispered: 'What's he doing?'

Marin walked past the bus driver who'd cheered him on.

Climbed the stairs into the bus.

Call it five minutes.

Then out of the bus stepped Marin. He wore his street clothes.

Without a glance toward Luc and the others, he marched toward the far gate in the field's chain-link fence. Out the gate. Walked the street back into town.

Gone.

Ten minutes later, the bus carried Blackhawk Elementary's football team back to their school where the next day, the 'experiment' of sixth graders playing football was declared over by Superintendent of Schools Makhem, officially because their coach had to take care of his broken-armed wife.

Silence rode that bus.

When they got back to the school, Luc, Jesse, and Bill Woon carried Marin's football gear into the gym. Put it on the pile. They put their own gear in assigned places against the wall. Walked through the haunted halls of their school and out to their sinking-sun hometown.

Luc didn't look at his watch as he swung onto his bike and pedaled furiously away from the school. He knew *when* it was: *Last chance.*

The sky bled as he pumped his bike pedals. Gasped as bone-sore legs pushed his race up Knob Hill. Past the street that would have taken him home. Past houses as lights inside got switched on for dinner. The breeze that fought his ride rustled through town trees to pluck off the most brittle of a million gold and russet autumn leaves and sail them down on him like drunken angels.

On his right: the brown house of Jordan Smith.

No, he told himself. *Not her. She's not from here. She won't know how.*

Go! he told himself. *Gotta go. Gotta get there. Gotta fix what I did.*

Make it right filled him. The certainty that *he* was the last guy who could make it right. Who wouldn't let what was happening to Marin… Would stop it.

Not Mom, he told himself. Not Dad. They won't make trouble. But I can make *him* see. He owes me. Owes *it*. He's from here. This is his place. In his blood like it's in mine. And he's part of it, so he can do it, he has to do it. *Has to.*

Luc braked his bike outside the house that didn't blow up back *when*.

Heard his sixth grade teacher's voice through the half-open door: '*Please!*'

Rita's voice threw her answer outside to Luc, the slur of her words not softening their jagged edge: 'All you can do is stand there 'n' say *please?*'

'What do you want me to do? What do you want me to say?'

'Don't give a damn what you say. But what you do, I damn well get to decide that. You think you're so smart and I'm such a dummy. Well, *Mister College*, guy I know finished law school. He done it and'll do it to you. You an' your Miss Perfect.'

'This isn't about her.'

'Like hell.'

'It's us. It's you. It's—'

'You don't give a shit about "us" and you sure 's shit give it all to her. Least you give her all that you can get away with. That shit better stop, too. 'Cause the one stone-cold certain thing you do give a shit about is your precious Ra'shel.'

'Don't do this to her!'

'I'm doing what law says I get to. I'm *the mother,* an' the law says that counts for everything. 'Specially when it comes to kids whose poppa's steppin' out and wantin' to take her away and *Daddy* her with some bitch. But the law won' let that happen. Bet you knew that even 'fore I talked to my suit and tie gunslinger on Main Street. He smiles at me just fine. Likes what my position is. Maybe he likes a little more 'n that, I ain't decided. But I own your adulterous ass in this town. And I got her, I got Rachel, your precious court of law'll see to that. You'd die for her, die without her. So that means I got you, now don't it, *Mister Please.*'

'You can have it all. The car. The money in our bank account. You can have the clothes off my back.'

'Yeah, you figure on doin' a lot of no-clothes stuff, don't you?'

'Look, she's your daughter, and I don't want to change that, but... you don't want to raise her. Be a mom to her like—'

'Like who? Like all the other biddies in this town? Like some teacher bitch from back east? Like somebody who's good enough for you?'

'I didn't say that.'

'You ain't man enough to say that. Well, don't you worry about *man* stuff. Not with Rachel. I'll take care of that. I'll teach her real well. Raise her up so she knows all about men. Unless, of course, you're livin' right here like a husband and a daddy supposed to and take care of that. Not livin' 'cross town with a new fancy wife. You do that, the two of you all happy-ever-after, I'll drive Rachel by your house. Point out where the son-of-a-bitch who's her daddy and his whore live.'

'You'll be too drunk to drive!'

'When has that ever stopped me?'

'Why are you doing this? You don't want me, Rachel – What do you want?'

Leaves skittered down the gutter near where Luc stood.

'I'm no loser! No got-nothing loser. I'm never gonna look in a bar mirror and see *loser* sitting on my stool. No loser going t' my high school reunion. I put it out on the line for you. I won you. You promised. So till death do us part. And there's not a damn thing you can do about that.'

Like a bullet through his heart, Luc knew that was true.

Not a damn thing Neal could do.

And not me either, thought Luc.

He got on his bike. Slowly pedaled away.

Houses he knew floated past him. Gravel crunched under his tires. Trees waved in the evening wind. His eyes fell on his watch: four minutes after six o'clock. Dad and Laura and Mom would be sitting at the dinner table in the yellow kitchen. Dad would say something like: '*Practice must have run long.*' Laura'd eye her plate, knowing better than to say anything. Mom's eyes would be nailed to the kitchen clock, to the constant sweep of the red second hand around that circle, each sweep screaming that this was not how things were supposed to be, that now it was time for everyone to be eating the dinner she cooked, that now the universe had been broken and Luc would know that was his fault.

He blinked back to where he was. Squinted in fading daylight. This wasn't the block he was supposed to be on. Not the way home. This was…

The block where Hal lived – *used to* live.

What Luc saw there and then hit him harder than King Kong.

Hit him so hard the bike skidded out from under him. He staggered over the potholed road as streetlights winked on in the evening glow.

Hal's house. Hal's ordinary American home.

But not anymore. *Not ever again*, thought Luc.

He saw twinkles from a brown bottle shattered on the porch floor.

Saw red paint scarring the house's white wall. Scarlet words as tall as him on the white house now painted in the Permanent Record. And no matter how much he wanted them not to be, Luc feared they were true:

TheRe IS NO JusticE in Vernon!

SOMETHING IN THE AIR

Laura drove the family car that warm Saturday after dinner.

Held the steering wheel steady in her left hand while her right hand tuned the radio for the eighty-seven-miles-away 'big' city station that played rock 'n' roll.

Luc rode shotgun.

Gramma Meg sat in the backseat behind Luc.

Windows rolled down. Warm September evening air brushed their faces.

'Can you feel it coming?' said Gramma Meg.

'Like a storm.' Luc shrugged. 'Or just the changing of the seasons.'

Laura shook her head. 'It's all gotta change.'

Luc looked in the rearview mirror.

Saw Gramma Meg staring out the windshield.

The radio crackled a chorus of four men lamenting: '*There goes my baby...*'

Sundown streaks appeared in the windshield as the car passed the Roxy.

Luc already knew what movie the marquee announced:

The Hanging Tree

Luc had gone to the Roxy that morning to pick up handbills to pass out door-to-door. When he got there, the theater manager Tom was sorting a stack of manila file folders at his downstairs desk.

A file folder yawning open on the desk caught Luc's eye with its contents of red, white, and blue pamphlets. One pamphlet showed lines of red names.

'What are those?' asked Luc.

'These pamphlets been sent out to movie theaters like the Roxy all over the country,' said Tom. 'The blacklists.'

'What's a blacklist? Who are those people?'

'Some big-name Hollywood stars that'd surprise you. Mostly it's directors and writers. Commies or sympathizers. Lefties. Freaks. Rebels. Theaters like us have to be on alert not to order movies from or with any of them. Pull them off our screens. Gotta keep you kids – hell, everybody – from getting hit with the wrong kind of thinking and saying. Gotta do what's right, be loyal Americans.'

'I always stand at attention, hand over my heart for the flag.'

'Good for you, son. Your aunts like to tell how you help with the flag up t' the hospital. Don't worry: nobody's ever gonna cancel anything you do.'

He closed the manila file folder and put it safely in his desk drawer.

Permanent record, thought Luc.

The handbills for *The Hanging Tree* movie said it came from a novel written by a woman from Montana. Like Luc was.

He heard whispers in his skull: "*If she could do it…*"

That evening, Laura drove past the Roxy's palace of dreams.

'What the hell!' said Gramma Meg. 'Let 'em wait. Let's ride around town.'

Laura's voice was calm.

'I know where we're supposed to go,' she said. 'And I'm driving.'

'Hell,' grumped Gramma Meg. 'After what happened last Easter, I figured you were finally letting loose a little.'

Their car drove past the west end of Main Street's Rainbow Hotel where lifetime bachelors like a town barber lived.

'Being loose doesn't mean you've got someplace to go,' said Laura.

Gramma Meg settled in the seat behind her granddaughter. 'I'm just trying to figure out what the hell you think you're doing.'

The car drove between Laura's high school and Luc's elementary school.

'Me, too, Gramma,' said Laura as her windshield filled with the vast blue sky coming on sundown. 'Me, too.'

Laura clicked the blinker for a right-hand turn.

Houses rolled past both sides of the car.

Garth shuffled on the sidewalk outside Luc's window.

Luc raised his hand to the man wearing ragged clothes, toilet-paper scraps over shaving cuts, a cap with its snapped-tight earflaps muffling all sounds.

Garth's right hand rose to his forehead in an answering salute.

Guess I'm one of the crazies now, thought Luc.

Don't kid yourself, he thought: *You've always been crazy*.

Laura parked the car across the street from the Tastee-Freez Drive-in.

Through the café's smudged window walls, Lucas saw teenage girls bustling to serve Cokes, hamburgers with French fries, and just-invented soft swirl vanilla or chocolate ice cream whirred out of a machine into cups and cones.

A curved line of cars in front of the café snaked past speakers on poles for customers to radio their orders to the servers. Beyond that cafe stretched the two-lane highway that ran through town toward dusk and dawn.

A white-roofed and turquoise-bodied Chevy with swooping tail fins slid into a parking spot near the walk-up window. The four doors of the Chevy flew open.

Johnny Russo's gray-haired wife Aunt Beryl rose out of the driver's side.

Iona stepped out of the shotgun seat. Popped a Lifesaver into her mouth while she looked away from her mother in a car parked across the street.

Luc's view of Iona got blocked by his Aunt Dory carrying Gramma Meg's crutches as she laughed "*Oh my Lord*" at the story she was telling.

The woman Luc and Laura called Mom stepped out of the driver's side back door. Her children read her: excited to be here and nervous *that*. Any *that*.

Luc and Laura opened their doors. Laura had Gramma Meg's door open by the time he could walk around their old car to help as their aunts drew near.

Laura told her gray-haired aunt: 'Nice ride.'

Beryl grinned. 'Your Uncle Johnny figured I don't drive taxi no more. He's got that barfly Roy working the calls. So I need a new ride. John thinks it's his.'

Iona said: 'Hell, you need a job, I can get Orville to let you work the rig.'

The sisters laughed.

'Ain't no way no man gonna let no woman work a rig,' said Gramma Meg. 'Women'd be too tough and end up taking the men's jobs.'

Meg worked her crutches toward the white-walled, drive-in treats factory. Her children and grandchildren fanned out behind her.

Like a posse coming into town, thought Luc. *Our hometown.*

He'd been raised knowing the Conners had been 'the first White folks' in 1884 to homestead a tarpaper shack in this merciless prairie valley after the Blackfeet beat the Crows in a territorial battle long before a railroad clerk'd kicked an empty boxcar onto a spur off the main line. Named the place it made "Vernon" after himself. Later blew his brains out with a Colt revolver.

'Doesn't make us special,' Luc's mom and her sisters told their children. 'Just means we were too stubborn and tough to move on to somewhere better.'

My family, thought Luc as he 'rode drag' behind Gramma Meg swinging herself through the soft September air on her crutches and steel-braced legs. Her daughters fanned out on each side of her. Laura walked a step away from them.

Their posse circled around the back of the white stucco Tastee-Freez to a patch of yellowing grass and fallen leaves that held picnic tables.

They swung two tables end to end so all of them could sit together.

As her family moved to their places, Dory told them how her husband Paul 'looked to be done pulling the farm together for winter by middle of next week.'

'They say this winter's gonna be a rough one,' said her sister Iona.

'They always say that,' said the mom named Cora.

'There's always some *they* that's always saying something,' said Beryl.

'What the hell else are they going to do?' said Gramma Meg.

All the Conner women laughed as their faces remembered brutal winters they'd lived through, winters like they knew would keep coming *forever*, though none of them on that fine 1959 autumn evening knew that that coming winter would be the last of those historic ones, lots of snow, four major blizzards, and nine days when the temperature sank to 40 degrees below zero.

Iona shrugged.

'Orville says job drilling south of town should carry him till around Halloween, and then he's heard tell things are gonna pick up again down in Butte with the mines and the Pit.'

AKA, the Berkeley Pit, that by the election of the third of four US presidents from Luc's generation had become a mile-long, geese-killing nine hundred feet deep and rising toxic lake and federal environmental disaster site/tourist stop.

Dory looked across 1959's picnic table at Luc and Laura's mom.

'So how's Don doing at the trucking company?' said Dory.

Mom snapped: 'Everything's fine.'

Nobody asked Beryl about her husband Johnny.

'Well, hell, kids,' Iona asked everyone. 'What's everybody gonna get?'

'Everybody' decided on Cokes – except for Gramma Meg, who wanted a Coke *and* a cup of 'that new fancy swirly chocolate ice cream.'

Wish I'd picked a cone of that! thought Luc as he and Laura walked the orders and a fistful of coins to the white stucco Tastee-Freez's walk-up window.

Where Irwin stood waiting for his order.

'We've got to decide on our projects for the science fair in November,' Irwin told Laura that September eve.

Laura said: 'I've already got mine.'

'Oh,' said the boy who'd once informed her in front of Luc that "*even though she was a girl,*" she was going to "*get to be*" salutatorian, the number two at their high school graduation to his number one valedictorian.

The teenage girl behind the window handed pudgy banker's son Irwin a triple swirl cup of white and brown ice cream with a plastic spoon.

Irwin told Laura: 'So I'll see you when I pick you up for school Monday.'

'Ah… *no*,' said Laura. 'I think… I think Claudia and I are gonna work out a carpool for the rest of the year.'

Irwin blinked.

Walked away.

Luc heard the *clunk* of that older boy's car door.

Laura gave their orders to the teenager working the walk-up window.

Luc asked his big sister: 'What's your science project?'

'I don't have a clue.' She smiled. 'And now neither does he.'

They delivered the treats. Took their places at the end of the picnic table. Luc faced houses for people he didn't know. Laura faced the road out of town.

They listened to the jabber of their aunts and Gramma Meg's pronouncements.

Their aunts passed empty soda cups and bunched-up napkins for the trash to the kids – to Luc first, because he was a boy and thus jobbed with cleanup.

A car in the long line of customers' machines beeped its horn as Laura and Luc dumped their trash in the garbage can beside the Tastee-Freez:

High schoolers Claudia and Chris.

Claudia scooted away from sitting beside Chris to lean out the passenger window and tell Laura: 'Come ride around with us! You can tell your mom and them you and Chris had Honor Society stuff to talk about,' said Claudia of her boyfriend driving the car she leaned out of.

Senior Chris was certain to win that year's scholarship that Laura needed the next year. His Elvis transgression happened before he'd gotten tapped for the Honor Society.

'Hell,' said Claudia, 'I'll just try to keep up with you two Einsteins.'

'You'd be the smartest one in the car,' Laura told her friend. Meant it.

'Don't tell Chris,' said Claudia – loud enough for him and Luc to hear. 'He likes me for my red hair, not what's under it.'

'Don't forget your cute butt!' called out Chris from behind the wheel.

Luc knew that Chris never ever wanted to watch her butt walk away.

The line of cars moved forward.

Laura and Luc walked beside Chris's car as it pulled forward.

Chris leaned across Claudia to the open window. Called out:

'Come on, Laura! We're going out east. We might be able to pick up that rock 'n' roll radio station in Oklahoma City that just went 50,000 watts.'

'You know you want to come,' said Claudia. 'Remember way back when we were sitting in the Whitehouse having Cokes and "Rock Around the Clock" came out of the radio? Knocked us out of our chairs.'

'*Naw*,' said Laura. 'I've got to get my gramma back to the nursing home, get Luc home. Besides,' she said, 'I don't want to be in the way of what you two hear.'

Claudia shook her head. But smiled.

'I gotta call you tomorrow about something,' called out Laura.

'I'll be there,' said Claudia.

Chris pulled the car forward to the order pickup window.

'I know you will,' Laura answered her friend so softly that only Luc heard.

They walked back to the picnic tables where their aunts told them that they were leaving 'but you kids sit here a bit with Gramma Meg.'

'But what if she has trouble getting back to my car with the crutches?' said Laura to the about-to-walk-away Conner sisters.

Gramma Meg snapped: 'You can handle it. I'll tell you how.

'Nice of you guys to show up!' she yelled to her walking-away daughters.

Laura sat on one side of Gramma Meg.

Luc sat on the other.

They watched Johnny Russo's snazzy car drive away.

The Conner sisters, thought Luc. Riding around. Laughing. Talking. Looking for what's going on. Looking to be. Looking to do. Like they had for years.

Like they always would, said something inside him. *Right?*

A whistle. A roar. A freight train tore through town.

'We gotta go,' said Laura. 'And I got an idea. You wait here. Get ready, Luc.'

She walked around the white stucco café toward their parked car.

Luc looked at the table where his grandmother sat. Her empty paper ice cream bowl and her Coke cup wobbled in the wind. He picked up her trash.

'What if I wasn't done with that?' said Gramma Meg.

Luc told her: 'There's nothing left.'

'The hell you say.'

He shook his head and walked away.

Looked up from dumping the trash to see Laura driving their car into the looping line of customers' cars. Realized that route would take her to a place on flat pavement only a few steps across the grass from the picnic tables.

No customer or employee at the Tastee-Freez that Saturday evening complained as Laura parked the car one slot back from the serving window. Got out to help her brother escort their on-crutches grandmother to the backseat of their car, *in*, door shut. Drove away without picking up a new order.

From the backseat, Gramma Meg snapped: 'We gotta go see something.'

Laura said: 'Gramma, you've already seen everything a thousand times.'

'But what Lucas seen! What everybody's talking about. I heard the nurses. I wanna see that house that got written on!'

She leaned forward from the backseat. 'You know I won't let it go.'

They were there in less time than it took for the radio to play one song.

But Laura wouldn't stop. Slowed down, but kept the car moving past.

TheRe IS NO JusticE in Vernon!

'What did Hal's mother expect?' mumbled Meg. 'Vernon's no different than anywhere else.'

They drove east along the southern rim of their small town. Turning north filled their windshield with the blue-cragged Buffalo Hills and Vernon's rooftops.

'How big do you think this town's going to get?' asked Luc.

'If it keeps going like this,' said his sister, shrugged, 'who knows?'

She parked at the end of the long spotlit sidewalk to the nursing home.

'You two stay put,' said Laura. 'I'm going to get a nurse and a wheelchair for you, Gramma. It's late, you're tired, and I don't want you to slip.'

'Thank you, honey!' Gramma Meg called out to the teenager heading toward the building's glass doors.

As soon as Laura was out of sight behind those swinging-shut glass doors, Gramma Meg jerked open her car door, swung out her steel-clanking legs.

Luc was out of the car before she yelled: 'Get my crutches!'

He got them.

Stood out of grabbing range of the Gramma-filled open back door.

'You're supposed to wait for Laura and the nurse, the wheelchair.'

'I'm the one in charge,' said Meg Conner.

Her grandson didn't move.

Didn't come closer so she'd have a crutch to stand on.

'So now you're running the *supposed-tos*?' she said.

Gave him a shake of her white hair, a knowing smile, emerald-hard eyes.

'They was *supposed to* have fixed you in there,' she said, nodding toward the nursing home that backed into the county hospital. 'Remember? You're *supposed to* be cut.'

'*NO!*' he shouted.

Gramma Meg blinked.

'No more,' he said. 'No more saying that, Gramma. No more telling people in front of me. If you do, don't care where we are, who we're with, I'll walk away. Out of there. Leave you on your own. I'm not going to take that anymore *ever.*'

He wouldn't break eye contact with her.

They heard the glass doors open behind where he stood.

Laura and two white-uniformed nurses with a wheelchair appeared. The three of them maneuvered Mrs Conner into the wheelchair. Wheeled the old woman into the nursing home. The glass doors closed behind them.

Luc rolled up the backseat windows. Shut the doors. Claimed the shotgun seat. Sat there with the autumn night coming in through his open window.

Didn't think about anything.

Didn't imagine anything.

Laura got in their car and closed the driver's door with a *thunk*.

'You ready to go?' she said.

'Yeah,' said Luc.

'Me too,' she said. 'Me too.'

Keyed the engine.

LAST KISS

Shouts woke Luc late that September Sunday morning.

Voices from inside the house. From the kitchen. *Dad*. And softer, *Mom*.

Luc hid his head under a pillow. Still heard their voices. Fury.

But he really, *really* had to pee.

Dad shouted: '*... for the whole damn world to see!*'

Luc eased into the bathroom. Shut the door. Parachuted tissues into the toilet bowl so they'd muffle the sound of his splashing. And then he *ohhhhh*.

Realized: *If I flush, they'll hear—*

—and they'll stop! They'll know I'm up so they'll stop fighting!

The toilet flushed. Its tank rushed full and fell quiet in a gone-silent house.

Now when I go out there we can pretend everything is OK and then it will be OK. He thought that. Knew that. Believed that.

Luc found them sitting at the kitchen table. A white plate of two fried eggs and buttered pieces of toast cooled in front of Dad. The pen Mom used for the crossword puzzle had so fiercely circled one story it gashed the newspaper page.

Luc sat at the table. Mom got up to get him breakfast. Dad trembled in his chair. Luc reached for the Sunday color comics.

'No!' said Dad.

Luc froze.

'Let him read it!' Dad yelled to Mom. 'Let him tell us what he thinks.'

'Don!' Mom's eyes burned the back of Luc's neck. 'I tell you it's nothing!'

'If it's nothing, it's nothing. If it's not nothing, he's already in it. We all are.'

'Just wait, Don. Please! Wait until Laura comes home from playing organ at church. She's older than Lucas. She knows more. Ask her. Wait.'

'Wait until what? Until I do nothing more than take what gets done to me?' Dad thumped the newspaper beside Luc. 'Read that out loud so I can hear it from someone else's mouth!'

Just get through it, Luc told himself.

Picked up the folded newspaper. The section called business. Savagely circled by ink was a paragraph under the headline:

TRUCKING BIZ REORGANIZES

'Read it!' bellowed Dad.

'*Alec Marshall, founder and president of Marshall Trucking of Vernon, announced that the business had been reorganized as Marshall Transport Inc. Mr Marshall will be corporate president. Ben Owens has been named vice president. Mr Owens is also founder and president of Montana Madison Avenue Adverts, an unaffiliated business. Mrs Alec 'Mary' Marshall will become secretary-treasurer of the trucking firm that specializes in—*'

'Enough!' yelled Dad. 'I sure as hell know what we – what *they* "specialize" in! Now everybody in the world does, too!'

Dad tapped the ink-bullseye-circled article.

'You say it, Luc. Say what this means.'

'Maybe it means…' Luc's stomach churned. 'Means Ben got made special.'

Dad's lips drew into a line so tight his words barely escaped. 'Special *how*?'

'Like… a bigshot. Kind of like… a boss.'

Dad whirled to his wife. Snapped a gesture that screamed: "*See!*"

'It's nothing, honey!' said Mom. 'It's just a couple lines in a newspaper.'

'"*Just a couple lines in a newspaper!*" An obituary is just a couple lines in a newspaper. I flip open my Sunday morning newspaper to find out that I'm dead!'

He crumpled the paper.

Threw it to the table where it unfolded like a waking bird.

Mom pleaded: 'You have to calm down!'

Don Ross. Husband. Father of two. World War II vet. Up from home-steading poverty to president of the Vernon Chamber of Commerce. Longtime boss of dozens of men and trucks. That Don Ross erupted from his chair at the kitchen table and two-handed flipped up his plate of fried eggs and toast.

Yelled: '*Just once I wish somebody was on my side!*'

He ran from the kitchen toward his bedroom.

'Don!' cried Mom as she ran after him. 'Wait! No, I am! I am!'

Dad's breakfast plate crashed onto the table's pile of newspaper pages.

A piece of toast fell on Luc's head.

Luc turned the fallen plate right-side up. Lifted the piece of toast off his head. Put it on that white plate. Another piece of toast lay on the floor by his bare foot. Luc put that piece of burned bread on the plate.

Looked up:

Two fried eggs stared down at him as they clung to the ceiling.

Like cinnamon moons came to him.

The mush of fried-before-they-died chicks plopped down on the table.

The ceiling bled yellow.

Luc made himself breathe.

Heard voices in his parents' bedroom. Maybe someone crying.

He shook the eggs off the newspaper and onto the plate. Cleaned the plate into the garbage can. Risked turning on the faucet to rinse crumbs and egg stains off the white plate while wetting the dishrag.

Stood on the kitchen table with his bare feet.

Wiped the egg smear off the ceiling.

Luc eased into his chair. Pointed his eyeglasses toward the picture window. Toward the autumn Sunday beyond that pane. Tried to vanish.

But couldn't. He was here. Heart pounding his ribs. Trapped in a kitchen chair. Shivering in pajamas. Bare feet on the kitchen tiles.

Came heavy feet clumping behind him.

Crunch-ding! as something got slammed down on the kitchen counter.

A kitchen drawer whirred open.

Luc turned around to see:

Dad, pulling things out of the kitchen drawer. The Mixmaster manual. A church cookbook. The phone book he jerked open with shaking hands.

Mom, by the stove. Her wet eyes mirrored her frenzied husband.

On the kitchen counter sat a black rotary phone dangling its cord ripped out of the wall: the black dispatch phone that for years had chained his dad to the Marshall Trucking Company.

'What's their home phone number?' said Dad. 'What's his damn number?'

'Honey, I… Don, they'll be in church now.'

Luc almost blurted out: "*The Lutheran church. Right across the street.*"

But stopped himself. That might have been the wrong kind of help.

'Luc!' yelled Dad. 'At the shop, damn truck office: What you got there?'

'My rifle. Mom likes it kept there with your shotgun.'

Then somehow Luc was dressed. Wearing his jean jacket as he walked down the front steps behind Dad, who carried that ripped-out black telephone.

Across the street, the breeze clinked the chain on the hospital's flagpole.

Neighbor Denton stood on his front porch while his mahogany dog Jack peed on the front lawn. Denton called out: 'Hey, guys, how's it going?'

Dad kept walking to the white-lettered Marshall Trucking station wagon.

'Get your bike.' Dad opened the trunk. 'Don't want you stuck there.'

Dad slammed the station wagon trunk shut on the loaded-in-back bicycle. Ground the station wagon to life. Luc rolled down his window. They drove through a beautiful autumn Sunday morning where gold and red leaves said good-bye to the trees, hello to bonfires.

Dad coughed. Blinked. His eyes were red.

Probably smoke from the bonfires, Luc told himself. *Nothing else.*

'Grab everything that's yours,' said Dad as they entered the office by the trucking company's garage bays. 'Get everything you want.'

Oh my God! thought Luc. *Does that mean Her?*

She's just hanging on the shop wall. McNamer once said something about being glad that the guy who put her there was long gone. So maybe she belonged to whoever had her. Mom would say *no*, but Dad said "*everything you want*."

What does She want? thought Luc.

Dad whirled from a cabinet as he jerked out files marked Family.

'Don't take nothing that's theirs! Not even a paperclip.'

Luc's heart sank.

Least I can sneak over there. See Her on the wall. Say good-bye.

Because he knew that was what this was: *good-bye*. Don Ross was…

Not quitting, thought Luc. *That's not Dad. That's not what he does. That's not what a man does. He's no quitter. He's…* Leaving.

We'll be poor, thought Luc.

So what, he said to himself. *I can take that. Laura's got the scholarship thing in her sights again. She'll be able to go to college.*

Eight years and I can go into the Army with the draft before college. I can babysit for Neal. Keep passing out handbills for the Roxy. Couple years, gandy dance in the summers on the railroad crew. Pick rock and buck hay bales.

Dad's key ring *clumped* onto the desk.

Don Ross looked beyond his son as he said: 'Get the guns.'

Luc found the two gun cases against the closet's back wall beside the Army surplus metal ammo box where Dad kept his shotgun shells plus the few rifle bullets that Luc always saved. Just in case.

Luc got his rifle for Christmas when he was nine, a sleek bolt-action .22. Dad would take him out of town on summer Sundays. Let him stalk gophers scampering across yellow prairie or standing straight up in their holes.

The idea hit him like a bullet:

If I sell my rifle, I can probably get enough food for three days for all of us!

Dad rummaged through a drawer to pile takeaway on the desk.

Luc leaned the guns against the desk. Set the ammo box on the floor.

A man's voice boomed into the office: '*Don! Am I glad to run into you!*'

Alec Marshall filled the doorway. He wore a go-to-church brown suit and a red tie. His battered fedora. His hands jingled coins in his pants pockets.

Words flew out of Alec: 'Did you see that damn *Tribune* this morning? I gotta give them a piece of my mind. Make them fix it.

'Hey, Lucas!' Alec sidled into the room. Nodded to the cased guns. 'I see you and your dad are going shooting. Or maybe already have. Yup, that's why you're here. How I got lucky to run into you.

'Wish I had me a son,' said the man who jingled coins in his pocket. 'I'm not much for guns. But I'd like to be able to walk out on a day like today with my son 'n' nothing more to worry about than spotting a gopher.'

Alec kept his eyes locked on the boy.

'That's the deal with kids, Lucas. You get one and suddenly who you are don't matter so much. You got them to worry about. Kids rope you to the future.

'And sometimes…' Coins jiggled in Alec's pockets. His words came at Luc like hammering nails. 'Sometimes, Lucas, you kids aren't smart or lucky. A father's gotta make the best of that. Lotta blood, sweat, and tears, lotta… sacrifice.

'A dad does what he has to do. Sometimes has to shut his eyes. Sometimes it adds up to seeming like a walking fool. But what counts is you're a father.'

Outside, a car rolled through this falling-leaves Sunday morning.

'You get more out of life if you pick up the weight of kids. Besides, lots of times, you don't get to choose. Babies happen. They're wonderful clouds and heavy as a boulder. They make you who you are, no matter what else everybody figured on.'

Alec let his fingers glide over the sheathed shotgun.

'I'd sooner put a gun to my own head than let my Fran suffer. Or have to worry about her having a roof over her head. That's what a father does. Carry boulders every day. Not run or shoot yourself gone or do what you could just because you're right and proud of it.

'Your dad does that for you. For Laura. But it ain't so hard for us in this here and now compared to what life is like for most of the world out there. We make what luck brought us into the best it can be.

'Listen to me rattling on about being a father when you got one of the best.'

Alec faced the man on the other side of the debris-covered desk.

'Did you see that damn article about us in the paper this morning, Don?'

A wave of Alec's hand blocked any reply.

'Course you did. You see more 'n most guys. Figured that when I got you to come work here way back when. This place couldn't work without you. But you know that. That's what makes that article mistake so damn funny.'

Dad said nothing.

'See, no article was supposed to get sent to the paper until *after* you and me had a chance to work on it. Lawyer Falk, he's a sharp one. Figured out a way to set up this place that'll keep us outta the tax man's gunsights. But Falk or *somebody* must have forgot and sent out a rough draft of the new deal.'

'So that story's not true.'

'There's true – and there's *true*.'

'No, there's—'

'True is, we're doing that legal move because my sick ticker could kick any day. Had to set it up so my girl's locked in safe with her mom and my grandkid. Come to know my daughter's new husband's in that box. Long as.

'True is, you're the sweat and brains of this place. The mistake is the paper didn't say so. Now we need to figure some way of saying you're the real boss. A title like "chief executive." That's the same title as the president of the United States. Does he work for the voters or is he their boss? The true answer is *yes*. I'll call Norm down at KRIP so if they read the news on the radio, it'll be right.

'All the rest…' Alec shrugged. 'We're two family guys doing fine in a world that's harsh and hungry. Doing what we gotta do, no matter what we'd like. When you look at it that way, nothing much has changed around here. Or needs to.'

Coins stopped clinking in Alec's pockets as he faced Dad's hard eyes.

'Unless you know something that matters more than all that,' said Alec. 'Unless you see a problem two guys like us can't work out. Ain't no man alive I'd rather work with than you. Neither of us likes to scare up problems just so we can prove how tough we are. Who needs that kind of tough? Who wants the kind of hurt it means for their family? I don't want to bring home hurtin' for my family, Don. How about you?'

The three of them stood there in that Sunday morning office. Two fathers and a son. The room smelled of dust and gun oil. Of paper files. Sweat.

Luc's heart slammed against his ribs.

Dad sighed.

'Luc,' said Dad, 'you go on. Get your bike out of the car and go home. It's all… We're done… You're done here. I'll put the guns away.'

'And I'll get out of the way,' said Alec. 'I better get on home and act like there's no better way to spend a Sunday than jawing with my mother-in-law. I'll walk out of here with young Mr Lucas.

'Come on, son,' said Alec. 'Let's leave all this here to the boss.'

Luc looked at his father.

Who stood behind his desk. Said nothing. Let Luc walk outside *not alone*.

'Hell of a day, Lucas,' said Alec as they stood in front of that office/house. A truck engine revved in the open garage bay.

Alec watched with his sick ticker as Luc unloaded his bike.

'Your dad's a good man.' Alec jiggled his hands in his pockets. 'Could be the best man in town. Sure as hell he's got me beat thataway. But, guess we all got our crosses to bear.'

'Dad doesn't go to church,' mumbled Luc.

'Sure he does. Look in his face, you see a man full of prayer.'

Alec leaned in. Froze Luc with a hard look that melted to a sly smile.

'When you get home,' said Alec, 'tell your mother I said thanks for running over to the church and grabbing me. Tell her I said "*much obliged.*"

'And do us all a favor,' continued Alec. 'Don't let nobody know about your mom and my chat. About me having you tell her thanks. Your dad's our town's good man. Don't bother him with what he doesn't need to know.'

Alec winked. Tugged the brim of his hat to Luc. Walked to his Cadillac.

The truck engine revved in the garage bay.

The man who owned it all drove his Cadillac away.

Luc watched him go.

Glanced at the garage bay.

Not today. Not now.

He didn't want to see Her so close, so far, so still here and never gonna be.

Didn't want Her to see him on this broken day.

Luc rode his bike through the streets of his life.

Chilly sunshine in a blue sky. A white cloud with wisps of gray.

Leaves in the trees were a million shades of gold and crimson. Luc knew they were all going to fall. Crumble to dust. Blow away. Or end up over on that lawn where the man of that house heaped leaf corpses into a pile he'd set on fire.

All around town, husbands and fathers, laughing moms, kids:

Everyone was raking leaves to burn in bonfires.

Luc biked across the blacktop road viaduct over the railroad tracks that split this town into two. Passed a nun sweeping her church's concrete steps.

Dead ahead sat the playground and Blackhawk Elementary School.

Where I'm in sixth grade, he thought. *On top. All I'm on top of is this bike.*

Luc swayed left at that intersection. Saw the brown-brick high school.

Where Hal's never gonna be again, he thought. *Where Laura's gonna flee just as far and as fast as she can. Where they're going to own me for four whole years – if I get out of junior high alive.*

Luc pedaled past the blocks for the public schools. Pedaled the direction he and Marin had walked last spring when they found a monster. Pedaled past the house where Fran who used to be Alec Marshall's little girl now lived with her own baby. With her husband. Who came to town. Who changed everything.

Blink and Luc knew where he had to go.

That small brown house stood quiet that Sunday morning. The sunshine carried the smells of the neighbor's burning leaves as Luc kickstanded his bike. Walked to the porch where a swing dangled empty and the door loomed shut.

His knuckles rapped on that closed door—

—and it swung open.

No sound came from inside the house.

The echo of his entrance surrounded Luc as he stood in the living room. The repainted white walls were bare. The brown hardwood floor was swept clean. No couch. No chairs. No books. No record player.

All that bare floor held was a black piano flecked with red tears.

Luc ran outside and jumped onto his bike.

Pumped up Knob Hill until he *whooshed* over the crest…

… became the caboose in a slow parade.

Leading the parade rode a green car with the radio that needed a punch.

Next came a maroon coupe whose engine rumbled with the strain of towing a wheeled cargo box packed heavy with no room for a black piano.

The green car parked in front of a small-frame house that hadn't blown up.

The maroon coupe with a trailer parked across the street.

Luc skidded his bike to a stop on the road between those two cars.

Neal Dylan climbed out of the green car.

The maroon coupe's driver's door opened, closed.

Neal got to Luc first.

'Sorry about sixth grade.' Neal's voice was hoarse. He forced a smile. 'And for Rachel, for all you did for Hal, for us, for all the trouble… Forever thank you.'

A man hugged a boy.

Walked into the house that held his wife and child. Left Luc in the middle of the road.

With her.

'Look at me,' she whispered. 'Lucas, look at me.'

Jordan crouched eye level with the boy standing trembling on a gravel road in just another Sunday town in the middle of one country *way back when*.

He whispered back: 'I'm not Lucas anymore. I'm Luc.'

'*Luc*.' Her voice sighed on this autumn morn. 'You chose that. I'm so proud of you. You're choosing who you want to be, not who we all say you've got to be. Like I try to do,' she said. 'All my life, I wanted one real chance. Just a chance. I refused to sit around waiting for it. Or hide in my bed and only cry. Or settle for what I could get cheap. Don't settle for cheap… *Luc*.'

She brushed the back of her hand on the boy's flushed cheek.

No tears there! he insisted to himself. No tears for her to touch.

'I came to town so proud and savvy,' she said. '*Wham*, lost my heart. The only way to get it back is to risk it all. I know you feel something big for me. We both know that can't happen. No chance. The clock runs us. That's our luck. Still, you might feel like I'm leaving town and running over your heart without even looking back. Without knowing or caring. So remember this.'

Her fingers warmed Luc's cheeks. She leaned so close that his eyes shut.

Electric pillow fire burned his lips.

All time fell away.

Until she leaned back. Stared at him.

'Your someday girl is the lucky one. But I got to be first kiss.'

She got back into her trailer-hitched red coupe.

BAM! slammed a thrown-open screen door on the front porch.

A woman screamed: '*Son 'bitch!*'

Neal carried jeans-sweater-sneaker-clad Rachel, her blue parka, and her favorite doll as he marched toward the red coupe. His face was stone.

Rita wore her pink robe over a white T-shirt. Carried a coffee mug. Her legs were bare. Floppy blue slippers slapped as she charged behind her husband.

'You son-of-a-bitch!' she yelled. 'Thin' you can do 'is to me?'

Neal kept walking.

'You think you can just take off to Vegas an' divorceland 'n' fuck me?'

The mug Rita threw missed her husband and daughter.

Shattered on the street.

Neal opened the maroon coupe's front passenger door.

As Rachel disappeared into that car, she saw *Ooo-cus.* Waved.

Clunk went the car door as it shut behind the woman and baby girl.

Clunk went the driver's door Neal opened, slid through, shut.

The maroon coupe groaned as it pulled away with the trailer's heavy load.

'Get back here!' Rita flip-flopped slippers to the middle of the road, her back to Luc as she shook her fist at the taillights of the trailer.

'You can't go anywhere!' yelled Rita.

The red coupe chugged farther away.

Rita whirled around. Spotted Luc.

'*You!*' She grabbed him so hard she knocked his bike over onto the gravel road. 'For once you're in the right damn place! You're the witness!'

'Let me go! All I want to do is go home!'

'Who cares what you want?' She marched toward the house as quickly as dragging Luc allowed. 'You think you get what you want? Grow up.'

She threw open the screen door – barely dodged it as it bounced back. Threw it open again and jerked Luc inside the house. His sneakers stumbled over the living room carpet. His arms flailed as she threw him into the kitchen. He hit the table with its bottle of whiskey. That glass cylinder wobbled.

'This isn't fair!' he yelled as Rita grabbed the phone on the wall.

As she spun the dial to call Zero, Luc yelled: 'This isn't right!'

She snapped her gaze off him to yell into the phone: 'This is Rita Dylan. Get Sheriff up to my house right now!... God-damn right it's an emergency!'

She slammed the phone down in its receiver.

Stabbed her finger at Luc.

'You never done what was right,' she said. 'You and them. Lying. Sneaking around. Like a preacher says, you gotta redeem yourself.'

The whiskey bottle caught her eye. She jabbed her finger at Luc to nail his sneakers to the floor. Stood on her slippers' tiptoes to reach into the cupboard near the white gas stove and pull down the canister of sugar.

'You think I didn't know what was going on?'

She banged the canister on the table.

'But if *you* think you know what's going on,' she said, slipper-flopping to the mugs hanging on hooks on the wall, 'you got another think coming.'

Rita popped the lid off the sugar canister.

'You don't know the half of it.' She shoved the green mug into the sugar canister. 'And the half you do know is a lie.

''N' that's life.' Rita pulled the mug out of the sugar canister. Shook nearly all of the mug's cargo of white crystals back into the metal canister. Marched to the white stove where the coffee percolator sat on a black metal ring. Poured the mug half-full of steaming brown liquid. 'So now you gotta fix it.'

She filled her mug with whiskey.

From outside came the sound of a wailing-closer police siren.

She jerked the phone out of its receiver. Spun the dial for local number.

'Yeah,' Rita said into the telephone. 'Put him on right quick… It's Rita, and take the shake outta your voice, honey, he's just my lawyer.'

She moved the receiver to drink from the black mug.

'Course it's me!' Rita snapped into the phone. 'He took off… Just now. Took the kid with him. You said the judge here in town'd rule mother-daughter crap an'… I got a witness an' I called the cops!'

The police siren wailed in the street outside the house. Stopped. Died.

'You make 'em catch him,' Rita told whoever was on the other end of the phone. 'Stop him 'fore he gets to the county line toward Vegas. That old rattletrap of hers, haulin' a big-ass trailer, won' make more 'n forty and they can catch him and custody up the kid and then, by God, we own his ass!'

Knocking on the front door shook the whole house.

In stalked Sheriff Wood, the star on his chest and the big iron on his hip.

Rita yelled: 'My lawyer'll tell you how you gotta chase 'em down!'

The sheriff took the phone. He and Rita paid no attention to the boy.

The man wearing the badge yelled into the phone: 'Don't

you tell me my duty, Falk… Yes, if I can catch them before the county line, but…'

Make it two songs on the radio later that Sheriff Wood strode away from that house. Got in the county's cruiser. Keyed the gas engine to life. Turned on the spinning red light and the siren as he raced away to fulfill the law.

What he saw if he looked in the rearview mirror was the dust from his spinning tires settling back on the gravel street where no bicycle lay.

Luc pumped his bike pedals as fast as he could.

Surged through the gravel street. Past blocks of houses. Through one set of black iron gates where marble slabs stood in the formations of the dead.

That brown field was where he'd found the monster on a barbwire fence. Wheels raced him forward. A bike. A wheelchair. '*How far can you push me?*'

He raced through prairie once ruled by Indians like Marin. Dead ahead: a black line, the river highway south toward Vegas, the getaway road.

Luc jumped his bike onto the highway of diamonds. White lines on the blacktop flicked past him. A rusted station wagon driven by a grave's eyes bride of Dracula. Trucks of Gold Star Mothers. Convertibles with college men. Blue taxis for customers of scarlet mansions. Green cars with tricky radios. Wrecked '57 Chevys. Black company station wagons with white letters for what used to be. Spinning-red-light police cars. Peeling white paint houses with bloody graffiti.

He's a sweat-soaked ten-year-old boy racing his bike over a black ribbon highway through chessboard gold and brown squares under a blue umbrella topped by a cinnamon ice cream eye and the heartless laugh of a calendar angel.

He's a heart-slamming *Bad Guy* running away from his crimes.

He's a geek.

There! Up ahead on the side of the road.

Coming closer, closer, closer…

Martin County's sheriff's cruiser nose down into the side of the road ditch. Sheriff Wood stood beside it. Turned to see—

Don't look at him! Luc ordered himself.

Did he see you swipe the sugar canister off Rita's kitchen table?

Fingerprints, the FBI book said fingerprints get the bad guys every time.

If they fingerprint the car or the canister in the garbage can up the street from that sad house, thought Luc, *then I'll be gone like Hal, gone for good.*

The sheriff and the sabotaged cruiser slipped past Luc.

Over there in that brown field: a whirlwind of dust where once a bald farmer lay dead. A whirlwind of dust where a rattlesnake coils and grins.

Luc's legs screamed. His chest heaved and burned. The thunder of his heart drowned out the sound of his tires on the blacktop and the wind he made.

The horizon ahead darkened to rolling bumps of the river hills.

Luc wobbled. The bike shook.

He crashed/flopped off the bike, let it tip over into the barrow pit. Stared.

The black highway.

White lines caged by yellow stripes all the way down to the bridge over the river, across the floodplain, then up again the other side of the river breaks. That highway snaked up those hills toward the blue sky and some invisible line. Call it the county line. Call it a border.

That highway ran empty and free.

Gone, thought Luc. *Has to be. Made it. The in-the-ditch sheriff's cruiser means 'not caught.' Means gone. No black piano, but the maroon coupe… Gone.*

Somebody has to get away, Luc told the universe. Let it be her.

Hell, let it be all of them.

He bent over to pick up his bike. Fell. Slid on it to the bottom of the barrow pit. As he lay there, he heard a car whiz past on the highway above him, knew that whoever was in that vehicle never even knew that he was there.

The slide off the road broke two spokes on the bike's front tire. Bent the back wheel. He muscled the busted bike up to the blacktop.

You don't leave your mess for somebody else to fix.

Nine miles from home, thought Luc, *and nobody knows I'm here.*

The air chilled inside his sweat-soaked jean jacket.

He turned to look across the river valley, a last good-bye.

Coming toward him up the highway slope from the river:

Not a car, a… pickup.

A pickup purring up the hill, coming closer, closer, straight toward Luc.

The pickup slowed for the boy on the highway holding a broken bike.

That's what you did. This was Montana in 1959. Everybody looked out for everybody. That was the right thing to do. The American – hell, the Christian thing to do if you believed in that kind of thing. The smart thing even if you didn't, because if you don't look out for everybody, nobody will look out for you. That's just the way it was. That's the way it was always going to be.

That Sunday's sun glistened off the windshield as the pickup pulled to the side of the road. Stopped. The engine shut off. The driver's window rolled down.

Harley Anderson leaned out. 'Kid, what the hell trouble are you—'

Man and boy blinked at who they saw.

The wind blew over autumn's golden fields.

Harley swallowed. 'You need a lift back to town?'

Luc told the truth: 'Yes.'

Harley climbed out of his pickup. Swung the kid's busted-up

bike into the back of his ride through life. Nodded the kid into the front seat.

The pickup fired to life from Harley's twist of its key.

KRIP radio's Afternoon News Roundup filled the pickup's cab: '—some symposium sponsored by the American Petroleum Institute back in New York City, Edward Teller – he's the most famous scientist out there now after Einstein. They call him "the father of the hydrogen bomb." Anyway, Teller said if we keep burning fossil fuels, we'll get something called a "greenhouse effect" and the polar ice caps will melt. The big news in college football—'

Harley spun the knob to turn the radio off that Sunday in 1959.

Dropped his pickup in gear and pulled back onto the blacktop highway.

Drove away.

Drove past a wrecker winching the sheriff's cruiser out of the ditch.

Harley stared at that taxpayer's calamity.

Turned back to the windshield.

Don't say anything, thought Luc. He meant those words for Harley. Meant those words for himself. Now there wasn't much difference between them. They'd both broken the law big-time. Sugared gas tanks and caused destruction.

What wreck on the highway will come from what I did?

First I'll confess to Dad and Mom so—

Luc shook his head.

No: If I get caught, if somebody else gets blamed… then fess up. Otherwise, let this end. Leave it be.

Don't pull Mom and Dad and Laura or anybody else into your crime.

Yeah, he told himself, *and you're doing wrong again by not confessing. Wrong plus wrong equals outlaw. That's who you are now. A crazy. An outlaw. That's who you have to live with for the rest of your life.*

But now, *this*… Let it all end. *There has to be some justice in my town.*

Make up some Permanent Record story for everybody and let it all end.

The pickup motored downhill toward the highway junction west of town.

'I'd've stopped no matter who you was,' said Harley as he kept his gaze on the town filling his windshield. ''Cause that's the right thing to do. I ain't no wrong guy. You remember that in case anybody asks. I'm a right guy.'

'Sure,' said Luc. 'We both are.'

Couldn't help himself, Harley said: 'Don't think so much of yourself, kid.'

Luc rolled down his window.

Autumn air blew in over them as the pickup motored down Main Street. The traffic signal by City Hall turned red. The pickup stopped.

'Kid… Are you OK? Under your glasses… Are you *crying*?'

Luc remembered that song.

Stared through that autumn windshield.

Lied and said: 'People burning leaves. Smoke gets in your eyes.'

ACKNOWLEDGMENTS AND THANKS

Roma Aikens • Tori Amos • Sherwood Anderson •
Ray Bradbury • Johnny Cash
Michael Carlisle • Janet Skeslien Charles • Bobby Darin •
James Dean • Dion
John Dos Passos • The Drifters • Bob Dylan •
Jamie Ford • William Faulkner
Benjamin Franta • Beverly Gage • Debby Gage •
Bonnie Goldstein
Donna Goltz Gladeu • Desmond Jack Wolff Grady •
Donna Grady • Jane Grady
Nathan Grady • Rachel Grady • Thomas W. Grady •
William Lindsay Gresham •
A.B. Guthrie • Bill Haley • Otto Harbach • Gary Harmon •
Wilbert Harrison
Chris Harvie • Claudia Harvie • Howard Hawks •
Alia Heavyrunner
Billie Holiday • Buddy Holly • Richard Hugo •
Evan Hunter • Dorothy Johnson • Julia Keller • Jerome Kern •
Stephen King • George Kipp • Len LaBuff • Sidner Larson
Sinclair Lewis • Shirley Malletta • Gene Mallette
Ron Mardigian • Marshiela Mariotte • Ziggy Marley
Marilyn Monroe
Patty Page • Phil Phillips • The Platters • Elvis Presley •
Lloyd Price

Alan Pulaski • Nicolas Ray • Marty Robbins • Cari Rudd •
David Rudd
Derya Samadi • David Hale Smith • Bruce Springsteen •
John Steinbeck
John Stewart • Roger Strull • Richard Thompson •
Francois Truffaut
Mark Twain • E.B. White • Holly Wilson
Hank Williams • Joshua Wolff

ABOUT THE AUTHOR

Photo Credit © Josh Wolff

James Grady has published more than a dozen novels and three times that many short stories, and worked in both feature films and television. His first novel, *Six Days of the Condor,* became the classic Robert Redford movie *Three Days Of The Condor* and the current Max Irons TV series *Condor.* Grady has been both US Senate aide and a national investigative reporter. He has received Italy's Raymond Chandler Medal, France's Grand Prix Du Roman Noir and Japan's *Baka-Misu* literature award, two *Regardie* Magazine short story awards, and been a Mystery Writers of America Edgar finalist. In 2008, Grady was named as one of the *Telegraph*'s 50 crime writers to read before you die, and in 2015 the *Washington Post* compared his prose to George Orwell and Bob Dylan. He has two children and lives with his wife inside Washington, DC's beltway.